BECOMING FELICITY

PRAISE FOR JAN STITES

PRAISE FOR *READING THE SWEET OAK*

"A charming new voice in women's fiction, Stites writes from the heart about friendship, love and what it means to find where you belong."

— SUSAN MALLERY, *NEW YORK TIMES* BESTSELLING AUTHOR OF *GIRLS OF MISCHIEF BAY* AND *HOLD ME*

"*Reading the Sweet Oak* will find its way to your heart by way of your funny bone."

— ELIZABETH ROSNER, AWARD-WINNING NOVELIST AND BESTSELLING AUTHOR OF *ELECTRIC CITY*, *BLUE NUDE*, AND *THE SPEED OF LIGHT*

"This sweet, well-paced work is concerned with the gathering of five women who live on the banks of the peaceful Sweet Oak River deep in the Ozarks. Each is in need of love, and the matriarch of the group gently guides them to their own best decisions through a romance book club."

— *LIBRARY JOURNAL*

BECOMING FELICITY

JAN STITES

Cover design by Mike Karpa

Author photo © Melinda Maxwell-Smith

Published by Mumblers Press LLC, San Francisco CA USA

https://mumblerspress.com

ISBN 978-1-963221-09-1 (paperback) | 978-1-963221-10-7 (e-book)

LCCN 2025919683

For Bert. So grateful we both ended up at that Sierra Club Singles potluck charades party way back when.

ONE

Cass parked her pickup in the Raven's Bluff Trailhead dirt lot and practically floated the full six miles of her hike. She was nearly back to the parking lot and nowhere close to calm. The *People* article had revved her so much and raised so many questions in her mind, she'd barely even registered the cold, the mounds of snow she had to skirt, or—

A shout pierced the silence. "Get down!"

Cass dropped.

Heart racing, she crouched and listened. Who had bellowed out that command—and at whom? After a few moments, hearing nothing more, she cautiously rose and looked toward the trailhead lot, from where she thought the sound had come. She saw only one other vehicle, a red pickup with a medium-sized dog that had not only disobeyed the shouted command to jump down from the pickup's bed but now yawned in the man's face.

His harsh voice cut through the crisp air. "You won't be yawning much longer, buddy."

Cass zeroed in on a rifle the man had rested against the

truck: a .270 Winchester, used by local hunters to bring down deer and elk. She might have thought the man was there to flout hunting regulations, a local pastime, except for the rage evident in his voice. And the threat. Could this guy, whose arms were ropy and gnarled like the handle of a whip, intend to kill the dog?

She knew most of her town of Loon's two thousand residents, at least by sight. She sure didn't know this guy, who wore only a t-shirt with his jeans and seemed impervious to the fact that the temperature hovered near freezing.

Cass stepped behind a cluster of firs, separating branches to watch. She wanted the man to stop, wanted her exuberance back.

"It's going to be a pleasure to put you down." The man clipped a leash to the dog's collar.

Cass shivered. Though the Northern Sierra Mountain air was biting, not surprising for late February, her hike had warmed her. Forced now to remain still, she felt the cold seep through her down jacket. Shooting a dog wasn't right. Felicity would say, *Be loud; be proud*. What Cass wanted was to say something that would stop the man while she remained safely invisible.

The guy dragged the dog off the tailgate and onto frozen ground. He looked around, perhaps searching for the best tree to tether the dog.

Before she really knew what she was doing, Cass—still behind the trees—blurted out in as loud a voice as she could muster, "Stop." Then she added, "Please?"

The man glanced around as if searching for something annoying. Like a bug he could swat.

Her phone chimed her jaunty ringtone. "Shit."

The man's head whipped around in her direction.

Cass fumbled with the phone until she managed to silence

it. Heartbeat sprinting, she pressed against tree trunks, hoping they might protect her.

The dog pulled free of the man's hand and bolted, running straight to Cass.

The man swore, "goddamn it." He walked toward her, rifle pointed down.

If only the man had long ears and a tail, Cass could judge whether he intended to shoot her. While she well knew the attack behaviors of dogs, people were a whole other matter. Running seemed pointless. *Loud, proud.* Cass stepped out from behind the trees and said, "Hi, I'm Cass," the only thing her frozen brain could come up with. She was lucky he didn't shoot her just for that inanity.

The dog watched her with unwavering eyes. Cass did what came naturally to her: patted his head.

The man halted about twenty yards from her, frowning. "You want that dog?"

She didn't really—she owned a kennel full of dogs—but she didn't want this one to die. "Yes. I mean, please." Cass cursed the trembling in her own voice.

The man shrugged. "He's all yours." He started back toward his truck.

"Wait," Cass said.

He faced her.

"What did he do to make you want to, you know . . . ?"

The man smirked.

Oh, how she remembered those smirks from all those boys —and girls—from her school days. Her miserable school days. Long gone, thank God.

The man walked back to his truck, calling over his shoulder, "This is your lucky day, Caesar. Good riddance to you." He put the rifle on the gun rack, started the engine, and peeled out onto the highway.

"Good riddance to you, asshole," Cass muttered. She closed

her eyes and shook herself all over, like a dog does when emerging from water, only she was trying to fling off not water, but adrenaline-stoked fear. She bet she could run nonstop up and down the trail for the next fifteen hours or turn circles and twirl all the way to midnight.

Cass looked at the dog that was looking at her. "Hey, boy."

Caesar—her friend Mackenzie would love the classical name —now cocked his head as if studying her. Slightly larger than a Blue Tick Heeler, he was mud puddle brown splotched with black.

"How come that guy wanted to shoot you?"

Caesar just kept watching her. He had one green eye and one brown, a pit bull's round head, a somewhat short snout, a thin tail, and crumpled ears. In a beauty contest, he was not likely to win Best in Show. Of course, neither was she. Her face was long, her hair limp, and her broad shoulders formed a fire-plug stout figure.

She wanted to tell somebody about what had happened, but with Mack away for two weeks, nobody came to mind. Then, "Oh my God: Jonas! I have to tell Jonas about everything, Caesar, especially the *People* article." She glanced at her watch: twenty minutes before five. If she hurried, she could get there in time, before Jonas closed up the library for the night. Cass rushed to her truck, opened the back passenger door, patted her thigh and said, "Caesar, come."

The dog sauntered over.

"Up." She gestured to the rear seat.

He put his paws on the truck's step, seemed to look in the truck . . . and promptly sat back down.

Cass glanced at her rear seat. "Oh. Right." She grabbed one of the trash bags she kept in the truck, swept up empty soda cans, old hamburger wrappers, and assorted other items she didn't take the time to identify. She then rescued her jacket from the floor, tossing it onto the front passenger seat. Her truck didn't look like she lived in it, exactly. More like she sometimes vacationed there.

Seat cleared, Cass patted it. "Come on, boy. I want to get going."

Caesar didn't respond. He was still sitting on his haunches with an expression that seemed to convey disapproval.

"Hey, may I remind you that I saved your life? At possible risk of my own, might I add."

He rose slowly, then jumped up onto the back seat.

"Good boy." Cass got in the driver's seat and looked at Caesar in the rearview mirror. He was standing, head out the open window, ignoring her. Well, fine. He was nothing like Matilda, her last dog, an Aussie who'd been Cass's idea of a perfect companion: responsive, curious, loving, enthusiastic, and protective, all that right from the start.

Cass drove out of the lot; Caesar stood the entire eight miles back to town. Her own body still vibrated with a weird mix of energy, fear, and relief that made her eager to talk to Jonas.

Thunk! The truck jolted as Cass struck something in the road. Her body lurched forward, the seat belt locking to keep her in place. "You okay, Caesar?" She turned to him.

He was still standing on the back seat; he looked at her and all but shrugged. At least, he looked like he could be shrugging.

"Okay then, good. Sorry about the jolt. If that pothole gets any bigger, the town could just add a lifeguard and declare it a pool."

Cass parked in front of the brick library, which had been built in the late 1800s as a grange hall. "Dogs aren't allowed in the library," she said to Caesar. "Promise not to destroy anything while I'm inside, okay?"

He stretched out on the seat, noncommittal.

Cass got out of the truck and glanced back. Caesar watched her with eyes that she would swear understood more than they should. She would need to figure out who to give him to, but that would have to wait. Jonas came first. She bounded up the library stairs and shoved open the door, the excitement she'd felt from the *People* article and her morning encounter heightened in the presence of so many books. So many stories. So many lives.

Jonas, a tall, whippet-bodied man of sixty-one, gray hair pulled back in a ponytail that reached his shoulders, stood behind the checkout counter. His purple T-shirt featured a book in the center captioned with scripted letters: *Books are the best food because they feed the soul.* Jonas—unusually for him—looked somewhere between glum and despairing.

"What's wrong?" she said.

"Guess who came by this morning."

"Who?"

"Rebecca."

Cass winced.

Two

Rebecca Oliver, Cass's chief tormentor during their school years, was the town mayor. "What did she want?"

"Nothing much. Except to tell me two things. One, she's closing the library."

"Wha- . She can't do that."

"I'm pretty sure she can."

"But why?"

"She said the building needs a new roof and a new furnace, among other things. To the tune of sixty-thousand dollars."

"Really? Sixty thousand?" That did sound like a lot. "Okay, but then move to another location, like where the bookstore was."

"That's what I suggested, but she said there isn't a suitable site because these old buildings aren't up to code."

Cass felt her brain spin. "What are people supposed to do for books?"

"Buy them online, according to Rebecca."

"Who can afford to? Besides, you do all kinds of in-person activities."

"I reminded her about all that: open mic nights, kids' story hour, tech help for the elderly. Not to mention that people without computers come here to use the library's. And kids hang out here after school. She didn't budge.

"A library is a basic right."

"Which brings me to her second point. Rebecca said the reason the council can't make the needed repairs is because the town's nearly broke."

"*Broke?*" True, eight months ago, the Brushstroke Gallery had closed its doors. Two months ago a *For Lease* sign had been slapped across the window of the defunct bookstore. Now this. Still, *broke?* "Did she say . . . how soon?"

"She's not sure, but she made it sound like it's not all that far away."

It struck her then. "If Rebecca did close the library, what would you do?"

"Try to find library work elsewhere."

Cass gripped the counter. "Move away?" Jonas had been the town's librarian for over thirty years. He'd steered her to so many great books with so many fascinating people and places. The books he picked had expanded the borders of her life far beyond the town's boundaries. The Felicity Benedict novels had been especially important; he'd loaned her the first right after it came out. "You *can't* move away."

"I don't want to," Jonas said, "but I have to work."

The very first time her father brought her to the library, when Cass was five, the normally reserved librarian turned her on to the magic of stories. Jonas didn't just read books when he held children's hour; he performed them. He'd wrinkle his nose rabbit-like, toss his head as if to flick his mane, or raise his arms and roar.

"No," she said. "No. The library *will* stay open. You won't have to leave. Nobody will. We just have to think of a way to bring in a whole lot more tourists."

"Oh, is that all?"

Cass's brain felt like it was on a merry-go-round. "Yeah, so, what does Loon offer tourists? For one thing, we've got gobs of gorgeous hiking in the mountains around us."

"So do a lot of other mountain towns, some of which are a lot closer to San Francisco."

"True." The Bay Area was more than five hours southwest of Loon; by contrast, Lake Tahoe, with nearby casinos, could be reached from the city in a little over three. "But we've got Moon Mountain. She's special."

"We're still too far from any major cities. And a lot of the other mountain towns around have already established thriving wine and/or marijuana businesses."

What was left? Cass sank onto the step stool Jonas used to reach the top shelf of books and rubbed her throbbing forehead. The ensuing silence was broken only by the sound of gusting wind rattling windowpanes. She looked around the library, her second home. Jonas had painted the walls a warm buttery yellow. Flanking the door, he'd posted newsprint on the walls where patrons of all ages drew pictures, created poems, or wrote comments about books. "Maybe we could get somebody famous to do a benefit for the library," she said. "Like a musician."

"I don't think Beyonce's coming to Loon any time soon, and the only famous people I know are authors. James Baldwin. Charles Dickens. Jane Austen. People like that. You know, dead."

"Wait a minute." Cass slapped her head. "Duh."

"What?" Jonas said.

Cass shot to her feet. "We *do* know somebody famous. Well, maybe we don't *know* him, but we know his books. In this week's *People* magazine, Kent Calloway told the world that Loon is the town that inspired his Felicity Benedict novels. Can you believe it? Felicity lives here!"

"Well, she's not exactly *alive*, but, yeah." Jonas pulled a copy of *People* from under the counter, "I know."

"We'll invite him to do a benefit for the library. I bet we could raise lots of money."

Jonas made a clicking sound. "Not sixty thousand dollars."

"Not alone, maybe, but the article says that the movie of the first Felicity novel comes out Memorial Day weekend. If we could convince Calloway to have the movie's premiere at our theater here in Loon, I bet that would bring in lots of tourists. And he could do a benefit that weekend as well. I know he'll come if we ask him. Authors care about libraries."

"Authors care about bookstores."

"Look at his novels. Kent Calloway's got to be a good guy."

"Not necessarily," Jonas said.

Cass rose and began pacing, her speech picking up speed with her stride. "We could time it so that the movie marks the beginning of our efforts to save the library. We could launch a big publicity campaign for the whole town around the premiere. I'll go home and look up his website. He must have an email address. I'll write him tonight, and I bet he'll come."

"I doubt he'll even answer, but . . ." Jonas held up both hands, fingers crossed.

Outside the library, Cass looked up and down Main, took in yet again the yellowing *FOR LEASE* sign plastered across the gallery window and the newer *FOR LEASE* sign slapped across the window of what used to be The Bookworm. Took in, too, the potholes. The town was almost broke? No wonder Rebecca hadn't had the street repaired in the year since she was elected.

Located at 4,500 feet in the Sierras of Northern California and founded as a mining town in 1850, Loon had thrived for a hundred years until the mines played out. The need for new houses had then fueled a logging industry, but now that, too, had dried up. All efforts to boost tourism had fizzled. Their population had dwindled below two thousand for the first time in a century. How long before the wind would be whispering down a street of shuttered businesses, scuffed footprints on the sidewalks the only remaining evidence that people had once lived here?

THREE

Wait. If the town failed, where would *she* live? She couldn't run a dog kennel without dogs. They required human owners. And where would Mack and Diego, her assistant, go?

Cass stopped. Who was in the front seat of her truck? Matilda? Oh, Caesar. Then Cass remembered: Matilda had died a year ago. It was the sorrow that still haunted her after losing Matilda to lymphoma the year before that made Cass not want Caesar, or any dog.

"Get a grip," Cass told herself. She'd been rattled by Jonas's news, but she needed to get her head on straight. She took a deep breath. She had to pick up a few things fast so she could get home and start on her email to Kent Calloway. Maybe *he* could think of something to save both library and town. Or at least the library. The town's fate was much too overwhelming for Cass alone. She would take it up with Mack when her friend returned from her family reunion. Surely Mack would come up with something.

Cass squared her shoulders and crossed the street into Grubstake Grocery. Loon's only food market, Grubstake consisted of eight aisles and a minimum of fresh produce: iceberg lettuce, sprouted potatoes, sometimes a squishy clump of broccoli or a bunch of asparagus you could practically knot, bruised apples, and bananas more brown than yellow. In the summer, the local produce stands overflowed. During winter, however, locals who wanted fresher produce had to drive an hour to the Safeway in Madison, the county seat.

On a stool behind the store's counter, Jewel, red-headed and petite, sniffed a vase of creamy white roses.

"They're beautiful," Cass said.

Jewel's smile was huge. "They're from Garrett. I'm pregnant, Cass!"

Younger than Cass by ten years, Jewel had moved to Loon, newly married, only three years before. She was always warm and friendly. "Congratulations," Cass said.

"I just passed the first trimester. That's why Garrett sent the roses. We didn't want to say anything until I got through those first three months." Jewel leaned toward Cass and lowered her voice. "I've had a couple first trimester miscarriages." Her voice caught.

"I'm so sorry," Cass said. "You'll be a *great* mother." Jewel would be warm and loving, unlike Cass's own mother, who could plunge the temperature in a meat locker.

"I hope so." Jewel patted her stomach, then suddenly stood straighter. "Did you see *People* magazine?"

"Yeah," Cass said.

"Loon inspired Felicity. How cool is that!"

"Totally cool." They exchanged grins. Cass felt more comfortable around Jewel than she did around people she'd gone to school with. If Jewel had been in Cass's class, she probably wouldn't have made cheerleader, but she'd have been an enthusiastic member of the pep squad.

"Kent Calloway said he loved his family's yearly vacations in Loon," Jewel said, "but that he hasn't been back since he was thirteen. I wonder why he never came back to visit. If I loved a place as much as he says he did, I'd want to see it again. Wouldn't you?"

"Yeah. It's a good question. I—"

A loud whoop made Cass and Jewel both look toward the door.

Zoe Oliver, Rebecca's teenage daughter, had blown into the store with a much older boy, laughing. Zoe handed her phone to the boy, who held it out and snapped a photo of the two of them feigning wide-eyed rapture, then another of them kissing in front of a cupcake display.

Imagine being so pleased with your looks, you were eager to splash them all over the Internet. The couple separated. The girl wore black everything: bra, camisole, metal-studded miniskirt, nylons, stiletto boots. No coat. No sweater. Black eyeliner and bronze eye shadow made her eyes look huge.

Cass headed to the pet section, where she picked out six cans of Grubstake's best dog food and a bag of kibble, enough to tide Caesar over until she found him a good home. There was food at the kennel, but she'd never raided kennel supplies for Matilda, careful to keep her business and personal expenses separate, and she wasn't going to start mixing them tonight.

She headed toward canned vegetables, but something caught her eye: Zoe, in the cosmetics section, palming a tube of lipstick and beginning to unzip her purse.

Cass froze. Zoe was intending to shoplift?

During Cass's school days, Zoe's mother, Rebecca, leader of the in-crowd, had specialized in spreading rumors: that Cass drank, cheated, shoplifted. If Cass exposed Zoe now, would Rebecca direct her wrath at her own daughter or at Cass? And if at Cass, what rumors might she spread? As Loon's popular mayor, Rebecca wielded a wide influence.

Damn it. She couldn't let Zoe steal; it wasn't fair to Jewel. Cass coughed, loudly, though she looked only at the fake eyelashes in front of her: thick black eyelashes that looked like long-haired caterpillars. From the corner of her eye, she saw Zoe set the lipstick back on the shelf and head toward the front of the store. Cass went on to the vegetable aisle, stuck several cans of green beans and two of spinach into the basket, then pushed the cart toward checkout.

Jewel was counting change into Zoe's boyfriend's hand as Cass lined up behind them. Like Zoe, the boy was dressed in darkness. Black shirt and pants, the pants with presumably deliberate tears. His name was probably Rip.

Zoe and Rip headed out, kissing. It looked like each was trying to swallow the other, python style.

Jewel watched them. "I suspect that Zoe shoplifts," Jewel said, "but I've never been able to catch her at it."

"You might be right." Cass told Jewel what she'd seen in the liquor aisle.

"I thought so. Thanks for stopping her." Jewel rang up Cass's groceries. "When Garrett ran for mayor against Rebecca, there were a lot of hard feelings. I don't want to stir all that up. I just wish I knew what to do about Zoe. Watch her more carefully, I guess."

Cass bid farewell. She put her purchases on the passenger side floor of her truck and glanced around; the pickup seemed intact. "Good boy," she told Caesar. She backed her truck out of her parking space and steered toward home. "I'm sure glad Zoe's not *my* problem. But can you believe Rebecca wants to close our library? Or that Jonas would have to move away? That we might all have to move away?"

Jonas had helped Cass survive the killing of her father, plus so many other hard times. He'd always known what books she needed, from *A Wrinkle in Time* through *To Kill a Mockingbird* to *The Art of Racing in the Rain*, and beyond for Cass's entire life. When Jonas gave her the first Felicity Benedict novel right after it came out, she'd been immediately smitten, transported into a kinder, more just world, where Felicity, who was an unofficial therapist and detective, made sure that all those she called Unsavories—liars, cheaters, thieves—either transformed or paid a just price for their misdeeds.

Cass practically throttled the steering wheel.

She glanced in the rearview mirror. Caesar stood looking out the window toward Moon's distinctive white dome. The mountain seemed like a soft cloud or fur she could pet if she could reach that high. At 9,000 feet, Moon loomed over the town. It was comforting to think that the mountain would be out there tonight when she tried to find the words she needed to convince Kent Calloway to come to town and fall back in love with Loon.

Yeah, right.

Who was she kidding? She couldn't convince a vulture to eat fresh roadkill. Her email would probably end up being little more than babble.

No. Cass commanded herself not to surrender to her usual self-doubts. She could do this. She just needed to channel the passion of the town's many Loonatics. She smiled. *Loonatics.* That was creative. By God, she could and would write a compelling email. Kent would return for his first visit in more than twenty years. And then, hopefully, Felicity—and the man who created her—would somehow save them all.

Four

Caesar trotted from one room to the other, his nails clicking against the hardwood floors in Cass's cabin. He seemed to take it all in: leaded windows; turquoise tub and pedestal sink; Navajo-patterned bedspread dotted with clothes she needed to hang up; and an open room that served as kitchen, dining area and living room.

Built in the 1940s as a vacation cabin, the house was small, but that suited Cass. It meant that on her mother's rare visits to Loon, she stayed with a friend. That alone was a good reason never to move to a bigger house. Besides, Cass loved her house: simple, cozy, nestled in the woods, sheltered by the pines and firs around it.

"You hungry, boy?" she asked.

Caesar barked.

His first "word." Cass smiled and fed him the dogfood she'd just bought. While he scarfed it down, Cass opened a can of green beans, took out some cold leftover pizza, and did some scarfing of her own. Her eyes fell on the photo she'd mounted on the wall. In it, she, Diego and Mack were sharing a dinner of *pupusas* that Diego had made in his apartment adjoining the kennel. The aroma of the Honduran pork-and-bean filled corn-meal griddle cakes had suffused the entire place, making some of the dogs whimper with longing. Cass understood. Diego's pupusas smelled and tasted delicious. She'd happily give up pizza—even fresh pizza—for *pupusas*.

After dinner, Cass rinsed her plate, lit a fire in the wood stove, plopped onto her gray sofa, and studied the *People* photographs. In one, Kent was shown working at an old rolltop desk, looking more pensive than he did on his books' covers. Husky, he had short, thick brown hair that jutted up like a hedgerow and wore jeans, a maroon T-shirt, and a diamond-quilted vest.

If it had been Felicity who interviewed Kent, she—unlike the *People* author—would have found out why he hadn't been back to Loon. In the first Felicity novel, a suspect who had danced around the sheriff's inquiries, confessed all to Felicity. The woman admitted to being the one who started a smear campaign against a competitor's catering business. The culprit bragged she'd gone beyond slander, sneaking into the kitchen and adding Phillips Milk of Magnesia to the ranch salad dressing her competitor had prepared for a client's bridal shower. All the shower guests became desperately in need of a toilet.

Kent would have told Felicity why he was just now announcing that Loon had inspired all three of his novels: *Matters of the Heart: Betrayal*; *Matters of the Heart: Passion*; and *Matters of the Heart: Envy*.

Cass closed her eyes to focus. After a few minutes, she felt something cold touching her hand. She opened her eyes to see Caesar's snout in her palm. She petted him. "Wouldn't it be something to meet the man who created Felicity Benedict?" she said to him.

His ears flicked toward her.

That's why she loved dogs; they listened. Plus, if you'd been gone a few hours, they greeted you with delight. Best of all, dogs loved you back despite your shortcomings. It occurred to her then, how much she'd missed that since Matilda died.

Cass turned her attention back to her letter. Surely the Felicity Benedict movie's Memorial Day release date, over two months away, allowed plenty of time for Kent to come do a benefit for Loon's library—and, hopefully, convince the movie's producers to premiere the film in Loon. That would generate a lot of tourists, which would bring in tax money to fund the library and keep the town from losing more businesses.

Cass cautioned herself not to get her hopes up—Jonas might be right—but she grabbed her laptop, googled Kent's website, noted his contact email, and started typing.

We need help. No. Too desperate. She deleted it.

You'll be looney for Loon. Too much like an advertising slogan. Delete.

Your books saved my life. Again, too desperate. Not to mention melodramatic. Delete.

Felicity Benedict is the smartest woman I know. True, sort of, but trying too hard to flatter? Delete.

She slammed her laptop lid down. Damn it. This was absurd. She was as qualified to write to a brilliant author as she would be to pilot a space shuttle.

She needed some canine support and dropped her hand to pet Caesar. He wasn't there.

She looked around. No dog. "Caesar," she called, "here boy."

He emerged from her bedroom carrying the football her dad had given her. They had played catch with it almost every day until he was killed in a hit-and-run while jogging along the road. It was the day after Cass's eleventh birthday. "Drop it," she ordered Caesar, suspecting she sounded every bit as panicked as she felt.

Caesar wagged his tail.

"Now! Drop it *now*."

He did. "Good boy." Cass grabbed the ball: no damage. She clutched it to her. She'd loved playing football with her dad. She was so good at it, he nicknamed her *Catch*. She closed her eyes and pictured him lobbing a spiral pass that seemed to float above her. She could hear her dad's voice: *Reach for it, Catch.*

She took *Matters of the Heart: Betrayal* from the end table where she kept it and reread the opening for inspiration.

> *Felicity Benedict was convinced that sheriff Lyle Smart was a very unhappy man. Maybe that was because of his name, one he could never hope to live up to. She understood hating your name. Born an unmelodious Gertrude thirty-nine years previously, she had changed her first name to Felicity before moving to the small town of Lonely. It was a beautiful town, population two thousand, two hundred and forty-three, nestled at five-thousand feet in the foothills of the Sierras amid towering trees and red, red earth.*

Cass had always marveled at the similarities between Lonely and Loon, such as elevation and population, but she'd never suspected that her town was the inspiration for Lonely.

> *Felicity chose her new name in part to entice its citizens into seeking her out for matters of the heart, including counseling, wedding vow writing, and the solving of small crimes, which seemed a valuable offering given how rarely Sheriff Smart solved anything. Felicity also gave herself that name to let people know that although she weighed over two-hundred-and-thirty pounds and stood just five foot two, she loved her ample body. It was perfect for comforting the brokenhearted, a soft pillow with which to enfold them when they needed to cry.*

Cass stared at the fire in her wood stove. The orange-and-purple flames mesmerized her. She concentrated until she heard Felicity Benedict whispering in her ear, then opened her laptop and began to write.

Felicity Benedict may not be real, but to many people across America, she seems like our best friend.

In the *People* article, you mentioned that you hadn't been back to Loon in years. We'd very much like to change that.

Should she be saying "we" or "I?" After all, she wasn't sure how many people in town had read the books, but if she used "we," it might be more persuasive than a single voice. She left the "we."

You also said that Loon had given you more than you could say. We would love to discuss with you the possibility of having the movie's premiere here.

The town hasn't changed much since you last visited. People are still friendly and help-ful. And we're all still in love with Moon and the other mountains around us.

Not entirely true. *Some* people were friendly and helpful. Still, it wouldn't help to detail the many ways in which a few of the town's residents had the compassion of a leech.

Like most small towns, of course, we're experiencing hard times. Our bookstore recently went out of business, and our library will have to close at the end of

```
summer if we can't find a way to fund needed
repairs. A town without books is a town
without soul. No one should live that way.

We need your help. If you would arrange to
have the premiere of the movie of your first
book here, you would go a long way toward
rescuing the town you loved. Maybe you could
even do a benefit before the movie comes
out. That would help fund the library
repairs.

Please come. We're confident that if you do,
one quick visit will rekindle your love for
Loon.
```

Cass signed her full name, *Cassandra*, because it sounded elegant. She added her cell phone number beneath her name but couldn't seem to convince her finger to hit the send button. "What do you think, Caesar? Is this good enough? Should I send it?" She would have sworn Caesar nodded. "Okay, then." Maybe she would keep the dog after all. Cass hit *send*. The *whiffft* sound confirmed that her message was on its way.

FIVE

Cass parked in the kennel lot on an early March morning and saluted Moon Mountain for luck before checking her email. She took out her phone and opened her inbox: nothing from Kent. It had been over two weeks since she wrote him. Apparently, Jonas had been right when he predicted Kent wouldn't respond. Damn, damn, and damn.

Caesar whined in her ear.

"Right," she said, getting out of the car. "Sorry." She and Caesar crossed the large ring that fell between parking lot and kennel. Occasionally, she or Diego used the ring to give bigger dogs extra room to romp.

The instant Cass and Caesar entered the kennel office, they were greeted by a familiar chorus of yips, barks, bays, and howls. Most people would consider the noise a racket; to her ears, it was a song. The office opened onto thirty-six pens in two facing rows twenty feet apart. In turn, each indoor pen opened onto its own outdoor portion, enabling every dog outside space. A metal barrier between the two sections of each pen could be raised or lowered as needed.

Above the pungent scent of dogs, Cass detected the seductive aroma of coffee. "*Hola,*" she called. Diego always made coffee for both of them, which they drank together while planning their day.

He came out of his cozy, one-bedroom apartment located at the far end of the pens. "Morning, Cass, morning, Caesar," he said. Dressed in jeans and a pale blue T-shirt, Diego carried two ceramic mugs, handing Cass the yellow one this time, keeping the purple for himself. Cass liked to vary which color of mug she used. Diego, however, preferred the purple. Always.

Cass inhaled the unusually fragrant scent. "What did you do to this coffee? It smells incredible. I mean, if rainbows had an aroma, this would be it."

Diego beamed. Nineteen, and a couple inches taller than her own five-feet-six, Diego had a broad nose and dark eyes that seemed to take up half his face. He fell close to—but shy of—handsome, but his heart was even bigger than his eyes.

"Try it," he said, petting Caesar under the chin, which transformed a doggy smile into a grin.

Cass sipped. The coffee was rich, dark, earthy, and incredibly delicious. "Wow. This is amazing. What's your secret?"

"Enrique sent roasted beans from our uncle's coffee farm."

Cass had met Enrique, two years older than Diego and still living with the rest of the family in Honduras, when he and Diego Zoomed; she envied the obvious bond the two brothers had. They also shared a bond with Arturo, their skinny, seven-year-old brother, who loved baseball and birds.

"We call Arturo *Bird Boy,*" Diego had explained. "He would rather watch birds than *fútbol.*" Diego had shaken his head. "Arturo is *loco.* Nothing is more important than *fútbol.*"

"True," Cass teased. "*American* football."

"Only your country plays your game," he'd said. "Ours, everyone plays. Even God."

Diego spoke lightly accented, almost perfect English. His

family had sacrificed to pay for bilingual schools in Honduras, seeing that as a way to guarantee their sons' futures. Judging from Cass's occasional conversations with them during Diego's Zoom calls, Enrique and Arturo both seemed to share his knack for languages.

Cass tried to hand him back the coffee cup, which was still mostly full. "I know how precious this must be to you. Thanks for sharing, but you keep it."

Diego held up a palm to stop her. "*We* drink it every morning until it's gone."

"I won't argue. Gracias." She sipped more of the delicious brew.

"Did you hear from the writer?" he asked.

"No. I guess he's not coming." She tried to shrug it off.

"I'm sorry," Diego said.

"Me, too."

They turned their attention to the list of the day's chores and boarders. Today they had twenty-four, six shy of their maximum.

Two hours later, after they had cleaned the pens, Diego drove the truck to town to pick up kennel supplies. Cass was rinsing off the brushes, the brooms and the hoes they'd used to clean when she heard a car door slam. She went to the doorway, still garbed in the stinky rubber gloves and clunky rubber boots she wore when cleaning.

Her gut knotted.

Rebecca Oliver was getting out of a black SUV. What on earth was she doing here?

Cass the Ass. She heard Rebecca's high school voice in her head. *Thief.*

Nearly twenty years had passed since their school days, Cass reminded herself, but that reminder did little to calm her. She yanked off the gloves that stank of a blend of dog feces and Clorox, wishing she had time to take off her boots, wishing she'd worn something other than her usual cargo pants and football jersey.

Rebecca, adorned in a snug tunic and form-fitting slacks, possessed a slender physique that, at first glance, some might call skinny. Upon closer inspection, however, every aspect of her face and head exuded perfection: natural red lips, a delicate nose, and long, palomino-hued hair. Furthermore, her graceful demeanor enhanced the overall impression. Cass, much like their school peers, viewed Rebecca not as skinny but rather as elegantly slender. When Rebecca entered a room, it was all but impossible to look away.

Cass walked outside, aware of her big boots on her big feet. Imagine having others look at you with admiration. Imagine them voting you prom queen. Voting you mayor. Imagine.

Her imagination wasn't that great.

Smiling broadly, halfway through the ring, Rebecca waved and called out a cheerful, "Good morning."

Cass glanced over her shoulder; surely Rebecca must be addressing someone else, but there was nobody there. She half-wished she were a turtle, so she could retract inside her shell. She nodded and said, "Morning." The faint scent of hyacinths reached her, presumably Rebecca's perfume or body lotion. Cass couldn't imagine what would have prompted Rebecca to seek her out. The closest Rebecca had ever come to owning an animal was probably a fur coat.

Cass's phone sounded. She'd changed its ringtone to the cry of a loon. She glanced at her phone's screen: area code 213.

An L.A. area code.

Where Kent Calloway lived.

Adrenaline surged through her. Cass started to push the talk button. *Cheater* echoed in her mind. Cass's finger hovered above her phone. She remembered how Rebecca's presence had always made her stammer, stumble, and sound like an idiot. She didn't want to do that with Kent. If Kent *was* the caller, surely he'd leave a message. If not, she would redial his number once Rebecca left. Cass pushed the decline button, strangling the loon's final wail.

Cass slid the phone back in her pocket and prayed that Rebecca would make this—whatever *this* was—short.

"Hello, Cass." Rebecca's smile looked strangely sincere. "It's been a while since we talked."

Yeah. Like nearly twenty years.

"I know we had some issues in the past," Rebecca said. "I suspect I could have been a nicer person."

Cass clamped her jaw tight to keep it from dropping open. Which astonished her more, that Rebecca was apologizing, sort of, or that the woman only "suspected" she could have been nicer?

"To be clear, I'm sorry for how I treated you. I was going through family stuff—but that's no excuse."

Cass half-nodded. God, she wished Rebecca would get to the reason she was there.

"I've heard great things about your kennel." Rebecca gave a big smile that seemed meant to convey warm affirmation.

Rebecca had gone from apology to compliment. What was going to happen next? It would rain unicorns?

"In fact, I've heard that you run the best kennel in the whole county. Which brings me to why I'm here."

At last.

"I have a favor to ask." Big, white-toothed smile.

Cass found herself leaning toward Rebecca. "Oh?"

Rebecca stepped closer and gave a quick glance around. If Cass were a cop, she would have thought Rebecca was about to offer her drugs.

"Let Zoe work here," Rebecca said.

Cass's whole body stiffened. She didn't dare criticize Zoe to Rebecca, but there was no way she wanted a loose cannon like

Zoe working with the dogs. "I don't have the money to pay her."

"You wouldn't need to. She'll be free help."

"I don't understand."

"Let me explain. My daughter's had some misfortunes of late."

No kidding. Among the rumors Cass had heard: reckless driving, vandalizing the principal's car, a DUI and a suspended license. And, probably, shoplifting, though Rebecca might not know about that. One advantage to small-town living was that you knew most everything about most everybody. It was also the disadvantage, because most everybody knew most everything about you. Not that she had anything to hide; Cass figured her own life would be about as interesting to others as a comma.

"I take it you've heard," Rebecca said.

"A little."

Rebecca rubbed her forehead. "Zoe was a great kid."

Her face softened into a look that Cass thought could only be described as tender.

"Then Hank left last year. She's never recovered."

When Rebecca got pregnant in high school, Cass had been secretly glad, expecting that Rebecca's pregnancy would tank her popularity. And maybe it would have, but Rebecca, a straight-A student, suddenly went out of her way to help other kids with their homework, to make suggestions to girls about make-up and beauty and how to attract guys, while making suggestions to guys about impressing girls, and was always ready to greet teachers with a friendly smile and offers of assistance. Rebecca still found time to insult Cass. Despite giving birth the summer between her junior and senior years, Rebecca was elected student council president as well as prom queen.

The most surprising thing about Rebecca's pregnancy was

the revelation that Hank Foster was the baby's father. No one had expected that. Where other students jostled friends or flirted in the hallways during passing periods, Hank walked the hallways reading. He never joined in taunting Cass, whether because he was kind or because he simply didn't register her existence, Cass had never been sure. Of course, Hank was also bright and ambitious and seemed likely to succeed at whatever he did. Rebecca had grown up poor. Really poor, from what Cass had heard, though Rebecca's fashion sense and sewing skills had turned thrift-store purchases into trend setters.

Maybe Rebecca had seen Hank as her ticket out of poverty. If so, he'd served his purpose. Cass wondered who had ended their marriage. And why.

"I . . ." Rebecca's voice broke, and tears welled in her eyes. "I'm losing Zoe."

"Oh." What *should* she say to something like that, and why was Rebecca confiding in her, allowing Cass to see what seemed to be someone both loving and vulnerable? Cass had never experienced Rebecca as either.

Rebecca sucked in air, then nodded as if to reassure herself. "The judge sentenced her to four-hundred hours of community service. It's that or Juvie. I persuaded him to let Zoe serve those hours with you. That's why you wouldn't need to pay her."

Rebecca had made the arrangement without first asking.

"I know I should have checked with you first, and I apologize. It's just that Zoe's been kicked out of a few other places. I'm desperate, Cass. I can't let my daughter go to jail. I really need your help. I've heard you're good with handling all kinds, including clients with obedience issues."

"*Dogs* with obedience issues. I haven't had much experience with people."

"But the techniques of working with animals and people must be similar."

A clicker and dog treats?

Rebecca lowered her voice. "Your kennel's just barely within city limits. She'd have fewer distractions out here."

Now Cass understood. Fewer friends would drop by. Or boyfriends. Like Rip.

"Will you let her work here?" Rebecca entwined her fingers in a gesture that seemed part plea, part prayer. "Please?"

Cass wanted to say, "No way in hell." Zoe was unreliable, apparently prone to stealing, and in all likelihood had no experience whatsoever with dogs. On the other hand, Cass had never seen Rebecca appear desperate. Nor did she feel certain that Rebecca wouldn't turn on her if she said no, starting rumors about the kennel, perhaps telling people Cass was drunk, dishonest, or incompetent.

The most important consideration, of course, was the dogs. "I'd need to meet Zoe before I could say yes." Excellent. If Rebecca had to go get Zoe, that would give Cass the chance to check her phone.

"Of course." Rebecca turned toward her SUV and yelled, projecting her voice with confident strength.

Damn. Cass hadn't realized Zoe was here.

A car door slammed. At the rate Zoe trudged toward them, by the time she arrived, Kent would have forgotten why he'd called.

If he'd called.

Zoe was even more gorgeous than her mother, despite her sullen expression. She wore eye makeup that made her green eyes zing and short spiky hair highlighted with blue streaks.

"Cass, this is Zoe," Rebecca said.

Cass held out her hand. "Good to meet you."

The girl hesitated a moment, then briefly shook hands with a limp grasp before turning to glare at her mother. "You seriously expect me to work here?"

"It's that or jail."

"I bet jail smells better."

"I'm out of patience with you, Zoe." Rebecca's harsh voice made Zoe's scowl deepen. "You *will* do this."

Had Rebecca tried the praise and reward approach? It seemed to work with dogs, but Cass had to wonder how it would go over with teenagers.

"Put her to work," Rebecca told Cass. "No playing with the dogs." She faced Zoe. "If you clean up enough dog shit, maybe it will inspire you to clean up your own."

Zoe crossed her arms again. "I am *so* not picking up dog shit."

Rebecca practically hissed. "Do as you're told, or you'll never get your phone back. Or your iPad. Or your computer."

"I need my phone. I'd rather go without food."

"That's the point. No social media until you have served at least twenty hours. Cass, don't let her use your cell phone or computer."

"Shoot me, please," Zoe said.

"Don't tempt me."

Too much negative reinforcement, Cass decided. "Zoe, *if* I let you work here, you'd have to promise you wouldn't do anything to hurt the dogs."

Zoe shrugged. "I don't abuse animals."

Cass hesitated. Did she want this sullen girl around, her anger possibly upsetting the dogs?

"Great! Thank you," Rebecca said.

Cass blinked. She hadn't said yes. Had she?

"Call me if Zoe doesn't cooperate." Rebecca wrote her cell on a business card and handed it to Cass. "We need to get going."

At last!

"Zoe will be back by 4:00 this afternoon after school gets out, then we'll be away for a couple days. She'll be back Saturday morning. Early."

"Early? On a Saturday?" Zoe's tone and facial expression combined shock with outrage.

"Yes, and you'll be here every weekday by 4:00 until you fulfill your community service hours."

Zoe scowled. "It's over a mile from school. How do you expect me to get here by 4:00?"

"Let's see, you could always curtail your social life and leave right after school gets out. You could probably hitch a ride with one of your friends. You could walk, jog or fly. Frankly, I don't care. You are to be here by 4:00. No excuses." Rebecca nodded to Cass. "If she's not here on time, please call me. And, thanks, Cass. I owe you."

For one dizzying moment, Cass would swear the planet had just turned upside down. Rebecca owed her? Then it struck Cass that this was her chance. "I, uh, I heard that the library has to close?"

"Unfortunately, yes."

"But, I mean, a lot of people rely on it, especially since the Bookworm went under."

"I appreciate that. Libraries benefit many people, but, unfortunately, we'd need around sixty-thousand dollars' worth of repairs. The town doesn't have anywhere near that kind of money. As you know, two of our stores have recently closed. What you may not know is that most of the rest are on shaky financial grounds. With their reduced revenues, there's less tax money coming in to support a library or anything else."

"Are you saying Loon could just . . . disappear?" Cass swayed.

"Not on my watch. I've been interviewing other small-town mayors about what they've done to shore up their economies and attract tourists. I'm sorry, I really am, but we need every penny we can scrape together to cover essential needs. Sixty-thousand dollars is a lot of pennies."

Cass watched mother and daughter go back through the

ring to their car, Zoe lagging behind, as if to say she had no relationship whatsoever to the woman walking in front of her.

The instant they reached the parking lot, Cass turned away and checked her phone. No voicemails. She hit the command to call the 213 number back, but all she got was a disconnect. She tried twice more, just in case. Same result. The call must have been part spam. Damn, damn, and triple damn.

Six

Aloud, bullet-like sound exploded somewhere outside the kennel office. Diego crouched, hiding beside the desk; fear distorted his face.

Cass whirled around: no one. She went to the doorway and looked outside. "It was probably just George's mess of a truck backfiring again."

Diego waited a moment longer, then rose—slowly—balanced on the balls of his feet, poised to run.

He'd never told her any details of the crime he'd witnessed, but it was the reason the U.S. had granted him asylum. She couldn't begin to imagine what it would be like at age seventeen—or any age—to see someone murdered. "You're safe here, you know."

"No." Sharp-voiced, he stepped away. "The gangs in our country, they started in yours. They are still here. And they pay rewards for finding people like me."

Diego had lived in Los Angeles for a year when he first came to the U.S., until gang activity at his school prompted him to drop out, head north, and seek work in a nonurban setting. "Even if they're looking for you, they'd never look here, right?"

He shrugged but said nothing. His whole body seemed to vibrate with adrenaline.

Cass took a step closer. "Is there anything I can do?"

"No, *gracias*." He grabbed four leashes from the wall. "*Necessito corer.*"

Diego usually only reverted to Spanish when stressed.

"Have a good run," Cass said. "Take as long as you need."

Diego soon set off up the mountain that rose behind the kennel with the three fastest of the kenneled dogs and Caesar. As she watched them go, Cass's shoulders gave a twitch when she recalled her own fear sparked by a man with a gun. As scared as she'd been, however, she'd also been lucky. Nothing much occurred. In fact, she'd gained Caesar. In Diego's case, things were different. Very different.

She hoped never to know the details of what he'd witnessed.

An hour-and-a-half later, just as Cass finally persuaded Blackie, a finicky Scottie, to take his medicine, which she'd hidden in liverwurst—he'd already refused peanut butter and crushed ice—she heard a motorcycle skid on the parking lot gravel. The driver was garbed in a black leather jacket with a rainbow peace patch on the right arm. The rider, who Cass now saw was Zoe, got off the bike and plodded toward Cass. The driver sped away, engine roaring.

"Glad you're here," Cass said to Zoe.

Zoe blew air through her lips audibly. "I'm not."

That was a verbal slap. Cass opened her mouth to respond, not sure what she wanted to say, when Caesar, Sadie, Cali, and Mookie ran up to her in a whirlwind of panting, Diego right behind. The dogs collapsed at Cass's feet.

Dark circles on Diego's shirt showed that the dogs weren't the only ones who'd run hard.

"How'd they do?" Cass squatted to give all four dogs some loving.

Diego glanced at Zoe. *"Bien."*

"And you?"

"Also *bien.*"

"Good." Cass gestured to Zoe. "Diego, this is Zoe. She's going to help us out for a while."

Diego's face brightened as he ran fingers through his thick black hair with one hand and held out his other. "Great."

Zoe shook Diego's hand far longer than she'd shaken Cass's.

Maybe Zoe would be a friend to Diego. As far as Cass knew, the only somewhat local friends Diego had were other Central American refugees he played bi-monthly soccer games with when he drove the hundred miles to Sacramento. Of course, given Zoe's recent history, Cass wasn't entirely sure what kind of friend she would make.

"Bean tore his pen again," Diego said. "I'll fix it."

Cass sighed. "That dog must be using the fence for dental floss." She turned to Zoe. "Can you give Diego a hand?"

Zoe took a step back. "I don't want to get my clothes dirty." She looked toward the parking lot and the road, as if pondering leaving. "I guess now you're going to narc on me to my mom."

"You're old enough to make your own choices. If you want to come here and sit on your butt all day, that's up to you. I'd be way bored." Cass turned away from Zoe and got leashes for walking the little dogs.

An hour later, Zoe was sitting on a boulder, Diego working outside, and Cass was at her desk reviewing the next day's boarders: all the usual suspects plus three dogs she didn't know.

"You do realize that dog is gnawing on your desk?" In his tan sheriff's uniform, Chance Garner stood at the door carrying a dog bed and chew toys, his German shepherd, Bullet, beside him.

Caesar was, indeed, gnawing the desk leg. "Caesar, stop."

He looked up and seemed to shrug but stopped his gnawing. Cass clicked and offered him a dog treat, which Caesar ignored. He walked over to Bullet. The two dogs sniffed each other, tails moving in tentative wags.

"Got room for Bullet tonight?" Chance said, his cheeks stubbled as always. He'd told Cass that no matter how often he shaved, his cheeks always seemed to need mowing. "I've got to go to Sacramento."

"Sure." A relatively recent transplant, having lived in Loon only fifteen years, Chance had always had a great relationship with his dog, which Cass assumed meant he was a man of good character. She ruffled Bullet's ears. "Hey, fella," she said softly.

The previous year, when Bullet was a romping pup, someone had stolen and abused the shepherd. By the time Chance found him, staked outside a shack during a heavy snowstorm, Bullet had become a quivering mess. Chance brought him to Cass. She—and often Diego—worked with Bullet every day for two months. A casual observer now wouldn't suspect anything amiss from watching him gambol about. Cass, however, could see the trace of caution in Bullet's eyes around people he didn't know; he wasn't so much scared as watchful.

She knelt beside Bullet. "How's your Friday going, boy?"

Bullet licked her face.

She translated that as, "great!"

Chance shook his head. "You're the only person that dog licks besides me. I swear, if you broke into our house to commit mayhem and murder, he'd just stand there and watch."

"Don't worry," she said, "I haven't killed anyone in years."

"That's reassuring." He smiled but shook his head. "I have

to go to some stupid conference. Never been to one that was worth a damn."

After Chance left, Cass checked her emails for the thousandth time. *Nada.* Nothing.

By the time she left for home, the glow of the setting sun transformed Moon's snowy dome an incandescent orange. What did she want to do for dinner? She was becoming less and less interested in cooking. Unlike Mack, she'd never been all that interested in the first place. Cass gave thanks for frozen chicken pot pies and pizzas, both with some semblance of vegetables, and for fresh fruit. Tonight, she would put her feet up, munch sausage-and-spinach pizza, and maybe an apple as well, and open a book. Some nights she liked to read a novel new to her. Others, she preferred to spend in the company of a familiar friend. Felicity. Atticus. Enzo, the canine narrator of *The Art of Racing in the Rain.*

She glanced in the rearview mirror. Caesar's muzzle stuck out the open back window, his lips stretched back in a wide doggy smile. "I should read Enzo's narration aloud to you," she said.

Her phone sounded. "Hello."

"Hi. This is Kent Calloway."

Cass braked so hard, she almost catapulted herself and Caesar through the windshield. "Really?" escaped from her lips before she could think of something more intelligent to say. Good thing there hadn't been any vehicles behind hers.

"Really, yes. Is this Cassandra?"

Cass swerved her pickup onto the shoulder, put it in park and turned off the engine. "Yes." Her mind spun. What should she say? Why hadn't she planned out a script in case he called? "I . . . I love your books," was all she could manage. Duh.

"Thanks. Those are an author's favorite words."

Caesar thrust his muzzle over her shoulder as if to better hear the conversation.

Cass's face flamed so hot she half expected her skin to blister. She felt tongue tied in a way she hadn't since English class her freshman year of high school when she gave that Godawful speech. She was sure that if she tried to speak now, she would stammer, so she stayed silent.

"You still there?"

"Yes, sorry." Take a stab at it, doofus. "Felicity has really helped me."

"I'm glad. She's a lot smarter than I am."

"But . . . you created her."

"I did, but she seems to have a life of her own. Hey, I was sorry to hear that the Bookworm went under."

"Yeah."

"And the library's in trouble? As you so rightly put it, a town without books is a town without soul."

He was quoting *her*. How many times had she quoted Felicity? Two hundred? Two thousand? She hesitated to ask the question, but she needed to know. "Any chance you might help?"

"Sure. I've been thinking about visiting Loon for a while now." His voice wasn't deep or resonant, but it seemed warm. "I'm having some trouble with the fourth book."

"I'm glad there's another one."

"There isn't yet. I was hoping a visit to the town might inspire me."

Cass felt almost dizzy with relief. "You'll really come?"

"You bet. And I'm happy to do a benefit reading or whatever you'd like, though I don't know how much money it would raise. Loon's a pretty small town."

"And getting smaller," she said.

"Like so many towns, unfortunately. How much does the library need?"

"Sixty thousand."

He whistled to underscore his surprise. "That's a lot. Is it still in the old grange hall?"

"Yes. It needs a new roof. And other things."

"Well, I'll do what I can."

"Thank you." She should be grateful for his willingness to do a benefit, no matter how small, and she was, she really was. But he was right. It wouldn't be enough. She took a deep breath and plunged on. "Actors attract tourists. Would you consider having the movie's premiere here in Loon?"

"I wish we could," he said. "Unfortunately, both the premiere and the accompanying publicity tour were booked months ago. I had no say in either."

"Oh."

He made a clicking sound, tongue against teeth, nearly identical to the sound her clicker made. "Tell you what," he said, "why don't I come up and look around, take some photos and make some notes. I bet I could get Penn Booth to come for a later visit. He's a very popular star and a great guy, which don't always go together. Plus, I'm helping him with a mystery novel he's writing, so he owes me. And you're right; movie stars attract much bigger crowds than authors."

"Which is wrong. They're reciting *your* words."

"More interpreting than reciting. And they're a lot better looking doing it."

"I still think it's not right." Cass was surprised by her own ferocity—and that she had, in responding to him, twice uttered a sentence that was longer than five words.

Kent chuckled. "You're a good advocate. You should be my agent."

Cass felt downright flabbergasted. For once she wasn't making a fool of herself. Maybe she was channeling Felicity.

"I'll fly in by small plane," he said. "Is Madison still the closest airport?"

"Yes. It's an hour from Loon. But I could, you know, if you want, I could, like, meet you there. And drive you."

"Thanks. I'll take you up on that."

Her heart was beating so hard, she was surprised he didn't ask who was doing the drumming. She took a deep breath, trying to slow her racing pulse. It would be just her luck to have a heart attack before she could meet him.

"I'll fly up in about two weeks on Saturday for the weekend. If you want to go ahead and schedule a benefit for that day, it should work. By the way, Cassandra, is the Miner's Resort still in business?"

"Oh just call me Cass, and no. It's been closed for a while. There's the Bonanza Hotel, the Motherlode Inn, and Placer's Gold B&B. The B&B makes great scones."

"I'm a sucker for scones. I'll make a reservation. Thanks for contacting me. I'll look forward to revisiting Loon. And to meeting you, Cass." He hung up.

Cass stared at her phone. What she wanted to do was throw it in the air and shout Hallelujah, but she was trembling too hard, whether from excitement or shock she wasn't sure. Kent Calloway wanted to meet *her*? Oh. My. God. Every trace of her earlier fatigue vanished in a swirl of energy. She fizzed with excitement; this must be how a shaken can of cola felt. To think she was going to be picking him up and chauffeuring him around Loon. How amazing was that! Even more extraordinary, though she'd been nervous, especially at first, something about him had put her mostly at ease.

Wait. Her car must *reek* of dog. What if Kent didn't like dogs, or was allergic to them? She would have to clean her pickup thoroughly, inside and out. Maybe she could persuade Diego—whose standard of cleanliness far exceeded her own— to give her truck a fine tuning after she'd cleaned it in exchange for credit at Hogan's ice cream parlor. Diego's love for mint chocolate chip surpassed even her own addiction to salted caramel. If only ice cream were unsweetened, nonfat, and still retained the same delicious flavor, the world would be a better place. She smiled. Until she remembered why Diego had come to the U.S. She shook her head to rid herself of such thoughts.

A million questions for Kent tumbled around her brain. Questions like had he set out to write a series with a character who cared about justice? If so, why was that theme important to him? How had he come up with Felicity in the first place?

Since the trip to and from the airport would take an hour each way, she would have lots of time to ask her questions. Assuming she could remember them. She better write them all down, prioritize them, memorize them, and bring the list with her, just in case.

She had to share this incredible news. The library was already closed, Jonas gone home for the day to his house halfway between Loon and Madison. Cass had never been there. Jonas was one of the most private people she knew. He could be living with a man or a woman, married or single.

Thankfully, Mack had returned home that morning from her family reunion. They'd planned dinner at Mack's tomorrow, but that was too long to wait. With a smile of anticipation, Cass put her truck in gear and headed toward her friend's.

SEVEN

The breeze created a concert as it soughed through fir, pine, and the many wind chimes hanging on Mack's porch: the *kloch* of pieces of bamboo blowing against each other, the ping of crystal, the shimmering silver sound of small aluminum strips.

Mack opened the front door. "What a nice surprise," she said from the front porch.

Cass waved. "Welcome home."

Silver hair cut short, Mack wore jeans and one of the flannel shirts she loved even in summer. Her two rescue pups—Socrates, a black Scottie, and Dante, an albino Dachshund that looked like a ghost dog—shot past her and barked at Caesar. Loudly. Protectively.

Caesar barked back.

Cass left Caesar in the truck and got out; she called to Dante and Socrates. The dogs came to her, their tails signaling welcome, but they still barked. Cass leaned over to pet them. "Hey, guys," she said. "How are you?" Dante licked her hand. Socrates growled at Caesar's head sticking out the window.

Mack joined Cass beside her truck. "I'm glad you're back,"

Cass said. She'd often thought that you could mark off sections of Mack—who stood tall and Army-straight—and use her as a ruler.

"Me, too." Mack indicated Caesar. "Who's this?"

"Caesar," Cass said.

"Great name."

"Yeah. I didn't pick it, though." Cass had never known Mack to name a dog anything other than something straight out of the classics. Mack had owned—or fostered—Aristotle, Athena, Apollo, Aphrodite, Antigone, Homer, Neptune, and Zeus. Her two latest dogs had come to her seven months before when a neighbor, whose house was foreclosed upon, had to move away. They couldn't afford to keep the dogs; Mack agreed to take them.

Cass wasn't sure what had drawn her to Mack's kennel, In Good Company, that day twenty-two years ago. Maybe she'd stopped there because the dogs' howls had given voice to her own loneliness. At twelve, Cass's father dead less than a year, Rebecca still going full tilt with her bullying, Cass had felt defeated. Mack spotted her looking at a chocolate-brown Lab, introduced herself as the kennel owner, and asked if she would like to help her by playing with Hershey, the Lab. Almost instantly Cass was petting the dog, rubbing his belly, playing fetch and keep away. Mack invited her to stop by anytime.

It became the highlight of her days. After Cass graduated from high school, Mack offered her full-time work at the kennel; when Mack retired four years before, she'd sold Cass the kennel for a dollar.

"Should I let Caesar out?" Cass said.

"Sure, assuming he won't think these little guys are hors d'oeuvres."

"He hasn't snacked on anybody at the kennel."

"Then, by all means." Mack clicked her tongue and pointed down. Both little dogs sat.

Cass opened the truck door and lifted Caesar's muzzle so that both his green eye and his brown eye looked into hers. "Be good," she said and stepped aside.

Caesar jumped down. Each of the three dogs sniffed the others' hind ends, the little dogs going up on their back legs to smell Caesar, their tails slowly wagging in cautious hellos. Then, apparently satisfied, all three dogs romped about the yard.

"Too bad people don't get along that easily," Mack said.

"Yeah. Maybe we should let dogs run free and kennel people."

"I know what you mean. So how'd you come by Caesar?"

Cass gave a brief accounting.

"Talk about someone who needs kenneling," Mack said. "I'm delighted you got another dog, but in the future, Cass, please don't come between a dog and a man with a gun."

"I didn't, really. Not deliberately."

"Still. Be careful, okay? There are some deranged people out there."

"I'll be careful. Hey, I want to hear all about your reunion."

"Speaking of deranged people." Mack winked. "In truth, it was great. A few little glitches here and there, especially Doris, who as you know is the family drama queen. I wish I could convince my sisters to move to Loon. Unfortunately, you'll have to wait for details till tomorrow night. I've got a historical society meeting in twenty minutes."

"I forgot." Cass heard the disappointment in her own voice.

"Something's got you excited," Mack said. "What's up?"

"It can wait."

"Tell me."

Cass quickly explained about the library closing, the discovery that Loon had inspired the Felicity Benedict novels, and Kent's promised visit. "Isn't that amazing?"

"It is. I know how much those books, and the library, mean

to you." At Cass's urging, Mack had read the first Felicity Benedict novel and pronounced it "excellent," but then went back to the history books she preferred. "And I love that you took the initiative to write to Kent."

"Me, too," Cass said. "I can't wait to tell Jonas about Kent's visit. And I guess I better tell Rebecca."

"Rebecca?" Mack looked like Cass had just vomited on her shoes.

"She *is* our mayor. I can't promote the town like she can. You know me. If I try to talk in front of more than two people, my tongue tangles."

Mack put her hands on Cass's shoulders. "Watch yourself when you deal with Rebecca."

"*Careful*'s my middle name."

"I mean it." Mack's expression softened. "I don't want to see you get hurt."

"I'll be careful, but people can change, Mack."

"Can they?"

Funny, she both liked and disliked Mack's fierce protectiveness. On the one hand, it felt reassuring to know someone had her back. On the other, it made Cass feel weak for wanting someone else's protection. After Cass's mom had moved away, how many times had Mack gone to the school and called out school officials for not stopping Rebecca's bullying? Never did any good that Cass could tell, but at least she knew that Mack cared enough to try. "I sure hope so. I mean, if Rebecca can't change, then neither can I." Cass longed to be more outgoing, more confident, more assertive. In other words, more Felicity.

Mack's expression softened. "I hope you're right about Rebecca, but I suspect she's still the bully she was in high school."

Cass decided to wait to tell Mack about Rebecca's apology and Zoe working at the kennel until their dinner the following night.

Mack glanced at her watch. "I need to go. Can you feed the boys?"

"Sure. You're not taking them?"

"Can't. Nate's allergic. I just need to get my backpack and keys."

Following Mack, Cass noted, as always, the Cecile Brunner rosebushes, not yet beginning to bud, that flanked her friend's porch. Mack's late husband, Seamus, had planted the pink roses as a birthday present when Mack turned 60.

The instant Cass stepped into the spacious, high-ceilinged, wood-beamed house, her chest seemed to expand, as it always did. "You know, Mack," she said, "your house sure looks a lot like the one Kent made up for Felicity. Any chance Kent was ever here?"

"Not that I remember. And Seamus would have told me if he'd had a guest."

Seamus had been Mack's husband and true love for nearly forty years, before he died in a botched hernia operation two years earlier. Mack still missed him fiercely. As did Cass.

Mack grabbed her things. "See you tomorrow night." She made her way out the door.

Cass filled two small dog bowls, then, hand on Caesar's collar so he didn't scarf down the food, set both bowls on the floor. Dante and Socrates chomped, tails wagging.

Caesar whimpered. Cass squatted beside him. "I know, boy. Sorry. But their food's a special mix for little guys. You need something heartier. I'll feed you as soon as we get home."

Once Socrates and Dante had finished gulping their food, Cass let them out to do their business and glanced at the collection of historical photographs of Loon that dated back to the mid-1800s. The photos covered one whole wall of Mack's living room: pictures of mining and lumbering and picnicking, of men and women, both at work and at play. Mack loved history the way Cass loved Felicity.

Maybe she should call Rebecca while she waited for Socrates and Dante. If she was lucky, a little of Mack's self-confidence might rub off on her. She found Rebecca's business card in her wallet, and called the number.

Rebecca picked up on the third ring. "Cass?" she said.

Cass didn't want to try explaining over the phone about Kent's visit. For all she knew, Rebecca had never heard of him or Felicity Benedict. "I, uh, I need to see you about something."

"About what?"

"Loon."

"What about Loon?"

"I might, you know, that is, I have an idea how to help the town, at least a little. Maybe more than that."

"You do?"

"Yes."

"Then by all means, let's meet. I'm tied up today and tomorrow. Come by my house Saturday morning. Let's say ten."

Before Cass could confirm, Rebecca disconnected the call.

Had Rebecca changed? Her manner was certainly brusque. Then again, if she was in a meeting or having dinner with someone, that would explain the curt call. Besides, she'd invited Cass over to say her piece. The old Rebecca wouldn't have done that, nor would she have apologized for her bullying. Whether she'd have apologized if she hadn't needed something from Cass, who knew? The thing to do was to give her the benefit of the doubt and see how Saturday went—but keep Mack's warning in mind.

Cass whistled the little dogs back in. They dashed for the house. Once they were safely inside, she started out, Caesar trailing her, and locked Mack's door behind them. Caesar gave her a clear expression of disapproval. "Okay, okay. I'm sorry. Feeding you will be my first order of business once we get home." She opened the truck door and whistled.

Still on the porch, Caesar sat.

"Look, I promise that next time we'll stay longer. Now get in the truck. Please."

He didn't budge.

Now what was he protesting? The back seat was clean. Well, that might be overstating a little. She shoved some kennel supplies to the far side of the back seat and called, "Caesar, come."

He sauntered over so slowly, she figured that by the time he reached the truck, she'd be eligible for Social Security. Once he finally—*finally*—climbed in, she closed the door and got in the driver's seat. Caesar turned away from her and stuck his head out the opposite back window. Cass suppressed a sigh. Sometimes her dog had the emotional maturity of a two-year-old child.

As Cass drove, her mind drifted yet again to Kent's promised visit. For him to create such a well-realized woman like Felicity—smart and strong and sexy and not traditionally shaped—he must be extraordinary. Cass's only regret was that she'd have to wait two weeks to meet him.

EIGHT

oud, heavy metal music blasted from the kennel office Saturday morning, vibrating the windows of Cass's truck as she pulled into the parking lot, scorching her eardrums. The dogs howled. She'd called Diego a few minutes ago to say she was on her way, but he never played music this loud anyway.

She left Caesar in the vehicle to afford him at least a modicum of protection from the din and shoved open the office door.

Zoe sat in the desk chair moving to the relentless, throbbing beat from Cass's old stereo set and speakers.

Cass yanked the cord from the wall and spun the chair so Zoe faced her. "Didn't you hear the dogs?" she demanded.

"Sure. They were singing along."

"They were howling because their ears hurt, damn it."

Zoe dipped her head. Her long bangs, today streaked with purple highlights, cloaked her eyes. She didn't respond, but her cheeks splotched red.

"Where's Diego?" Cass shot at her. She couldn't believe

anyone would have been unable to figure out that the music was too loud for the dogs' ears.

Zoe didn't look at her. "He took some dogs on a run."

"When?"

Zoe shrugged. "A few minutes ago."

Of course. He knew Cass would be there shortly. He'd reasonably assumed Zoe could handle things for a few minutes.

Cass struggled to calm herself. Was it possible Zoe really thought the dogs were just howling along with the music? "Dogs hear a lot better than people," she said. "Loud noises hurt their ears."

Zoe kept her eyes averted. "Whatever." She turned the chair away from Cass.

Whatever? Now facing the back of Zoe's head, Cass didn't bother to spin the chair toward her. "I told you and your mom I wouldn't tolerate anyone hurting the dogs. Get your things. I have an appointment with your mother."

"Fine." The girl grabbed her backpack.

If Cass didn't know better, she'd have thought that fear had flitted across Zoe's face, but Zoe seemed impervious to fear, not to mention common sense or remorse.

Cass flipped the sign on the door to *closed; back soon.*

Zoe, in fashionably torn jeans and form-fitting camisole, slouched toward the parking lot ahead of Cass. Zoe's clothes were far from the linen slacks and white sweaters Cass's mother had insisted Cass wear to school, at a time when other girls wore jeans and T-shirts. The very day her mother moved to Tucson, leaving her twelve-year-old daughter in Mack's and Seamus's care, Cass donated her slacks and sweaters to Goodwill, where she bought two pairs of jeans and three football jerseys. Other than switching from jeans to cargo pants in recent years, her outfits hadn't changed much.

Cass turned onto the highway. Rebecca wasn't going to be happy about Cass forbidding Zoe from working at the kennel on Zoe's first full day. The only question was whether Rebecca would blame Zoe, Cass, or both. She noticed she was white knuckling the steering wheel and made herself loosen her grip. She looked toward Moon Mountain, hoping to see cheering sparkle, but clouds hid it from view.

Neither she nor Zoe spoke. Zoe was turned away from her, chipping slowly away at the purple polish on one of her thumbs.

Damn it, Cass thought. What if this really did turn Rebecca against her—and Felicity? Then, too, Rebecca had said the kennel was Zoe's last chance before Juvie. Did Cass want to be the reason Zoe went to what was essentially jail? If only Zoe would express regret or apologize, Cass wouldn't have to eject her. Then again, maybe Juvie would be good for Zoe.

Or not.

Caesar nuzzled Zoe's neck. Traitor.

Cass stopped in front of Rebecca and Zoe's two-story house on Motherlode Drive, the more prosperous section of town. Painted creamy yellow with white trim, the house was a cross between Victorian and Cape Cod styles: a small front porch under a peaked roof supported by thin white columns, shuttered bay windows downstairs, dormers, and gabled roof. Cass wondered if the contrasting styles had reflected Rebecca and Hank's personalities. Rebecca would prefer the showy Victorian, Hank the quieter Cape Cod. He'd been almost invisible in the shadow of Rebecca's flamboyance. Maybe that's why he'd left. Maybe he'd wanted to be seen.

"Be good," she said to Caesar, leaving him in the truck as she and a scowling Zoe got out. "This won't take long."

Rebecca opened the door before they reached it. "Great," she said to Zoe. "Maybe Juvie's where you belong."

Cass's whole body tensed. That was the voice she remembered from her school days. When Cass's face had erupted in pimples, Rebecca and her buddies had added *Pizzaface* to their verbal arsenal.

Zoe just stared at her mother with an expression of contempt.

Did Cass really want the girl to go to Juvie? "There's been a misunderstanding," she said to Rebecca. "Zoe didn't do anything wrong."

Rebecca shoved her auburn hair behind her ear.

"I asked Zoe to join us for this meeting because I wanted to get a young person's perspective." Cass turned to Zoe, nodded, then flashed a smile at Rebecca that she hoped was convincing.

"You aren't kicking her out?" Rebecca's voice was just a note shy of incredulous.

"No. I mean, it's all a learning experience, right? You don't come to a new job knowing how to do it. You have to be trained. Just like the dogs." Cass surprised herself with that explanation. Maybe Zoe *hadn't* known about dogs' hearing. Hopefully Zoe really heard what she was saying, though she was looking at her fingernails. For all Cass could tell, Zoe could be thinking about her next rendezvous with Rip. Or about how lame Cass was. "I'm sure Zoe's a fast study."

Rebecca snorted.

Zoe rolled her eyes.

Rebecca looked from Cass to Zoe and back to Cass. Her shrug was almost an exact copy of Zoe's. "Come on in."

Cass took in the living room, which resembled a set piece for *House Beautiful*: a red, plush sofa with two matching easy chairs, nesting tables of bright colors, three gorgeous throw rugs in rich hues and geometric designs, abstract art on the walls, and vividly colored vases and lamps scattered around. It was a cheerful—no, Cass thought, an ebullient—room. She didn't know what she'd expected: dark leather upholstery perhaps. Rebecca gestured Cass to the sofa and took one of the easy chairs, Zoe the other.

"So what's up?" Rebecca said.

Cass sat on the edge of the sofa. "Have you read any of the Felicity Benedict novels?"

Rebecca shook her head. "Novels? I'm lucky to find time to read an ingredients list."

"Well, the books are really big sellers."

"Harry Potter big?"

"No, but *Hunger Games* big. *Twilight* big."

"And I care because?"

"The author just announced in *People* magazine that the books are inspired by and based on Loon."

Rebecca looked stunned. "Loon was mentioned in *People*?"

Cass handed Rebecca her copy of the magazine, opened to the two-page article.

Rebecca's eyes quickly scanned the story. "Hmm. Interesting."

"And," Cass said, "as the article indicates, a movie, based on the first book, is coming out Memorial Day weekend."

"Where'd they film it?"

"Canada."

"Figures."

"I contacted the author, Kent Calloway, inviting him to visit Loon. He's coming in two weeks."

"Coming here?" Rebecca said.

"Yes. And he's going to do a reading to benefit the library."

Rebecca looked puzzled. "Why does he care about the library?"

"He said he didn't want to see a town without books."

Rebecca frowned. "A town without books? Isn't that a little exaggerated?"

"Not if you close the library." Cass couldn't believe she'd just said that. Disagree with Rebecca? Apparently she could advocate for books as well as dogs.

"Hmm." Rebecca jotted something on a notepad. "I take it the author used to live in Loon."

"Not lived." Cass explained about Kent's family's summer vacations to the town.

Rebecca glanced back at the magazine. "Seems like there ought to be a way to get mileage from this guy's visit."

Cass scooted forward. "Kent said he could probably persuade Penn Booth, one of the movie's stars, to visit later. That might bring in some tourists."

"I like where you're going with this," Rebecca said, "but let's back up a minute. Tell me more about these novels and about the movie's stars."

"The heroine, Felicity Benedict, is smart and funny, and she's compassionate," Cass said. "She's part detective and part therapist."

"She's young and beautiful, I take it."

"No, she's forty and heavy."

"Fat and forty? Why are the books so popular? Is she a vampire?"

Rebecca looked genuinely puzzled. She didn't register that far more people looked like Felicity than like Rebecca. "I think because the books deal with problems we all face."

"Such as?"

"Oh, relationship issues. Lost pets or people. Robberies. Philandering spouses. Bullies. Dishonest people. Everyday stuff."

"Murder?" Rebecca said.

"No. They're gentle books. That's part of their charm."

"I thought sex, drugs, and murder sold books."

"Not in this case." Cass couldn't really explain how the novels had touched so many readers, especially women, herself included. Maybe if Rebecca read the books, she'd better understand their appeal.

"Plus, the Rain and Lucas relationship is straight fire," Zoe said.

"Huh?" Rebecca's voice sounded as puzzled as her expression.

Zoe once again rolled her eyes.

"You've read the books?" Cass said.

"Yeah."

That was certainly unexpected.

"Who are Rain and Lucas?"

Rebecca looked as puzzled as her voice sounded—but focused, so much so, Cass could practically see the wheels in Rebecca's brain spinning. "Lucas is an eighteen-year-old boy Felicity hires as her handyman," Cass said. "He falls for Rain, the seventeen-year-old runaway Felicity takes in. And Zoe's right." She nodded to Zoe. "Their relationship is torched. On fire."

"And you like these books?" Rebecca asked her daughter.

"Yeah. They show that kids can love each other."

"Teenagers don't know any more about love than they do about nuclear physics," Rebecca said. "They just think they do."

Zoe muttered something unintelligible under her breath and peeled away more polish.

Rebecca drummed her fingers on the chair's arm. "Who are the movie's stars?"

"Lana Kurth, who's really big, plays Felicity."

Rebecca chuckled. "Big in more ways than one, I take it."

Cass flinched.

"Sorry," Rebecca said. "Go on."

"The young stars are Olivia Golden and Penn Booth."

Rebecca scribbled something more on her legal pad. "They're popular?"

"Epic," Zoe said.

Cass would swear Rebecca's eyes were brightening by the minute.

Rebecca leaned forward. "If our stores sold Felicity Benedict merchandise like T-shirts and other souvenirs, that could bring in substantial revenue for the town, providing we can attract enough tourists."

"It would help fund the library, too," Cass said. "Right?"

"Of course."

"You should look up stuff on Forks, Washington." Zoe's eyes were on Cass. "It's the setting for the *Twilight* books. They get lots of tourists."

"Have you been there?" Cass said.

"No, but my friend Angelique told me about it."

"That's a good suggestion," Cass said.

A smile flitted across Zoe's face.

"How many tourists is a lot?" Rebecca asked.

"I don't know. Angelique just said it was really crowded."

"Get me my laptop."

Zoe shook her head like Rebecca had just asked her to hop up and down on an alligator, but she rose.

When Zoe handed her the laptop, Rebecca began keying. "Forks, Washington," she said. Her eyes scanned the screen . . . then widened further than Cass would have thought possible.

"My God," Rebecca said.

NINE

Cass leaned toward Rebecca wishing she felt confident enough to stand up and read over her shoulder. "What?"

Rebecca didn't look up. "Since the *Twilight* series came out, Forks has had over ninety- thousand visitors, sometimes more than three hundred a *day*."

Rebecca looked exactly how Cass felt: flabbergasted. "Seriously?" Cass said.

"So it says."

"In how many years?"

"Looks like three or four mostly." Rebecca startled Cass by moving to the couch to sit beside her. "Take a look at this." Rebecca gestured to the screen.

The physical touch with Rebecca made Cass want to scoot further away, but the screen held fascinating photos of Forks and its businesses selling all kinds of *Twilight* merchandise: T-shirts, caps, coffee mugs, water bottles, key chains, posters of the sexy stars autographed by the actors and the author. And more, including life-sized cardboard cutouts of the actors in front of stores that gleamed with fresh paint.

"Looks like they gave Forks a makeover," Cass said.

"That's exactly what they did. Three-hundred tourists a day would make Loon a boom town in a way it hasn't been since the gold rush days."

True. It would also mean traffic jams in a town that lacked a single stop sign or traffic signal, not to mention tourists crowding the town's sidewalks and businesses. Mack would be horrified. So would a lot of other people. But she brushed off those thoughts with the realization that crowds of tourists would mean tax revenue to fund the library and street repairs and maybe even a computer lab for the school, plus higher profits for businesses. It could be a true boon for Loon.

Rebecca kept reading aloud. "This says that Forks was floundering financially, like us, but thanks to the *Twilight* connection, it's thriving. People even move *to* Forks rather than away from it."

Zoe stood. "I'm going upstairs."

Rebecca didn't look up. "Do your homework."

Zoe walked quickly, Cass thought, perhaps to get away from her mother, who seemed to have trouble speaking to Zoe in anything but commands.

Rebecca closed the laptop. "I've been searching for a way to save the town since before I took office last year. I've solicited input from numerous people. The idea of tying Loon to the Felicity Benedict craze is inspired, Cass. It never occurred to me that I should ask you. I'm so glad you came to me."

"Me, too." Cass managed a smile, unsure whether she'd just been complimented or insulted.

"The question," Rebecca said, "is how to involve as much of the town as possible so that a big majority will support the changes. What should we call the overall concept?"

"The Felicity Benedict Connection?" Cass said.

"I like it." Rebecca tapped her finger on the keyboard. "The FBC for short. Good. Tell me more about the books."

"There are three so far, and Kent's working on a fourth. The series is called *Matters of the Heart*. Each of the books revolves around a different emotion. The first one's *Betrayal*, the second, *Passion*; and the third's *Envy*.

Rebecca listened, then frowned. "I do wonder," she said, "how Felicity can be so supposedly smart but weigh so much. She's got to know that being overweight poses all kinds of health problems. Given that, why would anyone assume she could solve anything?"

Cass didn't want to cross Rebecca but remaining silent felt like lying to the most important person in Cass's life apart from Mack. "Felicity's wise and really cares about people," she said. "She makes people happier and their lives better. How can you not admire that?"

"Okay, I see your point. When's the author coming?"

"On the 14th."

"Saturday, two weeks from today?"

Cass nodded.

"Doesn't give us a lot of time," Rebecca said, "but more people are likely to come on a Saturday. I'm good friends with Boyer August, who owns the paper. I'm sure he'll give us a terrific writeup. And I'll get all the towns near us to run articles to publicize our Felicity connection and Kent's coming. Maybe we can pull in a few fans."

"Good idea. I'm picking him up at the Madison airport." Just saying that made her smile. "He pilots his own plane."

"Hmm. We'll take my car. Be sure you bring a notepad to jot down anything he mentions on the drive back to Loon.

We?

"I'll introduce Kent at the library benefit. Unless you'd like to, of course. This was your idea, after all."

Cass paled. "I don't . . ." Her heart jackhammered her chest.

If any single high school experience had traumatized Cass, it was eighth-grade English when they had to give speeches.

She'd labored for weeks over her speech about *To Kill a Mocking-bird* and being kind to people who are different, the Boo Radleys of the world. She'd fantasized that her classmates would be so moved, they would cheer.

They didn't.

It began with Rebecca, who had scribbled something on a sheet of binder paper she was holding up so that Cass could see it, but their teacher couldn't. Cass squinted; it took her a minute to decipher what the sign said: *Loser*. Rebecca handed off her sign to her buddy Lindsey York, who snickered and passed it around. More snickers.

Cass stumbled, unable to recall what she'd planned to say next. The teacher reprimanded her for not being prepared. Cass slunk back to her seat, clawing her arm to keep from crying. She never got up in front of that class—or any class—again, preferring to take an "F" on all speech units.

"Don't worry," Rebecca said. "I'll do the presenting. I remember you never liked giving speeches."

Was Rebecca's memory that selective, Cass wondered, or had Cass overblown the incident in her own mind?

"I'll post Kent's upcoming visit on our town website today and will start looking into merchandising licenses for Felicity souvenirs. Plus, Loon needs a facelift. I'll get the council to start mapping that out, priorities and costs involved. But we can't mention Forks and our full promotion just yet. It's critical that we get the FBC in front of the town before the antis get wind of it."

Cass blinked. "The aunties?"

"People who oppose change. *Any* change, really. They're loud, mostly obnoxious and, unfortunately, quick to organize. That means you tell nobody. Including Mack."

Cass paused. "Why wouldn't I tell Mack?"

"Mack's an amazing woman," Rebecca said, "and she does a lot for this town with the museum and the historical society.

The town owes her. But look, Mack's focus is on the past. I suspect she'll oppose anything that smacks of development, or even the possibility of development down the line. And she's a formidable organizer. We want the writer to have an *enthusiastic* reception, so he'll sign on with continued efforts to promote Loon through media interviews, return visits, maybe even persuading movie stars to come."

"I don't know if I can do that," Cass said.

"I realize this is weird for you, Cass, and I don't ask it lightly. The way I'm seeing it, the campaign that you've inspired could literally save our town. Including, of course, the library. Do you want to jeopardize all that?"

Rebecca had a point. Mack probably would oppose anything that meant tourists and traffic. And Kent needed to have a positive experience if they wanted Loon's connection with him to really matter.

Rebecca was still looking at her.

"I already told her about Kent coming," Cass said.

"Did you mention anything about turning it into a tourist promotion?"

"No, I didn't know anything about Forks."

"Good. Look, Kent will be here soon. You won't have to hold off for long."

Cass shifted her weight. Was she really willing to withhold something so significant from Mack? But Rebecca was probably right that Cass's silence could help save the library, Jonas's job —possibly, even, the town itself.

"Once we have a better idea of what we're doing and what kind of numbers we can expect," Rebecca said, "we'll revisit the question of when to announce our plans. And in the meantime, we need some catchy slogans to advertise the Loon/Felicity Connection as well as the town's other assets. If you come up with anything, let me know."

"I know nothing about advertising."

"But you do know a lot about Felicity. No pressure, just if you think of anything catchy and easy to remember."

Rebecca's phone rang. Her ringtone sounded like *Hail to the Chief*, Cass thought, but surely it couldn't be. Could it?

Rebecca answered. "Just a moment," she said to whoever was on the line. She stood. "I'm really glad you came to see me with this, Cass. It's great to have you on my team."

Cass nearly tripped over her own astonishment. "I should check with Zoe about working at the kennel today."

"Her room's upstairs. It will be the one with the keep out sign. Ignore it." Rebecca turned away and walked to another room, closing the door behind her.

Cass took the stairs, her brain spinning. To think Rebecca wanted Cass on her team—and apparently respected her enough to invite her to come up with advertising slogans. Clearly Mack was wrong; people *could* change, at least some people. She'd love to come up with a slogan or something Rebecca wanted to use. After all, the way this day had turned out, almost *anything* could happen.

Big, bold black letters on Zoe's door did, indeed, proclaim KEEP OUT. Cass hesitated, but she had to speak with Zoe. She knocked on her door. No answer. She knocked harder. Still no answer. She turned the knob, knocking as she slowly pushed open the door.

"Go away," came the command.

"Zoe, it's Cass."

"Oh. Come in."

Zoe's room was surprisingly neat, bordering on immaculate. The room held a purple easy chair, a poster on the ceiling of the band Foo Fighters, and a vanity table that Cass suspected held more bottles and tubes of makeup than all the cosmetics sold by Grubstake Grocery. Cass couldn't help but wonder how much of it was stolen. Zoe, headphones on, was on her bed, legs stretched out, focused on something on a clipboard on her lap. Sketches of people adorned the walls. Each person was wearing distinctive clothes, and all seemed to swirl with movement and color.

"Doing your homework?" Cass said.

"Charting the life cycle of a worm? No way."

"What are you working on?"

Zoe handed Cass the clipboard. It was a detailed drawing of a dancing woman in a short green flared skirt, a dark red blouse, and a Bolero hat. The figure seemed almost alive. "This is good," Cass said. "Really good. So the sketches on the walls are yours?"

"Yeah."

"I didn't know you were an artist."

"A designer." Zoe spoke quickly. "I'm going to be a celebrity fashion designer. When I graduate, I'm going to New York City. Or maybe L.A."

"I hope it all works out just the way you want."

"Thanks."

"Are you coming back with me to the kennel?"

Zoe frowned. "I guess I have to. Unless you want to let me bail."

"Sorry. I don't think that's a good idea."

They walked down the stairs and got in the truck without further comment. Caesar gave Cass a reproachful look and once again nuzzled Zoe.

When they were on their way back to the kennel, Cass spoke in a voice as non-accusatory as she could make it. "Do you understand why I was angry earlier?"

"I didn't know about dogs' hearing," Zoe said, staring out the window.

"But you do now, right?"

"Yeah."

"And you won't play music that loud again?"

"No, I won't." Zoe turned halfway toward Cass and picked

at a thread hanging loose from one of the tears in her jeans. "Sorry."

The apology surprised Cass. "Okay, we're good," she said. Maybe Zoe wasn't unreachable. "Did you like the *Twilight* series?"

"The books, yeah. The movies sucked. Angelique thinks the guy who plays Edward is hot. As if. Angelique posted photos of herself in Forks kissing a cardboard cutout of the guy. Gross."

"What do you think of Penn Booth?"

"He's okay."

From what Cass was learning about Zoe, that was a strong endorsement. "When did you start reading the Felicity Benedict novels?"

"About a year ago. I really like Lucas and Rain."

"Not Felicity?"

"She's old and fat."

Cass sighed.

"You're not fat," Zoe protested.

"No, but I'm not that far from Felicity's age. By your standards, that makes me old."

Zoe turned a shade of crimson that would put an apple to shame.

"I'm just teasing you," Cass said as they pulled into the kennel lot.

The *closed* sign had been flipped to *open*. Inside, Diego was cradling Sniffles, a small, trembling Yorkie, rocking it back and forth while he whispered in its ear, "*Calmate, chico.*" There was such tenderness in Diego's voice and face. You couldn't learn that kind of tenderness. It made Cass glad once again to have hired him. He'd come to Loon to visit a distant cousin, who at the time worked for Caltrans on a road crew repairing a stretch of highway to the east of Loon. The cousin had since transferred to Oakland with his girlfriend. Luckily for Cass, Diego stayed.

"What's wrong with Sniffles?" she said. He and Thunder were the smallest of the dogs that day boarded with her.

"He thought Cali was charging him."

"*Cali?*" Cass had never known the boxer to be aggressive.

"He was just playing. Sniffles thought he was serious." Diego looked up and smiled at Zoe, who smiled back. "Poor little guy can't stop shaking."

Caesar walked over to them and licked Sniffles. The little dog's trembling seemed to lessen.

Zoe stroked Sniffles.

When the small dog was calm, Diego set him back in his pen. "I'll clean the outside pens, then give the big dogs some one-on-one time."

"You already cleaned the inside pens. You sure you want to do the outside?"

"It's a one-day special."

"I've never been one to pass up a special. Thank you." She'd certainly struck it rich today, on oh so many levels.

"You're good with dogs, Diego." Zoe's voice sounded softer than Cass had heard before, more intimate. More seductive.

"*Gracias.*"

"Can I help you?" Zoe said.

Cass was astonished that Zoe, dressed in designer jeans, had asked.

"Sure." Diego's smile was broad.

They headed outside.

Cass sat in her desk chair beneath the Dalmatian clock with its wagging tail. She would love to read more articles on Forks, but she needed to do her kennel chores first. Her phone sounded its loon call. She answered. "Hello?"

"How did it go with Rebecca?"

It was Mack. "Fine."

"She treated you okay?" Mack said.

"She did."

"That's novel. What did she think of your author coming?"

"She liked the idea." *Loved* it would be more accurate.

"You're okay? You sound a little off."

Naturally Mack would notice. "I didn't sleep well. I'm draggy." Boy was that a lie. She was revved and speeding on possibilities.

"Rebecca could exhaust most anyone," Mack said.

Cass made herself chuckle. "Yeah."

"Go to bed early tonight," Mack said.

"Will do."

"We'll talk tomorrow."

Cass disconnected the call. What would Felicity say about Cass withholding information from the one person whose love for Cass had always been unwavering? Cass squirmed. Then again, surely saving the library and, quite possibly, Loon itself, made it necessary to temporarily postpone the truth.

So why did she feel such a strong sense of unease?

TEN

At last: the honk she'd been waiting for. Cass grabbed her backpack and rushed outside into a day screaming with so much sunshine, Moon Mountain glistened like it was singing *The Hallelujah Chorus.*

"Good morning," Cass said as she got in front beside Rebecca for the hour-long drive to the airport at Madison, the county seat.

Rebecca grunted. She wore an all-black ensemble: leather jacket, short skirt, and high-heeled ankle boots. She remained silent as she drove. Minutes passed.

Cass had expected Rebecca to share her excitement. After all, Rebecca had seemed enthused about the FBC the previous week when she thanked Cass for her slogan suggestion—*Let the town that inspired Felicity inspire you.* Cass was proud of that slogan, which occurred to her in the middle of the night when she was waiting for Caesar to decide he'd peed enough so she could go back to bed. That was the only time prior to yesterday, when Rebecca had texted Cass to confirm their plans for this airport run, that Cass had heard from Rebecca since their

Sunday morning meeting some ten days previously. "What's wrong?" Cass asked.

Rebecca shook her head. "Nothing I want to discuss." She radiated a force field that was downright prickly. Cass hoped Rebecca's mood hadn't been triggered by problems with Zoe, for both their sakes.

She didn't mind the silence. It gave her the opportunity to review the questions for Kent she'd devised, written down, and then memorized. Her first question would be whether it was hard for him to write from the point of view of a female character and how he'd pulled that off so convincingly.

Rebecca reached for the car stereo. Cass wasn't sure what music to expect: rock? country? hip hop? classical? jazz?

Instead, it was NPR. Cass heard analyses of abused children, starving refugees, and suicide bombings. She willed herself to listen with only her head, not her heart. Although she felt a little guilty for it, she didn't want to get depressed, not now. She focused on two of Felicity's exhortations.

"Be loud, be proud," didn't have anything to do with actual volume. Rather, Felicity was counseling those inclined to think they had to always be "nice" or polite, to speak up and speak out.

Similarly, "stand tall and strut" wasn't about physically towering over others or literally strutting but about encouraging people—especially, but not exclusively, women—to own who they were. And to own their looks. When you saw your reflection in a window or mirror, you should smile at yourself and straighten to your full height, *whatever* that was.

If only.

Cass was eager to ask Kent about the books he loved, as a child and now. Maybe he liked one or two of her own favorites. She bet books had been a saving grace for him, much as they were for her. She couldn't explain the connection she felt with both Felicity and her creator. That connection had prompted her to stay up late finding the perfect quote from his first novel with which to greet him. She'd settled on Felicity's greeting for inviting new clients to spill their woes: *Welcome. Come share a little life with me.*

When they pulled into the airport parking area, Cass spotted a small, white-bodied plane landing. Her stomach lurched. What if her tongue got so twisted up trying to talk to him, all she could do was croak? No. She was being ridiculous. She would stand tall and be proud. She turned her attention to seeing what Kent might see: single landing strip, control tower, and a small squat building. It all reminded her of the accessories that came with model train sets. Trees. Stop signs. Railroad crossing barriers.

Rebecca opened her door without a word. As Cass got out, her throat felt tight. Was her presence what was upsetting Rebecca? She was afraid to ask.

They started toward the small building. Rebecca's phone chimed. She stopped, glanced at the screen, and answered with a soft, "Hold on." She pointed toward the building. "You go ahead," she said. "I'll catch up." She turned her back to Cass.

Cass gave silent thanks to whoever had called. Maybe she would have a few minutes to introduce herself to Kent without having Rebecca blinding him with her beauty. She walked faster.

The building contained a few plastic chairs in a waiting area and one window with someone working at a computer. Cass passed through the back doors out to the field.

A man was tying down a white two-seater with red trim.

Cass walked faster. She reached the plane just as he finished and faced her. Kent Calloway: a little huskier than he looked online, his body full and burly. Dark glasses masked his eyes.

He gave her a friendly smile, emphasized by the dimple in

his chin. Wearing a brown leather aviator jacket, he held out his hand. "Cassandra?"

He was here, really here. And extending his hand to her. Felicity's creator. Oh. My. God.

"Cassandra?" he said again.

"Sorry. Yes. Call me Cass." She took his hand, which was dry, warm, and large. "Thanks for coming."

"Thanks for reaching out to me. It's good to meet you."

Did she dare quote Felicity to him? She tried to take a deep breath, but her chest was too constricted. *Go for it, Catch.* "I'm glad you came to share a little life with us." She gave him a tentative smile.

"Thank you, Felicity." He smiled back.

Kent Calloway had called her Felicity. *Her?*

He was looking at her, watching her, no doubt waiting for her to say something. She'd love to ask him a Felicity question, but her mind had gone AWOL. She couldn't remember a single one. No! It wasn't fair! Not after all her preparations. She forced a smile through the lingering silence. *Think.* He carried only a single, small duffel bag. "You, uh, you travel light."

"You know how it is. A man can wear the same shirt three days in a row, and as long as it doesn't stink, he'll be praised as frugal. A woman doing the same would more likely be labeled tight. Hardly fair, but it's one of the many things that make it easier to be a man than a woman."

"Any, you know, minuses?" she said.

"You're expected to be athletic."

"You're not?"

"I'm about as athletic as a flagpole. Charlie Brown could kick a football farther than I can."

She gave a rueful smile. "I guess that, as Felicity says, we should all stand tall and strut. Then give thanks for the morning, thanks for the evening, and dance the night away."

"You really are a fan." He smiled, looking genuinely pleased.

Writers probably loved it when you quoted their books. That was easy. She knew all three Felicity novels from start to finish. And Felicity's advice seemed to be working. Cass wanted to keep quoting Felicity and keep talking, right there on the field, without Rebecca.

She ransacked her brain for questions. Still nothing. "You're a pilot," she said instead.

He smiled again. "Looks that way."

Brilliant, Cass. "I like your plane." Red stripes accented the top of the fuselage and the tips of wing and tail. "What kind is it?"

"A Cessna-152. Old plane, but she's served me well."

"Good thing," she said. "I mean, considering." God. What a flop she was.

"I'd say so."

Think of something intelligent to ask. "How'd you get started flying?"

"Went up with a friend. It was love at first flight. Commercial flying's become such a pain. The way they cram people in makes me feel like a sardine. Better yet, I'm in charge of my own fate. I like that."

"It must be amazing, the view from your cockpit."

"It is. And since this plane flies at less than half of a commercial plane's altitude, I see so much more. Rivers. Lakes. Ocean. Forest. Mountains. It reminds me of the hikes my dad and I used to take, the views when we reached a summit. I think that's what I love best. All that view, and you don't have to work to get it. Though I'd probably be better off if I did a little more physical work." He patted his stomach, which wasn't all that big, though he did have what some people called love handles around his waist.

"I think Felicity would say to just enjoy the view, however you get it."

"I think you're right. You *do* know her well."

Cass flushed again. This was going even better than she'd hoped, despite her brain freeze. Clearly Kent seemed impressed that she could quote his books, and she felt more confident speaking Felicity's words than her own. Maybe she and Kent would become friends. Imagine being friends with someone with Kent's imagination. "I could see Felicity as a pilot," she said. "She'd like that control."

"That she would. Maybe I should consider having her take lessons. That's another thing about flying. You escape everyday stress and strain. Frees your mind. I've come up with some of my best Felicity ideas while flying."

Damn. Rebecca was walking toward them.

"Good morning, Kent," Rebecca called as she neared.

Kent turned toward her, his face a map of his feelings: initial surprise, then curiosity, then deep appreciation.

Rebecca's glum expression was gone, replaced by a dazzling smile. She extended her hand. "I'm Rebecca Oliver, Loon's mayor. I can't tell you what a pleasure it is to meet the creator of one of literature's most delightful heroines."

Good lord, Cass thought. How bright would Rebecca's face shine if she actually meant what she said?

"The pleasure's mine," he said, shaking her hand.

"I love your books." Rebecca put her other hand over their clasped ones.

This from the woman who had insisted she would never consult a fat woman. Cass didn't know if Rebecca had even bothered to finish the book, let alone read the other two. She told herself to remember how convincingly Rebecca could lie.

"Thank you," Kent said.

Their handshake went on so long, it seemed more like a transfusion.

When they released hands, Rebecca gestured to Kent's plane. "That's a Cessna-152, right?"

Kent looked surprised. "It is. Do you fly?"

"Not yet, but I hope to. It must be satisfying to know your life's in your own hands rather than those of people who might sleep too little, drink too much, or think too slow."

Kent looked as impressed as Cass felt.

"Well put," he said.

No kidding.

"Are you ready to visit Loon?" Rebecca said. "She's been waiting a long time to welcome you back."

Good Lord. Where did Rebecca come up with this stuff?

"You bet."

When they reached Rebecca's car, Cass insisted Kent sit up front while she slid into the back seat on the driver side so Kent could easily see her. He got in, then watched Rebecca as she put her shapely rear on the seat, slid her shapely legs under the steering wheel, and inserted the key into the ignition with her shapely fingers.

"It's refreshing to meet a woman mayor," Kent said. "As I remember, the area's conservative. You must have some sort of superpower."

"Just some great supporters, a little patience, and a whole lot of luck."

"Men have made a mess of this planet long enough," Kent said. "It's about time we stepped aside and gave women a shot at it. Tell me, do you have any political ambitions beyond being mayor?"

"Maybe."

Cass wasn't really surprised. Curious, yes. What were those ambitions? County supervisor? Governor? President? Maybe Rebecca's ringtone really did chime *Hail to the Chief*.

"For now," Rebecca said, "my focus is on being the best mayor I can be and doing everything I can to help our town. Which is why I so appreciate your coming to Loon. And if I may be so bold, I want to thank you on behalf of women everywhere for creating such a remarkable heroine. Right, Cass?"

"Absolutely." Cass nodded with enthusiasm. "Your characters are so real, and you come up with all kinds of plot twists."

"Thank you both." Kent was beaming. "But be careful. All this praise is going to my head."

"It must take such imagination to write a novel," Rebecca said. "I could never do that."

"Well, I would never have the diplomacy to be mayor," Kent said, "so I guess it's a good thing that you're the politician and I'm the writer. What work are you in, Cass?"

"I run a dog kennel."

Kent didn't respond for a moment. Perhaps he was trying to think of something nice to say.

He looked outside his window. "That must keep you busy," he finally said.

Cass slouched.

"Maybe you could tell us a little about your writing." Rebecca glanced at Kent as she drove. "I mean, what inspired you to create the amazing Felicity?"

The amazing, *fat* Felicity, Cass wanted to remind her. Rebecca must be laying it on thick so that Kent would want to come back, movie stars in tow. After all, Kent couldn't be Rebecca's type. If anything, he was a little pudgy. Not fat, but certainly a bigger man than Rebecca was likely to be drawn to. Hank had been lanky. Given the way Kent was looking at Rebecca, her strategy seemed to be working. Cass was sure that if he had anything to say about it, movie stars would flock to Loon, and he would be right beside them.

Cass told herself to be glad Kent seemed attracted to Rebecca. It would be good for Jonas and the library, good for the town.

Kent turned from looking out the window and glanced at Rebecca, then Cass, then back at Rebecca. "I came up with

Felicity because I wanted to create a protagonist who's not all that attractive physically but is comfortable with her appearance and beautiful on the inside. You might say that writing my novels is a form of therapy."

That's when Cass thought she understood him, when she saw Kent's tentative smile and the slight shrug of his shoulders, things that told her that despite all the success he'd crafted, Kent Calloway shared at least some of her own self-doubts.

"We could use a Felicity in Loon," Rebecca said. "Someone wise who could solve any disputes or crimes that come up."

"You have a lot of those, do you?" Kent said.

"Not all that many crimes," Rebecca said, "but we are a small town. Sometimes we get on each other's nerves, just like any family. Did you grow up in a small town?"

"No. Fresno. I live in LA now, the Echo Park neighborhood. As you may know, when I was a kid, my family spent a couple weeks or two each summer in Loon. My dad and I explored so many different lakes and trails. I haven't been back in years, not since my dad . . . died."

Had Kent paused, or had Cass just imagined it?

"I'm looking forward to seeing how the town's changed," he said.

"Or hasn't," Cass said.

"Or hasn't, yes. How about the two of you? Are you both Loon natives?"

"Through and through," Rebecca said.

"Me, too," Cass said.

"Sounds like I'm in good hands."

Rebecca smiled at him; Kent smiled back.

Cass felt like the third wheel. Oh well. She just hoped she could get a little more time alone with Kent. They'd seemed to connect so well before Rebecca joined them. Still, she couldn't help but be impressed that Rebecca could come up so quickly with such great lines.

She was glad she *hadn't* told Mack about the FBC or the true number of tourists they hoped to attract. While she didn't know what Rebecca had planned for tonight's benefit, Cass was sure that Rebecca's presentation as to why the FBC would be good for the town would be effective. Indeed, she bet even Mack would be convinced.

ELEVEN

The first place they took Kent was Prospector's General Store, where Scotty Clemons, the bow-tied proprietor who was shorter than his store's name, put a set of Felicity novels on the counter. "They're my grandmother's."

Scotty's grandmother, Madelon, was an elderly woman whose scoliosis bent her over so far, her body nearly created a right angle, but who still smiled and laughed with ease. For years Madelon had read to kids at the library until stopping the previous August when she celebrated her ninetieth.

Scotty said Madelon now devoted her days to reading. That was the kind of old age Cass would enjoy. Books, books, books. And dogs, of course.

"Gran says she's learned more from Felicity than she has anyone real," Scotty said.

Startled to hear her own perceptions validated, Cass added an enthusiastic, "Me, too."

"Would you mind signing these for her, Kent?" Scotty asked.

"Happy to." Smiling, Kent took his pen from his front pocket.

The pen was nothing special, just a cheap black ink ball-point. Cass had fantasized that Kent's pen was made of gold and, instead of ink, would write fire, especially given how deeply Felicity's words were burned into her own brain.

"What's her name?" Kent said.

"Madelon but spelled kind of weirdly." Scotty spelled it out for him.

Kent autographed all three books.

"Thanks," Scotty said. "She'll be thrilled. And I'm glad you're here to help the library. I just wish you could help our stores, too."

"Business bad?" Kent said.

"Dire. My family opened this store over a hundred years ago. It will be lucky to last another year."

"A year?" Cass blurted out.

"At most." Scotty looked somber.

From comments Scotty had made when she picked up kennel supplies, Cass had known the store wasn't thriving, but she'd had no idea it was so close to going under.

"I'm sorry to hear that." Kent capped his pen.

"Don't worry," Rebecca said. "I've got a plan."

"The paper said you had something in mind," Scotty said, "but it didn't give any details."

"Come to Kent's benefit tonight for the library, and you'll hear all about it."

"I will."

"And spread the word," Rebecca said.

"Count on it. Incidentally, a couple of women came in earlier looking for Felicity Benedict souvenirs. Said they were from Sacramento and wanted to buy some from Loon for their book group."

Tourists already? Perhaps Rebecca really did have superpowers. Or magic in mind.

"Nobody in town carries anything like that, right?" Scotty asked.

"Not yet," Rebecca said.

Scotty's eyebrows went up. "Maybe I should start stocking some Felicity merchandise."

Rebecca just smiled. "Like I said, come tonight."

Back on the sidewalk, Kent glanced down the street and frowned.

Cass figured he was taking in the *FOR LEASE* sign that had been slapped over the bookstore's logo of a bespectacled worm reading a book.

"I'm glad to hear you have a plan to help Loon," he said.

"Absolutely," Rebecca said. "And you're a part of that."

"Oh? Which part?"

Rebecca linked arms with Kent, who Cass thought looked surprised but pleased. "I'll tell you all about it after our tour."

At Grubstake Grocery, Jewel positively beamed when Kent, Rebecca, and Cass entered. Dressed in a cotton candy colored sweater, Jewel got so tongue-tied she could only stammer out her love for Felicity.

"Thank you," Kent said, looking as appreciative as if Jewel had spoken with eloquence.

"Jewel's husband, Garrett, is our high school's P.E. teacher and football coach," Rebecca said. "Also, the school's basketball, baseball, and wrestling coach." She looked back at Jewel. "Are you both coming tonight?"

"I don't know about that. I mean, Garrett will."

"I hope you can make it, too," Rebecca said. "After all, Kent's generously given us his time."

"I'd really like to come. I'll try."

"Great," Rebecca said. "See you tonight."

Outside the store, Rebecca turned toward Kent. "If anyone's going to oppose our plans, it will be Garrett. He ran against me in the last election. The man's so contrary, he probably voted against himself."

Rebecca's wisecrack startled a smile from Cass. She'd been startled, too, to find herself voting for Rebecca because Garrett campaigned on an anti-change platform, which struck Cass as crazy even then.

By the time they'd introduced Kent to all the store owners, he'd received so much praise and gratitude, he seemed transformed, his face nearly as bright as Moon Mountain, which glistened in the sunshine. Cass was glad to have helped give back to him a little of the delight he'd given her and so many other readers.

They entered the library, their last stop. "Jonas," Rebecca said, "this is—"

"Kent Calloway." Jonas shook Kent's hand. "Thank you for coming to do a benefit for us." Jonas wore his jeans slung low around his hips and a rose-colored T-shirt emblazoned SAVE OUR LIBRARY.

"You're welcome," Kent said. "I'm just sorry you need one."

"Me, too." Jonas looked at Rebecca. "There are other things that should be cut instead. Especially with the bookstore closing. People need books, which have gotten expensive. Library cards are free."

"I agree," Kent said. "Libraries are essential for any community."

"Under the axe is never an enviable place to be," Rebecca said, "but with Kent's help, I'm confident we can save the library."

"I sure hope so." Jonas exchanged a look with Cass, who thought it was Jonas's way of asking whether Rebecca could be trusted. Cass answered with a gesture, showing him crossed fingers. She hoped Rebecca had taken in Kent's support for saving libraries. If *she* were mayor, libraries would top her "to keep" list.

"Are you hungry?" Rebecca asked Kent when they were back on the sidewalk.

"No, but I can eat something if either of you wants to."

"I'm fine. Cass?"

"Ditto. But, Rebecca, I was wondering, I mean, I knew some people had moved away because of the lack of jobs, that the library was endangered, plus the art gallery then the bookstore recently closed, and now Scottie's? I'm probably not the only one who was unaware of how bad things are. Maybe you should say something about all that tonight."

"Good idea."

"Absolutely," Kent said.

Cass felt her cheeks grow hot as she blushed with pride.

"What would you like to do?" Rebecca asked Kent.

"There's someone I'd like to see, but I can't remember his name. It's Irish. Patrick? Sean? He was maybe thirty or forty years older than I was. Big guy."

He had to be talking about Seamus, who'd been a lumberjack of a man. "Seamus?" Cass said.

Kent seemed to squint. "I think maybe that was him. He lived outside of town. Great house. It's the model for Felicity's."

"I thought so." Cass grinned. She couldn't wait to tell Mack.

"Does Seamus still live there?"

Rebecca beat Cass to it. "No, sadly. He was killed a couple years ago. Medical malpractice. His wife got a big settlement."

"I'm sorry to hear that." Kent's regret seemed genuine. "He made quite an impression on me."

"He was an amazing man," Cass said. "Gentle. Insightful. Playful. Did you meet Mack, his wife?"

"No, just him. Seeing that house again would be like walking into Felicity's home. Talk about verisimilitude."

Rebecca looked to Cass. "What do you think? Would Mack welcome us?"

Mack would *love* to know that Seamus's spirit lived on, at least in a sense. "Absolutely," she said.

It wasn't until they were heading toward Mack's that Cass wondered how welcoming Mack would be with Rebecca present. For all Cass knew, Mack might let Kent and herself in the house but bar Rebecca. Even though Rebecca was now her ally, Cass couldn't help but smile at the possibility of Rebecca finally getting to learn what it was like to be banished.

TWELVE

Rebecca stopped the car so close to the first row of flowers Mack was watering, Cass half thought she was going to mow them down—and Mack along with them.

Cass was first out of the car. "Mack, this is Kent Calloway, Felicity's creator."

Dressed in overalls and a flannel shirt, Mack hooked the hose on the deer fence and held out her hand, which Kent shook. He stood some two inches below Mack's nearly six feet.

"I've been listening to Cass rave about your books for a while now," Mack said. "She's your number-one fan."

"I believe it," he said.

Mack put her arm around Cass and gave her a quick squeeze.

Dante and Socrates shot out of the woods, barking, shivering with excitement and danger, alternating between growling at Kent and Rebecca, and jumping up on Cass. She knelt so she could scoop them up in her arms, "Boys," she said, "this is Kent. He's a good guy. And Rebecca. No need to growl. This is Dante and Socrates."

"Great names." Kent petted the small dogs with large hands, his knuckles hairy.

Cass set the dogs back on the ground. "Mack, Kent met Seamus years ago. Your house really *is* Felicity's."

"Is that true?" Mack said.

"It is, yes. I was sorry to hear about your husband. I'd hoped to see him again."

"Thank you." Mack put her hands together in a *namaste* expression of gratitude.

Mack looked genuinely moved, Cass thought, at least until she glanced at Rebecca. Mack's features transformed into a clear expression of disapproval that didn't disappear until she turned away from Rebecca and back to Kent. "How old were you when you met Seamus?"

"Thirteen."

"How did you meet?"

It seemed to Cass that Kent was blushing, but it must just be the way the sunlight was hitting his face.

"I was out hiking," Kent said, "on a really hot day. Being young and stupid, I didn't take any water. I must have been sweating up a storm because Seamus saw me as I walked by and asked if I'd like to come in for a few minutes to cool down. I was happy to do that. He gave me water and lemonade and showed me all around the house, which I loved. If I remember right, he designed it, no?"

"He did," Mack said. "And helped build it."

"Your house stayed in my mind," Kent said, "the way some things do. When I first started writing, I knew that eventually I'd write a story with your house in it. I didn't know anything more except that a woman would live there. Eventually I started thinking about it again and about the woman whose home it was. Living in your house, she'd have to be a dynamo. I didn't know much else yet, but I knew that. So, your house had a lot to do with my coming up with Felicity in the first place. All thanks to Seamus's kindness."

Mack passed her hand across her eyes. Then she seemed to shake off the sadness. "Would you like to come inside?"

"If it's not an imposition, I'd love to. I made Felicity's house as close to yours as I could remember, but I'm sure I got some things wrong. I didn't recall the roses, for one thing."

Mack held out her hand to gesture him in. "Seamus planted them after we'd been here a while. They were my birthday present."

"What a great gift. And thank you for inviting us in."

"Yes, thanks," Rebecca said. "I've long admired your house from the outside."

Cass put herself between Rebecca and Mack, who was giving Rebecca such a cool glance, Cass thought her friend might stand in the doorway to bar Rebecca from entering.

The instant Cass stepped into Mack's home, she saw again just how much like Felicity's it was.

Kent turned slowly, taking it all in. "The way Seamus talked," he said, "you could tell this house was a labor of love."

"That it was," Mack said, voice soft.

"Your house is stunning." Rebecca touched the fireplace stones. "I've never seen fossil rock like this. It's gorgeous. As I'm sure you know, some cultures revere spirals like this snail fossil."

How did Rebecca know that? Cass didn't picture her as someone who would be all that interested in other cultures' sacred symbols. What they used for currency, maybe.

Kent joined Rebecca. "I got the fireplace wrong." He frowned. "I'd remembered it as granite."

"You didn't get much else wrong," Cass said.

Mack looked at Rebecca. "Speaking of wrong, I hope that the plan the paper said you're unveiling tonight is a good one. What's your focus?"

"Just my proposal—and Cass's, we worked closely together on this—about how to bring in a few more tourists to help our library and businesses. You'll hear all about it if you come tonight."

Mack crossed her arms and studied Rebecca. "Oh, I'll be there."

Cass was torn between pride that Rebecca had acknowledged her contribution and guilt for not coming clean about how many tourists they really hoped to attract. She stayed silent, but she felt wobbly.

"I'm so glad to see the house again," Kent said. "And to do a mental salute to Seamus. Thank you."

"Thank *you*," Mack said to him.

"Me? For what?"

"For honoring Seamus. And for giving Cass a friend like Felicity."

Kent put his hand to his heart.

That gesture, Cass thought, conveyed his gratitude far more than any words could.

Mack and Seamus had been such a great couple, Cass recalled as Rebecca drove the three of them back toward town. They nurtured each other so well; it had been a pleasure to live with them. Cass doubted she would ever be lucky enough to marry a man like Seamus. Her thoughts drifted to Jeff Leavitt, whom she dated her senior year. Jeff wasn't much more accepted than she was, but he had a friendly, almost goofy, smile that reminded her of the open smile of a Lab. Plus, he liked both dogs and mountain hikes.

When he asked her out their senior year, Cass had been so excited about her first ever date, she hadn't slept at all the night before. They went to see the movie *Titanic*. A few weeks later, they slept together. Both virgins, they fumbled so much, that by the time they finally put everything where it needed to go, Cass had felt a searing pain and then nothing much.

She still thought of Jeff from time to time, wondering where he lived now and whether, had his parents not moved the family to Sedona shortly after that first bungled attempt at lovemaking, they'd have stayed together and maybe even, eventually, have married.

Jeff was the only boyfriend she'd ever had, the only guy she'd ever kissed.

"Here you go, Cass."

Cass snapped back to the present. Rebecca had stopped the SUV in front of Cass's home. Cass glanced at her watch: just three o'clock. She didn't want to leave Kent in Rebecca's clutches, but what was she going to say? No, I won't get out? No, come in with me? She wanted to propose dinner, but afraid of being rejected, got out.

Kent lowered his window. "See you tonight?"

"Sure. And maybe tomorrow morning I could drive you around, and you could point out other places that inspired you. I've got some ideas about what some of those places are."

"Let's save that for the afternoon so I can participate," Rebecca said. "I have two early meetings that I can't miss. Kent, why don't you sleep in?"

"I don't have that much time here," he said. "There's a lake I'd like to go to. It's about seven miles up from Grizzly Creek trailhead. I don't remember the name, but as I recall, it's at the base of a fairly sheer rock wall."

"Juniper Lake?" Cass said.

"That's it, yes. It was one of my dad's and my favorite spots."

"Mine, too." Cass had long suspected that just saying the lake's name and picturing Juniper made her eyes sparkle. Kent's seemed to be doing the same.

"If I remember right, the lake's a particularly striking blue, well worth the climb. The meadow about a mile in was the basis for the glen where Rain and Lucas go."

"I'd be happy to guide you there," Cass said. Would she ever!

"I'd like that," Kent said.

Rebecca's smile looked constricted.

"What time?" Cass asked.

"Is 7:30 too early?"

"Not at all. I'll bring my camera to photograph the meadow and anything else we see. I mean, who knows? Maybe we could put together photos and captions in some kind of brochure for tourists."

Cass looked at Rebecca, who pointed her finger at Cass. "Great idea," Rebecca said.

Cass couldn't help but smile, then turned to Kent. "Where should I pick you up tomorrow?"

"I'm at the B&B, as you suggested. I'm looking forward to those scones."

Rebecca drummed her fingers on the steering wheel. "Kent, I'll drop you here in the morning on my way to work."

Cass got out.

"See you tonight," Rebecca said, then drove away, taking Kent with her.

Diego wasn't expecting her back. How lucky Cass felt that in addition to having great instincts with dogs, Diego was so responsible. Still, she had no desire to sit around the house until the night's events. She was far too revved. Some of that stemmed from the prospect of the next day's hike with Kent, and some from anxiety about how the town would react to the Felicity Benedict Connection.

Especially Mack.

Cass licked her very dry lips with her very dry tongue.

Inside, changing into work clothes, her eyes fell on *Matters of the Heart: Passion*. Cass picked it up and searched for the passage where Felicity talks with Rain, the runaway 17-year-old girl Felicity takes into her protection, about perfection. Rain strives to be perfect in order to feel safe. "Forget 'perfect,'" Felicity counsels her. "Those who insist on striving for perfection live a black-and-white existence in a world vibrating with color."

Felicity's words on perfection resonated with Cass because they gave everyone, herself included, permission to be human. To make mistakes. Mack would understand that. Surely. She might even understand why Cass *couldn't* tell her the truth. It wasn't just Cass's fear of sparking a hostile reaction to the FBC, or her concerns for the town—especially Jonas and the library—that motivated her silence. It was also her own need to stay safe. Sure, she was thirty-two now and not, say, twelve or thirteen, and, yes, she should be able to be indifferent about Rebecca's opinion of her. *Should* be. The sad truth was, she felt a desperate need not to go back to being Rebecca's target. Not now.

Not ever.

THIRTEEN

"What's wrong?"

Mack's question came as they met in front of the auditorium that night, an almost-spring evening redolent with the sweet smell of daphne blossoms. Cass hesitated. Should she confess how many tourists they hoped to attract? It was, after all, too late to organize opposition for this night. Or was it? Mack might seek out Garrett and anyone else likely to oppose the FBC; they could stage a walkout that would throw the benefit into chaos, dismaying Kent and perhaps sinking their plans. Besides, Cass had agreed to keep silent until Rebecca presented it. "Just thinking about some kennel stuff," she said. "You well know how that goes. There's always something."

"True," Mack said. "So how was the rest of yesterday? Did you and Kent connect?"

"Oh, sure. He's a friendly guy."

"No, I mean really *connect.*" Mack raised one eyebrow.

"No. Rebecca did, I think."

"Hey Mack, hey Cass." Maya Browning's voice always seemed to be delivered by megaphone. The town's postal carrier, Maya wore her usual dark green sweatshirt captioned with the John Muir quote, *The mountains call me and I must go.*

"Hey, Maya," Mack and Cass responded.

"You folks as suspicious about what Rebecca's proposing as I am? I don't trust our mayor. Know what I mean?"

Mack nodded. "I do indeed."

Cass just forced a slight, noncommittal smile.

The way Maya hefted heavy packages, undaunted by the load or by bad weather or muddy rutted roads, made her seem to Cass to be a force of nature, right up there with earthquakes, hurricanes, and tsunamis. If Mack and Maya joined forces against the FBC, their protests could put the makeover—and thus the town—even higher on the endangered list.

They entered the auditorium together. Built in 1859 as a theater, the auditorium still maintained the original stage. It was used occasionally for weddings, memorials, plays, and official functions when a large turnout was expected—like tonight, the first such in a long while. Most of the three-hundred seats were already taken, and many in the audience clutched Felicity Benedict novels and jabbered with neighbors. The room was decidedly abuzz. A quick glance revealed to Cass that she didn't know quite a few of those present.

When Maya went to join a friend, Cass and Mack looked for seats. "There's two," Mack said, leading the way to seats midway down on the right.

Seated, Cass took in the gold curtains flanking the stage. Threadbare, they looked like one hard jerk might shred them both: appropriate, perhaps, given the town's threadbare economy. Two tall stools stood on the stage, with a detachable mic in front of each, while a folding chair had been set up at a table on the floor in front of the stage.

The woman to Cass's right wore perfume so strong and so sweet, Cass felt like someone had just stuffed cotton candy up her nose. The woman's white hair was pulled back in a ponytail that reached to her waist, but her eyebrows were black, making it hard to pinpoint her age.

She turned to Cass, lifting a bag of books from the floor to show her. The top book was *Matters of the Heart: Envy.* "For my book group. We *love* Felicity. I promised them I'd get their books autographed." She patted the bag. "Have you read all the Felicities?"

It was Cass's turn to smile. "Several times."

"I know. They're amazing, right?"

"They are."

"I'm Mindy Lucero. From San Luis Obispo."

"I'm Cass. From Loon. You made a long drive for this. What, six hours? Seven?"

"For most people. I drive an old 'Vette. Fast. I love driving, and I listened to Kent read his second book, *Passion,* the whole way. I'll listen to *Envy* on the way home. He's just as good a reader as he is a writer."

Cass had thought she was Kent's #1 fan. Maybe not. "How did you hear about tonight?"

"A friend in Angels Camp read about it and called me. She knows how much I love Kent. Plus, I wanted to see the place that's Felicity's real town."

Applause made her and Mindy turn toward the stage. Rebecca and Kent walked across the stage over to the stools. More applause, this time louder, signaled that the crowd was filled with Felicity fans, a fact that would explain why there were far more women than men in the audience. Typically, town meetings were sparsely attended, with men predominant.

Kent sat on one of the two stools while Rebecca picked up her detachable mic and walked to the front of the stage, her smile radiant. She wore a white silk pantsuit—straight legs, tapered jacket with turned-down collar, and a black belt—punctuated by a black camisole and black high heels. Somehow the suit looked both flowing and tailored, simple but elegant, suggesting a woman who was very much in charge but warm and welcoming.

On anyone else, that ensemble might look ostentatious, but Rebecca pulled it off. How one outfit could say such contradictory things and still look fashionable, Cass didn't begin to understand.

"Welcome everyone," Rebecca said. "Thank you for coming to celebrate a brilliant author and to raise funds to repair our library.

"Since most of you are here for Kent, creator of the hugely popular Felicity Benedict novels, we'll begin with him. A little later he'll be autographing books. And we will, as promised in the paper, share some ideas to help our struggling town. But first, anyone who traveled to get here to hear our featured speaker, and/or to see for yourself the town that inspired the book, if you'd please stand, we'd love to thank you."

Nobody stood at first, but then Mindy did, and so did some thirty others.

Rebecca led the applause. "Thank you for coming to join us." Her smile was so bright, Cass half thought those sitting near the front would need sunglasses.

"We expect you'll find the journey worthwhile," Rebecca continued. "We also expect that once you hear our plans for Loon, you'll want to come back with family and friends. Now without further ado, let's hear it for Kent Calloway and his remarkable heroine, Felicity Benedict."

Kent stood; applause reverberated through the auditorium. Once the audience quieted, Kent thanked it and Rebecca for such a warm welcome. He then opened *Matters of the Heart: Betrayal* and read the six-page first chapter.

Mindy Lucero was right, Cass thought. He was a great reader, using different inflection for different characters, reading with a deep, smooth voice that was almost a purr. Cass had always preferred print books to audio because print made it easier to focus, but in Kent's case, she wanted to hear him read all three books.

When he finished the first chapter, Kent looked almost abashed as the audience loudly applauded. He thanked them, then asked how many people had read at least one of the Felicity novels. So many arms shot up, some waving, the effect was like the instantaneous blossoming of a garden of long-stemmed flowers. Cass sucked in her breath at the sight of so many people—townspeople and strangers—so excited about the very books that delighted her. It made her feel part of a community.

What aspects of his books appealed to Kent's other fans, Cass wondered. Was it the plot twists, the humor, the wise and whimsical Felicity, the love between the two teens, the palpable heart in the novels? How many fans shared Cass's own appreciation for the fact that by each novel's end, the guilty—whether thieves, embezzlers, philanderers, sabotaging rivals—or hit-and-run drivers—got what they deserved?

Kent sat on his stool and spoke for some fifteen minutes about how he'd come up with the idea of Felicity Benedict while flying to Bend to attend a writers' conference. The idea so excited him, he said, he landed his plane in Redding and started writing his first book in the series, never making it to the conference. Kent spoke, too, of his family's many vacations to Loon, his love for the town, and how happy he was to be back.

When he finished his talk, Kent invited questions. Though it took a minute for someone to ask the first one—in this case, what Kent's writing routine was—other hands soon followed.

After twenty minutes, with a few hands still in the air, Rebecca rose. "I know many of you want Kent to autograph your books, which he'll do shortly. And Jonas, our librarian, will be selling Kent's novels in the back. However much we collect will be earmarked for the library.

"As many of you have heard, the town needs to raise sixty-thousand dollars to make the building repairs required to keep the library open. Make no mistake. It's not what I or the council members want to happen, but unless we can raise the sixty thousand, the library will close at the end of August. Tonight, we're going to take a collection; all proceeds will go toward the library. We hope you'll open your hearts and your wallets and give generously."

Kent nodded toward his microphone. "May I?"

"By all means."

"I want to thank you for your warm reception. And to say that libraries led me to reading, which led me to writing. We all need access to books. Not everyone's been lucky enough in their lives to be able to buy them. As your own Cass Enger wrote when she invited me to Loon, a town without books is a town without soul. However much you raise for the library tonight, I'll match it, up to ten-thousand dollars."

Calls of delight and applause rang out.

The four city council members passed hats around the audience: literal top hats modeled after the gold mining era. When the hats had been circulated to all, the council members took them to a table in the back that held Kent's novels for sale later. The men began counting the donations.

Rebecca spoke again. "Before we open this up for Kent to autograph your books, the council requested I tell you about our plans to make sure our struggling town doesn't become a ghost town. I've asked several people to help me present our proposal. Would you folks please come forward."

Four of the eight people carried what appeared to be rolled up banners. All eight joined Rebecca on the stage, grouping themselves in pairs.

"We've already begun to launch what we call The Felicity Benedict Connection," Rebecca said. "The FBC is a plan to tie our town to Kent's wonderful novels, which, of course, Loon inspired."

Rebecca took a few minutes to outline the kinds of merchandising and activities that had been so successful in Forks, Washington.

Glancing around the room while Rebecca spoke, Cass was surprised by how rapt most of the audience looked, many nodding their enthusiasm. A few people, like Jewel's husband, Garrett, scowled, arms crossed. Mack was frowning.

"To stage a successful campaign," Rebecca went on to say, "we came up with slogans for social media platforms like Facebook, Instagram and others, and for the town's website. We'll also place ads in carefully chosen newspapers and magazines.

"Here are some audiovisual aids with some of our advertising slogans."

Rebecca nodded to the first pair of people on the stage, Jon and Lily Lakin, owners of the Motherlode Inn. They unfurled a banner—white with purple lettering—that read, *Let the town that inspired Felicity inspire you.*

Applause.

They were applauding Cass's own slogan! Her cheeks went on high beam. She'd had no idea Rebecca was going to feature it. Wow!

Next, Sourdough Bakery & Café waitress Shirley Dawkins and Jackpot Gifts' Nate Pearl revealed a banner that proclaimed *Come for the Felicity rush, stay for the nature rush,* and featured an image of the first Felicity Benedict novel cover in the sky above a spectacular image of Moon Mountain's snowy dome.

Two youths Cass didn't know held the third banner. *You'll be over the Moon for Loon* its gold letters proclaimed.

Rev. Jackson and Rev. Corbett, ministers of rival congregations who were also drinking buddies, unfurled the last, its blue letters urging, *Make Felicity's Loon your destination location.*

"Next week, we'll roll out our social media campaign," Rebecca said. "We want to build on Felicity's appeal but also emphasize the historical gold rush aspect, plus the natural beauty of this area, so that if people come for Felicity, they'll come back for the history and for outdoor activities. Additionally, the first Felicity Benedict movie's coming out Memorial Day weekend. Kent believes he can persuade at least one of the movie's stars to come here after the premiere. We could do a major publicity campaign around that, so keep your fingers crossed."

Applause erupted.

Cass began to rejoice that Rebecca had not gone into the number of potential tourists.

"For those who are wondering how this campaign could help save our library, not to mention our struggling town," Rebecca said, "there's one last banner, and I imagine most of you will be as astonished as I was. To reveal this one, I'd like to invite Cass Enger forward."

If Cass thought her cheeks were hot before, they were freezing in comparison to how she felt now. She slumped in her seat, wishing she could just disappear.

"Come on, Cass," Rebecca said. "You and I have worked on this together. You deserve to be up here."

Mack nudged her on one side, and Mindy said, "you lucky thing" on the other. The nudge and the words helped her stand, but still she did not want to walk down that aisle, not with all those eyes on her. She squeezed past Mindy and the other people in the row, then walked slowly, eyes on the floor, down the center aisle. Although she told herself she was being ridiculous, she couldn't help expecting the jeers to start.

"We currently attract around fifteen-hundred visitors a year," Rebecca told the audience as Cass joined her onstage. "Not enough to be sustainable. Here's what we're aiming for in terms of how many tourists we'd like to see over the next couple of years." She nodded to Cass.

Cass pulled a string. The banner dropped down. It featured a thermometer with the number 1,500 at the bottom—and 100,000 in very large, bold numbers on top.

Gasps erupted, soon followed by thunderous applause. Although Cass averted her gaze from Mack, she was quite sure her friend would not be applauding. The vast majority of people were clapping enthusiastically.

Rebecca gestured Cass to the seat beside Kent. He clapped her shoulder, triggering a tremble she felt through her whole body.

"Some of you may think a hundred-thousand tourists is absurd, but consider this." Rebecca explained about the ninety-thousand tourists *Twilight* had attracted to Forks in just the first few years. "And remember that visitors generate money for local businesses, which means huge tax revenues. We can use that money to begin to address not just library repairs but street repairs, school needs, expanding police and fire protection. Eventually we hope to establish an acute care clinic. All these things will benefit the town and all who live here."

Cass marveled at how quickly Rebecca had put this show together: in two measly weeks. Rebecca was the real force of nature in this room tonight. The woman could command armies.

Garrett, Jewel's husband, shot to his feet. His goatee was so short, it looked like he'd dipped his chin in ink. He spoke with the commanding voice of a P.E. teacher and coach. "This plan is crap."

In the seat beside Garrett, Jewel slumped.

"Loon's not just a town," he said, "it's a *community*. You want to turn Loon into a tourist trap. How many of you," he looked around, "ever lived in one, because I did. My parents moved us from Angels Camp to Las Vegas, and it was a terrible place, where you knew nobody, and nobody knew you. Jewel and I moved here because we like seeing neighbors when we walk down the street, not a throng of strangers. I know we're not the only ones who feel this way. Your plan won't save our community. It will destroy it."

Garrett's warning was greeted with scattered applause—but louder boos. Now Cass understood why Rebecca had been intent on packing the evening with Felicity's fans. Smart.

"I'm Jack Kraft," a man called out.

His voice, which came from near but a little behind Cass, sounded familiar; she couldn't place it.

"I don't know Felicity Benedict from Homer Simpson," the man continued, "but this sounds like a great plan to me. We need tourists in order to make it possible for people to find work to support their families."

Cass remembered the man's bellowed *Get down*. He was the asshole who had intended to shoot Caesar.

"So stop whining and get your head out of your ass."

Garrett was on his feet so fast, Cass thought he'd hit an eject button. Garrett turned toward Kraft. "How long have you even lived in this town? Five minutes?"

"I'm registered to vote here," Kraft said. "I've got just as much right to speak as you do."

Mack rose then. She projected her deep voice well. "Garrett's right. Loon's charm is its small-town nature. If we start bringing in a hundred-thousand tourists, we'll have a traffic nightmare and, more importantly, property values will skyrocket. We have no rent control. That means huge increases in housing costs."

Cass shifted uneasily. She was on the same side as the dog killer and against the woman who had opened her home and heart to her? She glanced at Kent, beside her; his face as he watched Mack registered concern. Mack couldn't torpedo Kent's enthusiasm for the FBC, she just couldn't.

"A lot of people who live here now will be driven away," Mack finished. "Is that what we want?"

Again, some applause, with a few people booing while others yelled, "No."

Mack sat. Several people sprang to their feet. Postal worker Maya hollered loudest: "Rampaging tourists will drive offroad, and they'll hike off-trail. They'll scar our mother Moon. Some people here might be loony for Loon, but I'm loony for Moon. Don't desecrate our mountain for money."

Applause and boos.

Rampaging tourists? Cass pictured tourists with shopping bags wearing Felicity Benedict T-shirts, stomping lupine flowers. She didn't think so. She hid her smile with her hand.

Rebecca stood, calling for quiet. It took a minute, but people settled. "First, this isn't a town council meeting, and we don't need approval to proceed with the Felicity Benedict Connection. It won't be an added expense because we have thirty-thousand dollars that was set aside several years ago under my predecessor, a fund to be used only on a program to revive the town's economy. While I appreciate that there may be some drawbacks to the FBC, as there are to any plan, we're confident that the benefits will far outweigh potential problems. Naturally, however, the council and I care what our constituents feel. Let's find out."

Rebecca spoke with the confidence of someone who knew what the outcome would be.

"If you're *in favor* of our Felicity Benedict Connection, please rise."

Nearly four-fifths of the audience stood. Cass, too, rose.

"You packed the crowd," Garrett protested.

"I ran for mayor on a platform of bringing jobs and tourists to Loon. Let me remind you, Garrett: the voters chose *my* vision. Now, Council, how much money did we raise tonight?"

Lewis Jennings, a stocky councilman who had boarded his Irish setter with Cass, stood to report. "Including Kent's generous donation, we raised fourteen-thousand, three-hundred and seventy-one dollars."

Loud cheers. They were nearly a third of the way to the sixty thousand needed. Cass grinned.

"Thank you for that exciting piece of news, Lewis. And thanks again to all who donated, especially Kent. Before we adjourn so Kent can sign books, let's have another big round of applause for him." The applause was again thunderous.

"And for Cass," Rebecca said.

The applause was nowhere near the volume for Kent, but people did clap for her. Her! For a minute she sat taking in the applause, red-faced and giddy.

"Now let's put our attention back where it belongs, on the brilliant man who created Felicity Benedict, a girl's best friend."

Kent gestured to Rebecca, which brought renewed applause. She bowed. After a moment, Kent took the steps down to the floor level and sat at the table in front of the stage.

"If you have a book or books for Kent to sign, come on down. Remember, Jonas is selling books in back. Thank you all for coming tonight."

Mindy bolted to her feet and rushed down the aisle. There were a dozen people in front of her. She waved Cass over despite the heavy bag of books in her arms.

"I'm so envious," she said, startling Cass. "To have Kent Calloway quote you, and to live in Felicity's real town. Oh my God."

Cass couldn't suppress her smile. "Yeah."

It looked like at least half the audience, clutching one or more books, was headed toward Kent.

"A hundred thousand tourists?"

Mack's voice startled her. Cass hadn't seen her friend come down the aisle. She bit her lip before nodding, then said, "But not all in one year. And probably not nearly that many."

Mack's expression was one of puzzlement. "I take it you knew these numbers for a while."

Cass considered saying she hadn't known, but the idea of looking Mack in the eyes and flat-out lying kept her silent.

"Why didn't you tell me?" Mack said.

Cass opened her mouth to respond. Nothing came out. What was there to say?

"Cass?" Mack said.

"Rebecca made me promise I wouldn't tell anyone."

"*Made* you? How old are you, ten?"

"I'm sorry."

"And I guess I'm bewildered." Mack turned from Cass and started back up the aisle, toward the exit.

Should she go after Mack? Guilt made Cass slump . . . until she wondered how Kent felt after hearing Mack and the others speak against the FBC. Cass rubbed her clammy hands on her cargo pants. Hopefully the passionate but limited opposition wouldn't have discouraged him.

Much as she wanted to ask his reaction, the line for autographs snaked to the back of the auditorium. Rebecca was speaking with Boyer August, who was not only Loon's newspaper's main reporter, but also its editor, publisher and owner. Boyer was scribbling notes. Cass didn't want to go to bed late, given how early she'd need to rise for her hike with Kent. Besides, tomorrow she would have Kent all to herself. She could ask him every question she'd ever had about his books, his writing, and his life.

"Hey, Cass."

She glanced up to see Barbara Conway, the close friend Cass's mother stayed with on her rare visits to Loon. Barbara gave Cass an enthusiastic thumbs up.

That was a first. Barbara was Cass's mother's cheerleader, not hers. She waved to Barbara and headed toward the exit. She would go home and assemble the gear for their hike. Tomorrow, *after* the hike, she would swing by Mack's. Even if she'd been wrong to keep silent, Cass decided, she hadn't committed a capital crime. Hopefully by tomorrow afternoon, Mack would understand, if not support, Cass's actions.

Cass stepped outside. To think she had actually been applauded. Tears of gratitude warmed her eyes. She was so wound up, sleep might prove elusive, but even if it did, it wouldn't spoil this wondrous night—nor the coming hike. Nothing could.

FOURTEEN

Cass had parked and was strolling toward the kennel office to get Caesar when honking overhead made her look up. At first, she saw only dark clouds and a half moon. Then a flock of geese burst into view, sliding across the moon, calling, the flock shaped like a bow drawn taut. They disappeared into a black cloud, still calling, giving voice to the night.

She walked as softly as she could, hoping not to wake the dogs. Through the open office door, she saw Zoe and Diego at the desk table, sitting side by side in front of Diego's laptop, on a Zoom call with Arturo and Enrique. Zoe's leopard print leggings, huge gold earrings, and loose black sweater were a marked contrast to Diego's worn sweatshirt and jeans. On the floor beside them, Caesar appeared to be sleeping.

Cass suspected Zoe was long past curfew for a school night. Did Rebecca have any idea Zoe was here? Cass entered the office. Caesar stood up from his spot and wagged his tail. Her entry triggered barking and howling from the other dogs. "Quiet, guys, it's just me," she called. The dogs settled back into silence.

"Hi, Cass," Arturo said from the screen. His eager young voice reminded her of the enthusiasm of puppies.

"Hi, Arturo."

"*Hola*, Cass." Enrique appeared beside Arturo.

"*Hola*, Enrique."

"Arturo," Diego said to the screen. "*Es muy tarde. Very* late. *Buenas noches.*"

Arturo's thin arms and legs seemed birdlike. Cass wouldn't have been surprised to see him flap his arms and fly.

"*Te hecho de menos*," Arturo said, a tear seeping down his cheek.

"*Yo también.* So much." Diego's voice trembled. "*Ahora, vete a la cama.*"

When Arturo's face was gone from the screen, Diego asked Enrique, "Arturo is okay?"

Enrique spun a soccer ball on his index finger. "Don't worry. I'm taking good care of him."

Face somber, Diego leaned toward his computer as if to guarantee confidentiality. "Has anybody threatened him? Or you?"

Enrique wasn't smiling now. "Papa pays them, but they keep raising the price. I'm going to get a job. *Abuelita* needs a nurse to help her now."

Abuelita. Their grandmother.

"I should come home," Diego said.

"No." Enrique's one-word response shot from him. "Remember Jorge, the baker's cousin?"

"*Claro.*"

"He didn't want to join a gang. He sneaked across the border. The Border Patrol caught him and sent him back. The day he came home, a *pandillero* killed him. If you come back, they will kill *you.*"

Cass gave silent thanks that Diego was here and safe, though his eyes seemed moist now, the beginning of tears.

"I do miss your ugly face," Enrique teased, then slung his arm across the chair back and grinned, deepening the dimples that punctuated his smiles. "When I get a job, all the beautiful *mujeres* will be sad I have less time for them."

Diego wiped his arm across his eyes. "*Estas loco*. They are using your head as a soccer ball, *hermano*. *Las mujeres* don't want you. They want your cigarettes. Quit smoking or when you come to hike the mountains with me, I will have to carry my backpack *and* you."

"I don't smoke cigarettes," Enrique said. "I make clouds. Zoe, when I visit, you will forget all about Diego."

Zoe made a face of distaste. "Kiss a smoker?" Her light tone undercut her words. "I'd rather kiss a dog's butt."

"Ouch," Enrique said. "That hurts."

"Good night, *perdedor*," Diego said.

"Good night, bigger loser." Enrique saluted, and the screen went blank.

Diego touched the screen, his gesture an eloquent expression of his sadness.

Zoe faced him. "What's that word Enrique used, a *panda* something?"

"*Pandillero*. Gang member. Killer."

Cass hated to interrupt their exchange. "Zoe, don't you need to get home?" she said.

Zoe glanced at the Dalmatian clock: well past 11:00. "Shit. Will you give me a ride, Cass?"

"Let's go."

Zoe touched Diego's arm in a gesture of familiarity that made Cass wonder whether their relationship was more than platonic.

Diego leaned forward and kissed Zoe.

Question answered.

"*Hasta mañana*," Zoe said when they separated.

"Tomorrow," he echoed.

"How was the meeting?" Zoe said as they walked outside.

"Great. Your mom was terrific." Cass pushed the driver's seat of her truck partially forward for Caesar. He jumped in.

"She's always terrific. At work." Zoe's voice was flat.

Cass drove toward Rebecca's for the second time in thirty-two years.

"Please don't tell Mom I was with Diego." Zoe's voice had taken on a pleading tone. "She's convinced I'm going to end up pregnant like she did. I'm not stupid. I'm on the pill. She doesn't know that, though, so don't tell her. She should have been on it, too. What did she *think* would happen if she had unprotected sex? Like, seriously?"

Cass's mind whirled. First, she'd withheld information from Mack. Now Zoe wanted her to lie to Rebecca? It was Rebecca's prompting that had resulted in the applause for Cass, giving Cass her first taste of actual acceptance. "I won't lie to your mom."

"Please, Cass. If you tell, she won't let me work at the kennel anymore. I'll say I was with my friend Angelique. You don't need to say anything. That way *you* won't be lying."

Zoe's voice had an undercurrent of desperation that was hard to ignore. "If she asks if you were at the kennel," Cass said, "I'll tell her the truth." Just as she should have told Mack the truth.

"You don't understand what it's like living with her."

"Maybe not."

"Did you ever lie to your mom?" Zoe said.

"Sometimes." Her mother used to blame Cass's average-and-below grades on her many hours at the kennel. Cass had lied more than once about her whereabouts, knowing she could never successfully explain why the kennel gave her so much more happiness than any other part of her life. Working at the kennel had been the only thing that kept Cass clinging to whatever shreds of self-worth she had left. Remembering that made her sympathetic to Zoe's plight.

Zoe turned to stare out the passenger window, tapping her gold painted nails against her thighs.

The instant Cass stopped the truck, Rebecca stormed out of the house, triggering a motion detector that flooded the yard with so much light it seemed like morning. She still wore the white pants suit from the meeting, tall heels included. She probably hadn't been home long. Cass lowered the front windows.

"Where the hell have you been?" Rebecca practically shouted.

Zoe glanced at Cass with a pleading expression before answering. "At Angelique's."

Rebecca crossed her arms. She glanced toward Cass, then glared at Zoe. "So why didn't Angelique bring you home?"

There was a quality of harsh judgment in Rebecca's tone; Cass turned off the ignition.

"Angelique was drunk," Zoe said.

"Then you shouldn't have been hanging out there. And you sure shouldn't have been drinking."

"I wasn't."

"Out of the car. Now."

Zoe got out, slamming the passenger door closed. "I didn't have a way home. Angelique's parents were at the meeting."

"You should have called me."

"Uh, hello. *You* were at the meeting. I decided to walk. Cass saw me and picked me up."

Rebecca leaned closer to Zoe and sniffed. "Go inside. You're grounded for two days. And if you ever do come home smelling of alcohol, I'll ground you for a month."

"Whatever."

"Three days. Go on in the house before I make it a week."

Zoe looked like she wanted to argue, but she wisely kept her mouth shut as she stomped toward the house.

Watching Zoe go, Rebecca frowned. "Thanks for bringing her home."

"Sure."

Rebecca took a few steps toward her house, then faced Cass. "Most people tonight were really enthusiastic. We did well. Goodnight, Cass."

"Goodnight." *We* did well? If anyone had told Cass when she was in high school that Rebecca would one day want Cass on her team, it would have seemed about as likely as singing turtles.

Five minutes after Cass walked into her house, her cell phone sounded. Who was calling? Rebecca, having bullied the truth from Zoe, Mack to further protest, or Kent to cancel their hike? Cass unzipped her jacket pocket and reached for the phone. "Hello?"

"I'm proud of you."

Cass nearly dropped the phone. Those were words she'd never expected to hear from her mother. "For what?"

"Taking down the barricades."

"Barricades?"

"Walls, Cass. The walls you erected way back in middle school, all because of a few classmates."

Perhaps it had been only two or three people who initiated most of the taunts, but in middle school a *few* felt like a mob. Besides, most of their fellow students didn't dare contradict the popular kids and so went along with them. Cass didn't think her mother could begin to understand what intimidation felt like. Safer to switch topics. "How's the bathroom remodel coming?"

"Slowly, and don't change the subject."

Cass pictured her mother: attractive, dark-haired, looking at sixty-one more like forty-one, stylish clothes always fitting perfectly. It occurred to Cass, not for the first time, that her mother would have preferred that *Rebecca* be her daughter; she never would have left a 12-year-old Rebecca behind. Not that Cass wanted to live in Arizona with a hypercritical parent. What she wanted was a mother who would accept and love her like her father had, someone who wouldn't even consider abandoning her. Luckily, Mack had been just such a parent.

And now Cass had withheld critical information from the very woman who'd taken her in.

"Look, I'm not claiming Rebecca's perfect, or that she didn't treat you badly, but if you'd just stood up to her, she would have looked for somebody else to pick on. Your problem, Cass, was that you were always so touchy. If I looked at you cross-eyed, you'd slink to your room and hide. You'll never make new friends, male or female, if you're that touchy."

Cass sank to the floor and patted her knee for Caesar to come; she needed a dog to hold on to. Caesar nuzzled next to her, and Cass put her arm around his neck.

"Barbara said you invited some famous writer, and that Rebecca called you to the stage to acknowledge your contribution. See what I'm saying?"

As if that one act erased all the pain Rebecca had caused. "Sure."

Caesar yelped.

Cass released him. She must have tightened her hold too much. "Sorry," she said to him.

"What?" her mother said.

"Nothing. I was talking to Caesar."

"I take it Caesar's a dog." Her mother sighed. "I keep telling you, Cass, that you need to talk to dogs less and people more."

She wanted to say that dogs, unlike people, rarely bit.

"You hide behind dogs, Cass. Just like this call. Talking to a dog helps keep you distant from me."

Cass kept her distance? It was her mother who had created

distance, her mother who had moved away and left Cass behind.

"You need to step out from behind your walls and engage with the real world. Just like you did tonight. And didn't it feel good?"

It was the first thing her mother had said—in a long time—that Cass could agree with. "It did."

"Ally with Rebecca. Learn self-confidence and get to know people. If you don't, you'll never have a man in your life. It'll remain just you, Mack, and your dogs."

Maybe her mother was right. It would certainly be ironic if Rebecca, the very person who'd contributed so much to her lack of self-confidence, turned out to be the person who helped her regain it.

Be loud, be proud.

If her mother *was* right, and Cass had built walls behind which to hide, then maybe she had the power to take those walls down. Not all at once, maybe, but brick by brick. And wouldn't her hike with Kent provide her with a chance to try? Not to make Kent a boyfriend; that would never happen. She wasn't brilliant like he was, nor articulate and gorgeous like Rebecca. But maybe, tomorrow, she could think of enough intelligent things to say to Kent—he'd quoted her, after all— that he might want to be friends. Email friends anyway. *Should* she tell her mother about their hike?

No. What she needed was to end this call; she feigned a yawn.

"I know you're an early riser, and it's past your bedtime, but I do want you to think about what I've said. You can do this, Cass. You can choose to join the human race. I hope you do."

The connection went dead. "Good night to you, too," Cass said into the phone. She tapped her fist against her lips. Usually she found it easy to dismiss her mother's advice.

Tonight, she wondered if perhaps—*perhaps*—there was some truth in it.

"I wanted to abort," Cass years ago had overheard her mother say on a phone call to her pal Barbara, "but William pleaded with me not to. He promised me that nothing important would change. I believed him." She snorted. "Once Cass was born, *everything* I cared about changed. No more dinners out, no more dancing. We never went anywhere. William was so happy being a father, he forgot how to be a husband."

After Cass's father was killed, her mother hated the mountains even more than she had before: the snow, the silence, the nights as dark as fire-scorched trees. Ten months after Cass's father died, nearly a year after Rebecca started her tirades against Cass, her mother took a job in Tucson.

Cass hadn't wanted to move away, to keep living with a mother she knew would never forgive her for being born. Despite Rebecca's taunts, she wanted to stay in Loon. After all, there would be Rebeccas in every school. Moon and the surrounding mountains made Cass feel stronger—mountains that in some deep, elemental way, still held her father.

And now she'd hidden the truth from the very woman to whom she owed—and loved—so much. Cass felt a pang of guilt. It was too late to call Mack tonight, and too early to call before her hike. Besides, she wanted to apologize in person.

Caesar whimpered.

Cass took his head in her hands. "Whoozagoodboy," she said softly. Despite her mother's call, what a day—what a night —this had been. Between Kent quoting her, and Rebecca paying tribute, not to mention the audience's clapping, she'd known an approval that had eluded her most of her life. If that was what coming out from behind the barricades was like, Cass was pretty sure she could get used to it.

FIFTEEN

The thought of getting to spend the next few hours with Kent made Cass feel joyful, excited, and—what? —inflated with possibility. Felicity fans around the world would envy her. *Her*. Things like that just didn't happen. Maybe this day marked the start of a new page in her own life, one written with confidence and joy.

The peanut butter chocolate chip cookies she'd risen at 4:30 to make filled the house with a mouthwatering aroma she hoped would give Kent a tiny bit of the pleasure his books gave her.

Wait. She froze. What if he was allergic to nuts? She couldn't believe she hadn't asked. The last thing she wanted was to poison him: for his sake, hers, and Felicity's fans worldwide. She should have just bought Graham crackers; she'd bet nobody had ever died from eating those.

Don't be silly, she told herself. She shook her shoulders to try to loosen up and glanced at the table where she'd laid out a first aid kit, four bottles of water, a filter in case they needed to get more water from a stream, an emergency heat blanket, and lunch: smoked turkey sandwiches, apples and oranges, trail mix, protein bars, and the cookies. Seemed like everything.

After the hike, she would drive straight to Mack's to apologize. For now, she would put everything associated with Mack out of her mind.

The doorbell sounded; she practically flung open the front door. "Good morning."

"It is," Kent said, entering. "Perfect for hiking." Like her, he was dressed in a T-shirt, but he wore shorts to her cargo pants, and a puffy vest to her fleece jacket. "Something smells good."

"Thanks. I hope you're okay with peanut butter."

"More than okay."

She led him to the table. "No nut allergies?"

"No." He surveyed the spread. "You didn't tell me we were going for a week."

"I did a third-grade report on the Donner Party," she said. "Always be prepared, or you never know who you might have for dinner."

He chuckled and picked up a cookie. "Okay to sample one?"

"Sure."

With Kent's first taste of the cookie, his eyes widened. "These are amazing. What's in them?"

"Peanut butter combined with flour, eggs, sweet cream butter, a skosh more than a teaspoon of vanilla, and bittersweet chocolate chips."

"Please tell me we're taking some."

"We can take them all."

"I love this hike already," he said.

So did she.

K ent looked around Pond Meadow, a level half-mile in from the Grizzly Peak trailhead. "This is the spot where

Rain and Lucas go," he said, sounding as if he were talking about two real people.

"This meadow always makes me smile," Cass said. The grass—vibrant from the trickle of a stream that ran through it—was dotted with the flowers Kent described in his first novel. "I love your description in the book. I think it's *splashes of orange poppies, dabs of red Indian paintbrush, and streaks of purple lupine*. Something like that." She started to say more but stopped herself. She'd sound dumb.

"What?" Kent said.

She shrugged. "I don't know. I guess, it's probably stupid, but this meadow's kind of like a flower rainbow."

"I like that wording. Maybe I'll steal it one of these days. If you wouldn't mind."

She felt her cheeks flush. "I'd be honored." She looked around the meadow. "It's amazing you could nail your description of this meadow despite not having seen it for twenty years. Like with Mack's house."

"I have a good visual memory. Not much common sense, though. You know, one thing I'd forgotten is the way the meadow smells, like vanilla mixed with almond."

"You should use *that* in your next Felicity novel."

"Or somewhere."

Maybe Rain and Lucas were going to start meeting some place other than this meadow. The vibrant grass of what long ago would have been a small lake added to the beauty of the flowers, as did the Manzanitas, their bark the color of cinnamon; the clusters of lodgepole pines; and the needles of Douglas firs, silver in the soft sunlight of early morning.

"Do you have any doubts about tying the town to my books?" Kent said. "You know, the stuff Mack and others brought up last night?"

Good lord. Was he thinking of backing out? "No." She

didn't need to ponder it. "Without big changes, in a few years there won't *be* a town."

Kent was looking out at the meadow while she talked, his face revealing nothing.

Near panic constricted her throat. "Are you considering dropping out of the FBC?"

"I guess not. I do want to help."

"We'll never get total agreement," she said. "I bet if you announced a plan to give every person in Loon a million dollars, some people in town would oppose it. You saw all the people who stood up last night. Most of the town's excited about the campaign. It will create jobs so people don't have to move away. Your books will *save* Loon, not destroy it."

"You really may be my number one fan, Cass. Aside from my mother, that is. But she's biased. She'd like my books even if the pages were blank."

How wonderful it must be to have a mother like that. "And your dad?"

"He died."

"I hope he got to see at least one of your books published."

Kent shrugged, though his face looked anything but disinterested. "It's a complicated story. I'll fill you in someday."

Her stomach gave a flutter. Didn't *someday* sound like he anticipated knowing her beyond this brief trip? She didn't want to kid herself, but didn't it?

"Ready to move on?" he said.

"Lead the way." She tightened the straps on her daypack.

"I've got a lousy sense of direction," he said, "so feel free to correct me if I make a wrong turn. I'd rather we not end up in Guantanamo."

"Will do." They set off. He was such a humble guy for someone so successful. Did he really believe a woman who was overweight like Felicity, or plain with too-thin hair, like Cass herself, could still attract men? It felt safer to ask while they walked, so he couldn't see her face. "You know how Felicity's a big woman."

"Fat, you mean."

"Okay, sure, but a lot of guys still find her sexy. Do you ever get any flack for that? Like bad reviews or anything?"

He didn't pause. "A few on Amazon and Goodreads, but I pretty much ignore them. What matters isn't the gift-wrapping. It's what's inside the package."

Goosebumps dotted her arms. Maybe she really did have a shot at being friends with him.

The trail began a slight ascent. Fallen pine needles cushioned their steps. Only the squawking of jays angered by their presence broke the quiet.

"You know," he said as they walked, "I think the reason guys pursue Felicity is her self-confidence. That's a quality that attracts other people, whether it's sex appeal or charisma in general. If *you* think you're smart or sexy or whatever, others will, too. That's mainly why Felicity has so many admirers. She's confident."

"Must be nice," she mumbled to herself. Or thought she did.

"Yeah," Kent said. "Easier to write it than to feel it."

"Really? For you, too? Even after writing three huge bestsellers?"

"Sounds hopeless, doesn't it? But yes, sure. Growing up, I wanted to be an MVP, not a writer."

"What sport?"

"*Any* sport. I think that if you have a hard time as a kid, you never fully recover, and most boys who aren't athletic have a hard time, one way or another."

"Yeah. I still suffer from PTSD: Post Traumatic School Disorder."

He chuckled.

To think she'd made him laugh. Cass took a deep breath, her chest expanding.

She heard Grizzly Creek before she saw it. Usually a whisper, the creek was more of a roar. Two minutes more brought them to the bank. Water hurtled down the mountain. "Wow," she said. The rocks she usually stepped on to cross were nearly submerged.

"I don't remember the creek being this big," Kent said.

"Snow melt always increases it this early in the season. I don't think the water's all that deep. Probably not above your calves. It's fast, though. And cold. Do you want to try it?"

"Absolutely," Kent said.

"If we fall, we probably won't get washed downriver any further than, say, San Francisco."

"Funny." He nodded to her, smiling.

Good God. Had she just made another joke? And he'd found it funny? "Let's carry our shoes and wade across." There. She'd sounded confident.

Kent sat on a fallen scrub oak and took off his hiking boots while she shed hers.

He stood and stuck the toes of one foot into the creek. "Whoa!" He jerked his foot back. "*Cold* doesn't begin to cover it."

She rolled up her pants legs, tied her boots together, then slung them around her neck and plunged in. The instant her feet touched water, they felt attacked by wasps with stingers of fire. If she were alone, she would curse. Loudly. She splashed across.

"Impressive," Kent said, tying his shoelaces together.

Cass would have turned red, but most of her seemed to be turning blue. "It is cold," she said, sitting on a boulder and rubbing her feet.

He stepped into the water, grimaced and bellowed "shit" then quickened his pace, also splashing across. "I never knew water got that cold without freezing," he said, sitting on the rock beside her, rubbing his feet and legs.

"Me neither."

"Let's hope," he said, "that when we come back down, the creek will have warmed up."

"If we run back, we'll be too hot to notice."

He smiled at her. She smiled back.

"How'd you get started hiking?" he asked.

"Like you, with my dad. Sometimes we'd camp out for two or three nights. I still love it."

"I can see that," he said. "You still hike with him?"

"He was killed in a hit-and-run when I was eleven."

"That's rough. I'm sorry."

"Yeah. They never found the driver. One reason I love your books is that Felicity and fairness always win in the end."

"I can't stand books where the bad guy gets away with it. There's too much of that in real life." He picked up the fairly heavy pack and slung it over his shoulders. "My turn."

"I don't mind carrying it," Cass said.

"I'm good. You ready?"

"Lead on."

He walked with long strides—until the switchbacks started. They were the beginning of the hard part, three tough miles that gained over eighteen-hundred feet. Kent stopped. "I remember this." He looked around. "Gets pretty steep, as I recall."

"It does, yeah."

"I regret I never keep my workout plans." He gripped the pack's wide straps. "Plus, my lungs aren't used to breathing air I can't see."

Cass laughed. "You're also not used to the altitude," she said. "Let's just take it slow." All the better since it meant more time with him. She inhaled. The air smelled hot and glorious, like July had arrived early, bringing a memory of summer, hot dogs, and hiking with her father, out of reach of her mother's scathing voice.

Kent started up the trail. Gradually the trees thinned, with openings that revealed the peaks rising above the eastern side of the valley. So many white ribbons of water slid down the mountains, it seemed to Cass they were wearing necklaces of lace.

When they reached the spot where the trail cleared the tree line, it was marked with rock cairns.

Kent stopped to take several long swallows of water. He'd shed his vest. The underarms and back of his shirt were darkened with sweat. "I should have chosen an easier first hike," she said, taking a deep breath she didn't really need so he wouldn't feel bad.

"I *wanted* to take this hike," he said. "We'll get there. And by the way, you don't need to pretend to struggle. I can do the real thing for both of us. How about you lead the rest of the way?"

"Okay. We've got less than a mile to go."

Thirty minutes later they rounded the final bend. There below them, Juniper Lake nestled at the base of granite slabs that rose like cathedrals. At the far side of the indigo water stood a single juniper. Cass had always loved that tree, its branches knobbed and twisted like a witch's fingers.

"My God," Kent said between inhalations of air. "I remembered it as beautiful, but not *this* beautiful." He wiped his face with a red bandana. "This was worth the effort."

Cass had been unable to describe the lake's color until she saw a photo of a male indigo bunting a few years before, its feathers the color of the lake: sea-blue with just a tinge of green. Today there was no breeze to ripple the water, which was a perfect mirror, reflecting every intricate detail of the granite walls around it, yet so clear, you could see the sun-splattered rocks below the surface.

"It's my favorite lake," Cass said.

"It was mine and my dad's, too," Kent said, "for both fishing and swimming."

Cass wasn't sure if she was imagining a tremble in Kent's voice, or if it was really there. "I'll put our food out on that boulder." She pointed to one that was relatively flat.

"I'll give you a hand."

She spread the ground cloth while he began taking food from the pack. White cumulus clouds floated by, moving slowly in the sparse breeze. Something about this spot—whether lake or view or altitude—made Cass feel she could reach up and touch the sky. When all was set out, she felt herself bursting with gratitude.

"Thank you for guiding me," Kent said, as if he'd channeled her own feelings.

"Anytime."

"And thanks for lunch, especially the cookies."

She bit into a cookie, savoring the flavors of rich peanut butter and dark chocolate.

"I like how you think," Kent said. "Dessert first." He started eating one. "This cookie is the perfect reward for a hike like that."

Cass unwrapped the sandwiches; Kent opened two bags of chips. "What made you decide to become a writer?" she said as they ate. The sounds of chewing tart, crunchy apples and salty chips punctuated her words.

"I was such a klutz, I got made fun of a lot," he said. "My freshman year, I decided to go out for football. Offensive lineman. I'm built for it, right? I figured I could do it because I thought all linemen did was push. Wrong. During tryouts, I realized I had no clue and less athletic talent. Luckily, before I could make a complete idiot of myself, my left lung collapsed."

"That was lucky?"

"Absolutely. Gave me an excuse. I became the sports reporter for our high school paper, *The Quill*. When I interviewed Dave West, our star quarterback, we hit it off. Dave's friendship and popularity protected me. That's how I started as a writer. To escape being made fun of. To my surprise, I found I loved writing."

"Makes sense."

"I bet you were far more athletic than I was."

"I could catch. Footballs. Baseballs. That was my dad's nickname for me, *Catch*. He taught me a lot of the fundamentals of sports, especially football. The couple times I got to play with other kids, I really loved blocking and tackling, too. Bringing down the other team's players."

"Good for you."

"Yeah, only it wasn't good for a girl."

"So you got made fun of, too?"

"Yes."

"Too bad we couldn't have swapped talents. We'd both have been better off."

"Writing a book's a lot harder than catching a pass."

"I don't know. I mean, maybe for you, Catch."

Cass laughed and sat straighter, taller. It had been a long time since she'd heard her dad's nickname for her.

Kent wasn't finished. "Don't sell yourself short. You've come up with some creative things. Like Post Traumatic School Disorder and the 'flower rainbow.' Maybe you should try writing something. You might surprise yourself."

"*You're* the writer. I'd never be able to create anyone like Felicity. I can't wait to read the next book."

"Yeah. About that," Kent put down his sandwich, "there isn't going to be one."

"What?"

"There isn't going to be another Felicity Benedict novel."

"But you *can't* stop." Cass didn't think she could put any more feeling into that sentence than if she'd said, "You *can't* murder your children."

"She stopped talking to me. I don't have any good ideas for another book, and I've been trying to come up with a new story for months. That's a big part of why I came to Loon; I was hoping I'd get inspired."

"But you just got here. Maybe if you stayed longer."

"Maybe. I also wanted to see the town again. The mountains. And it's been great. This lunch is great, too."

Cass crushed the rest of her sandwich in a napkin and picked up a cookie.

Kent did the same. "To tell you the truth," he said, looking at the cookie before he bit into it, "I still can't get my head around why people love my books so much."

If only she could explain. "I can't speak for others," she said, "but I love them because Felicity is wise. And she's so, I don't know, so in love with life. Like she says in *Passion*, this planet brings us wars and famines, but it also brings us orchids and clown fish and just the most astonishing things. Her joy is contagious. And the way she tosses her scarf up in the air and catches it one-handed, then flings it around her neck? I love that. When I read your novels, I feel taller. Felicity gives me hope. *You* give me hope."

Kent looked at her, frowning.

"Sorry," she said. That was more sentences than she'd strung together with anyone other than Mack for a long time. She'd probably come across as a lunatic. A *fanatic*.

"No. *I'm* sorry, Cass," he said, and it seemed he saw her. Really saw her. "I just don't have any more Felicity tales to tell."

Any minute now and she was going to roll through the stages of grief. What were they? Anger. Bargaining. Sorrow. Something like that. She wasn't, however, going to reach the final stage: acceptance. Not when she still had so much to learn, and Felicity was such a good teacher. No way. No how. Never.

Kent opened his water bottle and took a long drink. When he spoke again, his voice was subdued. "My publisher wants me to finish a book a year, and I've tried. But it's made writing a job rather than a joy. Maybe that's why I've run out of ideas for Felicity. I don't know. I think I'll write a screenplay. They're mostly dialogue, so they're a lot quicker and easier than a novel."

Needing to fortify herself, Cass ate another cookie. "What would your screenplay be about?"

"A guy gets caught up in a bank robbery, and the police think he's an accomplice. He has to prove his innocence, but to do that he has to join forces with a hard-nosed woman, who runs a start-up, and her ten-year-old brother, who knows more about technology than either of them."

She blurted it out before she could think about what she wanted to say: "But everybody's writing those kinds of movies. You're the only one who can write a Felicity Benedict novel." She wanted to offer to help him, but it would be presumptuous. She knew nothing about writing. "Maybe you just need a little break," she said. "Write a quick screenplay, then go back to Felicity."

"Maybe."

He sounded as enthusiastic as if she'd suggested he hammer a corkscrew in his head.

There had to be more books. Not just for all his fans' sakes, including hers, but for Loon's. While she couldn't write a novel, maybe if she really tried, she could come up with an idea for one *he* could write. Preposterous, sure, but she had to try something.

When they'd finished lunch, they packed up. "Thank you, Juniper," Cass said to the lake.

"Yes, indeed," Kent added.

Cass took out her phone and snapped a couple photos of the lake, then looked at Kent, looked away, looked back. "Do you think—I mean, would you mind if we took a photo together?"

"Not at all. Want me to snap it? I've got longer arms."

"Thanks."

He put his arm around her, and she wondered if he could feel how fast her heart was beating.

"Let's take a couple," he said, putting his head closer to hers and smiling big.

Finished, they started down the mountain, not talking much, though Cass—despite her dismay about Felicity's looming demise—was practically dancing with the memory of his arm around her.

"I really need to get into a workout regimen," Kent said. "The next time I come to Loon, I want to be able to make this hike without puffing."

He was coming back. Was there any chance she was part of the reason why?

They were six-hundred feet further down and just passing a Manzanita that as always was shedding its distinctive red bark, when Kent said, "Is Rebecca dating anyone?"

Cass was glad he couldn't see her crimson cheeks or her blurring eyes. She doubted he had any idea how much she wished he hadn't asked, that he didn't care. "She's divorced," she managed to say. "I don't know if she's dating."

"It's silly to ask, of course," he said. "Someone who looks like her isn't likely to be attracted to someone who looks like me."

Cass winced. If people didn't care so much about *looks*, the world would be a far better place: happier, more peaceful, more just. Unfortunately, that wasn't the case and never would be. The Rebeccas of the world would always be the chosen ones. Everyone else should just accept that.

Sixteen

Cass steered her truck toward Mack's because she needed to tell Mack all that had happened—after she first apologized, of course. Caesar stood on the back seat, his head thrust out the window.

Cass stopped the truck in front of Mack's house. Kneeling on a pad, digging in the garden, Mack wore faded overalls and a red thermal top that clung to thin, taut arms. She didn't turn around, and she didn't just dig dirt with her spade; she stabbed it. Cass's stomach flopped.

Dante and Socrates chorused a greeting, leaping up against the pickup's door.

Mack still didn't turn around. At least the dogs were welcoming. If only Mack would do something—anything—to acknowledge her. Cass's throat got so tight, she doubted she could even swallow words.

The instant she got out of her truck, Caesar bounded down. He and the two little dogs chased each other around the yard.

"Hi, Mack." Cass spoke with all the enthusiasm she could put in her voice.

Mack grunted. Never a good sign.

"You're angry with me?" Cass said.

Mack stood. Behind her, the spade protruded from the soil like a knife stuck in a corpse. "You told me a few tourists wouldn't hurt," she said, "and I agreed." Mack wiped her arm across her forehead, streaking dirt. "Since when was a hundred thousand a *few*?"

"We won't get that many. *Twilight* was aimed at teens, who love vampires and werewolves. There aren't either of those in the Felicity Benedict novels, and teens make the most avid fans. Plus, Forks attracted that number over several years."

"We're still looking at maybe three hundred visitors—or more—a day, are we not?"

"Weekends maybe. In the summer."

"You need to spend a few weekends at Lake Tahoe this summer, sitting in stalled traffic, taking an hour to drive five miles. Then you come back and tell me how wonderful things are going to be."

"But, Mack, we need to do *something*. Look at the town. We're losing businesses. People have to move away to find jobs. Our tax base is shrinking, which means our library, our schools, our roads, and everything that matters the most, are all in danger. Wouldn't you rather put up with a little slow traffic than let the town die?"

Mack sighed, and as she did, it was like someone stuck a pin in her, allowing all the anger to seep out: her shoulders dropped, and her face transformed from angry to concerned.

"But what exactly *is* Loon, Cass? Just the buildings and businesses? Or is it the people, most of whom live here because they value what the town offers. The mountains. The serenity. The astonishing views. The neighborliness. If this becomes a tourist mecca, the people who move in down the road won't necessarily value what we do. They'll build golf courses and upscale condos, they'll put a Starbucks on every corner, and they'll snatch up available housing, forcing people currently living here to move away in even greater numbers than they are now. It won't be a place you'll recognize. So, when you say that with your plan, the town's not going to disappear, forgive me if I don't jump for joy."

Cass had no idea how to respond except to say, "I don't think that's going to happen."

"Then why did Rebecca make you promise to keep the numbers secret?"

Cass wondered about that for a split second, until she remembered. "We wanted Kent to have a good reception so he would push to convince some of the Felicity Benedict movie's stars to come to Loon."

"Why?"

"To attract enough tourists to support our businesses and keep our library open. Besides, Mack, I've learned so much from Felicity, and I want to introduce her to other readers." Cass startled herself with that realization. "It's a win-win."

"No, it's a lose-lose. For one thing, you don't learn how to live from fiction. You learn it from your family and your friends. Your *true* friends, who love and accept you just as you are. Friends who *act* like they love you."

Cass took a step forward, wanting to close the distance between them. "But I do learn from fiction, Mack. I always have. Since I began reading Felicity, I think I've become a little braver."

Mack shook her head in what looked like weary dismay. "Even if that's true, I'll tell you what the worst part of all this is. You think you're saving Loon, but you're wrong. By the time you realize what you've done, it will be too late."

What if Mack was right? Cass hadn't heard of anything close to that chaos happening in Forks, but she hadn't really looked. She glanced at her watch. "I need to get to the kennel. Diego's been covering for me. And, Mack, I want you to know, I really am sorry. I should have told you the numbers from the beginning." She meant it.

"Apology accepted."

A sense of relief flowed through Cass, and she turned to go, then turned back around. "We still on for dinner Saturday?"

"Of course. But no more discussion of the Felicity campaign. We need to agree to disagree and let it go. If we keep talking about it, I'll get upset all over again."

"Okay, sure." Cass opened her truck door but didn't release the handle fast enough. It snapped back on her finger, pinching it hard. Despite the fact her finger throbbed, she would rather have that pain, her finger already darkening beneath the skin, than the pain she'd seen on Mack's face. What if the Felicity campaign drove Mack and herself apart? *Then* would the campaign be worth it?

"You'll never be one of them, you know," Mack said.

Cass signaled Caesar back in the truck, then got in after him. She didn't look at Mack. "One of whom?"

"Rebecca's crowd."

Maybe she wouldn't, or maybe Mack was wrong. When Rebecca clapped for Cass at the meeting, spurring others to do the same, Cass had felt downright elated. She still did, on some level. "Because I'm a loser?"

"God no, Cass. Because you're kind and decent. You've never, ever been a loser, no matter what Rebecca and her buddies said."

"But she's changed. You saw that for yourself last night. She didn't take all the credit; she even got people to applaud for me. Not herself, Mack. Me." Cass lifted her chin and looked Mack in the eye. Tears stung. She wasn't sure whether they were tears of relief from finally shaking off so many years of disapproval or tears of regret that Mack didn't share her excitement, but she did nothing to wipe them away.

Mack squeezed Cass's shoulder. "I'm glad you were

applauded. That should have happened a long time ago." Her face was etched with concern. "But there are two things you need to remember."

"I'm listening."

"First, good people don't ask their friends to bury the truth, which basically means to lie."

Cass looked down, unable to bear looking into Mack's eyes. "And the second thing?"

"Perhaps some people change, but most don't, not really. A rattlesnake is always a rattlesnake. Sooner or later, you're going to put your foot in the wrong place. When you do, that snake will turn on you." Mack closed the pickup's door. "Be careful, Cass."

"I will. See you Saturday." Cass drove back to the highway. Surely the Felicity Benedict Connection would bring the right kind of people to town, no matter what Mack thought, people who loved Felicity and thus shared her values.

Rebecca's efforts were already bringing in desperately needed visitors. Was that why Cass was inclined to trust her, because Rebecca was doing all she could to save their town? Or was it something more selfish? Maybe she wanted to be friends with Rebecca in order to earn approval from the very people who'd ostracized her so many years ago.

If only she had someone to share all this with. She'd give anything to talk to her father. He didn't see what her mother saw. Tears stung Cass's eyes. "There's my beautiful girl," he'd say every morning. "My brave, beautiful girl."

That night, despite being tired from the intensity of the day and the exertion of the hike, Cass was unable to sleep. She wished she had someone to share her bed and hold her while she cried. Tears, after all, could be a balm for the heart, but when she cried alone, the solitude seemed only to magnify her sorrow.

She curled up facing Caesar, who was asleep on his pet pillow on the floor beside her. "Hey, boy," she whispered.

He didn't stir.

She spoke again, a little louder. "Hey, Caesar."

He raised his head, his eyes only half open.

"I feel really sad."

Caesar put his head back down and closed his eyes. His ears twitched, but that was his only response.

Apparently even her dog wasn't interested.

Seventeen

Although it produced a sound about as soothing as a weed whacker, Cass welcomed the daily chore of scraping dog feces across the concrete floor of the pens with a metal hoe. She found that the task helped keep her from obsessing over the previous day's transaction with Mack, unsure whether she was feeling sadness that she'd disappointed Mack or unease about her friend's warning regarding Rebecca and snakes.

Garbed in rubber boots and gloves, Cass shoveled the feces into a bucket lined with a heavy-duty trash bag, then mopped Poppy's floor with lemon smelling-germicidal detergent, squeegeed it down, disinfected it with bleach that made her nose curl, and rinsed it all off. Much as she loathed the bleach smell, she sometimes thought it was what kept her so healthy. No germs could stand up to all that Clorox.

She stepped out of Poppy's pen. All but three of the dogs were in the outside sections of their pens. Those three were with Diego, who had earlier driven her old Subaru, his to use whenever he wished, to Moon Mountain with three large dogs and Caesar. Diego liked to hike Moon because he enjoyed the challenges of its steep trails and its stunning waterfalls. Cass tended to prefer the trails that rose behind the kennel, like the one to Juniper Lake, hikes which afforded, on some trails, magnificent glimpses of Moon along the way. When she hiked Moon itself, because of the angle and tangle of trees, she was often unable to see the mountain's dome.

She was cleaning Tiffany's pen when the dogs erupted outside.

"I'm impressed."

Cass whirled around. Kent. He was dressed in T-shirt, vest and jeans. He looked good. She caught herself just before she raked Clorox/feces-stained gloves through her hair. "Hi."

"You don't delegate the dirty work?" he said.

"We divide it up." She hadn't seen Kent since their hike two days before; her pulse sped up. He'd sought her out. Why? "It wouldn't be fair to make Diego do all of it. And I wouldn't want to lose him."

"He's lucky to work for you."

"I'm lucky to have him." That was an understatement. For some reason, she wanted to share with him what had happened that night a year ago. "If it weren't for Diego, I wouldn't be here. Or anywhere."

"What happened?"

Sleet had turned streets and sidewalks slick, she told Kent, and she'd been distracted as she got out of her pickup in front of Scotty's store. Her feet slipped on the ice, and she closed the door harder than she intended, sending a loud clap into the night.

A snarl.

She turned, slowly, and took in the snarling dog standing in the street: no collar, mangy looking, chunk of one ear missing, burly. Fearful dogs' ears were usually back, their lips tightly together, their tails tucked. This dog's lips were lifted to reveal yellowed incisors, its eyes riveted on her, its ears and tail up. Hackles, too. This was a dog preparing to attack.

Her throat squeezed tight; air barely made its way into her lungs. Cass lowered her eyes from the dog's to avoid challenging it, though she kept him in view. "Easy boy," she said, as calmly as she could.

He responded with a low, guttural growl.

Her jacket, pockets laden with dog treats, was in the truck. Cass had no backpack, nothing to put between herself and the dog. Two careful steps backwards toward Scotty's store put her onto the icy sidewalk. Refuge was so close. She took a longer step, slipped and fell hard on her butt.

Teeth bared, the dog lunged.

Someone behind her reached over her and opened a black umbrella between her and the dog. *Fwop.*

It was a brilliant tactic. Cass couldn't see what the dog was doing, but his teeth weren't sinking into her.

A male voice spoke to the dog in soft, steady Spanish. The adrenaline surging through Cass erased her high school Spanish from her brain.

She slid the rest of the way backwards into the store still on her butt. The young man came in behind her just as Chance and his deputy, Bill Riley, arrived and shot the dog with a tranquilizer gun.

The umbrella was in shreds.

That would have been her. Or the man who'd saved her. Cass shuddered. Shock and her own fear must have kept her from hearing the dog maul the umbrella.

Cass thanked the young man, who switched from Spanish to fluent English. Her previous assistant had gotten engaged and moved to Colorado three weeks before. She'd interviewed four local youths for the job, but none had shown the dog sensibility she required. On impulse, she asked the young man, "How'd you like a job?"

Cass smiled, remembering. "I still give thanks for that impulse," she said.

"Impressive," Kent said. "I wonder how he came up with the umbrella idea."

"He said he'd seen the dog go into attack mode as he was looking at umbrellas, but I don't think most people would have put that together. I sure wouldn't. And I'm not certain I'd have had the courage to step out of the store and put myself close to that dog."

"No kidding. Remind me to thank Diego the next time I see him."

That night had been so cold and so dangerous, remembering it made her shiver. Wait. What had Kent just said? "The *next* time?"

"I'm going back to L.A."

"Oh." She tried to hide her dismay.

"I won't be gone long."

"Oh?"

"I'll be back in a few days."

"Really? That's great!" She'd like to invite him on another hike, but she wasn't sure she could stand a rejection. *Be loud. Be proud.* She took a deep breath and plunged. "Want to go on a hike when you, you know, get back?"

"I doubt I'll have time right away."

"Oh?"

"I need to write, and Rebecca wants to show me some of her favorite spots."

Of course, Rebecca. So much for "loud and proud."

"Then again," he said, "maybe Rebecca will want to hike, and we could all go."

"Yeah" was all Cass could manage. She would be willing to

bet that the only hiking Rebecca did was from her office to her car.

"We'll hike again eventually," he said.

"You're going to be a regular visitor?"

"Hopefully. I'll have to see how it goes with Rebecca."

Was it unusual for him to be so smitten with a woman so fast? Cass wasn't sure he'd want to answer her question, but so what? It wasn't like he wanted to spend time with *her*. She had nothing to lose. "Have you ever been in love?"

He flinched and glanced away. "A few times." He looked back at her. "Not always requited. You?"

"I've lost my heart hundreds of times, almost always requited. Of course, the objects of my affection have generally possessed four legs."

Kent had a kind smile that seemed to include his eyes, or maybe it was just that the creases around them turned up and made it seem that his eyes, too, were smiling. He took a step toward her and glanced around before speaking. "I don't know what it is about Rebecca, but something about her really attracts me, and I don't just mean her beauty. Maybe it's her decisiveness or her confidence. She's a remarkable woman, which of course you don't need me to tell you."

A whirlwind of panting dogs swept in and collapsed onto the cool concrete floor. Caesar, the pit bull Poppy, a Shepherd/Collie mix named Axel, and Matie, a blend of just about everything big, flopped on their sides, panting hard.

"Looks like they had a good workout," Kent said.

"Hmm." Diego had left four hours ago. Moon was only a twenty-minute drive each way. The dogs had clearly been run too hard for too long, and Diego was nowhere to be seen. Something was wrong. "I need to find Diego," she said.

"And I need to get going," Kent said. "Just wanted to let you know I'll be back. Take care. And thanks for setting all this up."

In an instant, he was gone. She filled water bowls, setting one in front of each exhausted dog. Where was Diego?

She started toward the door. Caesar rose to accompany her, but he limped. "Sit, boy." She lifted his front left leg; his paw pad looked reddened. Diego must have run them over rocks and boulders. That was not like him. "Stay." Cass signaled Caesar to lay down. He did, and she gave his head a couple strokes before going out to find Diego.

She located him in the far outside corner of the kennel, slamming a rock against a fence post, over and over and over. "Diego? What's wrong?"

"The dogs, they are lucky." He hammered the post. *Whack.* "They have shelter." *Whack.* "Food." *Whack.* "Nobody wants to hurt them." *Whack.* "They live better than *people* in my country." *Whack.*

"Please tell me what happened."

He stared at the rock in his hand. "My mama needs heart surgery. Stents put in."

"Oh, Diego, I'm so sorry," she said. "I can understand how you must feel."

"No." Diego all but yelled the word. He glanced at the rock he held with what looked like loathing. "No. You have no idea what it's like. If Mack needed surgery, you could be there. You don't have people wanting to kill you. You haven't had to run from all you love to stay alive."

"You're right," she said, cheeks hot. How could she—or anyone—really grasp the life Diego had been forced to live unless they were living a similar existence? She had no idea what to say.

"I want to hold Mama's hand and tell her how much I love her."

Cass spoke softly. "You can tell her that, you know. I mean, it isn't like being there, but maybe you could have a video call."

He hurled the rock he held into the woods so hard, Cass

heard it *thud* against a tree. Once it struck, air seemed to rush out of him, making him lean against the fence post.

"I'm sorry for what I said about understanding, Diego. You're right. I can't. And I'm sorry you can't be there. When's the surgery?"

"Tomorrow." Diego's voice quivered. "She is so far away." His eyes welled with tears.

"Your father and Enrique will take good care of your mom. I don't know your dad well, but I can't imagine Enrique letting your mom's doctors be anything but perfect. I bet she'll come out feeling a lot better."

"*Ojalá.*"

"Would you like to call your family now?"

He shook his head.

"Okay. Let me know if you change your mind. And remember, this is a day off for you."

"No. I want to be here." Diego looked at his hands, still balled in fists. He sucked in a deep breath and relaxed his fingers. "I ran them too hard."

"Yeah."

"I'm sorry."

"I know. The dogs are fine." She put her hand on his shoulder. "Do whatever brings you comfort today."

Diego stayed outside to give the big dogs one-on-one time. Caesar came up to Cass when she returned to the office. He wasn't limping now. The other three dogs were all still collapsed, but not panting as hard. She gave each a treat and some loving and put all of them except Caesar back into their pens.

Poor Diego. To be so far from those he loved, especially in a fraught time like his mother's heart surgery. He was lucky to have such a close family—not physically close, obviously, but certainly emotionally—but it seemed a mixed blessing: to love each other so much but be so far away.

Imagine if the situation were reversed, and she, Cass, had to escape to Honduras. She knew for certain that no matter how grateful she'd be to that country for granting her the asylum that saved her life, it would never feel like home, any more than this country did for Diego. She would miss the people she loved, miss the kennel, miss Juniper Lake and Moon, miss the sights, sounds, and smells of the mountains she knew, the mountains she loved, *her* mountains. Her home.

EIGHTEEN

Cass parked her truck in the closest space to Scotty's she could find—some four blocks away—and didn't mind at all. On the contrary. Before the start of the Felicity Benedict Connection nearly two months before, she'd rarely had to park anywhere other than right in front of whatever store she needed. Who knew inconvenience could be so appealing?

Her one regret during that time was not getting to hike with Kent. She'd seen him around town occasionally, mostly with Rebecca, on whom his attention always seemed riveted. Once when Cass saw him alone, in the grocery, she'd asked if he'd come up with any ideas for a new Felicity novel. He'd winced.

Now, walking toward Scotty's, she marveled at the town's transformation. Rebecca and the council had assembled a team of mostly local people who'd descended on Main Street like a locust swarm, only instead of leaving behind devastation, they'd left a town newly vibrant and welcoming. They'd repainted signs, dingy store fronts, and sidewalk trash containers, repaired every pothole, planted a circle of daffodils around the base of each streetlamp, and installed two cedar benches on each side of the street. Main had gone from looking like Death shopped there to looking like the Easter Bunny did.

Furthermore, Felicity Benedict merchandise had arrived in stores, while life-sized cardboard cutouts of the movie's three stars in costume stood outside several businesses along Main, including the Sourdough Bakery and Café. The cutouts featured: Lana Kurth wearing a muumuu and a purple scarf like Felicity's, Olivia Golden sporting a tight-fitting black T-shirt that revealed wiry arms like Rain's, and a shirtless Penn Booth, whose well-defined muscles were as developed as Lucas's in the books. The bakery had taped a sign to Lana's hand advertising that it sold Felicity's Fritters. The aromas of fritters, croissants, and cinnamon buns drifted across the street, tickling Cass's nose.

And every day, it seemed, more and more tourists came.

"Watson, stop!" a woman yelled.

Cass turned toward the voice just in time to spot a fleeing pug race down the sidewalk. She stepped on, then grabbed, his leash. Watson lunged, straining to escape.

The woman lumbering toward her carried a full bag of groceries in each arm while clutching a small boy's hand. Cass had seen the woman around town but didn't know her.

"Bad dog," the woman scolded as she reached the pug, but the little boy tugged free and dropped to his knees, hugging Watson. The woman just shook her head.

"Looks like you could use some help." Cass gave her the leash and took the groceries.

"Bless you. Between my husband, my four boys, and Watson, I'm reeling. There's way too much testosterone for one household. The boys kept pleading for a dog, and I kept pleading to get a *female*, but the boys fell in love with Watson. Naturally. I'm Rosalind Lamb, by the way. We live out on Lodestar Lane."

"Cass Enger."

Rosalind's eyes widened. "You're the one who's working with Rebecca on the Felicity Benedict thing, right?"

"One of the people."

"You are miracle workers. My husband Robbie's a painter. Before the Felicity campaign, he was having trouble finding work; we had to dip into our savings. We were worried because we love it here, but we weren't sure how much longer we could afford to rent. Since the improvements started, Robbie's had all kinds of work. So thank you, thank you, thank you."

Cass's smile had stretched before she even realized it. "Thanks for telling me that. And you're welcome."

"I'd never even heard of Felicity Benedict before all this," Rosalind said. "I've read all three books now and can't wait for the fourth."

Cass didn't have the heart to tell her there wouldn't be one.

"You know how Felicity says to be proud and loud?" Rosalind stood straighter.

"Sure."

The little boy tugged his mom's arm. "I want ice cream." His voice was in whine mode.

Rosalind shook her head and sighed. "Not now, Oliver."

"But I'm really hungry," the boy said.

"I'm talking. It's not your turn." She looked back at Cass. "I took Felicity's advice and demanded Robbie take care of all four boys one night a week. To my shock, he agreed. I've been going to the library the one night it's open, just to be by myself, whether to read or just stare into space. It's so quiet, so peaceful."

Rosalind's voice sounded pleased and dreamy.

"I'm really hungry, Mom. I want ice cream." Oliver tried to tug his mother toward the ice cream store. "You didn't feed me lunch."

"It's ten o'clock, Oli."

"But I'm hungry." He stomped his foot.

"Oh boy," Rosalind said. "We're heading toward a meltdown."

"Ice cream!" Oli screamed.

"I need to get Oli and Watson in the car quick." Rosalind scooped up Watson under one arm, Oli under the other, and moved fast back to her car, where she all but stuffed the yelling boy in his car seat, Watson beside him. Cass put the groceries in the rear of the hatchback.

"Thanks again, Cass, both for the help today and for the FBC."

"You're welcome." Cass waved as Rosalind backed out, pleased to know that she had helped introduce at least one reader to Felicity. Lifting her chin, she smiled.

The sign in Scotty's window was new, a large purple sign that proclaimed, *Headquarters for All Things Felicity*. Inside the store, anything that could conceivably be stamped with *Felicity Benedict* was for sale, including T-shirts, blankets, water bottles, key chains, and much more.

Three women Cass didn't recognize were lifting up the shirts that came in a variety of colors and Felicity slogans: *Proud to be Loud; Perfection Is an Ill-lusion; Focus on the how, the now and the wow*. Cass decided she would get a purple Proud shirt with silver letters for herself, a black how/now/wow one with gold letters for Zoe, and a rose one with the perfection slogan in black for Diego.

A teenager standing to the side of the Felicity tables was texting.

"If you'd like to try anything on," Scotty said to the customers, "there's a storeroom in back with mirrors."

"I might," said a plump woman, continuing to look through the shirts.

Scotty took out the dog bowls he'd ordered for Cass. "Business just keeps getting better," he said. Then he echoed her earlier thoughts. "Rebecca's gotten so many improvements done so fast, it's astonishing."

Cass's "I know" was drowned out by gift shop owner Nate Griffin, who stormed into the store, snatched the *Headquarters for All Things Felicity* sign from the window, and ripped it in half. "You're not the headquarters," the Boston-accented Nate shouted, practically frothing at the mouth. He towered over Scotty by a foot. "I carry everything Felicity you do. Your sign's a lie."

Scotty rose up on the balls of his feet and snatched back the strips of the sign. "I can call it anything I want." He, too, was nearly shouting.

"Liar!"

"Idiot!"

It seemed the men's rage might spill over, toxic, to anyone in range.

Three of the women shrank back from them, while the plump one moved in front of the teenaged girl, who peered around her, trying to see.

"I really do carry the same stuff he does," Nate told the frightened women.

Cass wanted to say something to get the men to stop. She wished she had a megaphone voice. "Please stop arguing," she said, way too softly.

Nate spun toward her, his entire face and his balding head red with rage. "That sign is *your* doing. *You* gave Scotty the *Headquarters* idea for his sign because he's your pal. Not to mention that the bench just happened to be placed in front of *his* store."

Loser.

Nate didn't say the old taunt, but he might as well have. Cass felt herself shrivel.

"*I* came up with that sign," Scotty said. "It's good advertising. If you'd thought of it, you'd have done it. And the *council* chose where to place those benches. Not Cass. And not me."

Nate glowered at Scotty. "Yeah, right."

"Go to Hell."

Rebecca strode into the store and stepped between them. "Stop it." Her voice wasn't raised, but it was commanding. Her eyes glared with such ferocity, it seemed like they could incinerate the men. She gestured toward the shoppers. "We have visitors. This isn't the way Loon welcomes guests."

Nate turned to face the women, who—except for the teenager, who was back to texting—still looked uneasy, shifting their weight, glancing toward the door.

Nate held up his hands. "Sorry. Sorry. Look, anything you can get here, you can get at my store, Nate's Nuggets, just across the street. If you come over, I'd be happy to give you a fifteen percent discount on any Felicity souvenirs you buy."

The women looked at each other and the T-shirts they were clutching.

"Twenty percent," Scotty said.

"Twenty-five." Nate.

"Thirty." Scotty.

"Thirty-five." Nate.

Scotty opened his mouth, then seemed to stop himself. "Thirty-five it is," he said.

The women were wide-eyed.

"Tell you what." Rebecca addressed the watchful shoppers. "How about buying some Felicity souvenirs here and some at Nate's, at the thirty-five percent discounted rates in both places. In fact, if you'll do that, you can tell Shirley at the Sourdough Bakery & Café that your lunch is on me, Rebecca Oliver, Loon's mayor."

"Sold," said one woman. The others slowly nodded.

"Thank you." Rebecca shook hands with each visitor. "And I

hope if you're active on social media, you'll spread the word about our town for other Felicity fans. By the way, we're going to have our official Felicity Benedict Connection launch on Saturday, July 13th."

Cass pulled back. Rebecca had scheduled the launch day without even bothering to check with her?

"That day we'll have events and prizes to commemorate Loon being named as the inspiration for Felicity's hometown. One of our special guests will be Felicity's author, Kent Calloway."

"Great!" chorused two women.

"Our other special guest will be one of the movie's stars, Penn Booth."

The teenager who'd been texting dropped her phone; it *clunked* against the floor. The plump woman grabbed it, frowning.

"Penn Booth's coming *here*?" the teen said.

Despite the disbelief apparent in the girl's tone, Rebecca smiled. "He is indeed."

"Mom," the teen said, "we *have* to come back for that. Penn's so hot. I'm in love with him."

"You and sixty million other teens," her mother said.

The girl clasped her hands together, prayerlike. "*Please.* I'll do anything."

"Dishes all summer without complaint?"

"Anything. Just say we can come back."

"Maybe. If he's really going to be here." She looked to Rebecca. "How will we know for sure?"

"He'll be here. He's a friend of Kent's. But you can confirm it if you follow Loon on Instagram or Facebook or check back on our town's website. For now, enjoy your discounts and your lunches. Scotty, Nate, could you step outside with me a minute?"

Cass followed Rebecca and the two men out to the sidewalk. Maybe she could learn something about defusing tension.

Rebecca spoke in a low voice. "This can't happen again. Bad online reviews could tank our campaign."

Nate sounded as aggrieved as he looked. "He can't call himself Felicity's headquarters. We're selling the same stuff. I mean, this is life and death for my store." His eyes never left Scotty's face.

"And mine," Scotty said, arms crossed.

"Tourism's growing every day," Rebecca said. "There will soon be enough business for both your stores. That much I promise you."

Eyes narrowed, Nate turned his gaze away from Scotty to Rebecca.

"This is what we're going to do," Rebecca said. "Scotty's stays as the headquarters. Nate, make a sign that calls your store something else. The best buy. The official site. Whatever."

"The official site," Nate said. "I like that."

Scotty seemed about to protest, then gave a kind of assenting shrug.

"Good. And no more of this crap."

Nate headed toward his store; Scotty went back inside.

Rebecca watched them go. "Idiots." She nodded toward a cluster of three leggy teens wearing very short shorts who had stopped beside the bakery's movie star cutouts and were planting kisses on Penn's face.. "Do you know any of those girls?"

"No. Do you?"

"No, but look at them. If we can come up with the right approach to take advantage of Penn being here for our launch day, it could be a game changer. Thank God Kent's been helping him with his book. Incidentally, I hope the 11th works for you. It was when Penn could come. Plus, the two weeks around July

4th are often the busiest of the summer for tourism. For a lot of people, July's the true start of summer."

The girls moved on. Penn's cutout likeness was smeared with multiple shades of lipstick.

"What if we did some kind of contest on our launch day," Cass said, "and the winner gets to spend time with Penn?"

"Now that," Rebecca said, "is a hot idea. What kind of contest do you have in mind?"

"I don't know yet."

"Let's both put our minds to it. The contest must be something anyone could win. And it has to appeal to teens."

"Here's another idea," Cass said. "We raffle off Kent."

"Huh?"

"Whoever wins the raffle gets to spend an hour or two with him. That way we'll attract not just teens who dream of Penn, but middle-aged women who identify with Felicity and would love to sit down with Kent." While she lacked Rebecca's presence, Cass was pleased by her own creativity.

"That's a *great* idea, Cass." Rebecca's voice was as bright as her eyes. "And you know what? We could offer one raffle ticket for every ten dollars of Felicity merchandise a customer buys."

Cass grinned. "That should make Scotty, Nate and all the other merchants happy."

"Indeed. We make a great team, Cass." Rebecca nodded to emphasize her point. "And how about this. Instead of calling it Launch Day for the FBC, we'll call it Star Day. To emphasize Penn and Kent's popularity."

"I love it," Cass said.

"Me, too. I'll tell Kent our inspired ideas. Brilliant." She flashed Cass a thumbs-up, then crossed the street back to the town offices.

Cass lingered on the sidewalk a moment, feeling taller. As she turned to get her water bowls from Scotty, she replayed his confrontation with Nate. Though the two men weren't close friends as far as she knew, she'd never seen them upset with each other, even during football season when they championed rival teams. The fact they didn't raise their voices over football but had shouted at each other—and her—over their Felicity merchandise was unsettling. She just hoped it wasn't a harbinger of things to come.

Nineteen

Caesar barked a joyful welcome as Zoe rushed up to Cass, thrust her cell phone at her, and proclaimed, "Cass, look!"

Zoe's face seemed on high beam, her eyes lit from within. Cass, standing in the doorway of the kennel office late Friday morning, a week before the Memorial Day weekend movie opening, looked at the phone expecting to see a selfie.

What she saw was a bug.

Diego was close behind Zoe, who wasn't at school because it was a teacher training day. Cass had never seen Zoe look so happy, but she wasn't sure what Zoe wanted her to see in the photograph. "I don't . . ."

"Look at the colors."

Zoe's enraptured expression astonished Cass. True, the bug, a beetle, was an improbable fluorescent green with splatters of neon orange, but if someone had told her that Zoe would get excited by a bug, Cass would have suggested that person should get on meds. "It's gorgeous," she said, meaning it. That Zoe was taking photos of bugs rather than herself seemed like a giant step forward.

"This bug's wearing colors together that most people wouldn't even put in the same closet," Zoe said. "It's epic. And look at this one."

Zoe swiped her phone's screen, producing a close-up photo of a butterfly with metallic blue wings speckled with orange and yellow dots. Cass had been struck by that butterfly's beauty when she was young, too. "Gorgeous," she said.

"Diego showed it to me."

Zoe swiped her screen again to produce a shot of the indigo Juniper Lake. Just seeing the photo made Cass want to grab her hiking boots and go.

"Does that color pop, or what?" Zoe said.

Zoe had never talked so fast or sounded so excited. "It sure does."

"I'm going to design clothes inspired by nature. Diego said I should call it *Zoe's Belleza Natural*. It'll be awesome. And I'll even donate five percent of all sales to endangered species groups or something."

"I'm impressed," Cass said. "With both of you."

Diego looked proud. Since his mother's successful heart procedure eight weeks previously, his mood had greatly improved.

Cass knew he loved nature as much as she did, but she'd had no idea Zoe had that same capacity, hidden until now. "You'd make a great teacher, Diego."

He raised his hands and stepped back as if in horror. "No. I would only like to work with kids like Zoe who are excited to learn."

"I'm not a kid." Zoe gave Diego's arm a shove. "I'm nearly seventeen."

Zoe was looking at Diego with what Cass would swear was longing, and Diego was reciprocating. Zoe's short hair looked tousled. "Did you go swimming?" Cass said.

"For like five minutes." Zoe shivered. "That water was too

fricking cold but so clear, you could see the rocks on the bottom."

Cass doubted Zoe had taken a swimsuit. The only bag they had was one Diego carried, and it couldn't have held much beyond water bottles and snacks. "Looks like you had an awesome hike."

"The best," Zoe said. "I've lived here my whole life, but before today, I'd never really seen it. I mean, did you know it was this epic, Cass?"

"I was lucky. My dad took me hiking a lot when I was little. I grew up loving it. Still do."

"I wish *my* dad had done that."

"You've got years to appreciate it. Some people *never* get their eyes opened."

"The day is beautiful, Cass," Diego said. "Go hike. I'll stay."

The kennel had been at capacity lately, meaning Cass hadn't had a chance to hike in a while, and Zoe's photos had made her ache to hit the trail. The fact that there were fewer dogs today made Diego's suggestion seem almost doable, but she didn't want to take advantage of his kindness. This was, after all, his day off. Much as she'd like to hike, she shook her head. "Not on your day off."

"I can help Diego," Zoe said.

"Go," Diego urged.

"Well. Are you sure?"

"Claro."

"Okay, maybe I will. Just a short one, if you're *really* sure."

A car pulled into the parking lot. Rebecca practically leapt from her SUV.

"Shit." Zoe slid her phone in the back pocket of her shorts.

Cass was surprised there was enough material to hold the phone against Zoe's rear.

Rebecca practically sputtered as she stomped toward them.

"What the hell were you thinking, Zoe? That having fun was more important than school?"

"Studying people who lived like ten trillion years ago? Who cares?"

"Wait," Cass said. "I thought this was a teacher training day."

Rebecca snapped her fingers. "Hand it over."

Scowling, Zoe slowly pulled her phone from her pocket and handed it to her mother.

Rebecca looked at the screen. "You're taking pictures of bugs? Get in the car. And, Cass, please remember that any time Zoe shows up here before 3:30 on a weekday, you're to take her directly to school."

Cass stiffened. Is that what Rebecca really thought of her, that she was nothing more than a shuttle service? "I can't just drive away and leave the dogs."

Rebecca gestured toward Diego. "He can watch them."

"Diego's not here all the time."

"Zoe, I said get in the car." Rebecca pointed, needlessly, toward her SUV.

Zoe turned toward Diego. "Thank you." She kissed his cheek, then sauntered toward the car so slowly the beetle she'd photographed could outpace her.

"Please don't either of you encourage Zoe's recklessness."

Diego nodded to Rebecca, then turned and headed toward the kennel office.

"Why didn't you hire a local boy?" Rebecca said. "There's lots of kids who need jobs."

"I interviewed several. None of them had Diego's gift for working with dogs. That's not something you can teach."

Rebecca scratched her neck. "Just keep him away from Zoe The last thing I need is for her to get pregnant.

Cass didn't say what she thought, that he was a good influence on Zoe and that if anyone needed protection in that relationship, it was Diego.

"Sorry for coming down on you," Rebecca said. "I'm just frustrated about Zoe."

"But she's changing." Cass flashed on an image of Zoe dressed in torn, black clothes. "For her to be excited about the color of a bug?"

"Whatever." Rebecca shook her shoulders as if to change the subject. "I have to tell you, our website and social media posts about seeing the movie's premiere in Felicity's own town are getting a ton of hits. We could have lots of tourists for that."

"Great!"

Rebecca looked toward the car. "I've got to figure out how to get my daughter to make better choices. I've tried praise. Didn't work. Tried rewards as well as punishments. Neither worked. Nothing works, and I'm running out of time. She turns eighteen in a little over a year. How do I train her to do the right thing?"

"The right thing?" Cass said.

"Achieve good grades. Be respectful. Don't lie or cheat. All that in a year."

Cass glanced at Caesar. If a dog could roll its eyes, that's exactly what he did. He then rested his head on his paws.

"She's honest and hardworking when she's here."

"Great." Rebecca's voice oozed sarcasm. Then she seemed to force a smile. When she spoke again, her voice had taken on a very different tone. "I mean it. That really is great, because I have a favor to ask. Kent called this morning."

Rebecca's whole bearing had changed. If eyes could dance, then Rebecca's were doing the salsa.

"He wants me to fly down next week for Thursday's official Felicity premiere."

"Wow," Cass said. The film would open in L.A. on Thursday

and nationwide on Friday. Cass tried to take every semblance of envy from her voice but doubted she succeeded. "Did you ever read his books?"

"Sure. All three. Once we decided to do the campaign, it would have been foolish not to." Rebecca's face beamed almost as bright as Zoe's had earlier. "Anyway, the plan would be for me to fly down Tuesday, then drive back with Kent Sunday. His car will be pretty loaded, so it's a good thing I don't take up much space."

"Why would the car be loaded?"

"Didn't he tell you?"

He hadn't told her anything. "No."

"He rented a cabin. He's going to use it as a kind of writer's retreat."

"Oh." So he was coming back to stay for a while. Maybe he'd have time to hike then. "How long did he rent it for?"

"That depends on what happens between us. He rented it month to month. Anyway, that's why Zoe needs to stay with you while I'm gone."

"Me?" Cass felt her jaw drop.

"Right."

"What about your parents?"

"My mother's a drunk, and my father's a bastard. I'd sooner *kennel* Zoe than put her in their clutches."

"Well, what about her friends?"

"I don't trust them, and I certainly don't trust Zoe, but she really likes you."

"Not *that* much."

"You like her. You said so yourself."

"Sure, but I've got too much to do at the kennel. I can't supervise Zoe."

"You wouldn't need to. Just make sure she goes to school and keeps curfew. And, of course, she should spend her free time working off more community service hours. She's still got a ways to go on those, right?"

"Yes."

"I'll pay you, naturally, for her room and board."

"That's not the issue. Have you mentioned this to Zoe?"

"It's not up to her."

"It won't work unless she agrees."

"Fine. Let's go talk to her. I'll make it clear."

"I don't imagine Zoe's going to like this arrangement," Cass said accompanying Rebecca to the car.

Rebecca waved aside Cass's doubts. "Like I said, it's not up to her."

Rebecca opened Zoe's car door. "I'm flying to L.A. next week to spend a few days with Kent. You'll be staying with Cass."

Zoe's nostrils flared. "I can take care of myself."

"I don't want you going to the house except to get what you need."

"What I don't need is a babysitter."

"Let me remind you that if the sheriff picks you up again," Rebecca said, "your next stop is Juvie. That's why you're going to stay with Cass. And if you don't, I will take away every piece of technology you own, only this time you won't see them until you graduate."

Zoe glowered at her mother. "How I live my life is up to me."

"Not till you're eighteen. You *will* stay with Cass while I'm gone."

"Why did Kent even invite you?" Zoe said. "Cass is his real fan. Not you."

Rebecca visibly flinched. When she spoke, her voice was harsh. "I don't want to hear any more about it."

Cass made her voice sound calmer than she felt. "Zoe, I need to know you'll follow whatever rules we agree to."

Zoe shrugged.

"A shrug isn't a commitment," Cass said. "What's your curfew?"

"Midnight on weekends," Rebecca said. "Nine on weekdays."

"Will you keep curfew if you stay with me?"

Zoe pursed her lips, then nodded.

"I mean it. You agree not to be late?"

"I'll keep the stupid curfew." Zoe reclined her seat.

Zoe's visible anguish when Rebecca attacked her reminded Cass of her relationship with her own mother. "Okay," she said. Maybe it would work. Maybe she would even enjoy having Zoe's company.

Rebecca took a folded sheet of paper and a key from her pocket. "Here's my contact info, Kent's info, my medical insurance policy info, our doctor's name and number, my house key, and our alarm code. I trust you to keep all this confidential. Anything else you need?"

Yeah. To get her head examined. "I don't think so."

"Thanks, Cass. You're the best."

The best what: idiot? Cass watched them drive away.

She went in search of Diego and found the door to his apartment open. He was inside the main room staring at 5 × 7 photos in his hands.

"I'm sorry," she said. "I didn't mean to intrude."

His gaze stayed fixed on one of the photographs he held.

"Is your mom okay?" she asked, fists clenched in case he said no.

He shrugged, then nodded.

"Are *you*?"

Diego handed her photos of birds and butterflies even more brilliantly hued than those in the pictures Zoe had taken. "Zoe should see *my* country. Our birds and butterflies, they are *maravilloso*."

Maravilloso? "Is that like marvelous? Brilliant colors?"

"*Sí.*"

His words seemed tinged with so much sadness and longing Cass wanted to put her arms around him. "I'm sorry, Diego. It must be rough to be so far away."

He swallowed hard.

The walls of his room, which he'd painted the blue of the Honduran flag, were covered with maps, photographs and posters that showed lush green mountains, sandy beaches, Mayan ruins and a jeweled ocean. "It looks *marevilloso* indeed," she said, handing him back the photographs.

"*Maravilloso.*"

A second *a*, not an *e*. "*Maravilloso*," she said. "I'd love to visit someday."

"No," Diego said. "Even God can't control the gangs." A shudder passed over him.

Cass leaned against the blue wall. "If you want to talk, I'll listen," she said. "Sometimes talking helps."

Arms hanging at his sides, one hand holding the pictures, the other clenched, Diego stared at the floor. She remained motionless; he remained silent. After a bit, she decided she'd misread him. Maybe what he needed was space. She started to push off from the wall to leave him alone.

Diego's voice when he spoke was as flat as a dead man's EKG. "We were kicking a soccer ball outside Alberto's house, Rodrigo and Alberto and me. Alberto tripped and fell. He started to get up, but a *pandillero* walked up. He jammed a rifle barrel into Alberto's mouth. I wanted to save my friend, but I was too scared. The *pandillero*, he said this would teach us not to refuse to join his gang." Diego shuddered.

"Alberto grabbed the gun and tried to push it out, screaming. But the *pandillero*, his body was alive, but his soul was dead. He laughed. Then he pulled the trigger."

Cass recoiled at the horror of that image. Poor Diego. Poor Alberto. Poor Rodrigo.

"Rodrigo threw dirt in the *pandillero*'s eyes. We ran in opposite directions. I fled to the park a few blocks away. I was hiding, shaking. I was so afraid the gang would find me."

Diego's voice remained flat, but he gripped his photographs so hard, his fingertips had turned white. Cass glanced down at her own hands, curled in tight fists.

"I waited till dark, then sneaked home, hiding behind things. When I reached our house, I went to the back door. I was so scared they'd killed my family."

Diego passed a hand over his eyes, his face anguished. Cass considered hugging him but decided he needed her just to listen.

"Mama heard me tapping on the door. My whole family hugged me, crying. The gang had come for me. Papa gave them all our cash, four-hundred dollars. They said he'd bought me six hours. I had only half an hour left to live. Papa put me in the car and we drove all night till we got to my uncle's farm. My uncle paid a man to smuggle me into the U.S."

Diego's eyes, so dark with sorrow and pain, suddenly glared. "Near the border, he pushed me out of the car to make room for people who would pay him more to get across. I got lost there, in the desert. I had no food or water, and it was so hot. After two days, I couldn't spit. Couldn't swallow. Couldn't pee. I stumbled across a woman who was wearing only her bra and underpants. She said she took off her clothes because she was so hot. She was all sunburned, only not the kind of sunburn that turns your skin red. The sun had turned her skin the color of burnt toast."

Cass wanted him to stop talking. Imagining that poor woman—and how close Diego had come to death—made it hard to take in air.

"That night, I was so tired, I fell asleep. When I woke up,

the woman was dead. I cried for her. For Alberto and Rodrigo. For my family and me. For all those who were lost. Only I had no tears because I had no moisture left."

The tears that Diego couldn't cry blurred Cass's eyes. "How did you make it across?"

"I was lucky. A Mexican priest found me. He said it was his mission to drive through the desert looking for people who were lost. He smuggled me to safety."

"I'm so glad he did," Cass said, "and I'm so sorry for all you went through." She made a slight gesture to show she was ready to hug him if that was what he wanted, but he didn't move. She so wished she could erase those memories from his mind—and those images from her own. She wiped her eyes before she spoke again. "What about Enrique and Arturo. Are they safe?" She wanted him to say yes.

"No one is safe, but Arturo is only seven. The gangs go after boys who are nine or ten. My mama and Enrique both have jobs. With what Papa earns, they pay the gangs to leave Enrique alone."

"And Rodrigo?"

"He's a *pandillero*. If he saw me now, he would kill me."

Cass wasn't sure whose fate was worse, Alberto's or Rodrigo's. But surely Diego's family could join him in the U.S. Her pulse picked up. His parents didn't want to leave his grandparents behind, she remembered he'd told her that. But to make your sons safe? "You got asylum here. Your whole family could."

"No. Your government now offers no home, not even to those who will die."

Cass didn't follow politics because it was so confusing, so upsetting, but even she knew how hostile the U.S. had become to immigrants. "How do you manage to smile being so far from home and after all you've seen?" she asked. She wasn't sure she could.

"Because I'm alive," he said. After a moment, he straightened. "Go hike, Cass."

"Another day, thanks." She wouldn't make any more jokes about PTSD being a school disorder, not when Diego suffered from the real thing. No wonder he'd cowered beside her desk. "You still have hours off. Do whatever would feel good."

"I want to be here, to work with the dogs."

That she understood, the solace of being with unconditionally loving dogs. "Big or little?"

"Big."

"Of course. And, Diego, the way you helped Zoe see the beauty around her? That's a huge gift. I hope you know that. And I hope that somehow Honduras will find its way back to peace so you can return if that's what you want."

"Yes, it is what I want. I miss my family. My country. My home."

He looked on the verge of tears. Instead, he nodded at her and strode from the room.

Cass went outside to inspect the fencing on each of the pens, but she kept picturing Alberto's murder—and a woman whose skin was the color of burnt toast.

TWENTY

Cass half thought she was going to be sick.

"Good God," Mack said, slowing her pickup as they rounded a curve because vehicles in front of them were barely moving, a line of cars with no more than a whisker's space between them. Some drivers began making turns onto side streets; others resorted to illegal U-turns, which were greeted by oncoming drivers with blaring horns, shouts, and curses. The ensuing cacophony was painful.

The stalled traffic looked like it stretched all the way to town. They were still a half-mile or more from Loon's stores, businesses—and movie theater. Cass prayed that the hour-and-a-half they'd allowed for getting to the movie's debut was enough.

"This has got to be Loon's first-ever traffic jam," Mack said.

"I'm sure it's just for tonight." Cass hoped she was right. "Rebecca advertised a lot for the movie's opening. And, of course, it's Memorial Day weekend. After Sunday or Monday, things will get back to normal."

"Will they? Have you noticed the number of out-of-state

plates recently? We may have become what Rebecca wanted, a tourist destination."

"Which could do a lot for the town."

"Or *to* it. But we agreed not to discuss this." Mack signaled a left turn. "If we don't get off Main, we're going to miss the movie."

It seemed to Cass that by the time an oncoming car slowed and waved them to make their turn, they were halfway to midnight.

Fifty-eight minutes and counting.

You're being ridiculous, she told herself. It was just a movie. How could she be so uptight about something so trivial, especially after what Diego had shared with her the previous week? But her voice of reason could not quiet her anxiety.

Mack drove residential streets looking for a spot. Cars were parked everywhere: in front of NO PARKING signs, cramming driveways, blocking hydrants, filling up every inch of space on Monte Vista and Moon Circle and Mountain Glen, on Diamond and Maple Wood and Frog Hollow. There wasn't enough room for a tricycle to park, let alone Mack's pickup. Cass tightened her grip on the armrest. Even if a spot magically appeared, it would take a good fifteen minutes to walk to the theater.

If they didn't get into the premiere, she couldn't go to the second showing, not with Zoe's curfew. Absurd though it was, she couldn't shake the feeling she was letting down Kent and—especially—Felicity.

She was, however, grateful that Mack wasn't proclaiming, "I told you so" about the traffic.

"You okay?" Mack asked.

"Just dismayed. I mean I know it's not *really* important. I do get that. But . . ."

"No need to apologize. The books mean a lot to you. If we can't get in tonight, I'm sure we could get tickets for tomorrow."

"Yeah." She suspected her voice sounded as knotted as her gut felt.

Unable to bear the sight of so many cars and no parking spaces, Cass closed her eyes. She told herself that it didn't matter whether she saw the film today or tomorrow, that even though she longed to be part of the movie's nationwide premiere, the reality was that Felicity didn't exist, Kent wouldn't care, and Rebecca wouldn't notice. Rationally, she knew all that.

Mack stopped the truck. "You better get out," she said.

Had Mack somehow found a spot? Cass opened her eyes. They were just two blocks from the theater, but Cass didn't see a parking space anywhere other than on someone's roof.

"You go on," Mack said. "I can catch it another time."

Cass frowned. "That wouldn't be fair."

"I know what this means to you. Go."

"You sure?"

"Absolutely. Enjoy."

"Well, okay, but . . ."

"Hurry."

Cass jumped down from the truck and jogged to the theater, where she confirmed with someone in line that the box office hadn't opened. She walked fast past strangers texting, strangers talking, and strangers taking photos with their phones.

The line snaked back from the theater for well more than three blocks. The moment Cass took her spot, the woman ahead of her turned toward her. "I sure hope we get in." The woman wore a gold *Stand Tall and Strut* sweatshirt. "I've been waiting forever for this movie to come out."

"Me, too."

"I hope they show the part where Felicity convinces Rain she's welcome to stay with her," the woman said. "I cry every time I read it."

"It's a great scene." Though Cass wished Mack could have

joined her, it was nice to be talking with someone who, unlike Mack, shared Cass's own enthusiasm for Felicity. She started to say how excited she was to see the Milk of Magnesia-in-the-salad-dressing-scene, but as Cass began to speak, the woman's phone quacked, her ringtone the sound of a duck. She answered, turned away from Cass, and plunged into animated conversation.

Cass looked up the line. The theater held two hundred. She tried to estimate the number of people ahead of her, but that proved impossible. Besides, they could be holding spots for family members or friends. Glancing behind her, she was comforted to see that the line now stretched back almost a block, with people still coming.

The line finally began to move. A buzz of excitement shot through the crowd—and Cass.

Chance materialized out of nowhere, fingers hooked over his gun belt. "Can you believe this crowd?" the sheriff said.

"No. I never imagined anything like this."

"I guess it's good for business," he said, "but it feels odd to see so many people I don't know."

"Yeah." It was comforting to have Chance beside her. He might not be a friend exactly, but at least he was familiar.

The closer Cass got to the box office, the faster her pulse sped. There were only a few people still ahead of her when Lily Diamond, theater owner, came outside. Wearing a long maroon dress that reminded Cass of the theater's curtains, Lily was a recent transplant to the town, having arrived only a year before. She'd bought the theater, refurbished it, and opened it on weekends. Rumor had it that Lily Diamond was as rich as her name and a genuine film buff who could afford for her business to fail.

"The first showing is sold out," Lily said, her husky voice projecting well.

Cass nearly sank to the sidewalk as groans greeted Lily's announcement.

"We'll begin selling tickets for the 9:30 showing in a few minutes."

"At least you'll get in to the second show," Chance said.

"I can't do that one."

"Kennel duty?"

"Something like that."

"Tell Lily."

"Wouldn't be fair."

"Hey, after all you've done to help with this whole thing, if you're willing to stand, I'm willing to overlook one person above the fire code limit."

"Sure," Cass said, hope lifting her spirits. "I'll stand."

"Lily," Chance called, just as Lily was about to go back inside. He waved her over, then lowered his voice, speaking softly. "You got a standing room spot for Cass?"

Lily looked amused. "That would violate the fire code."

"You're licensed for two-hundred people. The way I counted, you only let in a hundred-and-ninety-nine."

"Math was never my strong suit," Lily said, then looked at Cass, "but you really will have to stand."

"No problem. Thank you. And, Chance, thanks so much."

"Sure thing."

Lily opened the door and ushered her in. Cass took a ten from her pocket; Lily waved it away.

Cass chose a spot in the middle of the theater, leaning against the wall behind the last row of seats. While it wasn't how she'd envisioned seeing the movie, she was so excited, it was all she could do not to pump her fist and bellow "Yes!"

· · ·

What spoiled the movie wasn't her throbbing head, back and feet, all of which protested standing for two hours. What ruined the movie for Cass was the movie.

Judging from the sounds of approval—the whistles and cheers—called out by some in the audience when Penn Booth first appeared, and by others at various dramatic points, not to mention the audience's enthusiastic applause when the movie ended, she was in the minority.

Apparently, most of those present couldn't care less that Lucas and Rain didn't kiss until the *second* book. Or that they were lesser characters to Felicity in the novels but equal with her in the movie.

The audience also seemed willing to accept that at least half the dialogue wasn't from the books, events happened in the film that weren't in any of the novels, or that Felicity uttered only one of her favorite lines: *Be proud, be loud.* They didn't care that the woman who put Milk of Magnesia in the salad dressing of her rival's catering business was a complex character in the book but more one-dimensional in the movie than a cardboard cutout. Nor did they care that Felicity's trademark action of flinging her scarf around her neck was seen in the movie as tossing it in the air, then having the scarf float down in slow motion, settling around Felicity's neck as if by magic.

Then, too, Lana Kurth had been transformed. True, she was large, though not as large as Felicity, Cass didn't think, nor as large as she'd been in any of her previous films. Either they could photoshop a star in a movie to look more slender, or Lana had lost weight. Felicity in the books was a plain woman with big ears and long hair. Lana wore a lot of makeup, and her hair was cut fashionably short and styled. Her ears were petite, her eyes a brilliant blue, and her smile dazzling. Lana was a beautiful woman who looked about as much like Cass's idea of Felicity Benedict as did Penn Booth. The main point of the novels was that the only beauty that mattered was on the inside, but the film suggested otherwise.

Cass called Lyle's Loon-y Taxi Service for a ride home. Lyle employed only himself and his son, and they both drove clunkers, but they provided the town's sole ride service. While Cass waited, she noted that though her body ached, it didn't come close to hurting as much as her heart.

If she was this dismayed, Kent must be even more so. She was eager to hear his list of the many ways in which the movie failed to do justice to his book. She hadn't called him or Rebecca to see what they had to say about the Hollywood premiere the previous night, and she'd avoided reading any reviews, because she'd wanted to see the movie through her own eyes. Which she had. It was enough to make her wish she'd seen it through someone else's.

TWENTY-ONE

The night went from bad to worse.

By 12:45 Friday night—or, more accurately, Saturday morning—Cass still had no idea where Zoe was. She knew only where Zoe wasn't: at Cass's. Or at the kennel. Though Cass had hated to wake up Diego, she'd called him at 12:30. He'd said he hadn't seen Zoe since she left with her friend, Angelique, around 10:00, and she wasn't answering calls or texts either.

Since Zoe had kept curfew her first two nights, Cass had relaxed, assuming she would continue to do so. There were a million possible reasons Zoe wasn't responding, none of them good. Cass kept picturing her drunk, partying, sick, injured, or kidnapped. Well, kidnapped didn't seem likely, but the other four were all possible. Should she call Chance or Rebecca? No, not yet. But what *should* she do, stay or leave and search? She paced.

At 12.55, she grabbed her car keys and headed for the door. Caesar barked. When she glanced down, he had his leash in his mouth.

They were soon barreling in the truck toward the kennel,

Caesar looking out one side window, then the other, as if watching for Zoe along the roadway. The nearly full moon silhouetted the mountains and muted the stars.

"Zoe's okay, right?" Cass glanced at Caesar in the rearview mirror.

Caesar whimpered.

It was not reassuring. "Does that mean yes or no?" She half expected her dog to nod or shake his head, but he remained silent. Vigilant.

When she got to the kennel, Diego was nearly all the way to Cass's truck even before she could open the driver's side door. "Zoe?" he said.

"No."

His expression looked long past worried.

"I'm sure she's okay," Cass said, though she was anything but. "She's probably having too much fun with friends to notice the time."

"*Ojalá.*"

It was another word that surfaced from her high school Spanish: *I hope so.* "What was her mood before she left with Angelique?"

Diego looked away, shifting on his feet like he was uncomfortable.

"Diego?"

He still didn't look at her.

"Please tell me," she said.

"She wanted to . . . do more . . . than I thought was . . . safe."

"More what?" she said before she realized what he meant. "Oh." She looked at the steering wheel to give them both a moment to regain composure.

"I'll look for her," Diego said.

"No, please. I don't want the dogs left alone. Besides, Zoe might come here. Keep trying to reach her. Let me know if you hear anything, and I'll do the same. If I don't find her soon, I'll have to call Chance."

"If she drinks and drives . . ." he said.

"She'd be in big trouble, yes. That's why I haven't called Chance. I think she's too smart to do that. Hopefully she'll turn up in the next few minutes. I'll go check her house."

Cass was soon driving toward Rebecca's. She'd never gotten a speeding ticket, but if Chance or his deputy was patrolling these roads, she just might tonight.

She braked in front of Rebecca's. Rap music blasted from the house. Thank God. There were no cars around, just a huge black motorcycle. She leashed Caesar and led him to the front door. Doubtless the house was locked, but she had the key Rebecca had loaned her in her pocket. She tried the doorknob just in case. The door swung open.

And there Zoe was: lying nude on the couch, making love with an equally naked youth. His taut butt. Zoe's shapely breasts. Their slick bodies. Cass's relief battled with her anger.

The youth leapt to his feet. Rip. From the grocery. He grabbed his clothes off the floor.

Naked, he looked younger than he had in his black shirt and torn black pants, a boy. No longer a shadow.

"Cass, Dylan. Dylan, Cass." A stoned Zoe's words floated out slowly, as if they were being delivered by sloth.

Cass grabbed Zoe's clothes from the floor and handed them to her. "Get dressed."

Dylan thrust one leg into his pants.

Caesar growled.

Dylan darted out the front door, struggling to run with one leg clothed and one not. Cass would have smiled if she weren't so pissed.

Still naked, Zoe sat up, her head between her hands. "I feel dizzy."

"What did you take?"

"Just weed." Zoe pantomimed toking a joint. "Really *good* weed."

Cass handed Zoe her clothes from the floor. "Put these on." Turning her back to Zoe, Cass called Diego. "I have her," she said. "She's safe. We'll talk in the morning."

Zoe looked groggy. She took the clothes, dropping them on the couch, then pulled on her T-shirt, stood and swayed as she tugged on her tight jeans. "Dylan's cute, huh? He's got a great butt." Zoe lost her balance and crashed to the floor.

Caesar was there in an instant, licking Zoe's face. Zoe giggled.

Cass remembered thinking Rebecca should use positive reinforcement with Zoe, but she didn't see any way to apply that advice to this situation. It wasn't the sex she minded; it was that Zoe had given—and broken—her word. For the first time in her life, Cass felt sympathy for Rebecca. She stooped to link her arm through Zoe's, then pulled the girl up, steadying her. "Lean on me." She supported Zoe out the door and opened her mouth to reprimand her.

Zoe stumbled on the porch steps, nearly bringing them both down. "I'm so high," she drawled, "I bet I could touch the moon."

Zoe was so stoned, there was no point in Cass expressing her anger. She would save it until later, after they'd both gotten some sleep, but if Zoe thought Cass was going to let her slide, she was badly mistaken.

TWENTY-TWO

Anxiety dreams plagued Cass's few hours of sleep. Someone had opened all the pens and the dogs were lost and shivering. Zoe had ignored Cass's warning not to board a plane flying to the country where her dad worked. Cass had watched the plane take off, burst into flame and plummet.

Cass woke, heart racing, sweaty. It was a dream, she told herself, just a dream. No need to try to read anything into it. Everyone had a nightmare now and again.

She was startled to see that it was 7:00, late for her. Normally she was at the kennel before 8:00. What on earth was she going to say about Zoe's behavior that the girl would actually hear? On the one hand, Zoe had broken a promise. On the other, she had a mother who seemed just as critical as Cass's own, plus a father who was far away. Cass understood *lonely*. Zoe might well need a friend rather than a disciplinarian. Then again, she had acted irresponsibly. Could Cass just let that go? When she'd agreed to let Zoe stay with her, she hadn't signed on for trying to decipher how to discipline a teenager.

Good thing Mack was an early riser. Although she didn't

have kids, Mack was close to her nieces and nephews, who'd spent chunks of their summer vacations with her until they'd grown up and gotten jobs and families of their own. Plus, she'd pretty much raised a teenaged Cass.

Cass reached for the cell phone she kept on her bedside table.

"Good morning," Mack said when she answered. "How was the movie?"

That seemed like a lifetime ago. "I hated it. I'll fill you in later, but that's not why I'm calling."

"Oh? What's up?"

Cass explained about Zoe.

"How are you going to handle it?" Mack said.

Cass heard jays squawking on Mack's end. She was probably out watering her garden. "I don't know." Cass glanced out the window. The day seemed dim; clouds must be cloaking the sun. "Last night I was both worried and pissed. I'm calmer now. Given that Rebecca goes ballistic so fast, and that Zoe's dad's on the other side of the planet, I don't want to make her feel even more isolated."

"At Zoe's age, you were always polite," Mack said, "always going the extra mile. Seamus and I used to encourage you to act up. Never did any good that I know of. You were the perfect kid, and you know what Felicity says about perfection being an ill-lusion."

Cass chuckled. "I had no idea you could quote the book."

"I can't, but every third person I see is wearing that T-shirt. Hard to forget it."

"*Mom* sure didn't see me as the perfect kid."

"That's because your mother blamed everyone else for her troubles. Look, you know more than you think. If nothing else, you've had years of practice holding dogs accountable. Zoe gave you her word. That's what I'd emphasize. She knows better."

Sounds from the living room signaled that Zoe was awake. "Zoe's up. I better go."

"I'll check in with you later to see how it went."

"Thanks." Cass disconnected from the call. Mack was right; she needed to confront Zoe, but she wished she had a better idea of how to do that effectively. Her gaze fell on the stack of Felicity Benedict novels on her bedside table. Which one had the scene where Felicity confronted Rain, after Rain was arrested for a DUI? It was the third one, *Matters of the Heart: Envy.* Cass picked up the book and found the scene. She quickly skimmed the pages. *That* was the approach she would take.

She closed the book and slipped into sweats. Her mouth tasted like she'd been gnawing on roadkill, so she went to the bathroom, brushed her teeth, then headed into the living room.

Zoe was sitting on the floor, hugging a pillow. Crying.

"What's wrong?" Cass said.

Zoe just shook her head. Her smeared mascara made her eyes seem bruised.

Cass sat beside her and put one hand on Zoe's shoulder while Zoe hiccupped tears.

"I called my dad this morning," Zoe said when she was able to stop crying. "I really miss him. But he only had five minutes. He never has time to talk to me."

"That's hard."

"Yeah." Her lip trembled, then stilled. "I messed up last night, huh?"

Cass tried to keep judgment from her voice. "What do you mean?" She wanted to be sure what Zoe was saying.

"I wanted to hook up with Diego. I really, really *like* him."

"I don't understand. If you like Diego, why did you hook up with Dylan?"

"Because Diego wouldn't. I mean, we kissed and stuff, but he still wouldn't do anything more. So that's when I texted Dylan."

Cass realized she wasn't going to understand—let alone solve—Zoe's relationship issues. "You did mess up last night, yes." Cass paused, keeping her tone neutral. "You can't control other people's behavior. Not your dad's or your mom's, not Diego's or mine. There's only one person whose behavior you can control."

"My own?"

"Exactly. Your most valuable possession isn't your clothes, phone or computer. Those can all be taken away by someone else, and they can all be replaced. Your word can't."

"Oh," Zoe said.

"I was worried about you last night."

"You were?"

"Absolutely. So was Diego. And I was pissed."

"You're right," Zoe said. "I'm sorry."

Cass opened her mouth to say more, then closed it. Apologetic agreement was the last thing she'd expected. It was important to reward good behavior. "I accept your apology." That was the *click* she'd use with a canine friend. "I'm going to heat us up some coffee." And that was the treat.

"Thanks."

Cass filled two bright yellow mugs with coffee she'd brewed the day before, then set them in the microwave for two minutes. She spoke over the microwave's *thrum*. "While I accept your apology, there have to be consequences for breaking your promise."

Zoe didn't look happy, but she nodded. "What consequences?"

Cass thought of Felicity's words to Rain. "What do you think would be fair?"

Zoe's forehead furrowed. "You want *me* to decide?"

"Yes. Be honest with me. And with yourself." Cass set milk and sugar on the counter.

Zoe didn't say anything for a while. She stared out the back window. "I guess I should do something I don't enjoy, huh?"

"That's usually what consequences entail."

The microwave sounded. Cass took both mugs out and handed one to Zoe, who cradled it in her hands, blowing across it to cool it. "I guess I could clean the dog pens," Zoe said.

"Which ones?"

"All of them?"

"That sounds appropriate. Thank you for taking this seriously."

"Unless I could just do half?"

Cass let her eyebrows do her talking. They were the closest thing humans had to a tail.

"All of them, huh?" Zoe said.

"I think so."

"Can I listen to my music?"

Cass gave it a moment's thought. "Yeah. That would be okay."

"You going to tell my mom?"

"This is between you and me, assuming you do a good job today and keep your word the rest of the time you're here."

"I will. I mean it."

"We'll see how it goes. You owe Diego an apology, too."

"Yeah." Zoe rubbed her head. "Do you have aspirin? And cotton balls?"

"You have a headache?"

"Yeah."

"I'll get some aspirin, but what are the cotton balls for?"

"Stuffing up my nose while I clean the pens."

Zoe scrunched her face, almost making Cass smile. "We leave here in thirty minutes," Cass said. "You better hurry if you plan to shower."

"Okay. Thanks, Cass." Zoe headed toward the bathroom, coffee mug in hand.

Cass called Diego to tell him they'd be in soon. When she hung up, she gave silent thanks for help in confronting Zoe to Mack, Felicity, and Kent.

Kent. How would he feel about Rebecca after spending several days together in his world? Cass knew nothing about Hollywood other than what she gleaned from movies and an occasional *People* article, but she imagined that Rebecca—with her looks, her sense of style, and her quick mind—would be quite comfortable in what was doubtless a glamorous world. It was to be expected that Kent had fallen for her. It might have been fun to spend a few days with the Hollywood circle around Kent, but she, Cass, would have fit in with high fashion and glamour about as well as an elephant would fit in a gopher hole. Besides, if Kent and Rebecca had hit it off, that would help Loon and Loonies prosper. It was for the best.

Cass took her last swig of coffee. And spat it out. She must have messed up the proportions somehow; it was way too bitter.

Twenty-Three

Late Sunday afternoon—a hot, hazy June day when Moon Mountain's normal gleam was dulled by an inversion that had trapped pollution from the valley— Cass had just switched out the Yorkie, Sniffles, for Thunder, a tiny Chihuahua, giving the small dogs lap time while she balanced her books. The sound of a vehicle kicking up gravel set off the dogs in their pens. Diego wouldn't yet be back from his run, and Zoe was working in the outside kennels, so Cass set Thunder in his indoor pen and went outside to greet whoever it was.

Kent got out of the driver's side of a silver SUV, Rebecca out of the passenger side, a gray tote slung over her shoulder. They walked toward the office hand-in-hand, their smiles the very picture of bliss. Cass hadn't expected that. She wasn't surprised by Kent so much, but Rebecca's obvious delight caught her off guard.

The two were smiling and smiling and smiling—like zombies on happy pills.

"Morning," Cass said, forcing a smile of her own as they

approached. Kent's tight, olive green vest over a black T-shirt made him seem trimmer.

"Morning, Cass," they chorused.

"I wish you'd been with us," Rebecca said, echoing Cass's own longing.

Rebecca's sea-blue tunic top, tight jeans, and silver stiletto heels flattered her in every way, though her heels looked like they could be driven through a vampire's heart.

"Lana Kurth is just amazing," Rebecca said. "She and I went in a corner and talked about life and fashion for over an hour."

Cass wondered if her own face was turning green. What was she supposed to say? "Sounds like fun."

"More than fun. It was exhilarating. Lana's great. So are Olivia and Penn."

Kent's smile was wide. "Penn agreed to have a private lunch with whoever wins the scavenger hunt."

"Wow. That *is* exciting. The possibility of winning a date with Penn should lure a lot of teenagers. But, what scavenger hunt?"

Rebecca looked ecstatic. "We'll take photos of ten or eleven places that inspired the settings in the novels. Contestants will be given a map that has a photo of each. They'll have to find the spots and take selfies in front of them. Whoever locates all the sites first wins a private lunch with Penn."

"Great idea," Cass said.

"I know. We've got about six weeks to really promote Star Day, so that we have a good turnout. Better yet, a great turnout. Fortunately, we've got a good start on FBC publicity already."

"The scavenger hunt isn't the only good idea Bec came up with," Kent said.

Bec?

Kent smiled at Rebecca. "You suggested an idea for a new

Felicity Benedict novel that has me revved and ready to dive in."

Cass wasn't sure which she felt more: delight at the prospect of a new Felicity tale, or envy because Rebecca had been the one to come up with an idea, which seemed odd given that Rebecca didn't even like Felicity. "That's great news. What's the idea?"

Kent put his finger to his lips. "I don't want to talk about it yet."

Cass hoped she was masking her feeling of irrelevance. Her dismay.

"The reason is, I'd like to have you read the beginning chapters, Cass, as my #1 fan, and I don't want you to know the premise in advance."

"I'd love to read it. When?"

"I work best under deadline. By the time I write and revise the opening chapters, how about if we say a couple weeks from today?"

"Sure. Great." Was it ever! "And if you're done sooner, just let me know."

"Thanks for letting Zoe stay with you," Rebecca said. "Did she give you any trouble?"

"Nothing much." Cass waited to see if Rebecca would ask a follow-up question, but she didn't.

"Speaking of trouble," Kent said, "when I was eight, my best friend and I both got pellet guns for Christmas. We would hide in the bushes and shoot golf balls on the greens. Don't ask me why, but it was fun. Half those golfers couldn't figure out why their balls kept moving."

Rebecca touched his arm, a caress that seemed to Cass to be far more intimate than their earlier hand holding. "What about the other half?"

"If you want to improve your track speed, have an enraged

golfer with nine iron chase you. How about you, 'Bec. Ever get in trouble?"

"Yeah, Mom." Zoe entered the ring carrying the brush she'd been using to groom the collie, Bella. "Other than getting pregnant with me, that is." Did Rebecca notice that Zoe's jeans and T-shirt had actually gotten dirty?

"Hello to you, too." Rebecca's voice was chipper. She put her arms around a stiff Zoe and gave her a quick hug, then stepped back.

"So, did you?" Zoe said.

"I shoplifted some clothes and other stuff. Nothing expensive."

"Then how come you jump all over me when I do something wrong?" Zoe looked indignant. "It obviously didn't ruin your life."

"No, it didn't, but that's because I got caught. My parents never knew about the clothes, but my dad found my stash of things from the grocery. He made me sit and eat all four bags of M&Ms I'd stolen, then smoke every cigarette in the pack. By the time I finished, I was sick, sick, sick. Dizzy. Puking. Miserable. That was the last time I smoked. Or shoplifted. Or ate an M&M. And I never drove drunk."

"That sounds sadistic," Kent said.

"*Sadist* is a perfect word for that son of a bitch."

"You weren't Miss Perfect, though," Zoe said.

"Not even close. That would be Cass. She never did *anything* wrong. Right, Cass?"

"I wanted to."

"What stopped you?" Kent asked.

"I didn't want to give my mother anything else to criticize."

"How old were you when your dad died?" Rebecca said. "Thirteen?"

"Eleven." Cass was surprised Rebecca remembered that.

"That's way too young to lose a parent," Kent said.

"Yeah," Zoe said. "That sucks."

"It did," Cass agreed.

"Sometimes I feel like I lost *my* dad." Zoe looked at Cass.

"Your father's just working abroad." Rebecca's manner was breezy, dismissive. "You'll see him again."

"Well, duh." Zoe glared.

Cass expected Rebecca to go ballistic, but Rebecca glanced at Kent, whose expression softened as he looked at Zoe.

"I know it's hard for you, Zoe." Rebecca's tone seemed calm and understanding. "I'm sorry your dad hasn't kept in better touch. I know you miss him."

Zoe looked as surprised as Cass felt at this display of warmth. Was it genuine, or just a show for Kent's sake?

Zoe's face transformed from hostile to hurting.

"Since we're coming clean," Kent said, "my dad was great. We took so many trips together, hiked so many places. He's the one who got me to love mountains. But when I turned fourteen, he was arrested for embezzling money from the Fresno school district where I was a student. He went to prison."

Cass wasn't sure whose eyes had gotten wider—Rebecca's, Zoe's, or her own.

"Prison?" Zoe said.

"Why didn't you tell me?" Rebecca looked torn between concern and affront.

"It's not something I broadcast. We were ashamed of him. Kids at school gave me a hard time."

"Hard time how?" Cass said.

"The usual. Taunts. Shoving. Ripping my textbook pages so I'd have to pay for the book."

"I'm sorry you had to go through all that." Rebecca touched Kent's arm.

If Rebecca realized the irony, that that was exactly how she and her buddies had treated Cass as well as her other targets, she gave no indication of it.

Kent continued. "It got so bad, my mom changed both of our last names to her maiden name and moved us to L.A. It's the reason I never came clean about Loon being the inspiration for my novels. I didn't want anyone in town to figure out my real name. I was too ashamed of my father. Embezzling from a corporation is bad enough, but a school district?"

"Is he still in prison?" Zoe said.

"No, he got pneumonia and died there."

Rebecca put her hand back on Kent's arm. "I'm so sorry. Of course I'll never tell. Cass and Zoe, you can't either."

Zoe frowned. "Obviously."

"Of course," Cass said. "Thanks for trusting us, Kent."

No one spoke for a moment. Cass tried to wrap her mind around the idea of learning your father was an embezzler. And, yes, the fact he'd stolen from a school district seemed especially grievous.

"It's ironic," Rebecca said. "I'm the only one whose dad's both alive and living close by. I'd be better off if he was neither."

"He's mean," Zoe said.

Rebecca dipped her head in agreement. "That's on his good days. He may not have gone to jail, but he should have. He beat my mom, who would get so drunk she'd pass out, and he gambled away a lot of our money. Some days the only meal I got was the school lunch."

"What did you do in summers when there weren't any school lunches?" Kent said.

"Diet." Rebecca gave a low chuckle.

Cass felt as startled as Zoe looked by Rebecca's quip. She'd known Rebecca's family was poor, but she'd no idea Rebecca had had it so hard. All the more impressive that her combination of looks, brains, and sewing talents had kept her from becoming a pregnant pariah.

Kent took Rebecca's hand in his but looked at Zoe. "We all

make a lot of choices in our lives. A lot of mistakes. That's human nature, but it's hard when a parent messes up. It took me a while to get that I wasn't to blame for what my dad did. Kids are never responsible for their parents' mistakes."

Though Cass doubted Kent realized it, what he'd just said put the onus for Rebecca and Zoe's often fractious relationship on Rebecca, who drew herself up as if steeling herself for what might come next. When she spoke, however, she sounded care-free. "We got you each something." From her tote, Rebecca took out a package that looked gift-wrapped by a drill sergeant: crisp, tight corners, paper as smooth as water on a windless day. She held it out to Cass.

Cass had no idea what to expect. Rebecca's look of what seemed like excitement surprised her. Out of deference to the neatness of the wrapping, she peeled the tape off the box carefully.

"I'll take the paper." Rebecca smoothed it out. "I can reuse it."

Cass unfolded a long-sleeved, gray T-shirt that was unbe-lievably soft. On the front in elegant script were the words, *Felicity Benedict spoken here*. "This is great, Rebecca." She meant it. "Thanks."

"Check out the back."

Rebecca looked so eager, Cass half thought she was going to grab the shirt to hurry her.

The back featured four autographs: Lana Kurth, Olivia Golden, Penn Booth . . . and Kent Calloway. Cass was dumb-founded. That Rebecca would bring her any gift was shocking enough, but to give her one that was perfect? Cass's mouth all but dropped open. "I love it," she said, looking first at Rebecca, then Kent. She wondered whether her astonishment or her delight came across the most. "I mean, I *really* love it."

Kent held up both hands. "This was all Rebecca's doing."

"I had them sign it at the cast party with a special kind of ink that doesn't come out," Rebecca said, "but be sure you only wash it by hand in cold water. And line dry it, of course."

Cass felt ridiculously close to tears for reasons she didn't begin to understand; she smiled them away. "It's perfect. Thank you."

"It will look a lot better than those jerseys you always wear."

Ah, of course, Cass thought. Not Rebecca's bite of old, though. This one was only a nibble. And possibly not even intended.

Rebecca turned to Zoe and handed her a package that was also crisply wrapped.

Zoe squeezed it and groaned. "Please tell me it's not another cashmere sweater." She ripped the paper off.

Rebecca stayed silent, but a red splotch dotted each cheek. Cass wondered whether Rebecca was embarrassed, excited, or pissed.

When Zoe saw what Rebecca had given her, she appeared every bit as stunned as Cass had felt. Zoe held up a pair of distressed denim shorts that lived up to their name, being both distressed and short. Very short. In a pinch, Cass thought, they could double as underwear.

"These are epic," Zoe said. "Who picked them out?"

"Your mother," Kent said. "The saleswoman wanted to sell her some other style, but your mom knew what you'd like."

Zoe looked flabbergasted. "I can't believe you got me these."

Rebecca beamed. "I had fun choosing them. And yours, Cass."

"We'll have fun wearing them," Cass said. "Thank you."

Zoe handed the shorts back to her mother. "Would you take these home please? I don't want to get them dirty, and I need to get back to work."

"Sure," Rebecca said.

Zoe kissed her mother's cheek.

Both seemed surprised, Cass thought . . . and happy. Cass had mostly seen Rebecca angry with Zoe. Today she'd glimpsed how much Rebecca really loved her daughter. As Zoe headed toward the outside portions of the pens in the far back, Cass hoped this was the beginning of a better mother/daughter relationship.

"I'd say you scored big." Kent took Rebecca in his arms and kissed her.

The kiss seemed to go on and on and on. Cass looked up. She looked down. She looked away. She couldn't stand watching much more of their mutual bliss.

When they finally (finally!) ended their kiss, Rebecca spoke. "Cass, I heard Loon had an amazing turnout for the premiere."

"We did. Traffic was awful, though. We couldn't find a place to park, even ten blocks away."

"Wasn't the movie worth the wait?" Rebecca said. "We loved it."

Cass was dumbfounded. "You did?"

"What, you didn't?"

"I hated it." She looked at Kent. "You loved it?"

Kent looked sheepish. "Not really."

"But you said you did." Rebecca touched his arm. "You told everybody that, including the press."

"Complaining would be bad PR," Kent said. "And I want the other books to be filmed, too. What didn't you like about it, Cass?"

"Lana was beautiful, but Felicity isn't. Lucas looked so pale; I kept expecting him to bite someone's neck. Rain and Lucas connected much faster than in the books, and I'm pretty sure they had more screen time than Felicity. Plus, the movie made all the characters seem one-dimensional."

"Yeah." Kent nodded. "I felt like the people who made the movie had never read the books."

"I didn't actually like it either." Rebecca spoke quickly, turning to Kent. "I just pretended to because you said you liked it. But of course, your books are much, much better."

Kent put his arm around Rebecca.

Cass suspected Rebecca was lying. An attractive Felicity like Lana would be an easier character for Rebecca to relate to than the plain, heavier version in the books. Cass looked at the shirt in her hands. Which was the real Rebecca, the one who used to taunt Cass mercilessly, who had initially dismissed Felicity as fat and, essentially worthless, or the considerate woman who had come up with such perfect gifts and who seemed to genuinely care about Kent?

"We need to get going," Rebecca said. "Funny how five days away from your job means five weeks catching up."

"I'll let you know if I need to change the date," Kent said to Cass, "but how about if we shoot for two weeks from tomorrow? Mondays are my lucky day."

"Great."

"You mind coming to the cabin I rented? I'll provide brunch."

"No problem. And do you want to schedule a hike?"

He pulled back in apparent surprise. "Not right now. I'm on a roll. I'm going to hole up in the cabin I rented and knock out this book. It's been way too long coming."

Rebecca linked arms with him. "Thanks again for letting Zoe stay," she told Cass.

"It was fun," Cass said.

"Really? I should just board her with you." Rebecca winked.

Cass watched them go, her thoughts racing. Soon she would get to be one of the first people in the whole world—maybe even the very first—to read the start of the fourth Felicity Benedict novel. Wouldn't it be something if she could come up with at least one suggestion Kent would thank her for, one way to make this new Felicity book even better?

She glanced at the shirt in her hands and again marveled at what a thoughtful gift it was. Maybe she should frame it rather than wear it, though she would be sure to wear it the next time she went to Mack's. Rebecca was flawed, of course, just like everyone else, herself included, but surely Mack would have to agree that this shirt proved people really could change.

TWENTY-FOUR

At least Scotty had the decency to look guilty: glancing at the floor, fidgeting with his bow tie.

"Seriously?" Cass heard the dismay in her own voice. How had the price for kibble skyrocketed when just two weeks before, the day Rebecca and Kent returned, prices were unchanged? Scotty had mentioned that eventually he would have to raise prices, which seemed reasonable enough, but she'd expected two, three, or even four percent, not *twenty*.

Scotty motioned her to the back of the store, further from the tourists examining and exclaiming over the tables of Felicity Benedict wares. He raised his hands as if to show his helplessness. "What else can I do?"

"Raise it by five percent, not twenty."

"Sorry, but I've run in the red for most of the past two years. Plus, my lease is up in October. I'm sure Carlson will have heard about what we're doing and will jack up my rent big time. I need to make all I can now, during tourist season."

Edgar Carlson lived in L.A. Although he owned several properties locally—properties he'd inherited from his great grandparents, who'd lived in and loved the town—Cass didn't think Carlson had ever even visited Loon.

"The price hike's just for the kibble, right?" she said.

"No. It's across the board."

Cass felt paler than chalk. "Twenty percent on *everything?*"

"I don't want to." Scotty again fidgeted with his purple bow tie. "But I don't have much choice. Knowing Carlson, he'll probably triple the store's rent."

"I can't afford a twenty percent increase in *all* my costs," Cass said. "I might have to look elsewhere for my supplies." She much preferred to shop locally. Besides, she owed Scotty. Four years before, when several of the dogs in the kennel began vomiting, Cass had been sure the cause had nothing to do with the kibble because, after all, she'd used the same brand for years with no problems.

Scotty investigated on her behalf. His long experience and business contacts revealed that the brand of dog food Cass ordered through him had moved its plant from Canada to Arkansas. Cass didn't recall the exact explanation, but the gist of it was that the new facility was producing kibble with a high heavy metal content. That was what was making the dogs sick. They could have died. If that had happened, she might have been sued, might even have lost the kennel.

"You don't have to absorb all the increase," Scotty said. "Do what we're all having to do. Raise your rates."

"Tourists don't bring dogs to kennels; locals do. If I raise my rates, I'll lose business, maybe even the kennel itself."

Scotty rubbed his jaw, looking like he was reconsidering.

Cass put a hand behind her back and crossed her fingers.

A slew of car horns erupted from the street. Curious about all the commotion, Cass and Scotty went to the doorway

Weaving in and out among twenty or so trapped cars, were fifteen protestors wearing somber clothes and expressions.

Ranging in age from around twenty to eighty, they all held up posters. Apparently, they'd choreographed their movements, because they weren't leaving enough room for any driver to creep forward without hitting someone. Racket from horns and shouts swelled.

Maya and Garrett were among those who had stopped the traffic.

So was Mack.

Like the other protestors, Mack remained silent, ignoring the pleas, jeers, phone cameras, and threats aimed at them, continuing to walk back and forth, back and forth, back and forth.

Cass read their signs. Postal carrier Maya Browning's proclaimed *R.I.P. Moon Mountain: Murdered for Money*, which made no sense. Other posters did. Mack's showed a rocket blasting off with the words *Housing Prices* scrawled on the side. Garrett's featured a sketch in the shape of Loon's boundaries. The drawing was fractured, just as the town was becoming.

Angry voices from drivers and passengers were increasingly augmented by angry merchants. Daniel and Miranda Jacobs from the new outdoor gear shop, Nate from the gift store, Scotty, and others demanded that the protestors get out of the way.

Car horns ranged in pitch from blare to rumble. Dogs in trapped vehicles howled, while shouts rang out: "Move your asses!" "Get out of the street!" "I'm warning you!" Exhaust fumes from trapped cars created an acrid smell.

Tourists came outside from various businesses to investigate the commotion. Many, including a muscular man with a beard so white Cass half expected it to sparkle, were filming the scene with their cell phones. Scotty went back inside his store and emerged a few minutes later with a sign fashioned from ripped boxes: *Protestors = Loonatics*.

Jack Kraft got out of his trapped truck, waving his arms and hollering. He stopped in front of Maya. "*Murder* the mountain? Are you nuts?"

Maya simply walked around him. She and the other protestors stayed silent and kept walking, kept weaving. Cass admired their restraint and worried for their safety. And their logic. Maya's, anyway. If the town were proposing a strip-mine or ski resort, Cass could understand Maya's fear. Failing that, she had to agree with Kraft. Maya's protest did, indeed, seem crazy.

Kraft screamed. "You people better get your asses off this street, or I swear to God I'll run you down!"

Cass snatched her phone and dialed 911, heart hammering her chest, ears ringing with the racket. She got a busy signal. She redialed. Busy.

Kraft started his truck engine. Mack linked her right arm with Maya's left. They faced his truck. Cass started toward him shouting, "Stop!" but was drowned out by blared horns and voices. She linked her arm through a startled Mack's left. Though her legs were shaking, Cass spread them wide to face Kraft. He edged his truck forward.

"EVERYONE STOP RIGHT THERE."

Chance's order, boomed through a megaphone, came out thunder deep. If Cass hadn't recognized his voice, she'd have thought it was God speaking, which seemed to be the response from several of those caught up in the protest, who looked skyward. Cass didn't usually see the point of praying, but Chance's arrival sure seemed like a miracle.

Drivers stopped sounding their horns. The protestors lowered their signs. The shouting ceased. The abrupt silence was eerie.

"I'm Sheriff Chance Owens," he rumbled. "My deputy and I are offering free room and board to anyone who wants it."

Chance nodded to where his skinny, six-foot-six deputy, Bill Riley, stood on the other side of the street.

It seemed to Cass that there was a long, communal releasing of breath.

Chance continued. "Garrett and the rest of you, you've made your point. You also failed to get a march permit, so unless you stop now, you'll be facing charges. And those of you who disagree with the protestors shouldn't need a lawyer to know that it's illegal to make threats with your bodies—or your vehicles." He glared at Kraft. "Let alone hurt someone. All of you, on both sides, better behave, or I guarantee you'll *need* a lawyer. And to those of you on vacation, thanks for visiting. Let's all go on about our business."

It didn't take long. Within just a few moments, the protestors moved out of the street. Traffic started up and thinned out. The protestors, Mack included, set their signs in a stack in front of Grubstake Grocery under Garrett's watchful eyes.

"You joined our side?" Mack said to Cass after setting her poster down on the stack.

Cass shook her head. "No, but I wanted to protect you. Kraft's crazy. He's the guy who planned to shoot Caesar."

"Ah. Well, thank you."

Jewel came out of the grocery and handed the protestors flyers and clipboards. Mack joined with other protestors who were circulating through the crowd of sixty or so people, passing out flyers and motioning people to sign whatever was on the clipboards.

White Beard kept walking around, talking with people, filming their responses.

WHY ARE WE PROTESTING? read the flyer a teen Cass knew only by sight handed her. She scanned the copy. The flyer explained that the purposes of the protest were to slow tourism, strengthen opposition to the Felicity Benedict Connection, and serve notice to Rebecca and her cronies that they were being watched. The flyer urged readers to sign an online petition or one of the hard copies being circulated to demand a suspension of all further Felicity Benedict plans until the town council had published a full written summary of those plans and completed an environmental impact analysis. The council would also need to give people sufficient time to weigh in on the plans.

Another teen offered Cass a petition on a clipboard, with pen tied to it. Cass shook her head, and the teen moved on.

Soon, it was if nothing had happened.

Except it had. Some of the protestors, like Maya, might not have common sense on their side, but they had passion, a force that didn't always demand reason. The town's store owners and their employees had a passion of their own, one borne at least in part from trying to pay their bills, both business and personal. Plus, prices were indeed rising.

Cass looked back at the flyer in her hands. If the FBC saved the town's library and stores at the cost of its sense of community, would she consider that a success?

And what of collateral damage to people like herself if merchants and businesses raised prices precipitously? She needed to talk further with Scotty about his planned increases, but emotions seemed too fraught to do that now. She'd give him a day or two to reconsider, then approach him again.

Down the street, the white-bearded man was filming his conversation with Rebecca and Lindsey. Cass moved close enough to be able to hear.

"What would you like to say to the protestors?" White Beard asked.

Rebecca nodded, looking serious. "That I hear your concerns. Emotions are high on both sides, primarily because change is hard for most of us. Loon is more than a town; it's a community. Being good neighbors sometimes involves a little sacrifice. More cars, more people on the sidewalks. But those things mean more jobs, and more tax revenue for our library, our streets, our schools. I intend to grow our community so that one day people won't have to move away for work or a good education. Far from destroying our town, the Felicity Benedict Connection will *save* it."

When the man finished talking with them, Cass approached. "Did you see what happened?" she said.

Rebecca and Lindsey exchanged smiles. "We did," Rebecca said.

Cass didn't understand their smiles. "Someone could have been hurt."

"But they weren't," Lindsey said.

"Exactly." Rebecca moved closer to Cass and nodded toward White Beard, who was interviewing Maya. "That man's from the *San Francisco Chronicle*. He's doing a feature on Loon and the FBC. Some of the video he shot will be posted on the paper's website even before his feature comes out. I can assure you that this whole thing will get a lot of attention. With any luck, his or someone else's footage might even go viral."

Cass blinked. "I don't . . . ?"

"Publicity," Lindsey said.

"*Free* publicity," Rebecca added.

"But that wasn't *good* publicity."

"Any publicity's good publicity," Lindsey said. "Short of zombies on the loose." Lindsey grinned and bumped fists with a grinning Rebecca.

"Wait. You're saying people getting run over would be good publicity?"

"Of course not," Rebecca said, "but no one was hurt. Publicity means more people will hear about us and check us out online. They'll read about the FBC and our upcoming Date with a Star Day. And they'll come to see for themselves. The protest couldn't have gone better if we'd staged the whole thing. Which we didn't. To my shame. See you, Cass."

The two women got in their cars and drove off, Lindsey heading north, Rebecca south.

Cass stayed on the sidewalk, unable to get herself to move in either direction.

TWENTY-FIVE

Carrying a bottle of sparkling cider to celebrate the start of a new Felicity novel, Cass half-bounded, half-floated to the front door of what Kent had called a "cabin." It was a sprawling, two-story house with three-car garage located in a clearing in the woods a mile out of town. Not that Cass cared. It could have been a dilapidated shack, and she still wouldn't care, not when she would soon get to hang out with both Kent and Felicity.

Kent opened the door before she could knock. "Good morning," he said, his eyes practically aglow and all of him smiling, looking as eager as she felt. He wore his usual jeans, vest and T-shirt combo, his shirt a gorgeous teal blue that deepened the green of his eyes. "Come in."

"Thanks." She entered a living room that featured tan carpets and leather furniture, the sofa and chairs all a rich, copper hue. "Something smells delicious."

"Probably the cinnamon and nutmeg in the dip I'm mixing for the French toast."

"I love French toast." She handed him the bottle she'd brought. "To celebrate the launch of your new novel."

"Great, thanks. I love this stuff." He nodded toward a file folder. "The first two chapters. They're short. Do you want to eat first or read first?"

No contest. "Read first. Felicity feeds the soul, and right now my soul's ravenous."

"I like that. Sounds like something Felicity would say."

Cass suspected her own face now glowed like his.

He handed her the folder. "Remember, it's a first draft. I know there's room for improvement. Make yourself at home while I finish preparing brunch. Let me know when you're done."

She settled into the sofa. "Will do."

Kent left the room; Cass opened the folder and began to read.

Felicity Benedict thought about Lincoln Saunders, who'd recently opened A New Chapter Bookstore, as she stared at the numbers on her scale. She'd topped two-hundred pounds. Lincoln was a fine-looking man, who hadn't responded to her called hello when she'd seen him this morning returning from a hike. She wanted to be able to hike with him to mountain lakes—three or five or even ten miles—and for him to feel her sex appeal when she greeted him. Time to diet. She would be as ruthless with her excess pounds as she was with the other Undesirables: liars, killers, and thieves.

Cass winced. The Felicity Benedict she and so many other women admired wasn't just another desperate woman who craved weight loss. The real Felicity was healthy, confident, and sexy. She wouldn't try to change herself for any man. Nor had there been any indication in the first three books that she wanted to trek to mountain lakes, near or far.

Cass's breathing was shallow as she read the rest of the pages, hoping that Kent would reveal Felicity was joking. The Felicity in previous books would scoff at the idea of a diet. Not this one. Indeed, just because some boy calls her fat, this Felicity at the end of the second chapter joins Weight Watchers. Felicity should respond to the taunt by dismissing or enlightening the boy with a brilliant comeback that opened his eyes to the damage such taunts could cause less secure people. This Felicity seemed as insecure as Cass herself sometimes felt. Wanting to appeal to a man who didn't even bother to return her greeting? No way. And Weight Watchers, for God's sake? That wasn't Felicity talking; it was Rebecca. Could Kent really have that little understanding of the character he'd created?

"What do you think?" Kent sounded excited as he came into the living room thirty minutes later.

Clearly what he wanted was praise. Perhaps she should swallow her objections and give him that. Honesty could push —no, shove—him away. As much as she wanted to please him, however, she couldn't betray Felicity. Still, she had to think of something positive to say. "Your writing style's as sharp as ever," she said. "I loved the feel of this book."

"Good," Kent said. "Me, too."

Maybe she wouldn't have to tell him the rest of what she thought.

"What else? It doesn't help just to lavish praise. I know there's room for improvement, so lay it on me."

Cass tried to think of something that would remind him of the woman he'd created. "You know how much I love Felicity and your books."

"Sure," Kent said.

"I'm really glad you're excited about working on a new novel."

Kent's eyes narrowed. "But?"

"But I wonder if maybe, you know, Felicity could be a little less eager to diet."

"That's the point. It's what the novel revolves around. This one's called *Matters of the Heart: Loss*. That includes lost things, pets, and people, as well as the pounds Felicity sheds. It's a double meaning."

"I can see that, yeah."

His face scrunched. "But what?"

"It's just . . ."

"Spit it out, Cass."

If this were a discussion about herself, she would probably just zip her lip, the phrase her mother used to use when she wanted to silence Cass, but this wasn't about her. She'd be damned if she would sit here and let Kent destroy Felicity.

"I've read so many books and seen so many TV shows and movies where women are obsessed with their looks and turn to dieting," she said. "Felicity's unique in that she feels good about who she is even though she's a large woman. And she doesn't go after men; they come after her." Cass gestured to the pages in her hand. "Plus, she's not been into hiking or mountain lakes in the previous books. This isn't who she is."

"She's whoever I want her to be," he said, his body straightening into the rigidity of a tree trunk. Or tombstone. "*I* created her."

Damn her blushing cheeks. Cass looked down until she felt the heat diminish, but when she looked up, she was stunned to discover that Kent, too, was red-faced. It struck her then, how excited and proud he'd seemed when he gave her these pages to read. She hadn't meant to cause him pain.

"I'm sorry," she said at the very same time Kent did. She let him go first.

"I didn't have the slightest idea for a story until Rebecca came up with this twist," he said. "And while I'm glad you care enough about Felicity to defend her, weighing so much and standing just five feet two is inviting a heart attack."

Rebecca's line.

"It's not smart, and Felicity's a smart woman," Kent said. "She has to know the risk she takes if she doesn't slim down.

She doesn't have to get to slender, but losing forty or fifty pounds would make a huge difference. There's no way to attain that without eating significantly less."

Maybe Kent—and Rebecca—were right, but it felt like Rebecca had brainwashed him into betraying Felicity.

He took the pages from her hands and tossed them on the chair. They slid off, scattering across the hardwood floor. Cass bent to retrieve them.

"Don't bother," he said. "I'll get them later. Brunch is ready."

Cass wanted to run for the door, but she couldn't do that without making them both feel worse.

He served ample portions of French toast that would normally delight her taste buds, plus a fruit salad of blueberries, peaches, and cantaloupe. The sparkling cider seemed flat. "This is all delicious," she said, though she tasted little. She stabbed at a blueberry, which skittered across her plate.

The silence between them lengthened. Cass suspected that an x-ray of her insides would show her stomach twisted in a square knot: tight and hard.

"The thing is," Kent said, "if I don't have this book, then I don't have *any* book. I told you that when we hiked."

"You said this one was about loss. Couldn't you keep that and just delete the diet part?"

"No. The story would be too thin."

Cass nearly smiled at the irony of his word choice. "It wouldn't have to be. Loss affects all of us, right? You could write a powerful book about that. You're such a good writer, Kent."

"Not lately. I mean, here I'm desperately trying to change a character who has a huge following."

"And she has that following because Felicity speaks to so many women who have felt unattractive or inadequate throughout our lives. I love Felicity. Which is why it would be better that you never write another book in the series than write one that isn't true to who she is."

Kent blushed and sat up taller, shoulders rigid. "I thought you wanted another book. Now you're telling me don't bother?"

"No, I mean, don't write *this* book, but do write another. And another after that. Please."

"Like that's so easy."

She saw and heard his pain. "I'm not saying this very well." How had this day gone from delight to misery? "Wouldn't it be bad for sales of your earlier books? I mean, if you write this Felicity, then you undo the woman in your other three books. Right?"

"Maybe. Or maybe she just needs to grow. I could omit the hiking and Lincoln Saunders parts and have her decide to diet strictly because she's come to realize it's not healthy to be that overweight."

"Perhaps, realistically, but Felicity is an inspiration, with her confidence and sex appeal, even though she's not beautiful. Few of us are, you know. I mean, many of us try to improve our looks through clothes or makeup or dieting, but for most of us, *beautiful* is a dream we chase that doesn't come true."

Kent looked so devastated, Cass didn't know how she managed to swallow every bite, but when she looked down at her plate, it was empty. Much more of that, and *she* would need to enlist with Weight Watchers. She stood and reached for his empty plate.

"Just leave the dishes," he said.

"That's not fair. You cooked."

"No problem."

If her body got any tighter, it would wring out the tears she was choking back. "Thanks for the brunch." She couldn't bring herself to say thanks for the pages. She was anything but grateful for them. "I need to get going."

He walked her to the front door. "Thanks for coming."

"Sorry about . . ."

"I appreciate your honesty. Sort of."

"Well," she said. "Enjoy the rest of your day."

"You, too."

Fat chance.

The instant she got in her truck, Cass knew she needed to see Mack, who grasped all that Felicity meant to her and would understand her dismay. Luckily, Diego had welcomed the chance to earn some overtime, so she had the whole day off, her first free day in months.

M ack was sitting on the front porch, cuddling Socrates and Dante when Cass pulled up. Her face had an expression so forlorn, she looked near tears, which she rarely shed. Had someone, a sister perhaps, died?

Then it hit Cass. She glanced at her watch: June 8. Someone *had*, indeed, died: Seamus, two years ago this very day. How had she forgotten that date and its impact on her friend? Thank God she'd come to see Mack, albeit for a different and now insignificant purpose.

The small dogs barked and squirmed to get loose. When Cass got out of her truck, Mack released the dogs, who greeted Cass with tails wagging so fast, Cass was surprised they didn't give themselves whiplash. Socrates kept looking back at the truck as if expecting Caesar to jump down. "Sorry, guys," she said, "but Caesar's at the kennel with Diego." Cass petted them, then walked up on the porch and sat beside Mack. "Hard day."

"Yeah."

Ironic because it was a glorious day in most respects, full of sunshine and summer, the temperature hovering around 80, the sky a crisp blue. The Cecile Bruner roses Seamus had planted for Mack's sixtieth birthday were in riotous bloom, splashes of pink that released a fragrance so pleasurable, Cass would bet that if there was a Heaven, it would smell just like Mack's roses. Still, it seemed wrong, nature being so exuberant, oblivious to a day basted in so much sorrow.

Cass put her arm around Mack in a sideways hug.

Tears welled in Mack's eyes. She took a red bandanna from her flannel shirt pocket and wiped them away.

Cass scowled at the thought that a sleep-deprived surgeon had turned a routine hernia operation into a death sentence. Both Seamus and her father were dead because of others' carelessness. Unlike the driver who fled after killing her dad, the surgeon couldn't run away. At least he'd paid a price.

"I was thinking about Seamus's and my last date," Mack said.

"When you went to see *Hamilton?*"

"I *really* didn't want to go. I hated hip hop and rap, and tickets were pricey, but Seamus insisted. And then he got a speeding ticket. I wish someone could tell me how you get a speeding ticket going uphill in a 1968 Volkswagen van. Nobody else could have done that."

Cass knew all this, but maybe Mack needed to say it.

"I wanted to strangle him," Mack said. "He always drove too fast. I used to get so angry with him about that. If he'd had a red Ferrari like he wanted, he'd have spent more money on speeding tickets than he earned."

Cass smiled in remembrance.

"When we saw *Hamilton,* he danced in his seat for half the songs, and teared up for others. That he could cry over a sad story was one of the things I loved most about him."

"Me too," Cass said.

"Funny, I liked *Hamilton* okay. Didn't *love* it like Seamus did. After he died, I started really listening to the soundtrack and discovered how rich it is in terms of history and humor and even the music. Seamus was right. I regret I never got to tell him that."

Cass covered Mack's hand with her own. "Maybe he knows." She didn't think she truly believed that, but it felt good to say, comforting somehow, for herself as well as Mack.

"I hope so." Mack looked like she was going to burst into sobs. "Sometimes," she said, voice tremulous, "it feels like he died just minutes ago. Others, it feels more like a lifetime." Mack blotted her tears with her bandanna.

"One of my favorite Seamus memories," Cass said, "was my thirteenth birthday when he drove me to that humongous bookstore in Portland."

"That's right. To celebrate you becoming a teenager. I couldn't believe that stupid pipe broke so I couldn't go, too, but you'd been so excited, I just couldn't make you wait."

Mack had told her to write a list of the fourteen books she most wanted. Once inside Powell's Books, Seamus tore the list in half and challenged her to a race to see who could find the most the fastest. He won, of course, but Cass didn't care. After all, she had fourteen books to devour. "Did I ever tell you," she said, "that when it was time to pay for the books, Seamus came walking toward me with his seven balanced on his head?"

"That sounds like him." Mack shook her head, but she was smiling. "That man could make a game out of most anything."

"No kidding. I was sure he was going to sneeze, stumble, or do something that would make those books fall and break apart, but he didn't. 'How do you like my hat?' he said."

"What did you say?"

"I told him I thought it was gorgeous. He wore it well, all the way to the cash register, where he took those books down one at a time. Of course, he did get a speeding ticket, which he made me promise not to tell."

"Of course he did. But I open the mail. Let's just say that when I saw that ticket, I did not turn handsprings."

Cass chuckled. "I remember that when we got home, you gave me those four gorgeous granite bookends I still use, and you fixed your lasagna, my favorite, as well as a devil's food cake. Between the books, the food, and—most importantly—yours and Seamus's love, that was one of the very best days of my whole life."

Cass took Mack's hand as they sat in silence.

When Mack finally spoke, her voice was hushed, as if they were being stalked. "I never told you what I did with his ashes. Never told anybody."

"You spread them in the mountains, you said."

"I was planning to, but I couldn't. I needed him closer. I spread him around the roses." She nodded to the Cecile Bruner bushes. "When a breeze rustles them, I tell myself it's Seamus saying hello. This morning, when I heard them—heard *him*—I told him how much I love him still, how I always will. I also said that if he would come back, I'd buy him anything he wanted, even a red Ferrari."

Mack fell silent. Cass remained sitting beside her.

"Don't you need to get to the kennel?" Mack said after a while.

"I took today off to read Kent's new pages."

"How were they?"

"Awful. But it doesn't really matter, because Felicity Benedict, unlike Seamus, isn't real."

"Seamus was definitely real."

"I miss him, too," Cass said. "I'm glad to know he's close." She touched a petal and rubbed it between her thumb and fingers. When she let go, her fingers smelled of roses.

"If you have the day off, you should hike," Mack said. "I'm happy to have more time with Seamus. That man was a great storyteller and a prolific talker. I rarely minded listening, but a few times it rankled me because it could be hard to get a word in edgewise. Now I can say whatever I want, and all *he* can do is listen."

Cass smiled. "Yeah." Maybe Mack was right; a hike would do her good. "I think I'll do as you suggested and hike, but I'll come by later with dinner. We can eat it out here if you want to picnic with Seamus."

"That sounds lovely. Nothing fancy, though. I don't have much appetite today." Mack squeezed Cass's hand. "Thank you for remembering. And for coming to check on me."

Cass's face started to redden, so she rubbed both cheeks like she was massaging her head.

"What?" Mack said.

"Just a headache, but a mild one. I'll see you around six."

"Good. And, Cass, thanks again for coming by."

"You bet."

As Cass got in her truck, she gave silent thanks that she had remembered—albeit belatedly—what this day was. She needed to do a whole lot better job of keeping her priorities straight.

TWENTY-SIX

Astonishment dropped Cass's jaw and caused her to brake in the middle of Main. A bus was parked sideways in the second block of Loon's business district, taking up several parking spaces. And not just any bus: a tour bus. Was it possible that Loon had become a destination location?

A car was backing out of a space just ahead. Naturally. The first time in a while that there'd been a parking space on Main, and there was nothing in town she needed to do. Still, assuming this was anything other than a pit stop, the bus was clear evidence of the popularity of Felicity Benedict. Maybe it would help inspire Kent. She should investigate.

The instant she opened her door, Caesar climbed into the front, tail wagging. "Stay, boy," she said, snapping her fingers to command him to return to the back. "I'll be right back."

Caesar turned his hind end to her and laid down on the back seat.

Cass sighed, then headed toward the bus. She spotted the driver: close-cropped red hair, gray uniform, leaning against the rear wall of the drugstore, inconspicuous in the building's shadow, smoking and blowing rings with each puff.

"Good afternoon," she said, approaching him.

Jerry, identified by the plastic rectangular name plate pinned to his uniform, looked to be around forty. "Morning, yes. Good? We'll see."

"Oh." She wasn't sure whether or how to respond to that. "Can you please tell me if Loon is the bus's destination?"

"If it wasn't on the route, we wouldn't have stopped here." Smoke ring.

"Right, but I mean, is Loon the featured spot?"

"Nope. That's Reno's casinos. Loon's listed as a stop along the way. First time it was included on the itinerary. Some of the passengers were excited about it." He looked around. "Not sure why." Smoke ring. "Not much of a town."

Cass stopped herself from launching into a defense of Loon. She didn't want to alienate a driver who might be in a position to influence whether Loon was retained as a stop. "Thanks." She refrained from saying, "Have a nice day."

She took two photos of the bus and texted them to Kent with the caption: *Loon's a featured stop on the itinerary, thanks to your many fans.* She hadn't seen or heard from him since she critiqued his new chapter several days before. He might be avoiding her, but maybe seeing this evidence of his novels' reach would renew his enthusiasm for Felicity.

Her phone chimed with an incoming text.

KENT

I was coming to see you later. I'm at the Sourdough Cafe/Bakery. Join me?

Yes!

As she walked to the café, Cass came abreast of two

strangers with bulging shopping bags: a tall, gangly girl and her short, bejeweled friend.

"Penn Booth is so hot," said the gangly girl. "I have *got* to win the contest. Imagine a date with him. Maybe he'd even kiss me."

Slowing so she could listen to their conversation, Cass pretended to be absorbed by something on her phone.

"You don't even know what the contest is," said the shorter girl, whose pink tank top was an almost perfect match for her spiky pink hair. Large rings adorned each finger.

"Doesn't matter. I'm nailing it."

"You and every other girl."

"Not you. You'd rather kiss Olivia." The gangly girl gestured to the cutout of Penn as Lucas with his arms around Olivia Golden as Rain.

"True. Too bad *she's* not coming. We could double date, me with Olivia and you with Penn."

"No way. If I win a date with Penn, I want him all to myself. Anyway, I told my cousin about the contest. She's driving up from Oakland that weekend and bringing a bunch of her friends. She said she'd *run* all the way here for a chance to win a date with Penn."

"Don't tell too many people."

"Why not?"

"The more people who come, the less your chance of winning the contest, whatever it turns out to be."

"I hadn't thought of that," said the gangly girl, slipping her phone into her back pocket as they entered Nate's Nuggets: *Official Site for All Things Felicity.*

Cass felt like she had springs strapped to her feet. She passed lines of strangers waiting to get into the restaurant, the pizza place, the inn's coffee shop, and the new ice cream parlor. Ditto the Sourdough Café. She'd be willing to bet that Felicity's fans were every bit as devoted as Trekkies and Twi-hards. When she reached the café, she circumvented the line and headed toward the door.

"Hey, the line begins back here," someone called, the protest echoed by a "yeah" or two and "no cutting."

Cass faced the line. "I'm meeting someone who's already here."

There were scattered mutterings, but no further protest.

She entered the café and glanced around: no sign of Kent. That was puzzling.

"Hey, Cass."

Waitress Shirley Dawkins, with long gray hair and weathered skin but youthful energy, waved Cass behind the counter, where she was picking up several plates loaded with food: burgers and onion rings, fried chicken, and chef's salad. "So many folks were pestering Kent for his autograph, the poor guy was having trouble getting in a bite. We thought we'd give him some privacy." Shirley nodded toward the side door leading to a small room that could be reserved for private parties.

"Thanks, Shirley."

Shirley leaned close. "He's a sweetheart. If I were thirty years younger, I'd give Rebecca a run for her money." She started toward a corner table with the platters of food.

The door led to both the private room and the bathrooms. Cass hesitated. It seemed ridiculous to knock since Kent had just texted her. She would compromise: a quick knock, then walk on in. She knocked but couldn't help herself; she waited until she heard his "come in." She left the door partially ajar.

Kent stood. "Thanks for coming. I'm glad you're here."

"Me, too."

Shirley materialized in the doorway before Cass could sit. Cass would swear Shirley was batting her eyes at Kent as she set a water glass in front of Cass. "Anything for you, Cass?"

"No, I'm good."

"Anything else for you, Kent?" Shirley whisked away his plate—empty of everything except crumbs and a pickle.

"You make your own milkshakes?" he said.

"We do. What flavor?"

"Want to share one with me?" Kent asked Cass. "You can name the flavor."

"No, thanks."

"Strawberry, please," Kent said. "I like to pretend I'm eating healthy."

"Coming right up." Shirley closed the door behind her.

Kent picked up his water glass, took a sip, then set it back down. "I want to apologize for how I acted when you came over. The thing is, I really *want* to write another Felicity novel, but like I told you, lately my writer's block has been made from cement." He looked at his mostly empty water glass. "You were right. Felicity isn't a dieter. Or a hiker. Thank you for reminding me of that."

"You're welcome, but you'd have seen it eventually."

"Maybe. I'm afraid I'm getting blinded by dollar signs."

"Dollar signs?"

"As in, hurry up and produce the books because more novels mean more movies, which mean more book sales, all of which mean more money for my editor, my agent, my publisher. And, of course, me. So, thank you for keeping me from destroying my own character."

"You're welcome," she said.

He looked down a moment, then back at her. "The thing is, for whatever reason, usually no one tells me if I'm off track. I need an honest reader who will say when I go wrong, even if it's something I don't want to hear, even if I'm not the picture of grace. I can be an ass, as you saw, but eventually I get over myself. So will you be that reader?"

Had she heard right? He wanted her to keep reading for him?

"Will you?"

"Okay, sure. I'd love to. I mean, if *you're* sure."

"I am," he said.

Shirley entered the room and set a frosted silver milkshake glass in front of Kent. "Here you go. I hope you like it."

"Let's find out." Kent took a long slow drink and set the glass back on the table. "Now *that* is a milkshake."

Shirley looked pleased. "I brought a couple straws so you can share. I'll let you two be."

Cass would have sworn there was something off in Shirley's tone, and in the smiling way she looked at Kent and then winked at Cass, as if she thought they were a couple. Weird.

"I wish I could come up with a strong story idea for Felicity," Kent said after Shirley left.

"How do you usually get your ideas?"

"Sometimes I read something in the paper. Or scan police reports. Or glance at a variety of magazines. Whatever I can think of. Unfortunately, even though I've done all that, repeatedly, I can't think of a thing. As you know."

Cass wasn't sure what to say. She had no understanding of the creative process, how anyone could create characters and settings and stories from scratch.

"If you come up with any ideas," Kent said, "let me know. I could use some help."

"Don't hold your breath."

"Hey," Kent said, "I firmly believe we're all creative in different ways. Inspiration can strike anyone at any time."

"So you're an optimist?"

"For the most part, I'm guilty of optimism, yeah. You?"

"I guess I'd say I'm a hung jury."

He chuckled. "See? That was a creative answer."

Pleased by his praise, Cass willed herself not to blush. She was amazed when it worked. Maybe she'd finally found a way to keep from telegraphing her every emotion.

"You really should try this milkshake."

Why not? "Okay, thanks."

He slid the glass toward her. She removed the wrapper from a straw. The milkshake was thick and cold and tasted of ripe, sweet strawberries. She held it in her mouth several seconds before swallowing. "That's incredible."

"Yep." He took a drink, then passed the milkshake back to her.

The second sip tasted even better than the first. She'd had strawberry shakes before, but nothing that came close to this one. She handed Kent back the glass. Their fingers brushed. She felt something strange, sort of a jolt, sort of pleasant, sort of unsettling. Kent's eyes widened. Had he, too, felt it, whatever *it* was?

"Don't you two look cozy."

Lindsey, Rebecca's buddy, stood in the doorway to their room, her blood-red fingernails uncommonly long. Like claws.

Cass swallowed the milkshake in her mouth; it went down the wrong pipe. She sneezed. Coughed. Coughed again. Sneezed again.

"Do I need to do the Heimlich Maneuver?" Lindsey said.

Though Lindsey was smiling, Cass had the distinct impression of a scorpion.

"Cass, I'll let you catch your breath. Kent, I'll see you around. Maybe with Rebecca. In the meantime, you two enjoy that milkshake."

She sashayed away.

"What was that about?" Kent said. "I met Lindsey before, and she didn't act like that."

"She's not just Rebecca's pal. She's also one of Loon's biggest gossips."

"Oh." Kent stiffened. Blushed.

Cass rose, certain her cheeks were as red as Lindsey's claws. "I need to go."

Kent stood. "Me, too." He picked up his bill and slid a twenty under the glass.

Cass resisted the temptation to look toward the restroom for fear Lindsey was watching and would see their red cheeks. Which was crazy. They hadn't done anything wrong.

TWENTY-SEVEN

Raised voices arose from Diego's apartment when Cass got to the kennel the next day.

"That's stupid, Diego." Zoe's voice, loud and arrow-tip sharp.

"*No comprendes.*" Diego. Softer.

What did he think Zoe didn't understand? Cass hesitated at the office doorway. She didn't want to intrude, but several of the dogs were whining, probably upset by the fracas.

As she entered the office, neither Zoe nor Diego came out, but little dogs added their high-pitched barks to the clamor, triggering even louder barks from some of the bigger dogs.

"I'm not a virgin," Zoe blared, "and my mother's the last person I'd tell."

While Zoe's voice had gotten louder, Diego's dropped. Where Zoe shouted, he now murmured, so softly Cass couldn't hear what he said. She didn't want to eavesdrop, so she called out, "Diego? Zoe? It's me, Cass."

Caesar came running from Diego's apartment at the rear of the kennel and all but skidded into her. Cass didn't even mind when he jumped up, his paws balanced against her like he

"

wanted to dance. She petted his head, grateful that his welcome dispelled at least some of her unease.

Zoe appeared, storming from Diego's apartment, pulling on a green tank top over a mauve bra, her expression angry, her motions brusque.

"Is Diego coming?" Cass said.

"Ha. Not with me."

It took Cass a moment to realize that Zoe was thinking of "coming" in a sexual sense.

Diego emerged from the back, tucking his maroon T-shirt into his shorts. "Stop," he said.

Zoe faced him. "We did stop, remember? Almost before we started."

Cass sensed she might as well be a fencepost where they were concerned. She forced a cough, trying to awaken them to the fact that, unlike a fencepost, she had ears. "I don't know what's going on—" she began.

"Nothing, that's what," Zoe said.

Diego's voice took on an edge. "I can't go to jail."

Zoe waved both hands. "Jail? What are you talking about?"

"When your mom finds out about us, she'll blame me. She'll want me to disappear. It is not safe for me to cross people with power. My family needs me."

"*I* need you."

"It's not the same."

"I know that."

"No." Diego straightened, rigid. "You have no idea what it's like to live in my country. Or how easy it is to die there."

Zoe's shoulders sagged; her face softened. "But Mom won't find out. Cass wouldn't tell. Right, Cass?"

"No, I wouldn't."

"See?" Zoe's voice sounded imploring.

Diego, too, seemed to sag. He rubbed his forehead like it

hurt and looked at Zoe with an expression Cass thought was many things: sad, regretful and, above all, weary.

The silence that ensued hushed even the little dogs. Zoe looked toward Diego and seemed to really see him. She reached out to him; they embraced for several long, quiet moments.

"I'm sorry." Zoe stepped back.

"Me, too." Diego's lips quivered. "I want to make love to you, Zoe. I want things to be different. But they aren't."

"Yeah." Zoe's face and voice softened. "I just really want to be with you. In every way."

A car horn blared. Zoe froze, then glanced at her watch. "Shit. I forgot. My mom's taking me to the dentist. She's going to be pissed. I need to go." Zoe kissed Diego quickly. "I'll be back later." She rushed from the office.

Diego moved to the doorway, looking out, saying nothing.

Cass gave him a few moments before asking, "Are you okay?"

Diego's shrug seemed so vulnerable. She hated to see him like that.

"Hey, you're off this afternoon. Why don't you go for a run?"

"I already ran." Diego faced her. "I want to make dinner for you and Mack tonight. If you aren't busy. I'll turn on some music and cook *pupusas* and *pollo chuco*. Yes?"

"You bet. I already know your *pupusas* are delicious. *Pollo* is chicken, but what's *pollo chuco*?"

"Chicken, plantain chips, shredded cabbage salad, cheese and a special sauce."

"Yum. I'll give Mack a call," Cass said. "And later I'll pick up ice cream for dessert. I don't understand why you love cooking, but I'm sure glad you do."

. . .

"Really, Diego," Cass said as they sat around the office table her grandfather had crafted, "your mom's a bad cook?"

Mack's raised eyebrows suggested she, too, found this surprising, though Cass couldn't say exactly why they did.

"Terrible," Diego said.

"This *pollo chuco* is amazing." Mack wiped a crumb from her lip. "Light and delicious. The sauce is especially tasty. So how *did* you learn to cook like this?"

Diego's eyes took on a dreamy look, and Cass imagined that he was remembering good times, far away.

"*Mi abuela*. My mama hated kitchens. *Mi abuela* used to joke that if we had to eat my mama's cooking, we'd only grow up to be a meter tall. So she cooked, but Mama read to us every night. She taught us to read."

"My mom was like yours around kitchens," Mack said. "Couldn't stand cooking, but she did teach us to love books. I guess you could say she gave us food for thought. I learned to cook in self-defense."

"How about you, Cass?" Diego asked.

"I'm with your mom on that one. I hate kitchens. And I'm an inept cook."

"Your mama didn't teach you either?" Diego said.

"No, she hated cooking." Should she stop there? Something compelled her to continue. "Not wild about kids either."

"Other people's kids," Diego said, more statement than question.

Cass shrugged as if it didn't matter, but it did.

"Some people," Mack said, "thankfully not many, I don't think, are so self-absorbed they don't love anyone but themselves. Like Cass's mom."

"Do you visit her?" Diego asked Cass.

"Not much. She lives in Arizona."

"I'm just glad that when she moved," Mack said, covering Cass's hand with her own, "she gave you the choice of where to live."

Diego's face registered disbelief. "She moved away and left you behind?"

"Yeah."

"How old . . . ?"

"Twelve. But I was lucky. For my first eleven years, my father took care of me. We had such good times, and he taught me to love hiking the mountains. That made up for my mother. Not to mention that Mack and Seamus were terrific proxy parents."

"Two gifts then," Diego said. "Mack and a love of the mountains." He looked toward the door and the mountains beyond. "They are always here, guarding us."

"This might sound crazy," Cass said, "but when I hike, I sometimes get the feeling my dad's still here, watching over me."

"I like that," Diego said.

For a long moment, no one spoke.

Mack speared a piece of chicken with her fork. "Diego," she said, "you said your mom taught you to read. What kinds of books do you like?"

"Books about sports. Or music. Science fiction, too. I used to want to be an astronaut. To explore new planets where beautiful girls have many arms." He grinned.

Diego wanted to explore other worlds, but it struck Cass that she didn't even know her own. "What you said to Zoe this morning about things in Honduras, and considering everything you've been through, I've been wondering how the gangs became so powerful."

Diego's shoulders slumped.

"We don't have to talk about it, if you'd rather not."

Diego hesitated before replying. "When we elect a President

who tries to make things better for our people," he said, "like building schools and creating jobs that pay enough for people to live on, the Army 'gives' us a 'new' President."

"Overthrows the one you elected?" Cass said.

Diego's expression was one Cass couldn't identify. Not quite anger, not quite sorrow, not quite resignation. Or maybe it was a combination of all three. Or maybe he was just plain weary.

"Yes. The 'new' governments always have the same old people," he said, "those with money and power. They help themselves and their *compadres*. The rest of us?" He shrugged.

"I'm so sorry," Cass said. "Isn't there some way our country could help?"

Diego looked down; he nudged food around his plate with his fork but remained silent. His cheeks were a hot red.

After a moment, Cass said, "What?"

"Your country helped create the problems. And helps continue them."

That couldn't be true. "*We* do that? The U.S.?" She turned to Mack. "Mack?"

"May I?" Mack asked Diego.

"*Por favor.*"

Mack wiped her mouth with a napkin, then leaned toward Cass, who had the feeling she didn't want to know whatever Mack was about to tell her.

"For over a hundred years," Mack said, "our politicians have felt free to invade Honduras and every other Central American country. Many times. Honduras alone is up to eight or nine invasions. If we don't send troops, we send money and weapons to keep the rich and powerful in power, even those who deal in narcotics."

Cass couldn't bring herself to eat the last bite of *pupusa;* she set it back on her plate. "Why would we support gangs and drug traffickers?"

"Financial, mostly. To benefit corporations."

"Good God." Cass's head throbbed. "Diego, I'm so sorry. I had no idea. I feel ashamed."

"You don't run your country, Cass."

"God, no." She put her hands to her temples. "I find it challenging enough to run a dog kennel."

Cass didn't want to be someone who refused to acknowledge others' pain or her own country's role in creating it, but neither did she want to feel mired in despair. How were you supposed to balance the two? Clearly, her ignorance about The U.S.'s role in Honduras was her *choice*, whether deliberate or simply habitual.

It struck her that her ignorance wasn't limited to Honduras. She'd kept her head buried about Loon, too, hadn't known how hard up the town's businesses—and the library—were until she heard from Jonas, Rebecca, Scotty and other merchants. Plus, for months she'd not taken in the reasoning behind those who opposed the Felicity campaign, not even Mack's.

In *Passion*, Felicity tells a man who continually discounts his son's problems, that anyone who chooses to keep his head in the sand, has to be careful not to bury his heart along with it.

Maybe she needed to start paying more attention, to take her own head—and heart—out of the sand.

TWENTY-EIGHT

Cass wasn't surprised that the bank's outdoor thermometer displayed a temperature of ninety-three. She'd been wiping away sweat all morning and had to hoist herself out of her truck. She didn't mind *warm*, but *broiling* sapped her, making her feel like ice cream left to puddle in the sun.

Luckily a Hummer had vacated a parking place only a couple blocks from Scotty's. Since she had to pick up ten giant sacks of kibble, Cass gave thanks for this minor miracle. Parking spaces along Main had become about as rare as California rain.

Star Day was three weeks away; she had to dodge strangers as she trudged the two blocks to Scotty's. She was mopping her brow with her blue bandana for what she figured had to be about the ten thousandth time, and it was only 10:30. No doubt the temperature would soon surpass one hundred.

Across the street, Jewel stood at the tailgate of Mrs. Naomi Wagner's hatchback, clasping what appeared to be two heavy bags of groceries for the elderly customer, who the whole town knew didn't have much money after her husband died and his pension ended, though Cass couldn't have said how she or anyone else knew that. Mrs. Wagner fumbled with the key to her old van.

A teenaged boy in shorts and T-shirt sprinted between sidewalk and street clutching a T-shirt he held high, laughing as he weaved through the crowd. A shirtless boy gave chase. The boy with the T-shirt darted back into the street. He looked over his shoulder . . . and plowed into Jewel . . .

. . . who stumbled backwards and into the path of an oncoming car.

"Stop!" Cass screamed.

Tires screeched.

Jewel froze, dropping the groceries.

The car swerved. It struck the bags, smearing cans, cantaloupe, cobs of corn and more across the street.

Jewel covered her mouth with shaking hand.

Cass rushed over. "Jewel, are you okay? Did she hit you?"

Jewel shook her head.

Cass put her hand on Jewel's trembling shoulder. "Good. You're safe," she said.

The driver of the yellow-and-black bumblebee of a Smart car, got out. "I missed her, right?" The woman, who looked to be about fifty, wore a pink T-shirt with silver letters spelling out *loud and proud*.

A trembling Jewel didn't answer.

"Barely," Cass said.

"But . . . what's wrong with her?"

Jewel was practically gasping for air. Cass put her arms around Jewel, holding her tight, feeling Jewel's body quake. "Take some deep breaths," Cass said.

"I'm so sorry," the driver said. "She just . . . stumbled . . . right in front of me." The woman looked like she, too, was about to start sucking in air.

Jewel stepped away from Cass, her breathing coming in

shallow pants. "The baby," she cried. "I could have lost the baby."

"But you didn't," Cass said. "The baby's safe, Jewel, and so are you."

Mrs. Wagner looked at her now-destroyed groceries smeared across Main and raised her hands as if asking what she was going to do.

"Why don't you sit on the bench there in front of the store, Mrs. Wagner," said Shirley, who'd come out of the café. "Don't worry. We'll sort this out."

Cass was only now registering that people had stopped to watch.

"That was way too close." Nate from the gift shop gripped the arm of the boy who'd collided with Jewel. "I'm glad you're okay, Jewel," he said. "No thanks to you." He gave the boy's arm a shake.

Jewel didn't look okay, but at least her trembling had lessened.

"What do you have to say, Morgan?" Nate asked the culprit.

The boy, looking sheepish, mumbled, "Sorry."

The other boy, who'd been in pursuit, snatched the shirt back.

"Shirley," Nate said, "could you get us some trash bags?"

Shirley soon returned with the bags and handed two to each boy. "Shame on you," she said. "Shame on you both."

The boys looked away, cheeks red.

"Clean that up." Nate pointed to the mess in the street. He held up his hands to stop traffic in both directions while the boys picked up what they could.

Garrett ran toward them. "Jewel are you okay, honey?" he called with shaky voice.

Jewel fell into his arms, shoulders heaving as she cried.

"Can I go?" the bumblebee car driver asked.

"I don't know. Should we call Chance?" Nate looked at Cass.

"I don't know either," Cass said. "Jewel? Garrett?"

"I guess she can go," Garret said, but he glared at the driver. "But for God's sake slow down. It's not a speedway."

"Sorry. Yes, I will." The woman slid into her car and drove slowly away.

Nate told the boys they or their parents needed to replace Mrs. Wagner's groceries at no cost to Mrs. Wagner. "Do I need to call your parents?" he asked them.

"No," they chorused; both shook their heads. A lot.

Their movements were so similar, Cass thought they looked choreographed. She could imagine that calls to parents were the last thing these kids would want.

The boy who'd plowed into Jewel reached in his shirt pocket and pulled out a credit card wrapped in a twenty-dollar bill. He handed the card to Nate.

"I need to get back to my shop," Nate said to no one in particular.

Shirley offered to help. Assisting Mrs. Wagner from the bench, she linked arms with the elderly woman as they entered the grocery.

Cass looked at the growing crowd of pedestrians and automobiles. Traffic was getting dangerous. She needed to see Rebecca; the kibble could wait.

Entering the town offices, Cass noted that Marjorie Cummings, the town's elderly volunteer receptionist, wasn't at her desk.

Rebecca's office door was closed. Cass knocked once, then entered.

Rebecca glanced up. She moved file folders around on her desk. "Cass? What's wrong?"

Cass hadn't realized her adrenaline was spurting. "It's become way too congested out there, and it's not even Star

Day. Jewel was nearly hit. If the car had come literally just a couple inches closer, Jewel and her baby could have been badly injured or even killed."

"But she's okay?"

"Physically but not emotionally. When I left, she was still crying in Garrett's arms. We need some sort of traffic control out there or we could end up with a real tragedy, especially on Star Day."

Rebecca waved her hand as if brushing away the idea. Her silver bracelets jangled. "I'm not going to be the mayor who introduces this town's first traffic control device. Accidents can happen anywhere. We're still a small town."

"But we're drawing increasingly large crowds."

"Which is great, but you'd be surprised how much is involved in installing any kind of traffic control device, and I don't have time to talk about it. I appreciate that you're well-intentioned, but this proposal is a knee-jerk reaction to one incident. Let's wait and see if we need to do something further down the road, after we've had a chance to really study it."

"At least arrange for Chance and/or Billy to direct traffic on Star Day," Cass pleaded.

"That's not a bad idea. I'll call Chance later." Rebecca scribbled something on her desk calendar.

Cass felt somewhat mollified. Chance and Billy helping on Star Day should keep traffic reasonably sane.

Rebecca glanced at her watch. "Listen, I have an important meeting in half an hour, and I need to get back to work. Please close the door behind you."

Cass started to leave, but a wild-eyed Rosalind Lamb, this time unaccompanied by child or dog, barged in. Her red jacket was buttoned wrong, and her hair stood up in places, as if she'd been tugging on it.

"Rebecca," Rosalind said, "you have to help us. Please."

If Rosalind's shaky voice was any indication, she was frantic. Cass moved a little closer, hoping her presence might have a steadying effect.

"I know we've met," Rebecca said, "but I'm terrible with names."

"Rosalind Lamb. My family rents a house on Wilding Lane. My husband and I voted for you."

"Thank you for that," Rebecca said. "How can I help?"

Rosalind appeared to be near tears. "We moved here from San Francisco six years ago because we wanted to raise our children where they'd know their neighbors and get to explore nature. We love it here. We don't want to live anywhere else."

"So, what's the problem?" Rebecca again looked at her watch.

Rosalind thrust a typed sheet at Rebecca.

"Our landlord is doubling our rent," Rosalind said. "We don't have that kind of money. She can't do that, can she? A hundred percent increase can't be legal. Right?"

Rebecca was frowning at the page. "Lindsey's your landlord?"

"Lindsey York, yes."

Cass half expected to hear a snake's rattle.

Rebecca came around from behind her desk. "Unfortunately, Rosalind, Loon doesn't and never has had rent control covering single family homes. That may be something the council needs to revisit. There are also no statewide limits on single family residences. There's nothing official I can do."

"Please," Rosalind begged. "Please help us."

Rebecca put her hand on Rosalind's shoulder. "Tell you what, I'll talk to Ms. York myself on Monday."

"Thank you."

"I can't promise anything." Rebecca guided Rosalind toward the office doorway. "Leave your name and number on our receptionist's desk, and I'll call you Monday to let you know what I find out. Cass, can you show Rosalind the right desk?" Rebecca closed the door.

After Rosalind scribbled her name and number on Marjorie's notepad, Cass and she walked outside.

"Will Rebecca help us?" Rosalind said.

"I think she'll try." Cass wished she could be more reassuring. "In the meantime, maybe you could ask around for somewhere else to rent."

"We already have. My neighbors' rents are going up, too. My husband heard they're planning a golf resort."

"What? Who's planning a golf resort?" Cass said, walking alongside Rosalind.

Rosalind shrugged. "I don't know. That could drive up rents even more, especially with all the tourists coming for the Felicity campaign. Landlords can make more money from renting out their places for short term vacation rentals than for regular, long-term housing. And that's not all, Cass. There's talk of a ski resort on Moon or one of its satellite peaks."

Cass stopped walking. For a few seconds, she also stopped breathing. "On *Moon*? No way. Rebecca wouldn't allow it. Even putting a resort on one of the peaks around it would destroy Moon's magic."

"I hope you're right that Rebecca would oppose it," Rosalind said, "but that's what my husband heard. And, please, if you hear of anything that might help us, will you call me?"

"Absolutely."

Rosalind headed down the street.

Cass watched her, then glanced up at Moon. The mountain's dome gleamed in the sunshine. Rebecca never hiked any of the mountains, not even Moon. *Would* she oppose a ski resort? Cass went back inside. Marjorie was still away. Cass again knocked once before entering Rebecca's office.

Annoyance flitted across Rebecca's face. She again shuffled folders. "Yes?"

"You're not planning a golf resort here or a ski resort on Moon or one of the peaks around it, right?"

"Where did you hear that?"

"Rosalind's husband heard it." Cass waited.

"There's nothing imminent, no. Maybe somewhere down the road."

"That's a terrible idea. A golf resort alone would drive up housing costs across the board, but a ski resort? Moon's a one-of-a-kind mountain. People come here because of its air of mystery. Of magic. A ski resort would destroy that."

"Moon may be mysterious to some," Rebecca said, "but not to enough people to sustain the town. We didn't start the Felicity Benedict Connection because Loon was thriving. *Something* must change."

"But it's already changing. Tourism's taken off, and we've only just started."

Rebecca sighed.

Cass had never known a sigh to sound so dismissive.

"I know you love Loon," Rebecca said. "So do I. But face facts. Kent may never write another Felicity Benedict novel since you torpedoed his last idea. In Forks, once Stephanie Meyers stopped writing the *Twilight* series, tourism dropped off steeply. We must look beyond Felicity if Loon's going to survive."

"But we can't turn Loon into a town that the people who are here now, people who love living here, don't recognize and can't afford."

Rebecca steepled her hands against her forehead and peered out. "Look," she said, "doing *any* resort would require an environmental impact statement, public hearings, and the council's approval. There's plenty of time for discussion. I don't want to cut you off, but I really need to pull some numbers together. We'll revisit all this after Star Day. That should also give us more of a sense of how much tourism the FBC will generate."

It didn't feel like enough. "Okay." Cass reluctantly started to leave but stopped. "You will help Rosalind, won't you?"

"Like I already told her—*and* you—there's no law regulating rent increases on single family homes. I'll talk to Lindsey, but I can't force her to do anything. And remember this, Cass. No plan, no matter how carefully thought out, is going to benefit everyone. Now *please* shut the door behind you."

Cass left the building feeling like she'd split in two. She *did* want the FBC to attract tourists, wanted Star Day to be a huge success, but she *didn't* want people losing their homes because of that success. Let alone their lives. A couple inches were all that had stood between Jewel and tragedy. Wouldn't a golf resort increase the danger: not a golf *course* but a golf *resort*? Maybe Rebecca was right that the FBC wouldn't attract sufficient tourists to sustain the town, but a golf resort sounded all wrong, and a ski resort even worse.

Merchants like Scotty and people like Lindsey were wild about the Felicity connection. In their eyes, it was great for the town. But what exactly did that mean? The town didn't just consist of businesses and buildings. Above all, it consisted of people. The purpose of the FBC wasn't to jack up profits and prices so high that current residents were forced out to make room for newcomers who could afford to pay more.

Her thoughts drifted back to the antis' demonstration, which seemed like a million years ago. She remembered Mack's rocket ship blasting off, the words *Housing Costs* lettered on the side. Was it possible to attract lots of tourists *without* housing costs skyrocketing? And Maya's poster featured words about Moon being *Murdered for Money*. Maybe Maya and Mack were a whole lot smarter than she was.

Cass stopped on the sidewalk. Clusters of strangers parted around her and came back together. She had the sense of being a very small rock in the path of an oncoming flood.

TWENTY-NINE

loud, mournful wail erupted from inside the kennel as Cass neared the office—the wail so human, so long, so low that Cass froze. Her head commanded her to investigate, but her heart said no, said not yet, said that whatever the cause of that much anguish, her own life would never be the same.

She resumed walking. In the doorway, she stopped. Diego sat at the computer. On the screen was a somber face: his father. Cass entered the office, moving to the side so she could see both Diego's face and the computer screen. Tears slid down Diego's cheeks; snot ran from his nose.

Diego's father spoke Spanish in a low voice, nearly a rumble. Cass couldn't follow his words.

Diego took a bandana from his pocket, wiping his eyes and nose. "Arturo?" he said.

His father left. After a moment, Arturo appeared, sobs shaking his thin body. He looked so frail. Diego touched the screen as if he could touch his little brother. "*Lo siento,*" he said. "*Lo siento, hermanito.*"

I'm so sorry, little brother.

Tears sprang to Cass's eyes. Someone must have died. Had Diego's mother's heart given out? Had his beloved *abuela* died? But there was a blank place on the screen beside Arturo where Enrique should have been. Cass felt tears welling. Please, please, please, she thought, oh please. Please let Enrique be okay. Let them all be okay.

After Arturo left, Diego's father returned. He said a little in Spanish, then paused, apparently waiting.

Diego spoke Spanish in fast little bursts that sounded to Cass like gunshots.

"Diego, *no*," his father said, clearly not happy with whatever Diego was saying. "*No puedes. Comprendes?*"

Eventually Diego nodded. His father said something else. Diego raised his head, his eyes narrowed, his face full of venom. His father spoke again. Diego shut his eyes. Finally, he said one word. "*Comprendo.*"

I understand.

"Promise me," his father said, his unexpected English surprising Cass.

Diego stayed silent.

"Diego." It was a command. "*Prometeme!*"

Diego finally spoke, though with obvious reluctance. "I promise."

"*Otra vez,*" his father said.

"I promise," Diego repeated.

"*Cuidate, mijo.*" Take care of yourself, my son.

Diego shot to his feet and bolted out the office door.

His father's face still showed on the screen. "*Cass, Enrique está muerto.*"

Dead.

"*Diego no se dejes volver a Honduras. Comprendes?*"

Cass sat in front of the computer. "Diego *quiere estar con tu familia*. He wants to go home, to be with all of you." The need to conduct this conversation in her limited Spanish was, she knew, keeping her sadness at bay.

Miguel eyes welled with tears. He leaned toward the screen. "*Diego no se dejes volver a Honduras, Cass. Comprendes?*"

Tears welled in her eyes, too. What was Diego's word for a gang member? "*Los pandilleros* will kill him? Matar?"

"*Exactamente. Protégelo.*"

She didn't recall the word. "*Protegelo?*"

Miguel nodded. "Protect him. Keep him there, Cass, please."

Clearly, his English, though heavily accented, was a lot better than her Spanish. "I promise," Cass said. "And, Miguel, I am so, so sorry." Her voice trembled, and tears spilled down her cheeks.

Diego's father's tears echoed hers. "We cannot bury another son."

The screen went blank.

Cass remained seated, letting her tears flow. Enrique's death at the hands of a gang reminded her of her own father's death at the hands of another, but at least her father's death was likely not deliberate. To lose a child, a son who seemed so blessed with joy and love as Enrique? Dear God.

Cass reminded herself that she needed to focus on Diego's grief, not her own. Brushing away her tears, she stood. Where had he gone?

She found him in the back, clinging to Caesar, face buried in Caesar's mottled fur as he wept.

Cass sat beside him, one hand on his shoulder, saying nothing, trying to steady him as best she could, trying to let him feel her caring.

"I should have been home," Diego finally said. "I could have protected Enrique. We could have stopped the *pandilleros* I ran like a *cobarde.*"

Though Cass didn't know the word he used, she suspected she knew its meaning. "Oh no, Diego. You aren't a coward.

You're a *witness*. If you hadn't left, you would have been murdered, too. Then your parents would have *two* sons to mourn, and Arturo would have lost two brothers."

Diego gathered rocks and stood. He flung the rocks, one by one, into the woods. His tear-streaked face looked so young.

"I don't understand," she said. "I thought your family was paying protection money." She tried not to think about the fact that Enrique's killers murdered with impunity, partly because of a climate her own country had helped create.

"My mother lost her job. They missed a payment."

"My God," Cass said. That you had to pay to keep your child alive was grievous enough, but to think that missing one payment was a death sentence staggered her. "Enrique must have known he could be in danger."

"He didn't want to leave Arturo." Diego's voice hardened. "I want to make them pay."

"Oh, Diego," she said, more of an exhalation than actual words. Diego looked as though if he held a gun and Enrique's killers walked toward him right now, they wouldn't walk away. For a moment Cass wished that would happen. Right here, right now, where she could watch.

Tears again slid down his cheeks. "I can't even go to my brother's funeral." His face transformed again, from rage back into unspeakable grief.

"No. They would kill you, too. I'm so sorry. I can't imagine how hard this must be."

His tears increased.

"What about Arturo?" Cass said. "Who will protect him?"

"My father will try, but I have to bring Arturo here soon, before they kill him, too."

"Didn't he just turn seven? Surely at that age he's safe."

"In Honduras, no one is safe."

"Why don't you fly Arturo here? I could get another bed for your apartment. He could stay with you. A plane ticket couldn't cost more than a thousand dollars, right? I could help pay for it."

"No." The word came out sharp. "No. Your customs people would not give him a visa. They do not let people stay when they have no visa. They would say he's too young. They would stop him at the airport and send him back. My family would have to pay a coyote. But Arturo is too young to travel alone. My father would have to go with him, at least till he got across the border. For the two, a coyote now would demand twelve-thousand dollars. And might still leave them in the desert to rot."

Diego's words seemed spat out. Cass pictured the burnt woman from his flight from Honduras. She wished she had money, but she was maxed out on credit. "Couldn't he turn himself in at the border? I mean, since you got asylum, he would, too, right?"

"With this government?" he scoffed.

Of course. So many people were decrying immigration, people all the way up to the top. Diego was right. Besides, Arturo needed to live with his parents as long as he could. "Your parents should move here."

"Your country does not want us."

"How about another country that might be friendlier or maybe even cost less?"

"My grandparents are too sick to leave. *Mi abuelita*, she told them to go, but we are a family. We don't leave people behind."

Diego fell silent. Behind him in the distance, clouds hovered around Moon's dome as though they were trying to cloak the mountain in a shroud. A jay's loud, grating *squawk* seemed like protest or refusal: no!no!no!no!no!

Diego and Enrique had planned to hike these mountains together. Maybe, Cass thought, hiking or camping now would help him. Then again, she'd promised to protect him. If Diego went alone, she would have no idea whether he was safe. Or if he'd even come back.

Eventually he faced her. The rage had drained out of him again, his face the essence of grief.

"When my dad was killed," Cass said, deciding, "I was only eleven, too little to go camping on my own. But I did hike our favorite trails. The mountains comforted me in a way people couldn't. Would you like to camp in the mountains for a few days? You can use my gear, but you would have to promise me to come back. Or maybe you'd find it easier to stay here, around people, and dogs, who care about you."

"I want to camp, but who will help with the dogs?"

"Zoe can pitch in more during the day since summer school ends at noon now. I'll stay at night. If we run into any problems, I'm sure Mack will help."

"That is not fair to you."

"It's fine. We'll be fine. *If* you want to go. And *if* you promise me you'll come back. I promised your father I would keep you safe."

"Yes. *Gracias*," he said. "I will come back." Diego's eyes brimmed again, which made Cass, too, tear up.

"Diego? Cass?"

Zoe's voice. She must have come to the office. "Where are you?"

"I'll clean the pens first," Diego said.

"No." The word came out too loud; Diego flinched. "Sorry," Cass said, biting her lip to try to keep from crying again. She failed.

Diego started toward her. She opened her arms, and he stepped into them. They stayed like that, holding one another amid their tears.

"What's wrong?"

Zoe stood staring at them, her face showing her concern.

Diego moved back. Zoe started toward him, but Diego held

up his hand to keep her there, whirled around and headed toward the office and his apartment.

Zoe turned to Cass. "What happened?"

Cass brushed her tears away with her shirt sleeve. "Something terrible. Enrique was murdered."

"No." Zoe's eyes seemed to grow bigger, rounder. Her face combined disbelief with horror. "No."

"I wish."

Distress distorted Zoe's face. "Who killed him?" she said.

"Gang members. Cowards."

"Enrique isn't even two years older than Diego. He can't be dead."

"I know."

Zoe looked toward the apartment. Cass spoke quickly. "Let's give him a little space. Come help me get my camping gear out for him." Cass led the way inside to the storage closet. She told Zoe what little she knew while rummaging through her supplies for her stuff. Eventually she found it all, including backpack, tent, sleeping bag, and other assorted gear. They stacked it beside the door-desk.

Zoe spoke through the tears that slid down her face. "When we Facetimed, Enrique was always joking. How could he be so . . . And why didn't he leave like Diego did?" Zoe's voice broke.

"I think because he loved his family so much and wanted to protect Arturo."

"But it's not fair."

"No," Cass said. "It isn't."

Zoe looked so forlorn; she practically fell into Cass's arms.

While they hugged, Cass hoped that Enrique's killers would someday face justice and that the anguish felt by those who loved Enrique would be theirs to feel, at least for a while.

THIRTY

Though the alarm sound Cass had selected for her cell phone was called a *gentle* chime, the reality she woke up to was anything but. Diego had been gone for five days. She missed him. He'd been through so much in his short life. Cass had often wished she had siblings with whom to face their mother and the world, but if they would have met Enrique's fate, then she was glad she'd been an only child.

She sat up in Diego's bed in the kennel apartment. Would the Honduran-flag-blue he'd painted the room still be a consolation for him—or an omnipresent reminder of his brother's murder?

Beside the bed, Caesar rose, stretched, and whined. Even he seemed to feel sad. He thrust his muzzle at her. Cass took his head in her hands. "I know," she said. "Me, too." She kissed the spot between his eyes, then rose, pulled on sweats, and fixed herself a pot of coffee. Standing in the office doorway, hands cupping a mug, she hoped the morning's bulky clouds would disperse; she wanted sunlight for Diego. He didn't need the world to seem any gloomier. She hoped he was finding solace in the mountains.

And she hoped he would return soon. She had promised his father to watch over Diego, and now Diego's continuing absence worried her. Maybe she shouldn't have encouraged him to hike the mountains. Even if he wasn't trying to find a way back to his family, what about marauding mountain lions or bears? Not to mention a sprained ankle or broken leg. She couldn't very well protect him when he wasn't here. Wasn't encouraging him to backpack the exact opposite of what she'd promised?

The dogs were clamoring, ready to be fed and played with. Much as she didn't feel like it, playing with them almost always lifted her spirits.

Odd to think that Star Day was only two weeks away. It had seemed so important before. Now it felt frivolous. And yet she knew it wasn't; the town's future might well depend on it.

Cass watched Caesar, Cali, and Mookie make listless efforts to chase each other around the ring on a day that, despite dark clouds, had proven to be hot. Caesar and Mookie snapped halfheartedly at each other. Cass whistled the dogs over to her. They plodded to her and collapsed at her feet. The three dogs had to be missing their daily runs with Diego.

Cass regretted not being able to take them on a hike, but with Diego gone she couldn't spare the time. Zoe had been great, pitching in whenever Cass showed her what to do, exhibiting a willingness to work without complaint, including cleaning pens. She'd come a long way since the day Rebecca first brought her to the kennel. Zoe didn't yet have enough experience to work as independently as Diego, but she was learning.

Cass turned away from the dogs to savor the view of Moon Mountain, shimmering in the one ray of sunlight that pierced the darkening clouds. The glacier capping Moon's dome had shrunk over the past year, melting from the drought and the heat. Moon seemed exposed. Vulnerable.

Excited barks made her turn around. Diego squatted beside the dogs, who jostled and climbed over one another in their eagerness to greet him. All three jumped up on him. Unbalanced by his heavy backpack, Diego toppled backwards. The three dogs launched themselves at him in a frenzy of barks, licks, and hard wagging tails.

Cass grinned. "Need a hand?" she asked, walking over to them just as Diego managed to slide out of the backpack straps, shrug it off, and get to his feet.

"No, got it, thanks." He ruffled the dogs' ears and kissed their muzzles. His smile, while not exuberant, looked sincere.

"I'm glad you're back," Cass said. "So, obviously, are they."

Cali took off running, the other dogs in close pursuit. They were energized now.

"Where'd you hike?" she said.

"Mosquito Lake at first. Till I saw why they named it that. Then I dropped back to Juniper for the last couple of nights." Diego stopped smiling. "*Gracias*, Cass. The mountains, they . . ." He looked at a loss for words.

"Yeah, they do." Now it was her own turn to search for words. "Diego, I . . . I, uh . . . I'm sorry for what my country . . ."

"I know," he said. "Thank you."

After a moment, she nodded to the racing dogs. "I need to corral these guys then head to town to pick up Blackie's medication."

"I'll get the dogs," he said.

"Okay, thanks." She took the backpack from him. "And thanks for the loan of your apartment. I'll wash your sheets. I said this already, but I'm really glad you're back."

"Me, too," he said.

As she walked toward the office, delighted to see Diego and

relieved he was safe, she felt like jumping in the air in celebration. Before she could decide whether to follow through on that urge, her phone chimed a text message alert.

JONAS

News. Come by.

She froze. Good news or bad? She was afraid to find out. Enrique's murder was enough bad news to last a lifetime.

Cass's drive to town was slowed by a crush of traffic. Tourists swarmed the sidewalks and stores on Main, including a new souvenir shop that had opened where the Bookworm had been. Scotty and Nate both hated the store, named simply *Felicity*, but the store meant more revenue for the town. The closest parking place to the library was several blocks away. Imagine what Mack, Garrett, and others would say when they saw this turnout.

The instant she switched off the motor, the clouds ripped open. Torrential rain sent shoppers lunging for cover. Cass was usually prepared for weather changes, but today she'd brought no protection. Mountain summer cloudbursts were often intense but usually short lived. Rain had been so scarce in recent years, it was a welcome delight as it pelted her head and slid down her face.

She climbed the porch of the old Grange Hall that housed the library. Drenched, she shook her head, flinging a few spatters of water about, then ran her hands over her face.

She entered the library and took a deep breath. This was what she'd needed, the comforting fragrance of so many books. "Good news or bad?" she said, joining Jonas at the counter.

His lavender T-shirt showed a stack of books captioned, *My weekends are booked.* No one else was around. Lean and wiry, Jonas reminded her of a greyhound. In this case, a smiling one.

"Good," he said. "Very good."

Hanging from the ceiling was a new mobile. It featured a

huge plastic globe and a fleet of miniature flying books, each suspended by a different wire. She paused only a moment before making the connection: *Books can take you anywhere.*

"Rebecca came by a little while ago. She said the library fund has already brought in so much for repairs, that even without knowing the exact amount the town will collect through sales tax and other revenues, she could guarantee me the library will remain open."

"Wow. Already!"

"Rebecca said Kent's been playing it up in interviews, and of course there's the sign by the town office. Not to mention Kent's donation and what we collected at the benefit. Rebecca said one anonymous donor gave $3,000, another $2,000. Revenues in the town are way up. And that's not all. In addition to the library staying open, Rebecca's confident that once taxes are collected, there will be additional dollars that I can spend on books or technology, whatever I think the library needs." Jonas's face practically glowed.

"This *is* all great news." Cass meant it.

"The FBC has been a huge success. Thanks in no small part to you, Cass."

She frowned. "I *hope* it's been a success."

"What do you mean?"

"Traffic's a snarl. The town's stores and restaurants are mobbed. Jewel was almost hit by a car recently. And do you know Rosalind Lamb?"

"Sure. She brings her two youngest boys to story hour. Why?"

"Lindsey York increased their rent by a hundred percent. They have to move away from Loon to find housing, and it's all because of the campaign. Maybe it's changing Loon too much."

"A hundred percent *is* an enormous increase," Jonas said. "Then again, Lindsey and others have had to keep their rental rates way low for years because the economy's been so depressed. I imagine they'll want to recoup some of that by turning long-term rentals into short-term vacation spots through sites like Airbnb and VRBO. Can't really blame them."

"Still, a hundred percent increase should be illegal. Rebecca told me to work on getting the council to pass rent control, and I guess I'll try, but I'm not so sure they will. Plus, with all the cars, parking's a challenge. It's not usually a problem for me, but it's hard on people who are elderly or disabled. Our restaurants and stores are often crammed with tourists. All of which makes me wonder if we're ruining Loon rather than saving it."

"Locals will learn to adjust to shopping and eating out on weekdays when it's less congested," Jonas said. "In the meantime, I've heard there are a couple new restaurants coming, and businesses are thriving. As is the library. Give it some time, Cass. Things will get better."

"But—"

"Look, is the Felicity Benedict Connection good for everyone? Of course not. As Felicity says, perfection is an ill-lusion. You'll never come up with something that makes the whole town happy."

"So where do you draw the line? When do you say it's too much sacrifice?"

"Majority rules seems like a good approach. There's no reason to believe that, for most of our town, the campaign has been anything other than a blessing."

Cass had seen so many people wearing such huge smiles since the campaign started. "Maybe you're right," she said. And the library would remain open, the very goal that had led to the whole campaign. "Maybe overall it has been a boon for Loon."

"Admittedly I'm a little biased," he said, "but I think the library staying open, meaning the gift of books and reading, has been worth the downside. You've given people of all ages a source of solace that has gotten you, me, and a whole lot of other people through hard times. Not to mention that you've ensured people have access to computers, teens have a safe place to hang, little kids get story hour, and seniors can get tech help. I have ideas for even more services. You'll have to decide for yourself where you come down on this question, but in my eyes, we have far more reasons to celebrate than to mourn."

This time, Cass's smile was genuine. "Thank you, Jonas. You've made my day."

By the time she said goodbye and went back outside, the rain had stopped, leaving a fragrance both musty and sweet, while sunlight fell on drops and puddled water, creating tiny rainbows everywhere she looked.

Thirty-One

A crush of boisterous tourists created a din in the saloon, where Cass was celebrating the success of Star Day with Kent and Rebecca. Earlier, Cass had feared that excited fans were going to tackle Penn Booth and tear off pieces of him as keepsakes, piece after piece after piece, until the only thing left of the young star would be his shoelaces, and even those would probably be fought over. She leaned toward Kent and Rebecca and spoke as privately as she could considering she practically had to yell to be heard. "For a minute there, I was wondering if Penn was going to survive his fans."

"Movie stars get that all the time," Rebecca said.

Kent grimaced. "Which is why I'd rather be a writer than an actor."

Penn had been a good sport about it all. Cass had enjoyed the six hours he'd spent in Loon, talking with tourists, signing autographs, and taking the scavenger hunt winner to a private lunch at High-Grade Restaurant. It had been quite a day. The instant the scavenger hunt starter gun sounded, close to three-hundred fans, mostly teenage girls, had taken off in their quest to find all fifteen of the Felicity Benedict sites listed in the contestant brochure. Cass was glad the winner hadn't been a beauty but a plain, plump, acne-faced girl.

Much as Cass had enjoyed Penn and the day's many events, the most striking moment for her had been when the newspaper's Boyer August took a photo of Kent, Rebecca, and herself, saying he would caption it, *The Trio That Saved the Town.* Though it had felt a little awkward when Boyer instructed the three of them to scoot closer together for the picture, his insistence that Cass be included had left all of her, even her insides, grinning.

Sure, there were some people paying a high price for the campaign's success, but in her initial survey of the councilmen, two leaned toward supporting rent control, and two solidly opposed. The swing vote would be Rebecca, who had already told Cass she was considering supporting it.

The smell of popping corn from the machine in the corner suffused the dimly lit Moosehead saloon with a delicious aroma. Cass would have loved to grab a bag, but there were so many people thronging the saloon, it was next to impossible to get anywhere near the popcorn machine.

"Some five-hundred people signed the guest book at the visitor center today," Rebecca said. "We probably had well over a thousand visitors. That should be a real boost to our efforts to publicize the FBC."

"Fantastic." Cass beamed.

Kent, whose back was to the crowd, raised his glass to Cass. "To you. You got all of this started when you reached out to me."

A frown flashed across Rebecca's face before transforming into a smile. "To Cass," she said, bringing her martini glass to Kent's mug of beer.

"Credit goes to all of us," Cass said. "*You* wrote the books, Kent. And, Rebecca, you got the town a makeover *and* ran a kick-ass social media campaign." Cass lifted her glass, which held Felicity's Fizz, a delicious mix straight from the novels:

gin and tonic, plus Grenadine and mint. Cass didn't usually drink alcohol, but this day had seemed to call for Felicity's favorite. "To teamwork."

"To teamwork," the other two said.

They clinked glasses.

Cass was enjoying this moment, the way she, Rebecca, and Kent were grinning at each other. Set off by her sparkling, silver-and-turquoise jewelry—necklace, earrings, bracelet—Rebecca's face seemed to shine. Kent looked almost handsome in jeans and a maroon T-shirt under a quilted gray vest. Cass suspected she, too, might be beaming, wearing the Felicity shirt Rebecca had given her. It had seemed as if throughout the day, every store and business owner—as well as several newly employed locals—had sought the trio out to thank them. Cass was basking in the joy of being part of this Felicity Benedict team.

The bar's saloon doors swung inward. Mack entered. Stopped. Looked around. Cass was surprised and delighted that Mack had decided to join them. The place was so crowded, the lighting so low, they must have been hard to spot. She waved her hand and called out. "Mack. Over here."

Mack approached them with somber expression.

"What's wrong?" Cass stood to give Mack her seat.

"I told you *no*." Voice wavering, Mack ignored the chair.

"No what?" Cass said. Why was Mack upset?

"You know." Mack glared at Rebecca, then glanced at Cass and Kent.

"No," Cass said, "I don't." She looked at her companions. Both appeared as mystified as she felt.

Mack thrust the Scavenger Hunt contestant brochure at Cass. It was opened to the page labeled *Felicity Benedict's House* The photograph was of Mack's.

"I don't understand," Cass said. "It's supposed to be the Benjamins' house. They were excited to participate." Cass had taken several of the photos for the brochure and turned them over to Rebecca. Her shots included the Benjamin house. Not that it really looked much like Felicity's as described by Kent. Though sprawling and made of cedar like Felicity's, it was two-stories rather than one; the fireplace was brick, not granite; and the inside walls were lathe-and-plaster rather than wood. Rebecca had quipped that the Benjamin house looked about as much like Felicity's as Mickey Mouse looked like Taylor Swift.

Cass had laughed then. She wasn't laughing now. "Rebecca," she said, "I reminded you that Mack didn't want to be featured as Felicity's. The picture I gave you was the Benjamins' house, not Mack's. Remember?"

"No," Rebecca said. "I know you were disappointed when Mack said she didn't want her house to be featured. You might have intended to give me the Benjamin shot, but you didn't."

Cass blinked. Was that possible? "I didn't?"

Kent's eyes narrowed as he looked at Rebecca. "Did you substitute Mack's house for the Benjamins'?" he asked.

Rebecca put up both hands in protest. "I certainly did not."

"So, nobody's responsible?" Mack said.

"I guess it could have been the print shop's error," Rebecca said. "Or, Cass, you'd been working so hard, especially when Diego was away, and I can see how you might have accidentally given me the wrong photo. But, Mack, I hope you understand. Between the Felicity campaign and the extra kennel time, Cass has been on overload."

Rebecca had that right. Not to mention Cass's sadness for Diego. Although he smiled more, sorrow still shadowed his eyes. Cass rubbed her forehead, trying to recall exactly what she'd said and given to Rebecca, but the details of that exchange nearly two weeks ago eluded her. Her mouth felt dry. "Mack, if I'm responsible, I'm sorry," she rasped out. "We'll fix it."

"I'll pull all the remaining brochures," Rebecca said.

Mack shook her head, her disgust at something—or someone—apparent.

"Mack?" Cass reached out to her.

Mack rushed from the bar.

Cass went after her, pushing her way through the crowd. "Mack, wait."

Mack lengthened her strides. She was parked, windows open, in front of a fire hydrant, the only spot available anywhere. Mack yanked open the pickup door and slid behind the wheel, slamming the door closed. The lock clicked.

Cass reached the truck just as Mack started the engine. "Wait, please." Cass grabbed the door handle. "I gave Rebecca the Benjamin photo. I'm almost sure I did."

Mack's eyes glistened in the light from the streetlamp.

Cass's stomach churned. "I don't understand why you're so upset. It was an honest mistake."

Tears slid down Mack's cheeks; she backed out fast and drove away faster.

Cass watched the taillights of Mack's truck recede then trudged back into the saloon, concerned and mystified.

Kent was questioning Rebecca as Cass sat back down. "You're absolutely sure about that photo?" he said.

"Yes. No way I'd have risked exposing the town to a potential lawsuit. I hope Mack will come to her senses about this. After all, her house *is* Felicity's. But let's head over to the office to lock up the remaining brochures."

Cass sank into her seat. "Rebecca, I think when I gave you the photos for the brochure, I said Mack was still adamant. I'm pretty sure I even used that word."

Rebecca rose. "No, you didn't. Zoe told me you were upset that day about Diego, so it's understandable you'd forget."

Kent stood beside Rebecca. "Do you need a ride somewhere?" he asked Cass.

"No, thanks." Cass felt vaguely wobbly, and she didn't want

to go home alone, not yet, not to dwell on the image of Mack's tears. She sipped her Felicity's Fizz as Kent and Rebecca left. The saloon doors swung back and forth, back and forth, back and forth.

What should she do about Mack? Cass ached to talk to her, but if she just showed up, would Mack give her that chance? Cass gulped the remainder of her drink, then stood, swaying. She was too tipsy to drive. Mack's was just three miles away, not all that far. Walking would give her time to sober up.

She wanted to take something to make Mack feel better. Grubstake Grocery was closed, but she managed to persuade the bartender to give her a bottle of Merlot with the promise that she would pay him in private the next day since it was illegal for him to sell her the unopened wine.

Outside, bottle in hand, she started walking.

THIRTY-TWO

Wind whipped the towering firs and pines that flanked the road. Still dressed in cargo pants and her special shirt, Cass shivered. It wasn't all that cold. Upper sixties. So why was she shivering? And why had Mack gotten so upset over what was a simple mistake, regardless of who made it?

If their situations were reversed, Cass would be proud to live in Felicity's house. While Mack certainly had the right to opt out of the brochure and van tours, she'd way overreacted to being included. Rebecca was right; Mack's house *was* Felicity's. Hopefully Mack had had enough time to calm down. When Cass gave her the Merlot, maybe Mack would invite her in and they could trade apologies.

In the distance a coyote let out a long yipping howl. Cass had always hated that sound, which seemed to come from a place of dark, inconsolable sorrow. She rounded the final bend.

And gasped.

"Oh no," she moaned. "No. No."

Moonlight revealed the ruins of Mack's precious roses. Flanking the porch, the bushes had been stomped: limbs snapped, blossoms trampled. Petals smeared the ground like pink snow. Tourists must have destroyed the bushes taking selfies posed in front of Felicity's in their eagerness to "win" Penn Booth.

Cass stood frozen in the moonlight. Poor Mack. Poor, poor Mack. Cass could never make it up to her, the price Mack had paid for this "triumphant" day. Clearly Mack's *wasn't* Felicity's house, not really; Felicity Benedict wasn't real.

Tempted to flee, Cass forced herself to walk as quietly as she could toward the house, her heart pounding, not at all sure how she would be greeted but wanting so badly to comfort Mack. Her watch read 12:33. If Mack was awake, she would hear Cass's steps. If Mack didn't wake up, then Cass would leave the wine and return later in the morning. She stepped up on the porch.

Motion detector lights came on. Dante and Socrates erupted. She'd forgotten both lights and dogs. "Shh," she said, speaking as softly as she could. "It's me, Cass. Stop barking."

The dogs fell silent. Mack appeared in the living room. Cass tried to put all her regret—and all her love for Mack—in her expression.

Mack stood in her green and white plaid pajamas, arms crossed. Frowning.

Only a windowpane separated them, but Cass shouted to be sure Mack could hear her. "I'm *so, so* sorry. I know how much the roses meant to you."

Mack didn't move. Face impassive, she just stared at Cass.

Cass held up the wine bottle. "I brought Merlot."

Mack turned away. The house went dark.

"No." Cass put her hand to the window. "Mack, please."

Silence.

Cass turned and slid down until she was sitting, her butt against the hard-planked porch, her back against the door. The wine bottle had a screw top. She twisted it off and gulped. The wine tasted like vinegar. Or toilet bowl cleanser. Maybe on this night, anything would.

Cass drank more. The soft wind whispering through the trees seemed to be saying *hush*. The smaller wind chimes *pinged*. A mosquito buzzed her ear. The night air was full of the fragrance of trampled roses. And truth. It reeked of truth.

She'd set the wheels in motion that had rolled over Mack's roses. Mack had warned her more than once about the unintended damages the FBC would cause, but she'd been distracted from the start, desperate to heal the broken part within herself, to cultivate the self-confidence that had eluded her, to gain at least a glimmer of the light that always seemed to shine on Rebecca and her friends. She must have hoped on some deep, twisted, level that if she was good enough for Rebecca, then she would—finally—be good enough for someone to love. Obviously not Kent, but someone.

Cass took another drink. Another. Another. And another. Long minutes passed. Finally, she pulled herself up with the aid of the doorknob and swayed, unsteady. Gripping the mostly empty bottle, she stumbled off the porch and lurched back down the road.

THIRTY-THREE

Cass unlocked her door, stumbled to the bathroom, fell to her knees and heaved. She embraced the toilet to stop her head from spinning.

It was 1:45 in the morning. She ached to sleep. To forget.

She vomited again. And again. For an hour she knelt by the toilet. Wasn't she supposed to stay hydrated? She turned the faucet to fill the bathroom glass, then drank the water down. Almost immediately her stomach churned. Her head pounded. The room spun. She closed her eyes and clutched the toilet, but it wasn't just the room that was spinning. It was her. And the toilet. The house. The whole planet.

Everything seemed out of control. She'd never been drunk. Why had she downed so much alcohol?

Then she remembered.

Mack.

She was sick again. Done, she reached up and flushed; she didn't dare move away from the toilet. She stretched out on the floor beside it. If Caesar were here, he would snuggle against her, but at Diego's suggestion given Star Day's demands, she'd left him at the kennel.

Sick as she felt, she was also exhausted. She closed her eyes, hoping sleep would blot out all thoughts of this godawful night.

W hat was that racket? Cass opened her eyes. It was light now. There was another sound, a pounding. It made her head throb. She clenched her eyes and concentrated, trying to place the pounding. She wanted it to stop.

It repeated.

Then she got it: hard knocking on the front door.

Did she want to try to answer it, or would movement make her feel even worse? But maybe it was Mack. Cass pulled herself up using the sink. Movement gave her the dry heaves.

When finally she'd finished, she staggered to the front door and yanked it open.

Kent.

"You look awful," he said.

Why was he here so early? It couldn't be any later than 7:00 a.m. Dizziness made her clutch the doorframe. Kent moved beside her, wrinkling his nose. She must smell like a toilet. She glimpsed his watch: nearly 9:30. How could it be that late? She should be at the kennel.

Queasy again, she dashed to the bathroom and hurled air, then cradled her head on the toilet rim. She half thought she wanted to die. If there was a Heaven, she bet nobody vomited. Nobody was lonely. And roses never died.

"Here." Kent squatted beside her and pressed a wet washcloth to her forehead.

She hadn't realized he'd followed her into the bathroom. The washcloth seemed to leach out the heat and the dizziness. She wished she'd thought of it.

"Does that help?" he said.

She nodded, but even that little movement made the

hammering in her head worse. She should be embarrassed to be like this, sick and stinking, but she felt too bad to give a damn.

"Guess you aren't much of a drinker."

She wanted to be alone, with her sickness and her stench. "I'm okay," she said. "You should go. This is my own fault."

"No." Kent scowled. "Rebecca was handling the brochures. And Rebecca switched the photos. Deliberately. Rebecca, not you, Cass."

"She confessed?"

"Not at first, but I called the printer. He said Rebecca came by and substituted a photo of Mack's house for the Benjamins'."

Rebecca had lied so convincingly at the saloon. "Why?"

"She thought it should be the house that really inspired Felicity's. I told her a couple weeks ago that I was disappointed Mack didn't want her house featured since it was part of the inspiration for the books. Rebecca thought it would please me. She was wrong. Switching photos was bad enough, but then to blame you?" Kent shook his head like he was still stunned.

Cass's temples throbbed. She clenched shut her eyes, but that just made her dizzy.

"You don't happen to have any fresh ginger or Ginger Ale?" he said.

"No."

"Too bad, but I'll see if I can whip up something that might help. Do you have a blender?"

"Bottom pantry shelf."

"Don't go anywhere."

"Don't worry." The toilet bowl was her new best friend.

The blender soon whirred in the kitchen, pulverizing something. She wanted Kent here, and she wanted him to leave.

He returned, handing her a glass of a yellowish brown

liquid that looked like something that would come out of a dog's hind end. "What is it?"

"The best I could do. Tomato juice, banana, lemon, raw egg, coffee powder, and Tabasco. Drink up. It should help settle your stomach and ease your headache. I added a couple aspirin."

She sniffed it. "Eww." Well, what did she have to lose? There was certainly nothing left in her stomach. She took a taste and winced. "That's nasty."

"Pretend it's a milkshake."

"A milkshake?"

Kent pantomimed drinking.

Cass closed her eyes and sipped, a little at a time, until she'd swallowed the whole disgusting concoction. "Yum." She made a face that said the drink was anything but.

"My grandfather was a drinker," Kent said. "This was my grandma's recipe, or the closest I could come. My theory is Gram figured that anything that tastes that bad makes you shape up so you won't have to drink any more of it."

"You've tried it?"

He ran his hand through his hair, making it jut up oddly. "In college I went to a party school and had a double major: creative writing and carousing. For the first couple of years anyway. I had a few doses of Gran's curative. I think it's what finally steered me away from overindulging in booze. Come on, I'll help you stand. You'll be more comfortable on the couch." He put his hand under her arm and helped her up, then put his arm around her.

If she felt better, she would have thrilled to his touch.

He half carried her into the living room. "Doing any better?" he said when she was ensconced on the sofa. He spread the crimson throw from the back of the sofa over her.

"I think so." She felt enough better to care that she stank. "I'm okay. You don't need to stay. I mean, I'm grateful, but why are you here?"

He sat down on her recliner. That's when she really saw him: his cheeks stubbled, his hair mussed, his eyes shadowed by dark circles.

He looked grim. She wanted to put up her hand to stop him from saying whatever he was going to say, to freeze the moment, but it was pointless.

"First, to tell you about Rebecca switching the photos. Second, to say good-bye. I'm going back to L.A."

"Oh. Is Rebecca going with you?"

He seemed to ponder her question before shaking his head. "That's over."

"What is?"

"Rebecca. I ended it."

Cass blinked.

He rubbed his forehead. "I want to be with someone less complicated. Someone who doesn't lie and who has fewer demons."

"Demons?"

"Things that drive her to do the wrong thing. Rebecca has some great qualities, but I guess I was blinded to the bad by her beauty. I'd never dated anyone who looked anything like her. In some weird way, it made me feel good about myself."

"I get it," she said.

"You do?"

"Yeah." Her own blindness had come from something not all that different. Sharing in Rebecca's glow had made Cass feel good. Less alone. She pulled her blanket closer. "When are you leaving for L.A.?"

"In a few minutes. I'm packed up. But, first, tell me why Mack was so upset last night."

The memory of the stomped rosebushes made hot tears sting her eyes. "Because people trying to win the date with Penn trampled her roses."

"The ones by the door?"

She couldn't speak. Kent was leaving, and Mack had turned away from her. She nodded.

"The ones she said Seamus had planted for her?"

"Yeah."

"No wonder she was so upset." Kent rubbed his mouth. "Mack shouldn't blame you, though. *Rebecca* switched the photos."

"If I'd never started all this in the first place, the roses . . ." Cass couldn't finish.

"You reached out to me because you wanted to save the library. What's wrong with that? Along the way, you found out that the town, too, needed help. Loon. *Your* town. Your home. Helping Loon? Nothing wrong with that either. Were there unintended consequences? Yes. There often are. But Mack's roses are not your fault, Cass. *Rebecca* switched the photos. Rebecca alone. Would you like me to go by Mack's on my way out and explain to her what happened?"

"Please. Yes." Maybe Kent would say something that would help lessen Mack's pain. "Thanks."

Kent stood. "Thank *you* for all you've done for me and my books, Cass."

Cass pushed herself up to standing.

He took her hands in his.

She wanted to ask how he felt about *her*, and yet she didn't want to. She needed to know, but she feared his answer. Felicity would tell her, *Ask*. Cass hesitated, but she summoned up the will to say, "I enjoyed getting to know you."

"I enjoyed knowing *you*." Kent glanced down at their hands, then released hers.

He'd used past tense, not present or future.

"Will you come back to visit?" she said.

"I don't think so. I'm way behind in my writing. I'm not sure being here is all that conducive to my creativity."

She wanted to freeze time, but if he was leaving, then she wanted him to go.

"Take care of yourself, Cass," he said.

"You, too."

"I'll stop by Mack's."

"Thanks." She didn't trust herself to say more. If she opened her mouth, sobs might escape. She watched him walk away. Don't forget me, she wanted to say. Even if you never call or email. Please, just remember me. Don't let me be easily forgotten.

THIRTY-FOUR

In the kennel bathroom late that afternoon, Cass unleashed a steady stream of pee that went on and on and on, so long she figured she could have put out a small brushfire. She read over the three signs she'd posted years ago around the mirror: *It's really my dog's home—I just pay the mortgage*; *Wag more, bark less*; and *I want to be the person my dog thinks I am*. Normally, rereading them brought her at least one smile. Not today. Today she rubbed her aching head and wished she could burrow under the covers, to sleep . . . and forget.

A clamor of barks and howls told her that someone had come into the office. Maybe Diego, Zoe, and Caesar were back from their hike to Evelyn Lake, a small gem nestled amid rock and woods only a couple miles away. "I'll be right out," she called. It could also be the UPS man with a delivery, Maya with the mail, or a customer with a dog. Wait. Maybe it was Mack.

Finished peeing, she didn't even bother to rinse her hands, just pulled open the door, praying she would see Mack.

Rebecca blocked the doorway.

Cass couldn't step out of the bathroom without shoving her aside.

"What did you say to Kent to make him break up with me?" Rebecca's voice was threatening, her words deliberate, her eyes raging. Her perfume smelled expensive. Stifling.

"You deliberately switched photos, you tried to blame it on me, and you think Kent left because of *me*?" Cass felt more incredulous than enraged.

"You're supposed to be Felicity's biggest fan," Rebecca said, "but *I'm* the one who stuck her neck out. We all know that Mack's *is* Felicity's. I'm the one who cared. The one with the guts to be real."

Mack had been right all along. Cass had been living in a fiction of her own making: that she could transform herself into Felicity, that people—herself, Rebecca—could truly change. Her own desperate need to finally be accepted had been what really caused the trampling of Mack's roses.

Rebecca spat out words. "You wanted Kent for yourself from the minute he arrived. You were always trying to steal him from me. Lindsey told me how you flirted with him over that milkshake."

There it was, the tone that had haunted so much of Cass's life.

Rebecca smirked and stepped forward, bumping Cass back a step. "Well, he may not have wanted me, but he sure as hell wouldn't want *you*. You're a loser who runs a dog kennel. I bet even your own mother's ashamed of you. Why else would she move to Arizona and leave you behind?"

Cass felt like a balloon someone had popped, her energy and meager confidence seeping away. *Was* that why her mother was fine with leaving her for others to raise, because Cass was what Rebecca had labeled her all along: a loser? And, really, who but an incredibly cruel person would tell someone that, whether it was true or not?

"You—" Rebecca began.

The kenneled dogs exploded into barks. Diego and Zoe stood at the door.

In an instant, Diego inserted himself between Rebecca and Cass, which forced Rebecca to step back, allowing Cass to exit the bathroom.

It was a relief not to be trapped, though Cass felt ashamed she hadn't forced her own way out.

Caesar walked into the office, wagged his tail a couple times at Cass, then collapsed at her feet.

Hair mussed, Zoe stood in the doorway, dressed in halter top and the short shorts her mother had given her. Diego's hair also looked uncombed. Either they'd been swimming or love-making, Cass thought.

Rebecca turned toward Cass. "I told you Zoe was here to *work*."

"*I* get to decide who I love," Zoe said before Cass could speak. Zoe went to Diego, taking his hand. She sneered as she looked her mother up and down. "And who I don't."

Zoe's meaning seemed obvious: she didn't love her mother. For an instant Cass wondered if anyone ever had.

Rebecca swayed a bit, but only for a moment. She jutted her finger at Cass. "This round goes to you, but the next one's coming, and I *will* win."

Caesar rose, growling. Rebecca froze. Cass wanted to hug both Diego and her dog. Not because Rebecca scared her, but because in that instant she scared herself. She couldn't remember ever wanting to slap someone like she wanted to slap Rebecca. "It's okay," she said to both of her defenders, petting Caesar. He quieted but remained standing.

Rebecca softened her voice but moved in front of her daughter. "Zoe, you're done working here. And you," she said to Diego, pointing at him, "stay away from my daughter. Zoe, get in the car."

Zoe linked arms with Diego, but he moved her hand away. "Go with your mom," he said.

Rebecca glared at Diego. "Zoe, *now*."

Zoe looked toward Cass.

"Diego's right," Cass said, "but for you, my door will always be open."

Rebecca pointed toward the car.

Zoe cast Diego a last lingering look, then headed toward the parking lot, Rebecca right behind her.

"Thank you," Cass said to him. "I appreciated your help."

"Always," he said, nodding for emphasis. "What did Rebecca mean about winning the next round?"

"I've no idea."

"Are you worried?"

"I think she was just making empty threats. The only thing she could do might be to close the library, but she just announced publicly that it would remain open."

Both looked out at the ring and the parking lot. Zoe never even glanced her mother's way. When they reached the car, Zoe slid into the back seat.

"Will Zoe be okay?" Diego said.

"I think so, yeah." Cass stroked Caesar's head. "Hopefully we all will."

That evening, Cass drove to Mack's, dreading the potentially awful welcome she might receive. Kent had texted earlier to say Mack wasn't home and hadn't returned his phone calls.

Cass ached to tell Mack all she'd realized over the past two days, including her suspicion that she'd acted as she had in part from the confidence that Mack would always love her, and from the fear that Rebecca and the town would never even like her.

Holding her breath, Cass made the final turn. She arrived at an empty house. Mack's truck was gone. The dogs were gone. All that remained were the bits and pieces of trampled roses.

THIRTY-FIVE

ass stared at the paper she held in her trembling hands.

CEASE AND DESIST ORDER FOR
IN GOOD COMPANY KENNEL

BECAUSE THE NOISE AND SMELLS COMING FROM *IN GOOD COMPANY KENNEL* CONSTITUTE A HAZARD TO THE CITIZENS OF LOON, CALIFORNIA, YOU ARE HEREBY NOTIFIED THAT THE AFOREMENTIONED BUSINESS MUST CEASE AND DESIST ALL OPERATIONS NO LATER THAN 8:00 A.M., AUGUST 14.

BY ORDER OF REBECCA OLIVER, LOON MAYOR, ON BEHALF OF THE LOON TOWN COUNCIL

Cass put her hand against the wall to steady herself and released her hold on Rebecca's order, which floated to the floor. Rebecca had taken only two days to make good on her threat. Close the kennel? In three weeks? Cass tried to suck in air, but little could seep through her constricted throat. She had not seen this coming.

She was vaguely aware that Diego had entered the office, vaguely aware he picked up the paper she'd dropped.

"Close?" His voice seemed to come from far away and to tremble just as much as her hands. His eyes were wide, his face drained.

Cass willed herself to steady, for both their sakes. "No," she said. And then, louder, more emphatically. "No! This is bogus. You can't hear or smell the kennel from town. We're a mile away and barely within city limits. What stinks isn't the kennel. It's Rebecca."

Diego's face was ashen.

Cass put as much confidence in her voice as she could muster to reassure him. And herself. "Notice that the rest of the council didn't even sign this order. Rebecca's trying to punish me for Kent leaving. And for Zoe being so angry with her. I bet Rebecca didn't even mention this notice to the council members. Heck, Lewis has boarded dogs here. No way he'd go along with this. I'll go to the town offices and see if I can't find him or one of the other councilmen." She whacked the paper in her hand. "Rebecca's not going to get away with this. We have almost a month. If the council doesn't help, I'll think of something."

Diego didn't look convinced. Cass knew the kennel wasn't a hazard; she just hoped she was right about the rest of it. Her mouth was so dry, when she tried to lick her lips, her tongue felt like sandpaper.

Ten minutes later she was driving toward town, wondering whether the news in the morning's paper had any bearing on the order to close the kennel. The lead story reported that Rebecca and the council were negotiating a deal to bring a TBS box store to Loon. According to Rebecca, TBS—The Big Store (for Small Towns)—would bring in jobs and lower prices for

Loon's citizens, which would free people to spend more money on other goods and services, thus creating even more jobs. Rebecca also said that the council was looking into the possibility of building a golf course and condo development on the southern edge of town—and, eventually, a ski resort on Moon.

Cass managed to squeeze her truck into a space between two hulking SUVs a few blocks off Main. She hurried toward the town offices, barely registering all the tourists crowding the sidewalks, and entered the office building. Rebecca's door was shut, but Cass could hear her talking with somebody.

"Can I help you, Cass?" said elderly receptionist Marjorie Cummings.

Cass did her best to keep the rage from her voice. "No, thanks. Is the council in there with Rebecca?"

"Yes. It's a closed-door session. Should I have her call you when the meeting ends?"

"That won't be necessary, but thanks." Cass pivoted and covered the distance to Rebecca's office with quick strides. Ignoring Marjorie's protest, Cass thrust open the door.

Rebecca was seated behind her desk, the four council members grouped around it. All looked up at her intrusion. Cass could swear Rebecca's eyes gleamed. "My kennel isn't a hazard, and you all know it." Cass challenged each of the council members with a steady gaze. Two glanced down. One returned her stare, impassive. Only Lewis looked sympathetic.

"I told them that," Lewis said, his bright gold fillings glinting in the overhead light.

"Why are the rest of you going along with this?" Cass looked from one to the other. Was it regret, embarrassment, or guilt that had two councilmen staring down at the papers in front of them?

Rebecca tilted her chair back.

"Has any of you ever once heard or smelled the kennel from town?" Cass said.

No response except a sympathetic headshake from Lewis.

Cass tried to smooth the panic from her voice. "Look, Rebecca's doing this because she blames me for her personal problems. You don't have to approve it."

Still no response. Rebecca wore a triumphant smile. "Looks like you lose."

Cass had to fight the urge to wrap her hands around Rebecca's throat. "I'll appeal."

"Feel free." Rebecca shrugged. "Just file a formal notice and we'll schedule a public hearing on the order. By law we must publish a notice in the paper ten days before that hearing. You'll get to testify at the hearing, as will any of your supporters. And your opponents." Rebecca turned to the council. "Let's get back to business."

Cass's retreat, shoulders slumped, was far slower than her advance had been. Felicity would have persuaded the council to override Rebecca, but Felicity wasn't real. The real world was Lindsey doubling rents. It was Mack's trampled roses. It was Enrique's murder.

She *had* to find a way to win the appeal: for her sake, Diego's—and even Arturo's.

Cass started toward the outside door just as a mob of some fifty people tumbled through it, many screaming at each other, while others yelled at Rebecca, who had opened her office door and stood there, arms crossed and silent.

Cass could make out only snatches of what was being shouted: *jobs, TBS, Mother Moon, local merchants, desecration, prices, rent control, resort, lies, revenue.* She was startled to see Scotty and Garrett standing together, on the same side, the side opposed to Rebecca and the FBC. Scotty kept yelling the word "betrayal." He'd supported the Felicity Benedict Connection, he shouted at Rebecca, but now Rebecca wanted to bring in a big chain store that would undercut his prices and cause his store to fail.

Other people shouting at Rebecca and at those supporting the FBC included Garrett, Maya, and Rosalind Lamb. None of what they were saying was new to Cass, but what *was* new was how many people, once supporters of the FBC, now agreed with the antis and were yelling their rage.

On the opposite side of the room, Lindsey and fellow supporters, also passionate, shouted that the town needed to attract more people, that rent control would discourage potential investors, and that a TBS store would help save the town, not destroy it.

Jack Kraft squared across from Garrett. "Why can't you get that we need jobs, asshole?" Kraft said.

Garrett all but snarled. "Who are you calling an asshole?"

"You, asshole."

Cass felt like her insides were withering. She spoke before she even knew she'd opened her mouth. "Stop screaming. Please, just stop!"

She registered her own astonishment that she was speaking in public. Not just speaking but shouting to be heard. She glanced around the room. Some of the people looked as shocked as she felt, people she'd gone to school with. "Many of us grew up together," she continued, throwing her whole self into her words. "Most of us know each other." The screaming gradually subsided. Cass lowered her voice but continued, almost as if on autopilot. "None of us is perfect, but we all deserve to be heard. When you're screaming, the only person you can hear is yourself."

Although the crowd had fallen silent, the rage in the room hadn't dissipated. Cass had never before been in a room so brimming with scowls. She looked toward Rebecca's office, wondering why Rebecca was letting her speak. Maybe Rebecca, too, was shocked. Or maybe she hoped Cass would make a fool of herself, and maybe she would, but she had to try. "When I wrote to Kent asking for his help with our Felicity campaign, I only thought about what it would do *for* our town. I had no idea what it would do *to* it. That it would divide the town so badly we'd be standing here screaming at each other. Maybe the whole thing was a terrible idea. I just don't know anymore."

Some in the crowd were no longer scowling but instead looked confused, a few even ashamed. Oh, how to make them see? "Look, we do need more jobs and, sure, most of us would welcome lower prices, but we also need to protect our current residents and our local merchants. And we need to safeguard our mountains. Maybe we can't do all of these things, but maybe we can, if we work together. Really together. I mean, we're not bad people. So often we've come together, like when we built a new house for the Taylors after theirs burned down."

Cass put every ounce of passion she had into her words. "The thing is, if we change too much, we risk losing all we value, and if we change too little, we risk ending up like so many other small towns: extinct. I don't have the answers about what we should do except that maybe we should form a committee of people from all sides to look at how to go forward responsibly. One thing I am sure about: we should listen—really listen—to each other. We should be good neighbors. If you think that's not possible, come to my kennel. Dogs may growl at each other now and again, but most of the time they play together. If dogs can do that, why can't we?" There. She'd said her piece. Somehow, the words had tumbled out.

Applause greeted her—scattered and soft at first, then louder. Cass blushed. Was she dreaming? Her words had touched people and—incredibly—silenced the screaming. For one long, wonderful moment, she basked in her success.

"Cass is right," called Lily Diamond from the back of the crowd, her husky voice unmistakable. "We need to stop fighting."

"Nobody calls me an asshole." Garrett glared at Kraft.

Kraft curled his fingers into fists. "Then don't act like one."

"Screw you."

It happened so fast. The two men closed the space between them. "No!" Cass yelled. She stepped between the men just as they swung at each other. Garrett's fist missed her; Kraft's did not. His fist belted her face. She fell back. Maya's hands caught her, keeping her from going down.

It took her a few seconds to feel the pain. When she did, it exploded. Her face felt on fire. Her nose throbbed. Her cheekbone and the eye above it hurt. She wasn't sure whether the room had grown quiet, or she just couldn't hear above the jackhammering in her head. Her eyes teared up; she felt dizzy.

Shirley was first to ask, "Are you okay?"

Not even close, Cass thought, but at least the shouting had stopped. Her knees shook.

"You want a chair?" Scotty said.

Cass didn't know what she wanted. Except to go home.

"I'm an EMT," said a burly man she didn't know who pushed his way through the crowd. "Let me check her." He ran fingers lightly about her face, then shone a small flashlight in her eyes. "No concussion, good, and your nose isn't broken, but your face is going to hurt for a few days. And you're going to have quite a shiner."

Lily addressed the two fighters. "Shame on you."

No one spoke.

Cass thought she was going to be sick. "I need to go home."

Maya and Shirley helped her from the building.

The last thing Cass heard as she exited was angry shouts coming from the room she'd left.

The ice might lessen the pain in her face, but it didn't touch the pain in the rest of her as she lay on the couch in her home that night. She'd called Diego and told him she was sick and couldn't come back to the kennel until the following day, and that was true. She was sick alright: heartsick. The town would fracture further. Rebecca would keep Zoe from her. The kennel would be closed. Diego would have to leave for God knew where. Mack would never forgive her. She would never forgive herself for devising the plan that had sparked this disaster.

None of it would have happened if she hadn't tried to be someone who was nothing more than a fiction writer's fantasy. She threw the ice pack in the sink. So she had a shiner. So what? Besides, that was the least of it. She was surprised—even glad—she'd spoken up, but there should never have been a need to.

She got up and snatched the second Felicity Benedict novel from her bedside table, its cover a deep teal blue, and ran her callused finger over the embossed silver title, *Matters of the Heart: Passion*. This book, as well as the other two, had given her so much pleasure, so much hope. What crap. She carried all three books out to her backyard. It was a hot night, the waning moon but a sliver. She lifted the lid of the recycling can and dumped in all three books. From now on, there would be no more fiction for her—not in what she read, and not in how she lived.

When she went back inside, she brushed her teeth and went to bed, hoping sleep would bring her the rest she craved, but her mind kept circling back to the heartbreak she'd helped cause.

Caesar whimpered, his head resting on the edge of her bed. He wanted up. What was the point in never allowing a dog in her bed? It wasn't like anyone else wanted to share it. Cass patted the covers. Caesar jumped up, turned around once, then lay down beside her. Cass put her arm around him and tried to sleep.

THIRTY-SIX

Diego's expression of dismay the next day, a Thursday, confirmed what Cass already knew: she looked like hell. Which was also how she felt. The right side of her face was red, purple, and swollen, while the left looked hollowed out by scant sleep. Anything and everything above her neck hurt, from her chin to her hair follicles.

The dismay on Diego's face became resolve. "Who did this?" he said, voice steely.

Cass started to shake her head, but that just made it throb harder. "Nobody. I mean, not deliberately. Two guys were fighting. I tried to stop them."

"Go home," Diego said.

"Thanks, but I feel worse at home. I need the distraction."

"*Bueno*. But I'll clean *all* the pens."

"That would be great. Thank you."

A sudden din of barks worsened the hammering in Cass's head. She felt a flicker of hope that maybe Mack had heard what happened and was returning to comfort her.

Diego went to the doorway; he stiffened.

"Who is it?" she said.

"The police." He licked his lips.

"Don't worry," she said, though she understood his concern. When the police in Honduras paid you a visit, you had reason to fear. She joined him in the doorway. "I'm sure Chance wants to know if I'm filing assault charges. That or else he needs to board Bullet." She and Diego went outside, into the ring that bordered the parking lot. Clouds were forming above the peaks. Rain was predicted for that evening.

Chance ambled toward them.

"Good morning," Cass said. "Where's Bullet?"

"Cass, Diego." Gray hairs speckled Chance's short-cropped beard. "My granddaughter's visiting. She begged me to leave him home. Looks like Kraft's fist caught you square on, Cass. Your shiner's just getting started."

"It was an accident. I don't want to press charges."

"You sure?"

"Yeah."

"Sorry I wasn't there," he said. "It was my day off, and Bill was dealing with a drunk and disorderly."

"No problem."

Chance moved so fast, Cass had no time to act. He grabbed Diego's upper right arm.

"What are you doing?" Cass said.

Chance kept his eyes on Diego. "I'm sorry about this, Diego, but I have reason to believe you're in this country illegally."

"No, he's not," Cass said. "He was granted asylum." She put her hand on Diego's shoulder to reassure him, but he just stared at the ground, face pale.

"You need to come with me," Chance told him. "An ICE agent will meet us at the jail later. Hopefully you *are* here legally, in which case you have nothing to worry about."

Diego's eyes were wide, his expression stricken.

Cass frowned. He must not have asylum. He'd lied about

that, but with good reason considering what would happen if he was sent back. Dear God. Cass stepped in front of Chance. "You don't understand. Diego witnessed a gang killing. If he goes back, they'll murder him, just like they murdered his brother."

"Whether he goes back isn't up to me."

"Sure it is." She put all the urgency she felt into her voice. "Do the right thing, Chance. Let him go. *Please.*"

Diego trained his eyes on Chance; the sheriff hesitated.

For a split second, Cass thought maybe he would relent. Then another car churned gravel in the parking lot, and Rebecca soon appeared in the ring. Her gaze swept over the three of them. "I just came to see the show. Nice shiner, by the way, Cass. I warned you not to make me your enemy."

In a silver shirt, tight jeans, and silver heels, Rebecca looked like a bullet of a woman: straight and lethal. "*You* called Chance about Diego," Cass said.

"Of course." Rebecca looked at Diego. "I warned you, too."

"Let's go." Chance kept his grip on Diego's arm and walked around Cass, clearly headed toward the police car.

Diego wrenched his arm free and bolted; he sprinted toward the woods that bordered the kennel.

Before Chance could pursue, Cass hurled herself at him, locked her arms around his legs, and brought him down hard.

"Stop!" Chance and Rebecca yelled.

Diego kept running.

"Get off me, Cass." Chance shoved her with strong arms and eventually managed to slide out from beneath her. He lunged to his feet and ran after Diego, who had raced across the parking lot and disappeared.

Rebecca clapped. "Bravo, Cass."

Chance soon returned. Breathing hard, he glowered at Cass.

"I saw everything," Rebecca said. "She flung herself at you deliberately. Isn't that assaulting a police officer?"

Chance frowned and brushed the dirt off his uniform.

"I need to get back to the office," Rebecca said. "But hey, Cass, way to go. I hope you enjoy being locked up."

Ears flat back, Caesar snarled at her

"If that dog bites me," Rebecca said, "I'll have it shot."

Cass grabbed Caesar's collar.

Rebecca walked out of the ring and got in her car.

"Now I have no choice but to arrest you." Chance pressed the radio mic on his shoulder; it squawked. "This is Sheriff Chance Garner. I'm bringing in a female suspect who interfered with my arrest of a possible illegal immigrant, enabling him to escape. The suspected illegal, Diego Ordoñez, fled north on foot from the kennel In Good Company, located on Highway 83. I want him apprehended. And get the women's cell ready."

He put a pair of handcuffs around her wrists. "You made some poor choices today."

Cass's mind spun so fast, she nearly fainted. "Wait. Let me put Caesar in one of the pens."

Chance glared at her, but he nodded.

Cass commanded Caesar to come with her. The dog walked on one side of her, Chance on the other. Hands cuffed, Cass swung open the gate of an empty outdoor pen and kissed Caesar's muzzle. "Good boy." She signaled him in.

He took a step toward it, stopped, and looked at her.

"Go on."

He slowly entered the pen, but before she could close the gate, Caesar ran back through the kennel ring toward the parking lot, empty of Rebecca's car. In the lot he stopped, looking to see if Cass was coming.

"Caesar, come," she called.

He kept going.

Cass yelled and whistled; Caesar didn't respond.

Chance took her arm. "I'm sorry Caesar's run off," he said,

"but I'm taking you in. I just hope you knew what you were doing when you tackled me."

For once Cass's cheeks didn't burn. They paled.

Chance led her to the patrol car. "We'll catch Diego." Chance gestured her to the back seat. "Get in."

Cass's knees felt weak. She sagged. She hadn't had time to think about what the result of her actions might be. "Wait. There's no one to take care of the dogs. Or find Caesar."

"You should have thought of all that before you tackled me."

"Don't make the dogs pay for what I did."

"Call Mack from the jail. She'll tend them."

"She's away. And she isn't taking my calls."

"Great," Chance mumbled.

Zoe could help with the kennel, but there was no way Rebecca would allow that. "There's no one else who can take care of them."

"You can come back once you make bail. It shouldn't take long."

The dogs howled now as if in protest, as if pleading with Chance to let her stay.

Chance put Cass into the police car. She tried to think of something—anything—she could do to escape, but the grill between driver and suspect reminded her of a spider's web, and she was the insect trapped in its strands.

THIRTY-SEVEN

The mug shot Chance took of her at the police station made DMV photos look flattering. If the jury saw it, they'd think she ate little children.

"Tyson's on his way over," Chance said as he hung up the station phone.

"Who?"

"Lawrence Tyson, lead prosecutor in the DA's office."

"Oh." Cass leaned back in the hard metal chair beside his rickety looking desk: drawers that didn't close right, legs mangled as if a grizzly had used them for toothpicks, the part near her chair carved with initials. Three filing cabinets in the room looked like they'd been reclaimed from bomb testing sites. "Is that the normal procedure?"

Chance, grim faced: "no."

Wanted posters dotted the station's rust-colored walls. For a moment Cass imagined Diego's face on a poster. Or her own. "After Tyson comes, I can make bail, right?"

"Depends. He could keep you here till your arraignment."

"Which would be when? This afternoon?"

"He's got forty-eight hours—excluding weekends—to charge or release you."

"But that wouldn't be till Monday."

"Right."

"I can't be here that long."

"I wish you weren't here at all. Actually, I wish this whole day had never happened. Unfortunately, where this goes from here isn't up to me."

"Should I be worried?"

Chance frowned. "Of course you should."

Cass had never set foot in a police station. The closest she'd come to jail was living with her mother.

Chance lowered his voice. "Be careful with Tyson, Cass. I don't much like the man. He's as mean and smart as he is ambitious. That's a dangerous combination. Rumor says he's getting ready to run for DA and is looking for a case to help him make a name."

Something told Cass to call before Tyson arrived. "I'm allowed phone calls, right?"

"One, so choose carefully."

"Will you call Mack for me, please? Maybe she'll pick up for you. Ask her if she'll cover the kennel till I can get there."

He hesitated.

"What if Bullet was at the kennel?"

"Fine. Make your call, then I'll call Mack."

"I need privacy."

"This is a jail, not a spa."

"I'll hurry. And I promise not to call Diego."

"Why did you have to tackle me, Cass?" Chance rubbed the bridge of his nose. He looked like he was trying to shut down a massive headache.

"What would *you* have done, Chance, if it were someone who felt like family, someone you really cared about, someone you quite possibly owed your life to?"

"I remember that. How he stopped that Rottweiler from attacking you by opening an umbrella. Smart. And brave. I like Diego. Always have."

"He's those things, yes. He's also kind and loving. He deserves life, Chance, not death. Not to be murdered by a gang of killers."

Chance exhaled audibly. "Why didn't you just hire him a lawyer?" He handed Cass the phone he'd taken from her earlier.

"They could lose." She flashed on an image of the last paycheck she wrote Diego. "Hey, I paid Diego by check, and I paid his social security taxes, so he must be legal, right? To have all those papers?"

"They're forged, I'm sure. Besides, Diego ran. That should answer your question." Chance grabbed a set of keys from his desk and gestured her toward the door that separated office from cells. "You just have a few minutes. If you hear anyone approaching, hide that phone."

"I will. Thanks."

Chance swung open the door to the cell area. There was a small room with shower and sink, then two identical cells; the single window in each was high, out of reach. The freshly painted cell walls were white and blinding in the fluorescent light. Each cell held a cot and a steel toilet bowl. Cass entered the first cell. Chance pushed the cell door closed. It clicked, locking her in.

"Make it fast," he repeated, then left her alone.

The cell stank of body odor, vomit or both and some kind of cloying pine scent liberally sprayed in an unsuccessful attempt to cover it all up.

Zoe answered after only one ring. "Where are you, Cass? Diego called. He sounded so scared. We have to help him."

Zoe sounded scared, too. Cass wished she could hold her.

"Listen to me," Cass said, keeping her voice as calm as she could. "I don't have long. Is he safe for now?"

"He's hiking to Juniper Lake. I'm going to get his things and meet him there. We'll decide where to head."

We'll decide. Diego was probably out of cell range by now, so she wouldn't be able to call him even if Chance would let her. "Listen to me, Zoe. Don't you two leave Juniper until I can get there. I'll hike up as soon as I post bail, though I'm not sure when that will be. Maybe not till Monday."

"Monday! Wait. Bail?"

Zoe sounded as appalled as Cass felt. "It's a misunderstanding, no biggie." She didn't want Diego to know why she was in jail; it might make him reconsider fleeing.

"But why can't you get out before Monday?"

"It's up to the DA. But Monday would be the latest. I'll bring whatever money I can and any of Diego's personal things that you can't carry. You know where the camping gear is. Take it, plus his critical personal things like his wallet. Take as much food as you can, and clothes for both of you. Your pack's going to be heavy."

"You'll come for sure?" Zoe sounded all of about five.

"Definitely. Wait for me there."

"Okay. And, Cass, I *am* going with Diego."

Footsteps approached the door, boots clomping. "I have to go." She disconnected and shoved the phone under her mattress just as Chance, followed by a man, presumably the ambitious prosecutor, came through the door.

Cass knew the minute she saw Lawrence Tyson that she was in trouble. Tyson was so thin, Cass wasn't sure she'd see him if he faced sideways—but he was hard to look away from. His black smoldering eyes seemed to want to suck her in and burn her up.

Tyson nodded at Chance to dismiss him. "I'll speak with Ms. Enger alone."

Chance shot Cass a warning glance and left. Cass leaned against the back wall of her cell, as far out of range of Tyson's eyes as she could get.

"So," he said, straightening his already-neat tie, "I understand you leveled the sheriff. Where'd you learn to tackle like that?"

Cass didn't answer. Tyson's charcoal colored suit made him appear even more threatening. It took money to pay for a suit like that. It took success.

"Since you have no arrest record or experience with a jail cell, Cass, I'll spell this out for you. You have two choices. Choice number one, you tell me or Chance where the fugitive is and walk out of here today a free woman. Choice number two, you stay silent, which means you'll be charged with aiding a fugitive's escape and assaulting an officer of the law. I will personally prosecute you for the maximum sentence. You're looking at ten years in prison."

Ten *years*? Cass put her hand to her mouth before she could stop herself.

"A decade's a long time to be locked up," Tyson said. "I'd rather not have to do that, but it's up to you. Where is he?"

Cass tried to suppress the fear in her voice. "I've no idea."

Tyson's smile was as thin as the rest of him. "What do you have against Americans?" he said.

"What?"

"You could have hired a local boy. So why did you hire an illegal instead?"

Tyson would never understand. Besides, she wanted him to leave.

"Madison County has a higher-than-average unemployment rate," he said. "From what I understand, you started the Felicity Benedict makeover partly to bring jobs to Loon, jobs *Americans* need, but instead you gave yours to an illegal. I guess you want to open our borders to anyone who claims hardship, right? Is that your stance on immigration?"

"I don't have a stance," she said. "All I know is that Diego's older brother was murdered. If Diego goes back, he and his little brother will meet the same fate."

"I hope that comforts you when you land in a cell not much bigger than this that you share with someone who might not like you all that much. You know, of course, that, unlike the Bay Area, Madison County is made up of *real* Americans—the kind who will sit on your jury, people who will not be sympathetic to you or to illegal immigrants. Incidentally, did you know that Diego was given a fair hearing and denied asylum?"

Cass pressed back against the cell wall to steady herself. She summoned all the bravado she could muster. "If Diego was denied asylum, then he didn't have a fair hearing."

"If this country admits everyone who comes here because he or she has a sob story, we'll all soon be speaking Spanish. Or Arabic."

"A *sob* story. That's what you call murder?"

"That's what I call the fictitious stories illegal immigrants tell in order to pull on the heart strings of big-hearted but gullible people like you. He concocted a story, you fell for it, and now you face spending ten years in prison while he goes free. I appreciate that you are a compassionate person, Ms. Enger, but make no mistake; I am not. You have only two hours to tell me where he went. After that, I won't just prosecute you. I'll make an example of you to discourage other bleeding hearts from sheltering illegals. And I won't lose."

Cass all but gulped. She suspected she wasn't doing a very good job of hiding the panic that squeezed her chest, making it hard to breathe. Voice wobbly, she said, "When can I post bail?".

"Not before your arraignment on Monday. Remember, two hours. Clock's ticking."

The door closed behind Tyson. The instant he was gone, Cass sank onto the cot, her whole body shaking. By the time she got out of prison, she'd be in her forties. Her home would have been foreclosed, her belongings scattered, and the kennel long gone. Caesar wouldn't remember her, if he was even alive. Zoe would have gone who knew where, and who knew where Mack would be.

Maybe there was another option. Her pulse quickened. She could run a Go Fund Me campaign to raise money for Diego to hire a top-notch attorney to appeal the denial of sanctuary. He might get legal standing to stay.

Or not.

She couldn't do that. Much as she wanted to go home, there was no way she could betray Diego. He would never do that to her.

Chance came through the door and held out his hand.

"I need to make another call," she said.

"Sorry. Tyson ordered me not to allow more than the one. I need your phone."

Her hand shook as she gave it to him.

"I wish you'd reconsider," Chance said.

Cass's head was spinning. She couldn't think clearly.

"Mack didn't answer my call," Chance said. "Since there's no one to run the kennel, and you're stuck here till Monday, I notified Rebecca. She's having her staff contact the owners of the dogs. They'll transfer any dogs whose owners she can't reach to Paws Place, the kennel in Hidden Valley."

"Not there, Chance, please," she said. "That place is so disorganized, they're lucky to find their own feet. And they don't keep it clean, which is bad for the dogs. You've got to call Rebecca back and tell her to choose a different kennel." Where was Caesar?

"They'll have already started the calls. It's a done deal. And by the way, my deputy, Bill Riley's, staying tonight. I'd be careful what you say. He's a good guy but a Tyson fan. I'll be back in the morning."

Cass turned away from the sheriff. She didn't want him to see her despair. "I'm sorry for what happened," she said, speaking to the wall.

"Enough to tell me where Diego went?"

She wanted to tell him and get the hell out of this cell, but she didn't want to lie again, not to Chance, so she said nothing.

He closed the door into the office behind him: the *clank* seemed so final.

"Chance?" she called, quailing inside. She couldn't do this.

He opened the door. "Yeah?"

It seemed to Cass that she could hear everything: the cars speeding down the distant highway, the dogs barking at Paws Place, the snow melting on Moon Mountain. Diego's heart beating. She remembered Miguel's plea that she watch over and protect Diego. "Nothing," she said.

He closed the door again.

If only everything could be restored to the way it was before the Felicity Benedict Connection, back when Mack still had her roses and still loved her, back when Diego and she worked the kennel together and her worst problem was what to eat for dinner.

From the cot where she lay, trying and failing to sleep, Cass glanced at her watch: a few minutes past midnight. If only she could escape the horrors of what she faced through sleep, but she was too wired. And too cold. The air-conditioner must be blasting on this mid-July night. Perhaps in winter they unleashed the heater's full capacity, turning the cell into a sweltering place. Make prisoners more miserable. Impress upon them the undesirability of returning. If such was the goal,

Chance needn't have bothered; on that score, she didn't require reinforcement.

Cass stretched her aching neck. The pillow was about as soft as a rock; the bed felt hard and lumpy, like nothing more than a few pieces of straw. Sleeping on a placemat on the floor would be more comfortable than the cell cot. She pulled the blanket tight around her. Made of wool, reeking of B.O., the blanket felt scratchy, like she was trying to warm herself with a gigantic Brillo pad. She yanked it off: better to shiver.

If only she had someone with her. Mack. Caesar. Someone. Anyone. How was she supposed to bear all this alone? At least the light had been turned down so that it cast only a subdued glow, though the streetlight outside the jail was bright, revealing the light rain that struck the cell window.

Diego and Zoe were out there on the mountain in the rain: scared, desperate. She couldn't bear to dwell on their predicament. Or her own. Better to focus on something else. Anything else.

She chose a single raindrop to watch. Walter, she would call it. Walter's slide down the window was slow, languid. She bet he was lazy, that he couldn't be bothered to move more quickly. Or maybe he was in tune with the natural pace of the universe, not rushing to get from one place to another. Then again, Walter could be arthritic, crippled, unable to rush, which was why he slid so slowly. Finally, he joined with other drops where they pooled at the bottom of the pane.

Loretta, she dubbed the next drop. Loretta seemed drunk, her path unsteady: start, stop, swerve left, start, stop, swerve right.

Yet a third drop, Daniel, stayed at the top where he landed, seemingly unwilling to join with other drops.

If only she could step outside and open her arms, letting the rain drench her.

Twelve-thirty. The night seemed interminable. Cass willed

her mind to erase the thought of ten years in prison, closed her eyes, and tried counting slowly to a hundred, then back down. No help. Sleep seemed as far away as Saturn.

She recalled a night long ago when her father made her a batch of snow ice cream: fresh snow, vanilla extract, sugar and milk. She must have been four or five. He'd set out a variety of food colors—crimson, amber, orange, blue, emerald—and told Cass to choose one to color the ice cream. Cass had loved all the colors and been unable to decide. While she dithered, the ice cream began to melt. Her mother would have erupted, but her dad simply smiled and said he understood; it was like having to choose just one color from a rainbow. He put the ice cream in the freezer while Cass decided.

She eventually chose crimson. Her father mixed it in. The ice cream, more pink than red, melted on her tongue, cold and sweet and delicious. Cass had not tasted store-bought ice cream since then that came close to being as good as what her dad made that night. She would give anything to taste that snow ice cream again. She would give even more to have her father with her now.

Cass closed her eyes to staunch her welling tears. It didn't work. They slid down her cheeks. Her nose ran. A decade in prison? She started to tremble. For a long time, she wept, terrified and shaking.

When she had no more tears and was unable to get comfortable on the bed, Cass rose. She spent much of the rest of the night huddled in a corner of the cell trying to sleep, but between the cold hard floor and the cold hard truth, she barely even dozed.

THIRTY-EIGHT

By 10:00 Friday night, Cass was so tired, she stretched out on the cot, too exhausted to care about the blanket's stench or its prickly texture. She pulled it over her and slept.

"Damn it, Chance!"

The shout jolted Cass half-awake, wondering who was yelling at the sheriff.

"I'm telling you, Zoe has run away."

Of course. Rebecca: blaring, harsh.

Cass couldn't make out what Chance was saying. Unlike Rebecca, he spoke in a low murmur.

"Zoe told me she was going to stay with her friend for a couple days," Rebecca said, still loud. "She said if I didn't give her have some space, she'd take off and never come back. A little while ago I decided I'd waited long enough and went by her friend's to check. Angelique hasn't seen my daughter for several days. Zoe's with Diego. I know it."

More murmuring.

"*She* knows where they are."

Rebecca flung open the door from the office and gripped the bars of Cass's cell. "Where's my daughter?"

Cass turned her back on Rebecca.

"I *demand* that you tell me where Zoe is. Chance, make her tell."

Chance sauntered into the cell area. "How do you suggest I do that? Thumbscrews? Waterboarding?"

"Whatever it takes, damn it."

A phone sounded in the office; Chance went to answer.

"Zoe's with Diego, isn't she?"

It didn't matter anymore, what Rebecca thought of her, what anyone thought of her other than the people she cherished. That realization gave Cass an ironic sense of freedom as she turned back around. "None of this had to happen," she said. "There was no reason to close my kennel. Or to report Diego. This is all on you, including Zoe's running away."

Rebecca stepped back. "Zoe and I were just fine till she started working for you."

"Oh right. That's why she had to do community service, because she was fine."

"You turned her against me." Rebecca again gripped the cell bars. "If you don't tell me where she is, I guarantee you I will . . ."

Cass, too, grabbed cell bars, her face only inches from Rebecca's. "You'll what? Close the kennel? Have me arrested?"

"I'll convince Tyson to prosecute you for the maximum prison time."

Cass just snorted. "That's the best you can do?"

After a moment, Rebecca released the cell bars and spoke in a calmer voice. "I can do the opposite, too, Cass. I can convince Tyson to drop the charges."

Cass, too, backed up. The DA's cold burning eyes loomed in her mind. Could Rebecca really get Tyson to let her go?

"Or at least I could get him to ask for the minimum sentence."

In Tyson's eyes, the minimum on a ten-year sentence was probably nine years, eleven months, and three weeks.

"And I will," Rebecca said. "If you'll help me find Zoe."

"Help you? If Zoe even saw you, she'd run in the opposite direction."

Rebecca winced. "I realize I'm not a perfect parent."

"You think?" Cass hoped Rebecca heard her sarcasm.

Rebecca's nostrils flared, but she paused before she spoke. "I do love Zoe. You act like you have all the answers, so answer me this. Zoe's barely seventeen. Do you really think it would be good for her to run away with Diego?"

"Maybe not, but what do you suggest I do from a jail cell?"

"Tell me where she is."

"I won't put Diego at that kind of risk. Zoe may be too young to do what she's doing, but if she's found she doesn't face death."

Rebecca again grabbed the cell bars. "So she *is* with him."

"How would I know?"

Rebecca sagged; her shoulders slumped. "Please, Cass." Her voice was more plea now than demand. "Please find her."

Cass cursed the tendrils of sympathy she felt for Rebecca. If the woman deserved anything, it would be a barbed wire fence slapped around her frigid heart. "How do you propose I do that?"

"Chance?" Rebecca called.

He reappeared, Bullet walking beside him. "Yeah?"

Bullet went over to Cass, tail wagging. She knelt to pet him through the cell bars. "Hey, boy." His tail sped up. Where, she wondered, was Caesar? She prayed he was somewhere safe.

"Let Cass out," Rebecca said. "I'll pay bail. Charge whatever you need to. I don't care how much."

"First, I don't set bail." Chance hooked his thumbs in his

belt. "And second, Tyson spoke with the judge. No bail will be set before Cass's arraignment Monday."

"But she's the only person who can find Zoe."

"Maybe so, but Cass is charged with two felonies. As you well know."

"She isn't any danger to society."

"No kidding. But I enforce the laws; I don't make them."

For a moment the only sound was that of Bullet whimpering for Cass to pet him some more, which she did.

"You *have* to let her out," Rebecca said.

Chance just shook his head.

"I know." Rebecca spoke quickly. "I'll call Tyson. If he called the judge, I bet they'd set bail."

"Good luck," Chance said. "Tyson's the keynote speaker at some conference in L.A. Said he needed to 'network.' He won't be taking calls until tomorrow evening."

"That's perfect," Rebecca said. "He won't be by to check on Cass. You can release her to find Zoe."

"No way."

Cass pictured Zoe: so in love, so sure of herself. So young. Though she'd probably bounded up the mountain to be with Diego, how would she fare in a life on the run? Would it push her to revert to the sullen girl she'd been: drinking and driving, shoplifting and vandalizing, a danger to herself and others? Furthermore, she would endanger Diego simply by her presence. Rebecca would do everything conceivable to find Zoe, including printing up and posting flyers, hiring a private investigator, and offering a substantial reward for information. If they found Zoe, they'd find Diego.

Rebecca was right. Cass needed to find Zoe and Diego: not for Rebecca's sake, but for theirs.

What could she say to Chance to persuade him? For a moment they all—Chance, Rebecca, and herself—seemed frozen. Cass was first to speak. "Remember how frightened Bullet was when you found him and brought him to me?"

"Sure," Chance said.

"I worked with him for sixty-one straight days and never charged you a cent. Diego helped a lot."

"Yes, and I appreciate all that, but it's irrelevant."

"You know what it's like to have a child run away." Chance's middle daughter, sixteen, had run off with her boyfriend and come back seven months later—pregnant.

Chance frowned.

"I'm on good terms with the county Board of Supervisors," Rebecca said. "I'm sure I could get them to fund that new communications system you've been wanting."

Chance glared at her. "I don't take bribes."

"Rebecca, be quiet," Cass said. "Chance, I'm not trying to bribe you. I'm just saying that Zoe's too young for what she's doing."

"Fine. Tell me where she is, and I'll bring her back."

"I can't do that."

"You mean you won't."

"No, I won't. Sometimes we need to do what's right, even if it's not what's legal."

Chance's frown seemed to deepen by the minute.

"When Bullet recovered," Cass said, "you told me that if I ever needed anything, I could count on you. I'm asking you now to please let me find Zoe."

"No," he said, though his voice seemed shaky.

"You said Tyson wouldn't be available till tomorrow evening. I promise to return before that. You can take me to the kennel in handcuffs, just in case. If somebody does spot us, you can say you're taking me there to look for clues to Diego's whereabouts."

Chance scowled.

"I know that at heart you, too, are concerned about Zoe and

Diego both. Please let me out. Not because anybody's bribing or blackmailing you, but because it's the right thing to do."

Chance's hands seemed clasped in prayer. He looked down at Bullet, who stood in front of Cass, nose through the cell bars for more petting. "You have to give me your word you'll come back by 10:00 tomorrow *morning,* with or without Zoe."

Cass held Chance's gaze. "I promise."

"Spell it out."

"I promise I'll return before 10:00 a.m. tomorrow. Even if Zoe refuses to come with me."

Chance stared hard at her, then unlocked Cass's cell, shaking his head in apparent disbelief at his own actions. "I must be nuts."

Cass pantomimed putting one hand on the Bible while raising the other. "I'll be back. So help me God."

"I'm going with you," Rebecca said.

"No way." Cass looked back and forth between Rebecca and Chance. "Drop me at the kennel, Chance, then you leave. I'll do my best to find Zoe and bring her home. If either of you tries to follow me, I won't help. Understand?"

Both nodded slowly; neither looked happy.

"Rebecca," Cass said, "does Zoe have any credit cards?"

"Yes. I didn't cancel them because if she uses them, I'll know where she is."

"You cover for me," Chance said to Rebecca, cuffing Cass. "Answer the phones. If something happens to change Tyson's mind, and he calls or—God forbid—shows up, tell him I've taken Cass to the kennel to look for clues. Then call me immediately."

Rebecca nodded with obvious reluctance. She plopped herself behind the sheriff's desk. "Bring her home, Cass."

Handcuffed, Cass stepped outside into a clear night that carried the scents of jasmine and cedar. She longed to just sit and savor the fragrances of freedom.

Chance opened the backseat door of his sheriff's car. "Let's go."

Cass slid in behind the grille. Chance drove toward the kennel. If Tyson ever learned what Chance had done, the sheriff would lose his job, if not his own freedom.

"Get down."

Headlights were coming toward them. Cass slumped in her seat the rest of the way until she could feel the car making the sharp turn just before the parking lot.

"If I were sheriff of a bigger town," Chance said, "I couldn't do this. I've known you a long time, and I got to know Zoe during her wild days. She was a pain in the neck, but I always thought she had something solid at the core. And I appreciated yours and Diego's help with Bullet."

They pulled up to the kennel. Chance turned off the engine and lights. "I wish I could help you, too, but with Rebecca as a witness, my hands are tied."

"I understand, and I appreciate your doing what you're doing now. Just so you know, I wasn't making anything up. Diego really will be killed if he's sent back."

"I know. I read some articles on Honduras while you were dozing."

A surge of affection for Chance swept her.

He got out of the car, opened the backseat door for her, took off her handcuffs, then handed Cass her cell phone. "Come back. By 10:00 tomorrow morning."

"I will. I promise."

THIRTY-NINE

Cass had the willies standing in her darkened, empty kennel, wishing she could hear the comforting sounds of dogs. Especially Caesar. She would give anything to know where he was and whether he was safe.

Though it was dark, a little after 10:30, she didn't dare risk turning on the overhead lights. By now, much of the town would know of her arrest, and she didn't want to give away her presence. Few would understand what she'd done; they'd probably just think she'd blown it again.

She clicked the flashlight app on her phone and scanned the inside pens. Whoever had transported the dogs to Paws Place had left behind the dogs' familiar comforts. There was the Chihuahua, Thunder's, worn stuffed rabbit with its torn right ear, as well as a much-gnawed rawhide bone belonging to Tiny, a St. Bernard who slobbered so much, you could practically shower in his drool.

She reminded herself she needed to hurry.

She quickly searched Diego's apartment. Zoe had taken everything of significance, plus the camping gear Cass had shown her and the packable food. Good girl. Cass strapped on the headlamp she kept for emergencies and stuffed water bottles plus a worn but warm parka for Zoe in case in her rush Zoe hadn't thought to pack one.

Cass added the two hundred dollars she kept in her safe for emergencies, wishing she had more but unable to get to a bank. She also packed the few foods Zoe hadn't taken, including string cheese, and a bag of peanut butter crackers, then told herself she had this. "Nothing to it but to do it," she said.

The instant she stepped outside into the dark, moonless night, her pulse ratcheted up. She never hiked in the dark, for good reason. It was dangerous, easy to trip on an unseen rock or branch, easy to twist an ankle or worse. She'd be easy prey, too, for whatever creatures roamed the night. Well, she didn't have much choice, not if she was going to be back on time. Hopefully, Diego and Zoe would be waiting for her at Juniper Lake.

A loud bark spun her around. She half expected to see bloodhounds accompanied by a posse, but it wasn't a posse. It was Caesar. She knelt. Caesar launched himself into her arms, licking her face. "Good boy," she said. "Good, good boy." She hugged him tight. Where had he been? Had he eaten? Maybe not. She went back inside the kennel and, by the light from her headlamp, poured him a bowl of kibble. Caesar wolfed it down as she poured more kibble into a bag and stuffed it in her pack.

If she went to prison, what would happen to him? He might end up with a brutal owner or be put to sleep. She couldn't— wouldn't—let that happen. Her first order of business after paying bail would be to find him a home.

Caesar stood watching her, tail wagging tentatively, like he wasn't so sure this was going to end the way he wanted it to. "It's fine, boy." Giving thanks to the universe that he was safe and that she wouldn't be hiking alone, Cass opened the office door. Caesar dashed past her to take the lead. Improbably, he headed straight for the trailhead in the woods behind the kennel. It was as if he had a map.

A coyote yipped somewhere in the distance. Goosebumps dotted Cass's arms.

Caesar trotted ahead, tail wagging.

Cass had trouble keeping up. Though the flashlight lit the trail, she stepped carefully, hoping she didn't run into anything four-legged and big, let alone something legless and slithering.

Caesar seemed unconcerned. Too bad he couldn't make conversation—or sing some happy song, but his wagging tail buoyed her spirits whenever he was close enough to be in her flashlight's beam.

After a mile, she was dragging. No wonder, given the last 48 hours. But she needed to go faster: for Diego's sake, Zoe's, Chance's and her own. If Tyson found out she'd "escaped" jail, doubtless he would add another decade or so to her sentence. And she might well not be the only person Tyson would go after. Gratitude for Chance's decency and courage flooded her.

Cass trod as fast as she could, hoping that if anything menacing appeared, she would have time to take evasive action. Whatever that would be. Drop her bag or climb a tree or yell for help. If that's all she could come up with, she was doomed if she ran into something big and hungry. Bear. Cougar. Vampire.

Crack.

Cass's heart raced so fast she half expected it to trip on itself. "Caesar, is that you?"

Nothing.

"Caesar, here boy," she called.

He didn't come. Cass would have moaned, but she didn't want to sound like she felt, which was terrified. She was pretty sure fear signaled vulnerability to animals of prey, so she straightened, whistling loudly. There were no more snapping twigs or other sounds. After a few minutes, she relaxed and picked up her pace. She came to her first hill and decided to charge up it. Her long, quick steps soon brought her to the summit.

And face to face with a bear.

A dark, enormous bear.

Cass froze.

The bear rose up on its hind quarters, looming over her.

From behind Cass came another *crack*. She moaned, hoping it was Caesar and not this bear's cub. She and the bear kept facing each other. If the bear wanted to kill her, it wouldn't take more than a swipe or two of its lethal claws. *Please help me*, she prayed. Her legs shook so hard she could barely stand. For a moment, she yearned to be back in jail.

The bear sniffed the air. Cass doubted she stank as much as the bear did, its scent musty, like the odor of rank B.O.

This wasn't fair. She shouldn't even have to be here. Damn Rebecca. Damn the council. Damn Tyson. Damn that bear. And damn the injustice of this universe. Well, she'd had enough. No way was she going quietly. No way in Hell. She straightened to her full height, waved her arms like she was hailing a rescue vessel, and roared, "No. NO. I am NOT your dinner. Leave me alone. Go away, damn you. GO AWAY."

The bear's ears went back: a bad sign.

Caesar dashed between her and the bear: barking, baying, howling, growling. He seemed to be trying to figure out which sound would make the bear back off.

None of them.

And no wonder. That bear could easily shred them both. Cass could have sworn the bear rolled its eyes before dropping to all fours and ambling back down the hill.

Legs too weak to stand, Cass sank to the ground. Caesar licked her face. Clutching him, she remained on the ground until they'd both stopped trembling.

Fear that the bear was waiting prompted her to walk slowly,

cautiously. Eventually she decided the bear had gone off. Relief surged through her, her excess adrenaline propelling her to walk fast for the next mile until a gurgle told her she was nearing the creek. There was far less water in it now than there'd been when she hiked the trail with Kent. The creek's roar had subsided to a murmur, but it was still too far for Cass to jump. If she wore her boots into the water, they would tighten, making it harder to hike. She undid the laces, slung the boots around her neck, and hesitated. The creek would still be cold, the rocks slippery.

Caesar scampered across then barked as if encouraging her.

"That's easy for you to say. You have four legs." Steeling herself, she stepped into the cold water. Immediately her feet ached.

Though she slipped and slid, she made it across without falling and dried her feet on weeds. She put her boots back on. Despite the lateness of the night and the thinning air, despite her hunger and lack of sleep, despite the fact she still faced three more—steep—miles, she needed to keep going. She began reciting the chant she and her dad used to say when they hiked: *Left, left, left my wife and forty-nine kids in a starving condition without any gingerbread. Hope I did right, right, right by my country but golly I had a good job when I left. Left. Left my wife* . . . The chant, recited over and over, helped her walk faster.

The trail soon began the steep switchbacks that would take her to the last ridge before the granite rimmed bowl where Juniper Lake nestled. The switchbacks slowed her.

After another forty minutes, she was all but panting. Her fear for Diego and Zoe, however, pushed her to maintain a quick pace. They *had* to be at the lake. She couldn't be making this trek for nothing. Of course, she had no idea how she was going to persuade Zoe to come back with her. In Zoe's place, Cass wasn't so sure she'd be willing to return to living with Rebecca.

The world around her was quiet and still, the air redolent with the scents of fir and pine. No insects sang. No birds hooted. No coyotes yipped. Walking through the dark, moonless night seemed like walking through black velvet. It was a world at peace. Maybe if she inhaled, she could take in at least some of that sweet stillness.

It was nearly 2:00 when Cass crested the final hill that led down to the lake and got her first clear view of the night sky. The Milky Way was an almost solid brush stroke of stars. By the time she reached the lake a few minutes later, her eyes had adjusted enough to take in the massive granite walls that towered straight up on three sides, slabs of rock rising above crystalline water. She smiled, remembering the many times she'd come here with her father.

When she reached the lake's shore, she hollered. "Zoe? Diego? It's Cass. Where are you?"

The echo of her own voice, bouncing off the rock walls around the lake, was her only answer.

"Zoe? Diego? It's just me and Caesar." She strained to hear their voices.

Nothing.

Caesar lapped water from the lake.

Cass's spirits plummeted. Zoe had already run off with Diego. Zoe couldn't have put her hands on much cash, not with so little time to pack and flee. Damn it, why weren't they here? She'd promised Zoe she would be coming for them.

Joyful barks.

"Caesar! Cass!" Zoe's voice came toward her from a darkness lit only by Cass's headlamp and Zoe's small flashlight.

Zoe fell into Cass's arms. Diego came up behind her. Cass held the girl until Zoe stepped back, then embraced Diego "Are you both okay?"

"Yes," Diego said.

"Cass, your face." Zoe sounded horrified.

Cass had forgotten all about her purpled eye, her swollen cheek. "It was an accident," she said. "I'm fine. How are the two of you?"

"Psyched," Zoe said. "We're going to Oregon. It'll be an adventure."

Oh boy. Convincing Zoe to leave Diego was not going to be easy. "Where's your camp?"

Diego pointed. "Behind some boulders."

At nearly 7,600 feet, the lake was above tree line, except for the lone juniper that somehow had survived.

"Bears have come close. Twice." Zoe shivered. "Do they kill people?"

"Not as often as people kill them," Cass said, "but given their size and their claws, they can be a little intimidating."

Diego snorted in mock-derisive humor. Cass smiled. He smiled back.

"I brought you some things," she said. "Let's sit over on that boulder."

Zoe clung to Cass's hand. Cass squeezed and then let go as they sat on the rock so she could open her pack. She took out the jacket she'd brought for Zoe. "Sorry I don't have more. I didn't have much time."

"If I don't come back," Diego said, "they will put you in prison?"

If he knew the truth, he might insist on returning. Cass waved away his concern. "Oh no. They already dropped the charges against me. It was just a misunderstanding about parking tickets."

"I told you," Zoe said.

"That's true?" Diego asked.

"Yes. You're the one in danger." She didn't want to give Diego time to think about her situation. "I brought my map of the Pacific Crest Trail. It runs from Mexico to Canada, though you might consider Nevada. Reno's just a few miles on the other side of the pass and has a big Latino population."

"The mountains call to me," he said. "I hear Enrique."

Like she heard her dad. She took out the cash she'd brought. "The trail north is dotted with occasional stores where you can stock up on food and supplies. I wish I could have brought more." She extended it to him. She couldn't pledge to send more, because she didn't think you earned money in prison.

Diego put up his hands. "No. You need it. I saved some."

She admired his sense of principle, but he needed the money a lot more than she did. "Unless you saved a lot more than I think, please take this. I don't need it. You would do the same for me. Besides, it's for Arturo's sake, too."

"Thank you." He slid the money in his pants' pocket.

They fell silent.

"I'm sorry I lied about having asylum," Diego said.

"Don't worry. I get it." Her father and Enrique, both robbed of life. At least in her own family's case, she and her mother had not been forced to flee for their lives. "Do you know where in Oregon you'll go?"

"No. But I'll find somewhere."

Zoe took his hand. "*We'll* find somewhere. Cass, I've got it all figured out. Diego and I will live somewhere we can blend in. I'll find the people who can get him new papers. We'll both get jobs, and I'll start my fashion business on the side. I'll buy vintage clothes like at Goodwill and turn them into something really cool. I've been studying Instagram. Some kids who design clothes have thousands of followers. I'll buy a stock photo of somebody and put her picture on my website, then I'll write a fashion blog, and sell clothes online. When my company takes off, the first thing we'll do is get Arturo up here. And in a little over a year, when I'm eighteen, I won't be a runaway. Mom couldn't do anything. I'll post my real picture.

It'll be epic. Can you believe it, Cass? I thought of it all myself."

"I can sure hear your enthusiasm," Cass said.

Zoe's body went rigid. "But . . . ?" Her voice held the tone of belligerence Cass had often heard Zoe use with Rebecca.

"What will your mother do to try to find you?" Diego asked.

"Oh, *everything*. She'll print up fliers with my picture and make sure they're posted in every store, post office, and police station. I bet she'll even hire some ex-cop to find me. Which he won't." Zoe made a brushing motion with her arm as if sweeping away the possibility. "My mother can do whatever she wants. That's *her* problem."

Diego took Zoe's hand. "No. It's *my* problem, Zoe. Mine and Arturo's. My family's."

Zoe opened her mouth to speak, closed it, then suddenly brightened. "I know! We'll make enough money to hire a really good lawyer, and they'll figure out how to make you safe."

Cass and Diego's eyes met. "What if they can't?" Diego said.

"Are you willing to risk Diego's *life*?" Cass said.

"Why are you saying this stuff?" Zoe looked from one of them to the other, her expression shouting her determination and her rage.

It was a rage Cass could well understand.

"If you're trying to talk me into going back to live with my mother, forget it. After what she's done? No way. I'm going with you, Diego. I'll protect you. I've got credit cards. I can get cash advances. You'll need money for food and stuff."

"If you use those cards," Diego said, "your mom will know where you are. And where I am."

"Diego?" Zoe's voice was a plea.

"I don't *want* to tell you goodbye," he said. "But I can't get caught."

Tears slid down Zoe's cheeks. "You don't want me?"

Cass's heart went out to her. Zoe looked so devastated, so young.

"Of *course* I want you. But I can't take the risk of being sent back to be killed."

Zoe flinched, let out a wail, then collapsed, sobbing, against Diego.

He clasped her to him. "Shhh," he murmured. "It'll be okay. Shhh."

Cass looked up at the Milky Way. A shooting star streaked across the sky. She closed her eyes and made a silent wish that both Zoe and Diego would live long, joyful lives, and that Diego's family would be safe.

Another star fell. Cass wished for Mack's return, and for their friendship to be rekindled—preferably outside of prison.

Another. A wish for Caesar to be adopted by good people. Another star. A wish for Loon's citizens to stop fighting and come together.

"Look up," she said. "I think it's a meteor shower."

Zoe's "ohh . . ." and Diego's *Dios mio* gave voice to Cass's own sense of wonder. She glanced out at the lake that looked as dark as a raven's wing. Reflected in the water, the stars seemed to shoot across both sky and lake, at a rate of one or more per minute.

Cass leaned back on the boulder and watched, vaguely aware that Diego and Zoe had lain back, too, the girl cradled against the boy.

At this elevation, and in the absence of a moon, the streaking stars were incandescent. Cass had never seen so many. The long, thin trails of meteors looked like someone was trying to stitch up the universe and make it whole.

Odd to think that she was but a speck in a world with billions of stars. And people. It wasn't a bad feeling so much as a humbling one. By the time the meteor shower stopped, she and Diego and Zoe still lying there looking up at the sky, her fears had melted. Spending a few years in prison certainly wasn't anything she wanted to do, but she would survive. Maybe she could even grow. She might take some college classes, if they had them.

For her, prison would be temporary. She wished the same were true about the violence in Honduras and elsewhere.

"Even though we live in a world with so many terrible things," Diego said softly, "I hope I can remember that it's also a world with so many stars."

Amen, Cass whispered. If only the world could experience what she felt now. Acceptance. Serenity. She was unlikely to sustain that feeling forever, but at least she had this night, this memory, that she could bring out and blow on, like a small flame she could kindle so that, from time to time, it would blaze bright again.

FORTY

"Zoe's gone."

Diego's words jolted Cass awake from the boulder where she'd dozed. She'd stayed up most of the night, savoring the stars, the silence, and the gentle ease with which darkness slid into light. "Gone where?" She glanced around: no Caesar. Had he left with Zoe?

Diego's frown formed deep vertical creases between his eyes. He set his bulging backpack on the boulder beside Cass and handed her a note. "She left this."

On a page ripped from a notebook, torn holes fringing its left side, Zoe had written in purple ink, her handwriting full of elegant loops.

> Diego & Cass: I can't live with my mother after what she did. I'll go somewhere and use my credit cards. That way Mom and the police won't look for you heading north, Diego. Don't

*worry. I know what I'm doing, and I'm fine.
Love, Z.*

"And this." He handed her a second note.

*Mother. I can't live with you after what you
did. Goodbye.*

Rebecca was not going to like this. Cass folded the note and stuffed it in her pocket.

"I will go after Zoe," Diego said. "She hasn't hiked the mountains enough. It's not safe."

Cass couldn't search for Zoe without endangering Chance. And herself. Nor could she explain that to Diego since she didn't want him to know she'd lied, that she still faced criminal charges.

What surprised her was the discovery that she felt sure Zoe would be safe. It seemed to Cass that she was still in touch with the stars, the universe. Or maybe that was just wishful thinking. Either way, there was nothing she or Diego could do.

"This might seem strange," she said, "but I'm pretty sure Zoe will be fine. She's been hiking with you enough, and she loves the mountains."

"What if she falls? She could get hurt."

"It's possible, but not likely. The thing is, the longer you hang around, the greater the chance the police will find you. And send you back."

Diego looked torn. "Can you search for Zoe?"

"Which way? East? South? West? We've no idea, and I don't know how to track people. Caesar, wherever he is, isn't a bloodhound. Plus, I need to get back to the kennel."

Diego didn't look convinced.

"You know, I've come to realize that Zoe's got a lot of moxie," Cass said.

"'Moxie?'"

"Spunk. Strength. Determination. She's got *all* that, right?"

He smiled. "Yes. Zoe has moxie." His smile faded. "I'll miss her," he whispered before turning to face her. "And you, Cass. I'll miss *you*."

"And I you, Diego." Cass felt the heat of beginning tears, a reflection of those forming in his eyes.

He opened his mouth to speak.

A loud bark from the trees near the lake was soon followed by Caesar bounding toward them. Diego knelt and buried his face in Caesar's fur.

Cass paused to give Diego and herself a moment to move beyond grief. Not because sorrow was bad, but because saying goodbye hurt so much.

"Goodbye, amigo," Diego said to Caesar, then rose and hugged Cass in a long, warm embrace.

When they separated, reality hit her; she might never see him again. "I hate the word 'goodbye'," she said.

"*Hasta luego*, is better." Diego released her. "*Till then*, or *till next time*."

"Promise me there will be a next time, one way or another."

"Claro, *hermana mia*. We are *familia*."

Family. For her, after her father died, family didn't exist until Mack and Seamus opened their hearts and home to her. Now Diego, and his family, had become part of hers. She was having to say goodbye to all of them. Cass coughed to avert her tears. She wanted to grab Diego and not let go. "Always," she said, using one of Diego's favorite words. "Always, *hermano mio*."

The sun would soon rise over the peak. "It's going to be hot today," she said. "You should go."

"Thank you, Cass. You have done so much for me."

"No. Thank *you*. From the first time we met. I was a stranger and you—that dog—the umbrella." Her voice caught. There was more she wanted to say. Cass clenched her fists, squeezing hard, trying to lessen her grief. She wanted to thank him for all the ways he'd helped her with the kennel—and so much more. Like sharing the incredible coffee from Enrique, that beautiful young man with the cocky grin. And for sharing his family on Zoom calls, from his parents to Enrique and little Arturo, *bird boy*. Not to mention all the work he'd done around the kennel. She tried to suck in air, but her throat, too, seemed to brim with tears. All this time, Diego had not been just an employee. Rather, he was someone she'd come to respect, admire, and love, someone who had done more for her than she'd ever done for him. She wanted to tell him that, but if she opened her mouth to speak, she didn't think she could restrain her sobs. She took a few breaths to calm herself. When she thought she could choke out her words, she tried again. "Thank you . . . for being . . . the amazing young man you are . . . despite . . . all you've witnessed."

Diego's eyes seemed to echo the sorrow in hers, but then he straightened and wiped his bandana across them. He seemed to wrest control of his sadness. He even smiled at her.

The sun was rising high enough to blister the land. He needed to go. "Be safe," she said. "*Hasta luego*, Diego."

"*Hasta luego*, Cass." He shouldered his pack, saluted her, turned, and headed north.

Cass stood watching until Diego crested the ridge and disappeared from view. Beside her, Caesar whimpered. "Yeah," she said. "Me, too."

Cass released her tears, which streamed down her cheeks, tears for Diego and Zoe and a few for herself. She would miss them so much.

She walked down to the lake and surveyed the indigo water. Undisturbed by even a slight breeze, the water was still, the early morning reflections of the mountain peaks that ringed the lake crisp.

The last time she'd been at this lake, Kent had been with her. It seemed like a lifetime ago, in someone else's life.

Kneeling, she splashed water on her face. She felt like she was communing with the lake, the mountains, the universe, felt again the certainty that Zoe would be fine. "Please, Universe," she said the words aloud, "please protect Diego. And Zoe, too. And please, if it's safe, bring him back. Bring them both back."

Caesar's bark startled her. She glanced at her watch. "Oh." She hadn't realized it was so late. She stood.

Caesar wagged his tail, looking eager.

"Okay, boy," she told him. "We've got to keep up a good pace so we don't give Chance a heart attack. Nothing to it but to do it."

They set off back down the trail, Caesar trotting in the lead. As she walked, Cass tried to take in every boulder, every wildflower, every weathered tree she passed. It could be a long time before she saw them again.

FORTY-ONE

"Wait there," Chance instructed Cass when she called him as she neared the kennel.

Cass glanced at her watch: 10:13.

Chance arrived, brakes screeching, almost before Cass could disconnect the call.

"You're late," he said as he came through the kennel door.

"I know. I'm sorry. But it was only thirteen minutes."

"Thirteen *long* minutes." Dark bags shadowed his eyes. "Where's Zoe?"

"Gone, but not with Diego."

"Gone where?"

"I honestly don't know. She wrote this for Rebecca."

Chance read the note she handed him. "Great," he said. "Rebecca will probably call out the National Guard. Not to mention the Army, Navy, Air Force and Marines." He slapped handcuffs around Cass's wrists.

"Sorry about stressing you," she said. "Just one second." From the closet where she kept a few clothes for emergencies, she grabbed the only good clothes there: clean cargo pants and a navy-blue shirt, glad she didn't have to wear a football jersey to court. "I thought I should look more like an upstanding citizen, less like a serial killer."

He grunted.

"I need one more favor," she said before they left the kennel office.

"Uh-uh. No way. Whatever you're about to ask, forget it."

"I know I owe you, not vice versa."

"You got that right."

She didn't have anyone else to turn to. "Could you please just keep Caesar until I can make bail Monday?"

Chance glared at her but looked down at Caesar, who sat on the floor and looked right back. "Oh, why not?" Chance said. "Bullet will be glad, and Caesar will be a lot more fun to have around than Rebecca." He glanced at the note in his hand. "Especially when she reads this."

Caesar gave a single wag of his tail.

Chance squatted and petted him for a few seconds, then stood. "Let's get a move on."

He put both Caesar and Cass into the back of his patrol car. Caesar lay across Cass's lap, grinning as she scratched his stomach.

Chance drove at a speed considerably above the limit, though he didn't turn on the siren. He must have been so scared, Cass thought. "Thank you," she said to him when he ushered her out of the car.

Air puffed from his lips. "You're not welcome. That was the longest twelve hours of my life. And all for nothing."

If only she could tell him that the time he'd courageously given her had allowed her to give Diego the money she had, and gave him time to talk Zoe out of going with him. Both had made Diego safer. Cass just hoped her instinct that Zoe was fine was right. "One day," she said to Chance, "I hope to tell you why it *wasn't* for nothing."

"Thank God" burst from Rebecca the instant they entered the office. She jumped up from the desk chair. After a moment, her look of joy faded into one of confusion. "Where's my daughter?" She glanced back at the door, waiting for Zoe to appear.

Though Chance looked like he'd rather do just about anything else—including eat live tarantulas—he handed Rebecca Zoe's short note. Rebecca glanced at it, then scowled at Cass. "You promised to bring her back."

"I said I'd *try*. She refused to come."

"She's seventeen," Rebecca said. "It shouldn't have been up to her."

"How would you have suggested I *make* her return?"

"Where did she go?"

"I've no idea," Cass said. "I dozed off, and when I woke up, she was gone."

"You're lying."

Cass started to respond with sarcasm but stopped herself. Rebecca looked so hurt, so forlorn, so desperate, Cass softened her voice. "No, I'm not. That's the truth."

"Chance," Rebecca said, turning back to him, "you need to put out a bulletin about Zoe being kidnapped."

"She wasn't kidnapped," Cass said. "She left of her own free will."

"You'd say anything to protect *him*. Even at Zoe's expense. I bet you didn't even try to bring her back. You told her some sob story about going to prison. You upset her so much, there was no way she'd come home. You want revenge."

"Not revenge. Justice."

Rebecca's nostrils flared. "Oh, you'll get that. I'm the DA's star witness. I'll make sure you get all the justice you've got coming. All ten years' worth. See you in court, Cass." Rebecca slammed the door behind her.

"Sorry, Cass, but . . ." Chance gestured her to the cell area.

Cass smiled. "It's okay. I'll be fine." She reentered the cell, Caesar right beside her.

Forty-Two

The shower had only dribbled water, and the fragrance of the mottled green and white bar of soap had been nothing like Cass imagined an Irish spring would smell, but it was good to feel clean again. Once she'd finished her shower and dressed, Chance locked her back in her cell until time to head to her arraignment.

"That's a flat-out lie." Chance's voice a few minutes later: shouting.

Cass prayed for his sake that nobody, especially not DA Lawrence Tyson, had spotted her outside of jail on her search for Diego and Zoe. She strained to hear, but if Chance's shout had been a hurled brick, the response was a cat's purr: soft and steady and just below Cass's hearing.

Chance swung open the door to the cell area.

Cass gripped the cell bars. "Mack!"

"Hi, Cass." Mack greeted her like it was just another routine day. From their old routine, pre-Felicity.

"Nobody will believe you," Chance said, hands on his hips. "You were *not* there."

Unlike Chance's agitated voice, Mack's sounded calm,

matter of fact. "Just because you didn't see me doesn't mean I wasn't there."

It was as if every word Mack spoke was followed by a period.

"You weren't where?" Cass said.

"You're really going to perjure yourself?" Chance glared at Mack.

"What's going on?" Cass looked from the sheriff to Mack, who stood an inch or so above Chance and wore gray slacks and tailored shirt, rather than her usual denim and flannel.

"Chance doesn't believe I was there when he arrested you," Mack said, "but I was."

"You were?" Cass said.

"I was in the back playing with Bella. I saw you hurry after Chance, pleading Diego's case. You tripped and fell forward. You weren't *trying* to tackle him."

"Then why didn't you make yourself known?" Chance said.

"Cass and I were feuding. I thought some time in jail might bring her back to her senses."

"That's bullshit." Chance was again close to yelling.

Mack just smiled.

Chance expelled air as he rubbed both temples in an apparent attempt to calm down. "If my heart survives all this, it will be a miracle."

"Not at all. You have a big heart," Mack said.

"I already told Tyson that Cass tackled me."

"Was he there?"

"Of course not, but Rebecca was."

"Rebecca? Her tormenting of Cass goes way back. Ask anyone who went to school with them. Rebecca's mistaken or lying. I saw it all quite clearly. Cass was so busy pleading with you, she just forgot where her feet were."

Chance looked directly at Cass for the first time during this talk. "Damn it, Cass. Why did you have to tackle me?"

She held his gaze; he knew the answer.

"Only she didn't," Mack said.

"Yeah, yeah."

Mack added, softly, "Even if you don't believe me, isn't it possible? And whether my testimony's accurate or not, do you want to put Cass in prison for *ten years*? For helping Diego?"

Chance looked at his watch. "It's time to go. Mack, please tell me you aren't going to interfere with my taking Cass to the courthouse."

Mack held up her hands. "Of course not. In fact, I'd like to ride along if that's okay."

"Fine." Chance snapped handcuffs on Cass. He led her to the police car and opened the back door. Cass slid in. Mack scooted in from the other side for the nearly hourlong drive to the county seat and the courtroom. Chance turned on the ignition. The car coughed, sputtered, and died.

"Jesus," he muttered. "I can't wait for this day to be over."

Cass's mind reeled. Mack was risking prison to make up a defense for her? No way. But she didn't want to blurt it out. She leaned over and spoke as quietly as she could. "I'm not letting you perjure yourself."

"It's not perjury if it's true."

Cass pictured the trampled rose bushes. "I'm sorry about your roses," she said. "If only I'd listened to you in the first place, they wouldn't have been destroyed. I'm so, so sorry."

Sadness flitted across Mack's face, then vanished. "Me, too, but you mean more to me than they did. Besides, you didn't stomp my roses or switch photos. Kent kept calling till I finally answered. He explained that Rebecca deliberately changed the photo at the last minute. I shouldn't have blamed you."

"I guess I wanted so desperately to believe she'd changed. Really changed."

"It's tricky, isn't it?" Mack said. "When to hold on to the past and when to let it go."

"Obviously I let it go too soon."

Mack squeezed Cass's hand. "I'm sorry, too."

"You didn't do anything wrong."

"I shouldn't have run away," Mack said. "I apologize for that."

"Where did you go?"

"To Monterey. I stayed at the inn where Seamus and I used to vacation." Mack's eyes took on a moist, faraway look. "I wanted to reclaim him after what happened to the roses."

"I wish I'd never suggested changing the town," Cass said. "Everything just backfired."

"You cared enough to try to make things better. And got clobbered for it, I might add. That's a striking souvenir."

Reflexively, Cass brought her hands up to touch her face, which made it hurt. She dropped her arms.

"Actually," Mack said, "some of the changes have been good for the town. We do need more jobs and more revenue. You got that conversation started."

"I should have been upfront with you about how many tourists might come."

"Water under the bridge."

"Let me get this straight." Chance looked at them in the rearview mirror. "Mack, you ran away, and now you want to make it up to Cass by lying to defend her?"

"I'm not lying."

Mack spoke with such conviction even Cass wondered if her friend's version of events could be true. No. She knew better. She looked out at the day. A billowy white cloud seemed to be balancing atop a massive fir. "Maybe we could think of a way to change some of the things about the town's makeover," Cass said. "You know, the parts that cause the most problems."

"We should try," Mack said. "We should all try."

When they made the final turn onto the main avenue of the county seat, Cass thought a parade must be about to start.

People lined the block leading to the courthouse, some of them waving signs. She wondered what the occasion was.

That's when they got close enough to read the signs: *Free Cass*.

"Great," Chance mumbled. "Just great."

He parked, then opened the door for Mack and an astonished Cass. As Chance led her up the courthouse steps, a chant broke out: *Don't be an ass. Free Cass*, spoken over and over by most of the crowd.

There had to be well over a hundred people. All of them had come for her? Cass's head reeled. Mack must have done something to mobilize them.

Near the courthouse door, a very pregnant Jewel brandished a very white poster board, its *Free Cass* message sparkling in the sunshine. Standing near each other, Scotty and Garrett waved similar signs, and they weren't arguing. Shirley Dawkins from the café was there, as were Jonas and Lily and Rosalind and Maya, plus a whole lot of other people.

"We're with you, Cass," Jewel called.

"Amen," Jonas said.

"I know you're a great organizer," Cass said to Mack, "but how did you pull this off?"

"I just suggested it to Scotty, Jewel and Jonas; they ran with it. These people aren't here for me, Cass. They're here for you."

How was that possible? Unless, maybe, what she'd thought she'd seen in so many people's eyes wasn't judgment, but acceptance.

Chance escorted her into the courthouse, Mack at her side. Cass blinked. It had been so bright outside. The dark, wood-paneled courtroom looked somber, but it didn't summon up the fear Cass had felt when she was first arrested.

Chance led her toward the defendant's table. A man sat with his back to her, working on some papers. He must be her lawyer; she hoped he was a good one.

Chance uncuffed her and handed her off to the man, who reached out his hand. "James Dunne," he said. "I'm your public defender."

The cuffs of the man's brown suit jacket looked worn, well on the path to frayed. That plus his stark white shirt and green bow tie were a far cry from chief prosecutor Lawrence Tyson, at the prosecution table, who looked like he'd spent the night in a refrigerator drawer, everything about him crisp: short hair, charcoal pants and jacket, white linen shirt, purple-and-blue tie.

Cass hoped James Dunne was a better attorney than dresser. "You're my public defender?" she said.

"Yes, Ms. Irvin."

"I'm not Ms. Irvin." How could this man defend her when he thought she was somebody else?

"Oh." He checked a paper in front of him. "Right. Sorry. You're Ms. Enger. Cass Enger. Good thing for you. Ms. Irvin's charged with murder." The attorney took off his glasses and rubbed his eyes. "I assume you'll be entering a plea of not guilty."

Cass leaned toward him. "But I'm, I mean . . ."

James Dunne held up his hand. "Stop. Let me point out to you that the burden of proof is on the DA. Let's not do his job for him. There's usually room for doubt. It's your choice, but I strongly urge you to plead not guilty."

Cass's pulse sped up. She was sitting beside a lawyer who thought she was someone else, in a courtroom for the first time in her life. She *was* guilty . . . of doing what was right. How *should* she plead?

A bailiff dressed in a khaki uniform called that it was time to settle down. That's when Cass turned around and saw that people from outside were trying to cram into a room that held maybe fifty. It was a standing room crowd. Jewel, seated near the front, flashed her a thumbs-up. Her encouragement helped

Cass settle.

Chance took a seat beside Tyson, who leaned over to whisper something to the sheriff.

The bailiff commanded all to rise for Judge Eugene Burdick. Tyson sprang off his chair.

Judge Burdick lumbered into the room and plopped down in his seat, his stomach growling so loud Cass thought his robe must be hiding a poodle.

The instant they sat, Mack rose. "Your honor, I'm Mackenzie Macdonald, and I just want to let the DA know that I was at the kennel the day Cass was arrested. I witnessed everything. She did not tackle the sheriff. She tripped and fell into him. It clearly wasn't intentional."

Tyson shot to his feet. "If Ms. Macdonald so testifies under oath, I will bring perjury charges."

"The defense can call you as a witness during the trial, Ms. Macdonald," the judge said. "You can testify then."

Mack sat. Jewel stood, cradling her pregnant girth. "I was there, too, your honor. And I saw the same thing."

Jonas rose. "Me, too."

Scotty stood. "Ditto."

Beside Cass, her attorney smiled.

Tyson practically sputtered. "These people are lying. All of them."

The judge rapped his gavel. "How many of you folks in the audience claim to have been at the kennel and are prepared to testify that Ms. Enger tripped?"

Lily stood. So did Rosalind. And Shirley. Councilman Lewis Jennings pushed through the crowd to join those standing. Cass's eyes widened. Eight people were willing to go to jail to save her? *Her?*

Tyson leapt to his feet. "I'll prosecute all of you." He pointed at Jewel. "Your baby can visit you in your cell."

Judge Burdick's stomach rumbled even louder as he again

rapped his gavel. He looked at Chance. "Sheriff, let me ask you this. Is there any chance Ms. Enger did not take you down deliberately?"

Tyson stayed on his feet. "Your honor, this is an arraignment. None of these witnesses has been or can be sworn in for an arraignment."

"I'm aware of the law, but I'm curious. None of this goes on the record, true, but it might affect how high I set Ms. Enger's bail. I trust you'll indulge me, counselor. Sheriff?"

The courtroom fell silent, except for the judge's lingering digestive noises. Cass clasped her hands on the table, waiting for Chance's response.

"Judge, Ms. Enger was behind me. I assumed it was deliberate, but I suppose it's possible that she tripped."

Tyson turned to his witness. "You're an officer of the law. Act like one."

Chance just shrugged.

"Will you be calling any other witnesses at the trial, Mr. Tyson?" the judge said.

"Yes. Loon's mayor, Rebecca Oliver, witnessed the assault on Sheriff Garner."

"Rebecca, where are you?" the judge said.

"Here, Judge." Rebecca walked part way down the aisle.

Could the woman walk with any more confidence, any more poise? If Cass didn't know better, she'd have been ready to believe Rebecca's every utterance.

"How are you doing?" the judge asked. "Enjoying being mayor?"

"I am, your honor. Thanks."

"Good. Now, please tell the court what you saw."

Rebecca glared at Cass and all but smirked, clearly savoring this moment. She opened her mouth to speak, but the voice that broke the silence was not hers.

"Mom, wait!"

Cass turned.

There was a commotion. Zoe nudged her way through the pack of standing onlookers.

Thank God her instincts had been right, Cass thought; Zoe was safe and dressed in a burgundy cashmere sweater. Cass would swear that Zoe looked more like Rebecca than she had a few days ago.

"Remember, Mom, what you told me?" Zoe said. "I'd texted you about having another detention. You were all angry, and you were looking down at your phone, so you didn't see what happened."

Tyson was on his feet and pointing at Zoe. "That young lady has a track record that clearly establishes her unreliability. A perjury conviction will land her in Juvie. Keep that in mind, Zoe, before you tell lies."

"The young Ms. Oliver is not on trial at the moment," Judge Burdick said. "Rebecca, what did you see?"

Rebecca looked at Cass, at the judge, at Tyson, at Zoe. She visibly tensed, like whatever she was about to say was being ripped from her. "Zoe's right. I got her text, and when I looked back up, Sheriff Garner was already on the ground."

Tyson's jaw dropped.

"Counselor," Judge Burdick said to Tyson, "it appears you have no witnesses, which means you have no case unless you wish to prosecute the defendant for being clumsy."

"Your Honor, Ms. Enger deliberately tackled the sheriff to keep him from arresting an illegal immigrant. These are dangerous times for first responders." Tyson put his hand on Chance's shoulder. "We can't tolerate assaults on officers of the law. Furthermore, Ms. Enger enabled an illegal immigrant to escape and is withholding evidence about his location. This is a critical case. We need to send the message that such behaviors will not be tolerated." He pounded his fist against his palm for punctuation.

"You may be right," Judge Burdick said. "Then again, given that you can't prove obstruction with intent, you might want to drop the charges to a misdemeanor and ask for time served. It's up to you. We can proceed and schedule a trial date. Of course, if you lose, it won't enhance your reputation, and judging by this crowd, you might have trouble getting a jury sympathetic to your case. If you go with a misdemeanor, we can put the accused on probation with the understanding that if she repeats this alleged offense, she will be charged with a felony. What do you say?"

Tyson scowled at the judge, scowled at Cass, scowled at the others present. "Agreed," he said finally, the word sounding squeezed out of a very tight tube.

"Ms. Enger," the judge said, "how do you plead to a misdemeanor offense of hindering an arrest?"

Cass didn't ask her lawyer before answering. "Guilty, your honor." It felt more honest to admit to *something*.

"Very well, and you do understand that a repeat offense will mean felony charges?"

"Yes, sir."

"I sentence you to five years' probation and time served." Judge Burdick rapped his gavel hard. "Court's adjourned. Ms. Enger, you're free to go."

Spectators cheered, many of them crowding around Cass, hugging her, shaking her hand, all of them plus Mack, smiling. By the time she'd received everyone's congratulations and turned back to her public defender, he was gone.

So was Rebecca.

Zoe came up to her. They embraced, then Zoe stepped back, giving Cass an accusatory look. "You lied. You said the charges were dropped."

"I didn't think Diego would leave if he knew," she said. "How did you find out?"

"I called Angelique. I'm glad I did."

"Me, too." Cass shook her head, bewildered by all that had happened this day. "What are you going to do now?"

"I want to live at the kennel and help you."

"The kennel's closed."

"I can change that."

"Even if you could, your mom would never let you live there."

"It's not up to her. Either she reopens the kennel and agrees to my plan, or I'm gone, and she'll never see me again." Zoe spoke softly when she said, "Maybe Diego will find his way back, at least to say hello."

"I hope you know how much your mom loves you. She changed her testimony to protect you. You do understand that, right?"

Zoe shrugged. "Yeah, well she's the reason all this happened. She's got a lot to make up for."

Mack strode up to them. "Way to go, Zoe. You saved the day."

Zoe blushed, which made Cass smile. Zoe didn't get caught off guard very often. She herself had certainly been caught off guard today by the unexpected and undeniable support of so many people.

Mack put an arm around Cass. "Let's get out of here before Tyson or the judge changes his mind."

Flanked by Zoe and Mack, Cass walked out of the courtroom into a morning vibrant with sunshine.

Zoe glanced around. "I wonder where Kent went."

"He was here?" Cass said.

"Yeah. In the back next to me. I called him because I figured he'd want to know."

Oh well. A *Free Cass* poster lay on the courthouse steps, a footprint smeared across her name. She picked it up. She'd keep it so that any time she felt unlovable, she could look at the sign and know better. Even she, as slow as she sometimes

was about matters of the heart, would have a hard time forget-
ting what had happened here this morning, this very unexpected morning. She was disappointed that Kent hadn't
lingered, but that did nothing to diminish her glorious sense of
wonder.

FORTY-THREE

It was one of those hot August days when the sun beat down so hot, it seemed to Cass like the land would blister. Still, in the past few days, there'd been hints—in a few yellowing trees, in the softening of the light—that autumn was whispering, *Here I come.*

Cass watched Caesar romp with Coco, a white Dalmatian with a single black spot, in Coco's pen. The two dogs had become inseparable when given the option. Once they collapsed, panting in the heat, Cass turned the hose on the two. As always, they leapt up into the spray, snapping at the water, issuing happy barks.

Sweat rolled down Cass's neck. Lucky dogs. She would love to have someone spray her.

Wait. That was silly. She didn't need someone else to do that. She lifted the hose overhead and turned it on herself. The spray struck her head, then streamed down her body, cooling her, creating what felt like rainbows all over her skin.

Thoroughly wet, she turned off the hose. The dogs flung water as they shook themselves. She chased them around the pen, smiling, something she'd done a lot of since her hearing three weeks before.

Cass towel-dried the dogs, then herself, wiping mud off all their feet, then went inside and sat at the desk. Zoe, attending the last day of summer school, had told Cass she'd be back at the kennel by 2:00. Right after Rebecca rescinded the kennel's closure order, Zoe had moved into the kennel apartment and taken on Diego's chores. If Zoe didn't quite have Diego's natural instincts with the dogs, she came close. And she was learning. Cass was happy to pay her.

Cass pulled out her account ledger to update information she'd need to calculate her estimated quarterly taxes. She had no idea she'd drifted off until a clamor of barking woke her. Footsteps were approaching.

"Hi," Kent said.

In her half-awake state, Cass was so astonished to see Kent standing in the doorway that she almost wondered if he were a figment of her imagination. "Hi."

"Congratulations on your hearing."

"Thanks."

Kent leaned back against the wall, dressed as always in a T-shirt, vest, and jeans. "And congratulations for all the well-deserved support you got."

"Sometimes I still have trouble believing I didn't dream it."

"I would've hired you a good lawyer if you'd needed one."

"I'll keep that in mind."

"Oh? You planning to get rearrested?"

She smiled. "You never know."

"There's something I need you to do," he said.

"What's that?"

"I've got a good start on a new Felicity novel."

"Really?"

"Yep. I threw out the version you didn't like. You were right about it. I'm on a roll, and I'd like you to critique it for me in three or four months when I'm done with the first draft. Will you? I promise not to get defensive."

She'd never told him she'd dumped his books in her recycling bin, not because she was angry with him—she wasn't—but because she'd lost her faith in books. In fiction. Reality had seemed to trample hope. Now she had room to dream again. "I'd love to read it," she said.

"Good. It's about the risks we take to protect those we love, even the risk of imprisonment."

Shock jerked Cass back . . . two-hundred volts worth of shock. "Seriously?"

"Do you mind?"

"No, I guess not. I thought you were finished with Felicity."

"That's what I thought, but the idea of risking so much for those we care about opened all kinds of story possibilities."

Cass had been shocked enough to have so many people rally behind her, and now *this*. "Zoe said you were at the hearing. Why didn't you stick around to say hello?"

Kent tapped his fist against his mouth a couple times. "Well . . . it's, uh . . ." He shrugged, looking like he wished he'd just kept his mouth shut.

Curious what had him tongue-tied, Cass wanted to prod, but she suspected it was better to let him decide whether to explain.

Scattered barks punctuated the ensuing silence. Caesar thrust his muzzle against Kent's leg. Kent petted him, but his mind seemed elsewhere.

"Okay." Still standing, Kent shook his shoulders. "I don't know if you remember this. You must have been eleven or twelve. You were walking down the sidewalk past a trio of boys hanging out in front of the outdoor gear store drinking Cokes. As you went by, the boys hooted and called you stuff."

"I remember that, sure. Before that happened, I could sometimes tell myself it was just Rebecca, but to have strangers do it? That was one of the worst days of my life."

Kent reddened.

"Wait. How did you know about it?"

Kent looked down. "I was one of them."

"What?"

It took him a moment to meet her gaze. "My folks had said I could invite a couple friends for our usual summer vacation here. We were thirteen and that odd mix of cocky and insecure. I didn't see your face when you went by because I was looking at the mountains, but when the other boys taunted you, I joined in."

"Why?"

"I wanted to fit in. I wasn't brave like you were with Diego. You risked far more than scorn."

"Thirteen's a harder age to be brave than thirty-two. Besides, with Diego it wasn't a matter of bravery. It was a matter of love."

"I can see that." Kent rubbed one hand with the other. After a moment's silence, he continued. "That day when we taunted you, that's how I *really* met Seamus. He saw us and chased us. The other guys were a lot faster than I was. Seamus caught me. And shamed me."

"He was a really good man," Cass said.

"Yeah. He had a kind of charisma, I guess, because when he invited me back to his house for lunch, I went. We didn't talk about what had happened. He asked me how I felt about school and sports and stuff. I never told my friends. And I never made fun of anyone again."

"I see." Cass petted Caesar, standing beside her. She was unsure what she thought about what Kent had revealed.

"There was more to it, though," he said. "When we taunted you, you kind of raised your head. Like this." He raised his chin, and his head went up in a way that suggested strength.

"Huh?" she said, confused.

"Don't you see?" Kent sounded excited. "That small act of defiance. It stayed with me."

"I was probably just straightening up so I didn't choke on my tears," she said.

Kent sat in the chair beside the desk and leaned toward her. "Cass, that's what inspired me to create Felicity."

"What is?"

"You. That strength of character, that defiance amid so much pain."

"That inspired Felicity?"

"*You* inspired Felicity."

She almost pinched herself. Was this conversation real?

Kent's eyes brightened. "I wanted to explain to you what happened and to thank you for being Felicity's role model. And, although it's way late, I wanted to apologize and ask for your forgiveness."

"Well, sure. I mean, that was a long time ago. We were both just scared kids."

"Thank you. You're doing it now, you know."

"What?"

"Your head. You raised it up, just like you did back then. And in the courtroom. You did it there, too. That's when I knew you were the girl we'd mocked. I was ashamed; *that's* why I didn't stick around."

Cass had trouble absorbing what he was saying. Had she really inspired Felicity? Was it possible that she had a kind of strength she'd never allowed herself to see?

Neither Kent nor she spoke for what felt like a long time. Dogs barked occasionally. A fly buzzed into the room, landing on Caesar's nose. He twitched. Cass brushed the fly away.

"Thank you for telling me that," she said. "I suspect it wasn't easy."

"Thank *you*," he said.

Their eyes met for a lingering moment. He stood. "I need to get back to L.A. to write while the book's flowing. Don't want to lose the momentum." He handed her a business card. "That one's got my private cell number. If anyone hassles you about Diego, or anything else, or you just need to talk, call me."

"I will. Thanks."

"Take care of yourself, Cass Enger."

"You, too, Kent Calloway."

He turned and was gone.

To think that all this time, she didn't need to struggle to become someone else. She simply needed to become who she was.

She would get new copies of the books she'd thrown away, to reread them with today's revelations in mind. And she wanted to read other books, too, to meet new characters and explore new worlds. Not to mention that she would like to get to know more real people with worlds of their own.

Caesar barked, sprinting from the office. What had gotten into him? Oh well. He'd be back.

He soon reappeared with a set of keys dangling from his mouth. Cass bent to take them. They were coated with slobber that she wiped off with a paper towel. "Where did you get these?"

Kent appeared in the doorway looking so befuddled she couldn't help but laugh. She handed him the now-dry keys. "Sorry about that. I guess he didn't want you to go."

Kent nodded. And then he leaned toward her. "May I kiss you?"

She froze. "Kiss me?"

"Right. You know, on the lips. Like people do."

"Oh. Okay. Sure." He didn't put his arms around her, but he leaned down and put his lips to hers. They kissed for a long moment.

He pulled away. "I don't know . . ."

"I don't either." Cass had so many questions, but for this day, this moment, she didn't need answers. She just looked into Kent's soft green eyes and smiled.

"See you in a few months," he said.

"I'll be here." Cass walked him to the parking lot and watched until his car disappeared from view.

On the way back to the office, she and Caesar stopped in the outdoor ring. The aspens would soon turn that glorious, shimmering gold. And today, as the sun started to set, Moon and the peaks around her would be touched by the setting sun's rays, creating the soft alpine glow that seemed a blend of red and gold, fire and ember, darkness and dawn.

Cass squatted beside Caesar, who sat with his tongue hanging out his mouth, his lips pulled back in a grin. She gently shook her dog's head. *Whoozagoodboy?* she said. "Are you a good boy, Caesar?"

He barked.

She took that as a yes.

THE END

A Request

Reviews are the lifeblood of independent publishers and authors. If you liked meeting Cass and her friends and frenemies, please leave a review on one of the many sites that review books. Sign up for the Mumblers Press newsletter at https://mumblerspress.com. to get the latest news on *Becoming Felicity*, Jan Stites, and Mumblers events, books and authors.

Warmest thanks,
Mumblers Press LLC

Discussion Questions

1. Who's your favorite character? Was this true from the start of the book? What drew you to the character?

2. In Cass's position of having been bullied so much, do you think you'd have been able/willing to reach out to and work with Rebecca? Have you seen many bullies in action? Have you ever intervened on behalf of someone who was the target of bullying?

3. There are basically two approaches to the town's future. Do you side more with Mack's position or Rebecca's? Do you see any other options that might be ways to build Loon's economy without sacrificing its essence/community?

4. Should Chance be punished for what he did in allowing Cass to leave jail to search for Zoe? Can you think of any situations that might make you break the law to this degree?

5. Which books, if any, do you find yourself rereading, the way Cass reads Felicity? Have any books been so

important to you that you turned to them in difficult times?

6. Have libraries played a big role in your life? In the age of A.I. and the Internet, do you think we would lose anything essential if libraries were to close?

7. Do you believe Diego and his story belong in this book? What do you think happens to him? What do you think you might do if your family were similarly threatened?

8. Do you think a romance between Kent and Cass is realistic? How might such a relationship work?

9. Do you think Rebecca did more harm or good for the town? Would you have voted for her the first time? Would you vote to re-elect her when she runs for re-election?

10. If you are or were writing a book, where would you set it? What settings in other books have stood out for you?

AUTHOR INTERVIEW: BECOMING FELICITY

Memoirist, poet and essayist Tarn Wilson* interviews Jan Stites about *Becoming Felicity*.

What was the original inspiration, or seed idea, for the book?

Some years back, I saw an article in a newspaper about Forks, Washington, which is the setting for Stephenie Meyer's *Twilight* series. The article described how the actual Forks gave itself something of a makeover to model itself after the fictitious town in the book. Tourism prospered.

I thought what a fun idea, to write a novel about a town that remakes itself—and the divisions that arise while doing so. Loon, however, is a fictitious town. The events, including the fracturing of the community and the courtroom thread, aren't based on Forks or any other town.

Why did you set the book in Northern California's Sierra Mountains?

Initially I thought I'd set it in the Ozarks, which was the setting for my last novel, *Reading the Sweet Oak*. Over time, however, my love for the Sierras deepened, and I decided I'd like to write about a fictitious small Northern California mountain town. Also, I enjoy both experiencing and creating many different settings. My first novel, *Edgewise*, is set in Oakland, a town I live in and love; my second takes place along the banks of an Ozark's river, and this one is set in the mountains. My next novel, *Genevieve*, features at least some scenes set oceanside. City, river, mountain, ocean: all places that inspire me.

Your book includes a nuanced exploration of economic development in small towns. Did you do any research on the topic or find yourself having a deeper understanding of the complexities as you wrote?

For research, I traveled to several small Sierra mountain towns and interviewed store owners, town officials, environmentalists, and tourists. I also read a lot about the financial challenges small towns face. I wrote 17 drafts of *Becoming Felicity*. (Yes, 17; I write fast but have to revise a lot.) The more I wrote of this book, the more I could see factions and fractures develop. That's one of the storylines I most enjoyed portraying.

Which character do you feel the most affection for and why?

I adore pretty much all of them: Cass, Diego, Caesar, Mack, Zoe. Even Rebecca has her moments. But I feel special affection for Chance, the town sheriff. Chance is a decent man who cares about his dog and upholding the law, but who wants to uphold justice even more. He shows immense courage in the choices he makes.

Why did you decide to include Diego and his story? What do you think his experience adds to your book or your themes? What research resources were most valuable?

My first post-graduation job was teaching in a village school in the Yucatan peninsula of Mexico. I met amazing people, who greeted me warmly. I felt so at home, it was hard to leave. In my early versions of *Becoming Felicity*, there was no Diego. I felt the book lacked something. Then I thought about who might work at the kennel helping Cass, and Diego took form. He's based in part on students I met while teaching in Mexico, and later in Kenya; on immigrants I've met here, and on my own experiences working abroad. Diego has suffered a lot in his young life. Cass, too, suffered when young at the hands of a very popular, very cruel Rebecca. I thought Cass and Diego would share a close bond. In some ways, their pasts echo one another, though Cass's experiences are obviously far less traumatic than Diego's.

For research, I interviewed several Hondurans as well as other immigrants and read many articles about conditions in Honduras and elsewhere in Central America.

Have any books helped guide you in the way the Felicity series guides Cass?

Not quite as much, no, but many books have helped me along my own journey. One is Fyodor Dostoevsky's *The Brothers Karamazov*. His challenges to beliefs I had long held led me to change some of my own beliefs. Another book that carried a lot of impact for me, as it has for many, many girls and women, is *Little Women*, by Louisa May Alcott. As a tomboy who loved playing sports, I remember telling my best friend that I wanted to grow up to be a football player, a cowboy, or President. Fortunately, I didn't try to pursue any of the three, but the character of Jo helped give me permission to take paths that were somewhat unusual for a girl/young woman at the time. Finally, *To Kill a Mockingbird,* by Harper Lee, is a book I've read and reread, both for the power of its depiction of racism and, in later years, as a model of the quality of novel I aspire to write.

Which character do you most identify with and why?

Cass because I identify with her uncertainties about herself and her perhaps flawed assessment of Rebecca. Tho never bullied in school the way Cass was, I'd love to be more assertive, like Mack is. And Felicity. When you grow up with a lot of self-doubt, it can be hard to rid yourself of it. I identify with Cass's flaws . . . and strive to cultivate her strengths.

What emotions or messages do you hope will linger with your readers after they have finished reading?

I hope we can all feel encouraged to be Casses, to grow into the best versions of ourselves we can. I hope, too, that we can all experience a sense of the importance of community and connection in our lives. One other message I'd love to transmit for readers is to remember, if they've forgotten, as I sometimes do, how much enjoyment and enlightenment books offer us.

In the book, there are essentially two camps on how to sustain the town. Which approach to community building/financial strategy do you embrace? Why?

Both. Which is to say I can see plusses and minuses of each and am glad I'm not in a position to have to choose the best strategy.

Bullying is another theme in *Becoming Felicity*. What made you want to include it?

Certainly when I was teaching middle school, I witnessed a lot of situations where one or more students bullied others. Those experiences helped me understand the dynamic. If you truly value yourself, why would you need to bully others? Bullies try to build themselves up by pulling others down. As such I pity them. I hope that we can all—myself included—better perceive and stand up to bullies, be they family members, friends, colleagues, teachers, peers or politicians.

Rebecca ends up being a villain, but she is a complex one. How did you create her, and did your understanding of her change or deepen over time?

In initial versions, she was one-dimensional, kind of a James Bond villain without all the money and power. I had to work to understand her: what might motivate her and how to make her more complex, like most of us are. Shoutouts to writing friends who—I think, I hope—helped me shape her into a more rounded character.

The life-giving power of books and libraries is one of the main themes of this story. What led you to it?

I was fortunate to have parents who read to us and valued books. Life can be stressful for anyone. Books became my escape valve. I couldn't afford to buy a lot, so libraries were one of my happy places. Like Cass, I loved traveling via books to places I couldn't go and meeting people I'd never encountered. Also, without computers or the internet, libraries were the main repository of knowledge. My friends and I often went there to do research for school assignments. Though I appreciate and have certainly availed myself of the Internet, I think we lose something when libraries are ignored, let alone closed.

Excerpt from Edgewise

Read the first chapter of Jan's novel, *Edgewise*, which three-time Oprah's Book Club author Wally Lamb called "courageous, heartfelt and unforgettable."

CHAPTER ONE

There must be some mistake. Simone stood before a chain link fence tipped with spiked points. Plywood barricaded some windows; the piercings in the wood looked like bullet holes. Black bars striped other windows, either to keep local people out, or patients in. At her feet: shattered glass. This wasn't a hospital; it was the set for a horror movie.

Oakhill Hospital Day Treatment Center, the sign had originally read, but the *i* had been spray painted to read *Oakhell*. This was not the part of Oakland she had expected, the region of prosperous hills. She was in its crime-infested flatlands. Probably not just the hospital's windows but its patients were bullet bait. What was she doing here?

She picked up one of the glass shards from the sidewalk. It stank of whiskey. She considered slashing her wrists. Then she wouldn't have to worry that she was not going back to her classroom to teach any time soon.

She stared at the hospital's four trailers, grouped in a loose square, all of them the brown of dead flowers, bare and squat and drab. Fog drifted over them, as if the hospital were smoldering after a patient riot. She had nowhere else to go. Sighing, she smoothed the loose blouse she wore over leggings because she was tired of men staring at her breasts and started picking her way through the broken glass to the front trailer, its door the only part of the hospital not barricaded behind the fence. Locked.

She knocked, waited. The door opened to an Asian man wearing jeans and a pink T-shirt emblazoned with a chest-sized Tweety Bird.

"Hi," he said, smiling. "Can I help you?"

"I'm supposed to be visiting the program."

"You are?"

"Yes."

"No. I mean, who are you?"

"Oh. Sorry." *Way to go, idiot.* "Simone Dupre."

"No problem. Welcome. I'm Jun Gambia, one of the counselors."

Tweety Bird gestured to a gate in the fence that barricaded the complex. "Members enter there."

"'Members'?" Simone asked.

The man smiled, or didn't; Simone wasn't sure. "General meeting starts in five minutes. I'll explain our outpatient program right after the meeting. Just wait out in back with the others. The gate combination is three-two-one." He closed the door.

Simone went to the gate. A small brown bird with a black head like an executioner's hood that she hoped wasn't an omen perched on the fence, watching her try to work the lock. She forced herself to take a deep breath. She could do this. After lining up the right numbers, she entered the compound.

A huge black man, arms flailing, lumbered toward her, yelling words—all Simone could make of his rant was *aliens* and *Jesus* and *Eddie Murphy*. Panic gripped her. She stepped back. He kept coming, his eyes on her now. She stepped back again, but he was almost within striking distance. She pivoted, ready to run and scream. The flailing man veered away from her, heading back behind the front trailer. She could still hear him, still smell his sweat.

Heart pounding, she lingered at the gate, hoping someone sane would appear. No one came to save her. Finally, she walked hesitantly forward. As she neared the corner of the front trailer, she detected murmuring voices behind it and followed them, emerging into the glare of a dusty courtyard that held a scattering of round concrete tables with concrete benches, a volleyball court, and a basketball hoop.

Some two-dozen people seated at the tables turned and stared at her. Their conversations stopped as if her presence had flipped a switch. They were black, all of them. Expressionless, they scrutinized her. Smoke curled from their cigarettes, dispersing into the fog. Simone yearned to be that smoke.

"Hi," she made herself say in a full voice. She slid onto the concrete seat of the nearest table; the two women sitting there regarded her as if she were three-headed. "I'm Simone."

The woman across from her scowled. Her hair stuck out jaggedly from her head. Her purple sweatshirt stretched against her sides. She wasn't fat, Simone decided, just big, a fullback of a woman.

Simone refocused her attention to the other woman at the table, who was slight with curly hair and an unsettling grin. She gave the woman her best first-day-of-school smile. "Hi." The woman's face barely changed. Simone felt more alone than she did when she was by herself.

"All right, y'all, who's gonna cover my bet?" demanded the big woman in the purple sweatshirt.

"What odds you giving, Satch?" asked a skinny woman with long, pointed earrings seated at the next table.

The woman named Satch ran her eyes over Simone and snorted. "Three to one against."

"Ten."

"Five," Satch said. "Bet's a dollar."

"What are you betting on?" Simone asked.

"Count me in," said the woman with the large earrings, their tips touching her shoulders.

"What are you betting on?" Simone asked again.

"Got a dollar say you ain't coming back tomorrow. White folks visit. Don't come back."

Simone put her fist to her mouth and glanced at a table where a balding man, the joints of his glasses bandaged with tape, was cradling three brown teddy bears as if they were his triplets.

"You staff?" another man asked her, his languorous eyes on the smoke rings he was blowing.

"Shit, no," Satch said. "She come in the nuts' entrance, just like us. I seen her come round the corner." Her eyes bored into Simone. "What you doing here?"

Simone wasn't about to mention her crying jag in front of a roomful of tenth graders, or what her thighs looked like under her leggings, or her principal's declaration: "I can't allow you back in the classroom. Get help." She shrugged.

Satch narrowed her eyes and curled the corner of a lip crowned by a dark brown mole. "Got to have qualifications to join this club. You schizophrenic? Bipolar? OCD?"

She wasn't any of those things. But she had to say something, and it might as well be true. "I guess I'm just really tired."

"Tired?" Satch said, glaring at her. "Oakhill ain't no spa. Don't got no hot tub."

"I know. I didn't mean..." She really was tired, too tired to finish her sentence.

"*Tired!*" Satch said. "What right you got to be *tired*." She waved at the cadre of faces behind her. "We all tired."

At first Simone made herself hold Satch's gaze, but finally she looked away and, in relief, let her eyes follow a tall, umber-skinned woman wearing a batik pants suit and matching red beads in her braided hair.

"Good morning, everybody." Batik Lady nodded to Simone, who wanted to kiss her feet in gratitude for the greeting.

"Hi, Muslimah," said the teddy bear man, tucking his head down like a bashful child.

Muslimah smiled at Marvin then turned to Satch. "I'm glad you're back," she said.

Satch kept her eyes on the table. "Had the flu."

"Have you seen a doctor? You seem to get that flu a lot," Muslimah remarked.

Simone detected the slightest hint of reprimand.

Muslimah straightened the file folders in her hands. Satch didn't respond. "We'll talk later," Muslimah said. She crossed the courtyard to the far trailer.

Simone saw her chance. "Did you get a flu shot? I teach, so I'm around a lot of sick kids, but since I started getting flu shots I never get sick."

"Fuck you, bitch!"

Simone's gut cramped.

"If you so damned healthy, why you here?"

"She was just trying to help," said the slight woman with the unsettling smile.

"Yeah," agreed the man with the teddy bears triplets.

"White folks always be telling black folks how to live,"

Satch said. "And I *know* you ain't coming back, 'cause Oakhill ain't white enough."

A car screeched down the street, the sound keening into their eardrums.

"Noooo!" screamed the slight woman. She clamped her hands over her ears, scrunched shut her eyes and screamed again, rocking back and forth. *"Noooo!"*

Satch instantly moved into action; she took the screaming woman in her arms and glared again at Simone, as if she'd done something to cause the screams.

"Noooo!" The woman kept screaming.

The teddy bear man buried his face in their fur.

Simone's heart beat fiercely. She reached out her hand to touch the woman, to help comfort her, but Satch's scowl stopped her.

"I got you, Viola," Satch said gently to the screaming woman. "You safe." Her dark, blazing eyes never left Simone's.

The huge man reappeared, his arms flailing wildly.

"Noooo!" The woman kept screaming.

Simone covered her mouth—the screaming was a siren summoning her to scream along and never stop.

Tweety Bird—Jun, that was his name—came out the first trailer door and dashed over to Viola, taking her hand. "Feel my hand, Viola," he said. His voice was barely audible over the yelling but so steady that Simone decided he was talking to her too. Her pulse ratcheted down to triple digits. "You're not on the sidewalk. You're safe."

"Noooo!"

Another woman, this one with straightened hair flipped up at the ends, stood and clutched her hands to her chest. "I'm having a heart attack!"

Was she? Should Simone do something? Everyone else was ignoring the woman. She must be crazy. They were all crazy. Muslimah hurried over. Satch released Viola, whose screams eventually subsided into tears. The two staff members put arms around her and escorted her inside the trailer. The woman having the heart attack jutted out her lower lip, clasped her shoulders, and sat down.

Simone felt like she was breathing air through a pinched straw. She stood and squeezed her arms around herself. She might dissolve in front of a classroom, but she had a life—and a car that could take her away.

"Figure I'm gonna win my bet," Satch said, studying Simone with a withering smile. "Leaving now and ain't coming back tomorrow, huh?"

Simone fled out the gate.

ACKNOWLEDGMENTS

In my experience, it doesn't take a village to write a book. Rather, it takes a whole (densely populated) city.

The inestimable Mike Karpa and I fortunately met and formed a writing group with fellow writers in Jim Frey's Novel Writing Seminar more than thirty years ago. We're blessed to have the amazing Wendy Schultz and Melinda Maxwell-Smith in the group, providing insightful counsel into both writing and life. Luckily, so far we've taken turns feeling that writing and/or the world are hopeless. Were we all to arrive at that conclusion simultaneously, we might have given up long ago.

Tarn Wilson, fellow writer and friend and stellar human being, is always ready to talk through problems and solutions for mine or my manuscript's rough patches. Ditto gifted story-teller Ernie Grafe, and exquisite poet, Gail Onion.

Wouldn't feel finished without a huge thank you to my late great friend and writing buddy, Madelon Phillips, who taught me so much about how to write full spectrum and how to live and love accordingly.

Numerous MPC delightful writing groups have sprung up over the decades since dynamo Margaret Irving launched a writing program. Huge shoutout to Margaret, Anna Dabney, Margaretha Derasary, Lin Gentry, Jean Gregory, Melinda Maxwell-Smith, Patricia McBroom, Barbara Miller, Sharon Noteboom, Gail Onion, Bertha Reilly, and Patricia Scheiner-Ovenfors.

Thanks to several readers who tackled earlier drafts for their insightful comments and pep talks: Lynn Beittel, Matt Binder,

Francie Chan, Gayle Durbin, Dianne Elise, Bette Felton, Jean Roggenkamp, and Yul Ailea Stites.

Editors who helped shape BF and hence share the blame for its flaws* are Susie Hara, Heather Lazare, and David Corbett. (*Just kidding. The flaws are mine.)

I'm grateful to Mumblers Press for expertise in publishing and for the books it's brought to light, all of which deserve a huge readership! (I may be biased, but it's true.)

I'd also like to thank Meg Ruley. Your critiques of earlier drafts pushed me to make substantive changes. You were right.

For moral support and encouragement over the years, special thanks to my brother, Steven, and our late brother, Ron, and to my sister-in-law, Sandra. Gratitude, too, for years of delight to James, Sierra, and Yul Ailea Stites, and appreciation to Ricky Jacobs for saying yes when I've wanted to say no.

In two previous novels, I've thanked my husband, Bert Felton, foremost. At the risk of being repetitious, I do so again. Thank you, my love, for all that you've been and remain to me. You're the kindest man I've ever met.

And thanks to whoever reads this book for taking the time to do so.

About the Author

Jan's path to novel writing began with her love of books and movies, which led to screenwriting. She optioned several projects and taught screenwriting classes at San Francisco State University and the University of California-Berkeley for several years before belatedly realizing that screenplays are written to be *seen*. Jan wanted to write something to be read. *Becoming Felicity* is Jan's third published novel.

Jan lives with her husband in Northern California.

ALSO BY JAN STITES

Edgewise

Reading The Sweet Oak

www.ingramcontent.com/pod-product-compliance
Lightning Source LLC
Chambersburg PA
CBHW021436310726
48971CB00005B/1386